THE DIVIDE

Also by Jeremy Robinson

Standalone Novels
The Didymus Contingency
Raising The Past
Beneath
Antarktos Rising
Kronos
Xom-B
Refuge
Flood Rising
MirrorWorld
Apocalypse Machine
Unity
The Distance
Forbidden Island
The Divide

Nemesis Saga Novels
Island 731
Project Nemesis
Project Maigo
Project 731
Project Hyperion
Project Legion

Post-Apocalyptic Sci-Fi
Hunger
Feast
Viking Tomorrow

The Antarktos Saga
The Last Hunter – Descent
The Last Hunter – Pursuit
The Last Hunter – Ascent
The Last Hunter – Lament
The Last Hunter – Onslaught
*The Last Hunter – Collected
Edition*
The Last Valkyrie

SecondWorld Novels
SecondWorld
Nazi Hunter: Atlantis

The Jack Sigler/Chess Team Thrillers
Prime
Pulse
Instinct
Threshold
Ragnarok
Omega
Savage
Cannibal
Empire

Cerberus Group Novels
Herculean
Helios

Jack Sigler Continuum Novels
Guardian
Patriot
Centurion

Chesspocalypse Novellas
Callsign: King
Callsign: Queen
Callsign: Rook
Callsign: King 2 – Underworld
Callsign: Bishop
Callsign: Knight
Callsign: Deep Blue
Callsign: King 3 – Blackout

Horror Novels
(written as Jeremy Bishop)
Torment
The Sentinel
The Raven

THE
DIVIDE
JEREMY ROBINSON

For David Berube,
Good friend, librarian supreme, and slayer of dragons.
Welcome to the party, pal!

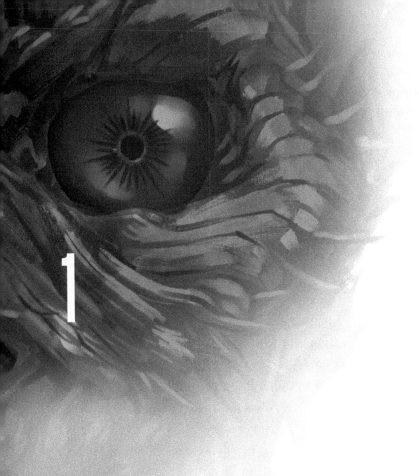

1

Stark naked, hair tied back, body and weapon poised for optimal aerodynamics, falling still makes noise. Pockets of air collect and swirl. In the ears, the eye sockets, between the breasts, and against a slender belly. In the silence of a still forest, the whisper of churning air screams. That's a lesson best taught, hunter to apprentice. I learned from experience, and the four long scars across my belly serve as a constant reminder. The mountain lion below, fur glowing yellow in the morning sun, wearing scars of its own, confirms this simple fact by turning to face me as I descend.

Ten feet above the ground, I have a choice to make: throw the spear, or hold on to it. The first choice, if successful, prevents a dangerous fight. Missing means death. The second choice guarantees a fight, the outcome of which will be determined by whichever of us is the more experienced killer.

The lion has more scars.

It kills to survive.

But so do I.

At birth, I was given the name Davina. My friends now call me Vee. To everyone else, I'm known by an assortment of official titles—mother, former elder's daughter, present elder's wife. While they all sound nice, noble even, the words used in conjunction with my titles are far from flattering. Runt, scrap, outcast, dirty, and wild are common but my favorite is savage.

Though I am a wife of Micha, Elder of Essex, and daughter of Jesse, the county's former elder, my status is lower than most common people. I am sometimes called 'dirt.' To be 'walked on, brushed off, or spat upon.' Micha's words. I call him a 'delightful man,' which his sarcasm-deaf ears hear as flattery.

As the youngest of eight children, and the last of eight wives, I am an afterthought, most often referred to—when people believe I'm not present—as 'Eight.' A woman of few offspring and many names. Had I been a better breeder, I could have elevated my status. Bearing children, especially to an elder, is a blessing. Sixty percent of children die from disease, from exposure to the elements, or from predators, by the age of two. Of those, only fifty percent make it to adulthood. Without large broods, humanity would cease to exist.

But I wasn't married for children. My body was used for pleasure, not for reproduction. Despite frequent visits to my bed, Micha worked hard to make sure I never conceived. And when I did, no thanks to the man I was forced to marry, his visits came to an end. My unspoiled womanhood was all that had drawn him to me. Swollen with child, he lost interest. Had I known that earlier, I would have sought out a donor far sooner. Yet another lesson learned through experience, and not without scars of its own.

The lion's ears fold back as it bares its teeth and hisses, angry at the interruption. I land, spear still in hand, its point creating a small, but effective barrier between my soft flesh and the lion's jaws. The small gathering of deer that the lion had been hunting see both of us for the first time and bound away through the forest, hooves thumping the soil, white tails flashing. The lion leans toward the fleeing creatures while keeping its eyes locked on me, warring instincts simultaneously telling it to give chase, and to defend itself.

But it can't do both, and since I don't want it killing my deer, I hiss back and give the spear a thrust, challenging the beast, making this a territorial dispute between rival predators...even if that is not my job.

I am not here to kill the deer. I am simply a shepherd. In their small minds, the deer are free, living out normal lives in the forest. In reality, they are stalked, day and night, and on occasion, guided away from—or protected from—danger. When meat is needed, hunters come and kill the oldest, weakest, and least productive animals. In days past, such animals might have been confined by a fence, but even the simplest technological advances are forbidden.

To be present in any meaningful way is to be detectable, and detection means death, not just to the individual, but to the species. To all of humanity. So says the Prime Law—the guiding force that shapes every aspect of our lives.

I really only know two things about the law's origin—its many rules, regulations, and guides protect the human race from unseen dangers, and it was, without a doubt, written by men. As a woman with just one child—a son—my life, and the resources I consume, are in direct conflict with the Prime Law.

But murder is also forbidden. So I have been given a job for which the odds of surviving are lower than a newborn baby's, not because of disease, or even the elements, but because of dangers like the one now staring me down.

"Easy," I say, creeping to the side, circling, showing no fear, asserting dominance. The encounter will end with one of us dead, or one of us running—and I'm not going to run. Not because I *want* to fight, but because outrunning a mountain lion that can outpace and outleap any human being, man or woman, isn't possible. The moment I show my back is the very moment I will die.

With the deer long gone, the big cat that probably out-weighs my two hundred pound husband, gives me its full attention. It's not going to run. I'm too small for it to be intimidated into retreat, and while I've cost it a meal, I've also offered myself as a replacement.

Only its eyes move as the beast tracks me. The rest of its body is coiled, frozen, and ready to spring. A living trap, waiting to be prodded. And when the trap springs, a flurry of movement lasting no more than a second, will leave one of us unharmed, and the other transformed.

Even killers can become meals.

Such is the life, and usually the death, of a shepherd.

What no one knows is that I'm happy with my 'low' status. Facing the jaws of a lion is preferable to a loveless husband. And while I am not a loyal wife, I would die before breaking the law. I'm happy to push the limits on occasion, but I understand what's at stake.

Freedom is death.

My father used to say that to me while my siblings were out being groomed for lives greater than mine. He would talk to me while I tended the chickens, fished the river, and dug for edible roots. He would expound on the world, on the forbidden knowledge he kept safe, and skirt around secrets which only elders were allowed to know. He was unaware that I was listening, *really* listening, and getting a better education than my siblings because of it. 'Freedom is death' was his favorite subject. I believe he was paraphrasing something from the Time Before, but he would never confirm it. To speak of the Time Before to anyone other than another elder was against the Prime Law. He broke that law, on occasion, during his ramblings, but always without realizing it.

The result was a youngest daughter whose opinions on the world were better informed than most, but it did not matter to anyone.

The lion is considering how to kill me—by snapping my neck, by choking me out, or by disemboweling me—and it's paying me more attention than any person ever has. And I return the favor. Two solitary creatures plotting the demise of the other.

"I don't want to kill you," I tell the beast, the sentiment true, but the words uttered as a growl communicating the opposite. "Leave!"

A quick thrust sends the lion's paws scrambling. It nearly lunges, but spots the spear tip just a foot from its open jaws.

I'm not the first human being this creature has encountered. It recognizes the spear as a threat, which works in my favor. But the lion is also standing before me, which means its previous encounter—perhaps *encounters*—provided the lion with a full belly.

Spear or not, it's going to attack.

The lion moves, stalking in a slow circle, as I continue my own, predators both.

But only one of us is a mother.

The male lion has felt pain, but it has never had a life taken from its belly, never experienced its insides tearing away, never shared its life so fully with another living being. My son, Salem, though distant and severely misguided, is my tether to this world. As long as there is hope of his return, I cannot die. He is my strength, and this lion's weakness.

The cat misreads my smile, hissing to intimidate.

"Come then."

The cat goes rigid again. I steady myself, taking a deep breath. The air is rich with salt from the ocean, miles at my back, and the sun-warmed scent of pine needles beneath my bare feet. A hand against the spear's flat base, my feet planted against the soil beneath the pine needles, I prepare for the attack.

Tension builds in slow waves, me bracing, the lion lowering, our eyes locked. There is a moment between us, a kind of kinship, where it doesn't matter who lives and who dies, where we are partners in a cycle beyond us both. For a moment, I feel love, and respect.

Then I blink.

And the lion springs.

2

Blood is warm.

I remember it well, from a hundred different wounds on a hundred different days, but none as poignant as the tacky wetness that marked my wedding night. It leaked, not from my recently broken-in womanhood, but from a wound on my forehead, tracing a path from brow to cheek, from chin to chest, from bare breast to the deer-skin floor. The gash, delivered by my new husband, was meant to teach me respect.

What it achieved was a delirious stupor. Before that moment, I thought I understood the world and my place in it. Low as my station was, I was confident and proud of my heritage—my father, Jesse, was an excellent elder. At the end of that night, the scales of blindness had flaked away. I saw the world through new eyes. Micha's word, beliefs, and actions were not to be questioned. As an elder, such things are his right, but I had hoped he would be different as a husband. My father had been fooled by Micha's charming public persona, and by marrying me to him, had allowed Micha to inherit my father's position. Being the second son of an elder meant Micha could not inherit his own father's legacy. Marrying the daughter of an elder, even if she was the eighth daughter, meant he could challenge the elder's own sons to the right of inheritance, which Micha did.

By the time I was grown, my eight siblings had been whittled down to five. A better survival rate than most families, but two of them were brothers. The first was slain by Micha, legally. The second, an effeminate man, relented his position. My husband took what he wanted through manipulation and force. For a time, what he wanted was me. So I distanced myself, held back my thoughts, dreams, and desires and waited for the opportunity to improve my life by lowering my station.

Three years into my marriage, on the eve of the summer solstice—the only day of the year when elder families from all of *New Inglan* come together, and imbibing is permitted—I found a man too drunk to recognize me. I allowed him to plant the seed that would become my son, and my freedom from a tyrannical husband—which is not forbidden, but also often leads to death.

The warm blood is mine.

Some of it.

The lion's grappling claw raked over my ribs, bouncing over the bones to create a series of short dashes.

The rest of the blood, spattered over my face, chest, and arms, belongs to the lion—now impaled on my spear. The cat leapt high, claws splayed wide. It had meant to wrap them around me and hook them into my back while its jaws closed over my face, a suffocating mask. Its teeth would have burrowed into my skull. Instead, I thrust with the spear, its tip sliding through the lion's open mouth, then the back of its throat, and then its spine.

Momentum carried the predator's paws around to my exposed side, the claws cutting as gravity tugged them down-ward, but the wounds are not deep.

Still braced, I grunt as the cat's full weight falls on the spear. Then I lower my kill to the ground.

The deer are long gone, and they won't return to this area until the scent of lion piss and scat—currently leaking from the loose-bowelled lion—is rinsed fully away. Months at least. It will take a few days to track them down, but their migration routes, guided by former shepherds, are predictable.

I put a finger to my wounded side and wince. The cuts aren't deep enough to require stitching, which would mean a return trip to the village, but they will need a treatment of herbs and oils to prevent infection. But that, I can handle on my own.

Before I can tend to the wounds, I need to retrieve my belongings.

Scaling the tree holding my gear is a painful affair, the gashes stretching with each reach, threatening to tear wider. So I move slowly through the branches, climbing into the thick-leafed oak the way a porcupine does. Safe in the leafy canopy, I rest on the branch holding my clothing, wiping tacky blood with a clean cloth and then holding it in place until the bleeding stops. Two loops of twine, tied tightly around my chest, hold it in place. Then I dress. The clothing is well made from wild cotton fibers, dyed black to help conceal me at night, and thin enough for the summer-time heat and humidity. But they're also loose fitting, easily snagged, and loud when moving fast. I had shed them upon spotting the lion's approach.

Bandaged and clothed, I put my gear bag—containing a bed roll, water skin, knife, food pouch, and leather boots not meant for scaling trees—over my shoulder and scrape my way down the bark.

Back on the ground, I face the lion once more. Boots returned to my feet, I step on the lion's head and withdraw the spear with a hard tug.

"You should have listened to me," I tell the slain beast, and stab the spear into the ground. Then I draw my knife and crouch. Lion is not a preferred food source. No one actively hunts them. But fresh meat should not be wasted. It's not enough food for me to make the journey home, but I will eat my fill, and then beyond it, stuffing my gut and consuming enough meat to fuel the days it takes me to find the deer again.

My knife is an ancient weapon forged five hundred years ago, when technology wasn't just allowed, but always advancing and a part of daily life. I draw the sharp blade down the lion's sternum, slicing skin and sinew. A firm whack to the pommel punches the knife tip through bone. A hard twist cracks it in half. My fingers wriggle between the two jagged halves. The ribs flex, fighting against my pull, but then yield. They crack wide to reveal layers of connective tissue, lungs, and after a few more cuts, my prize. Severed arteries, no longer under pressure, ooze blood as I cut them away and remove the heart.

Some believe eating a lion's heart infuses those who consume it with the creature's strength and cunning. I think it's bullshit. For a lion's heart to be eaten, the beast must first be slain, and if it is killed by a person, who is truly stronger and more cunning?

I've chosen to eat the heart, not because it grants power, or tastes better, but because it provides the most nutrients. When I'm done with the heart, I will consume the liver. And if I am not full to bursting by then, I will consume what I can of its brain.

Preparing my meal is simple. I take the blood-soaked organ, raise it to my lips, and bite.

My father told my child self, as I plucked trout from a river, that people once cooked food using devices that generated heat without fire and smoke. I'm not sure how such a thing was possible, but I have often dreamed of it. Now we would have to use fire, and an open flame for cooking is forbidden. In the winter, wood fires are necessary for survival, and thus, deemed legal when more than two miles from the Divide. Most of the smoke is collected by large, damp, cloth tarps stretched over the blaze. What escapes into the air dissipates long before it can be detected. Forest fires occasionally fill the air with towers of smoke, and they have never attracted unwanted attention, confirming the safety of burning wood—in moderation. But burning meat?

The scent of heated oils and crispy singed flesh?

My mouth waters at the thought. I have little doubt such smells would draw every predator from the forest, and those beyond it, perhaps even from across the Divide.

I have consumed cooked meat just once in my life. I was seven. My brothers, during their rebellious teenage years, captured, killed, and cooked a squirrel. I was offered a morsel as payment to stay quiet about what they had done, making me an accomplice. It wasn't until the meal was complete, and the arrival of a hungry bear, that the full weight of what we had done crashed down upon us.

How long had it taken to attract a predator? Thirty minutes? How far had we been from the Divide? Two miles? Less? No one had kept track, and as we fled the scene, we pledged two things: never to tell, and never to repeat our act of insanity.

Every meal—meat, vegetable, or insect—since that day has been fresh, and raw.

I chew my last bite of heart, relishing the taste, and then spit out a ring of artery. Too rubbery for my liking. The bit of blood vessel hits the pine needle carpet and bounces three times. In the still silence of the forest, broken only by the distant chirping of small birds, I hear the *pat, pat, pat* of it bouncing, and then, when it stops, I hear the sound once more.

From behind.

Knife gripped in hand, I turn my head, tilted upward as though admiring the trees. The sun is higher, shimmering between a patchwork of needles and leaves scraping together as a breeze sifts through, bending and creaking the trees.

Though my eyes are turned up, I focus on my periphery. The aberration is nearly invisible despite being in the open. It's hidden in a patch of sunlight, the creature's coat matching the yellow light. The black nose and rings around its unblinking eyes reveal the beast—the male lion's mate.

Before I can retrieve my spear, or turn, the lion pounces, and I feel the warmth of blood on me once more.

3

The journey home is made out of duty—the meat from two lions is enough to feed several families. It's also made out of necessity—the four puncture wounds in my thigh need the kind of attention that I cannot provide on my own. The twelve hour hike is drawn out by the two cats' weight, which I drag behind me, staked on two fresh-cut poles. My limping gait doesn't speed things up, either. While it was once preferable to eat raw meat within two hours of a kill, human beings' guts have adapted—so says my father, who once explained how we now have enzymes that our ancestors lacked five hundred years ago. Some people even prefer the flavor of rot.

The village is all but invisible until you're inside it. The structures are made from wooden poles and layers of animal hides, all of which are already perfectly camouflaged. Some of the structures, like the elder's dwelling and the meeting hall, are quite large, but everything is designed for mobility, able to be broken down and transported within hours. The village is relocated once a year, allowing the forest to erase all evidence of our temporary dwelling, leaving no footprint behind.

In my lifetime, the tribe of Essex has migrated thirty-five times. Mobility is essential to concealment, which is paramount to survival, and thus, it's the law. The location is never the same, but we also never leave the county borders. As a people on the Divide, it is our responsibility to protect our eight hundred and thirty miles of land, primarily the thirty mile-long stretch bordering the Divide. And as the only tribe to border both the Divide *and* the ocean, our responsibilities are twofold. Though we are able to fish our coastal waters, fishermen must enter the water naked and tethered to shore. If evidence of our occupation was swept out with the tide, it could wash up on shore further south and be found. The water protects us, so says the Prime Law, but no one knows if the Divide can be crossed, and no one wants to find out.

I'm spotted by lookouts hidden in the trees. I don't know they're around me until I hear twin pairs of mourning doves cooing at my approach. The soft coo tells the guards on the ground that a member of the tribe is returning. Had they been crow calls, I would have been greeted by spears instead of helping hands.

Two young men rush out to greet me, their hair cut short to prevent lice and to deter ticks. Neither of them say 'hello,' or welcome me home. Despite their age, and social standing, I am still less. A shepherd. One of them lingers, eyeing my wounds, and then the lions, his eyes showing a flash of respect as he realizes who killed the beasts. Then they take the poles from my shoulders and drag my kills away. I won't see them again. I won't taste their flesh. If anything, I will be berated for consuming the heart, which should have gone to Micha or to his child-bearing wives.

But I will likely hear nothing of it. Micha prefers to act as though I don't exist, waiting for me to die in the wild, while he leads the tribe by proliferating and pretending to be as knowledgeable about the world as my father.

"Vee." The voice is friendly, familiar, and then concerned. "My god, what happened to you?"

I smile at Grace as she approaches and points to the lions being dragged away. As my father's assistant for forty-five years, she helped raise me, despite never having had a romantic entanglement with my father, who only married once. My mother died giving birth to my younger brother, who did not survive his first winter. That's not to say my father doesn't love Grace. She and Father were, and are, inseparable. But their love did not comingle with lust. They are, as Grace puts it, best friends. I find the term unusual, as I have no friends.

Grace looks back at the lions, *tsks* loudly, and frowns. "The forest is no place for a lady to be on her own."

"It's a good thing I'm not a lady."

She rolls her eyes. The title 'lady' is generally reserved for members of elder families, of which I belong to two. But as the lowest member of both families, cast out by my husband, bearing only a single child, and generally covered in filth and blood, the term is never used in reference to me—nor would I want it to be.

Ladies are dominated.

I am independent.

That is dangerously close to saying I am free, but only in a personal sense. I am as bound to New Inglan as every other living person.

"Pretty sure neither of us are ladies," I add.

Grace responds with a partially-toothed grin and a wink. "I'd rather be skewered alongside those cats."

As I wonder if that is the real reason she and my father never married, she takes my wrist and tows me along. We pass the butchery, where my lions are already being dismantled, hungry people lining up for their portions. Like me, the people of Essex are brown-skinned, brown-eyed, and brown-haired. Our ancestors had a variety of skin colors, eye colors, and facial features. But a limited population after the time of the Great Divide, and five centuries of breeding, blended many races into one. According to my father, we are similar to the people who populated this land one thousand years ago. Even our way of living and customs have more in common with those people than with our amalgam of more recent ancestors.

As a child, listening to my father's ramblings, it all sounded like fairy tales, that for a brief time, mankind could do things that sounded like magic, that the world was larger, that people looked different than they do now. And then I had a son with eyes like the ocean, and I understood that everything my father had told me as a child, was true. I also knew I could never discuss what I had learned. To do so would be a death sentence for both me, and for my father. Aside from the cooked squirrel, the knowledge passed from my father to me is my only offense against the law.

After passing through a sliver of forest, we give the elder's dwelling a wide berth. I can hear the voices of women through the layers of hanging hide, no doubt chattering on about the tribe's latest drama, which they most likely conjured in the first place. Our path takes us uphill toward a natural, rocky clearing, where my father dwells like some kind of wild recluse.

After hustling us through the village mostly unseen, Grace says, "I didn't expect you to return so soon."

"Soon? My watch doesn't end for another month. I'll be leaving in the morning."

She pauses long enough to furrow her brow in my direction, then she's moving again. "The runners didn't find you?"

"Runners?"

"Your father sent out four. Two days ago."

Runners are most often young men training to be guards, soldiers, hunters, and trackers. They carry messages between tribes, and on occasion, to deployed tribe members. But never to a shepherd. That four of them had been sent to find me reveals my father's enduring influence, and the severity of whatever I've been summoned for.

"Is it Father? Is he—"

"Jesse is still a cranky, old bastard." She spoke the words with a smile. My father was required to relinquish the position of elder at the age of sixty-five, an arbitrary number he claimed harkened back to a day when men and women of that age were expected to do little or nothing for the rest of their lives. Now eighty, my father has surpassed the normal life expectancy of an elder by ten years, and that of the common man by thirty.

Grace pauses again, her smile melting into a frown. "It's about your son."

Your son.

As dear as I might be to my father, and to Grace, neither of them accepted Salem, even before his betrayal. He was too smart, too curious, and too impetuous for a young man whose station in life will never change, partially because of his mother, but mostly because he is a dissident. He is what's known as a Modernist, obsessed with the ancient ways, technology, and what lies beyond the Divide. Discussing such things is forbidden, the punishment for which is lashings. Actively pursuing technology, which could announce our presence to the world beyond the Divide, is punishable by death, often in brutal and very public ways.

Salem and two of his friends were caught discussing an ocean voyage and were beaten for it—by Micha himself. When they recovered, all three boys disappeared. For a time, I believed Salem dead, and then I learned his fate was worse than death. He had sought out and fallen in with Plistim, the Modernist leader and former elder of Aroostook. It is a wild, untamed place far in the north, more than two hundred miles from the Divide, where it is rumored that meat is cooked and homes are constructed as permanent structures.

If Salem returns he will be tortured for information, and then killed.

If he is caught with Plistim, he will suffer the same fate.

At the age of sixteen, my son's life will, like most wild creatures in the forest, end in violence.

It is not the fate any mother wishes for her child.

And yet, I respect his conviction. But respect doesn't change the law.

Freedom *is* death.

"What about him?" I ask.

"Best if your father tells you," Grace says, failing in her attempt to hide the despair in her eyes.

I dig my feet in, the same feet that stood against a mountain lion, and Grace jerks to a stop. She turns to face me, wilting some under the weight of the questions I might ask. So I'm merciful and limit myself to a single query. "Is he alive?"

"He is," she says. "For now."

4

The hairs on the back of my neck rise as I clear the forest and hike up the open hillside, limping through knee high grass. Eyes straight ahead, my view is composed of large granite stones, a small, almost frail looking hut, and a very blue, cloudless sky. Insects buzz in the warm sun. Sweet pollen from blooming flowers tickles my nose. Straight ahead, the day is magic.

But behind me...

Curiosity digs its relentless talons into my head, pulling me around to look, but I resist.

"You should look," Grace says. "We all need a reminder sometime."

Her prodding is all it takes for curiosity to win. I turn and feel the deep sense of dread that is instilled in us as children. The Divide is just three miles away. It's invisible from the forest below, but from atop Father's hill, it is in clear view. No one knows exactly how deep the gorge is—it has never been explored, and even walking to its precipice is forbidden. The tree line ends several hundred feet from the edge, the land there mysteriously barren. Venturing beyond the trees is against the Prime Law. I've only been to the forest's edge once, a year ago, while redirecting the herd. Three of the deer ventured into that barren, craggy land. None of them returned.

The far side of the Divide is visible here, but diluted by a permanent haze rising up from below. The Divide is an estimated three miles across at its narrowest point, and at its widest...no one knows. What we do know is that it keeps us safe, and alive, and is impossible to cross—for us, and for the Golyat.

I've never seen the Golyat. No one has. But we know it exists, and not just because the Prime Law says so. On rare occasions, the setting sun projects the monster's silhouette into the fog rising from the Divide, warbling as it stalks the lands beyond the horizon. With such a clear view of the horizon and the Divide from here, I imagine my father has seen it more than a few times since his hut has been located atop this hill.

The Golyat is our enemy. The Divide protects us from it, not because its vastness is insurmountable, but because it keeps us hidden. If the Golyat knew we were here, it would find a way across.

So says the Prime Law.

And my father.

Morbid curiosity satiated, I turn and find my father standing before his hut, body curved forward, twin canes bearing the burden of keeping him upright. His eyes linger on the view, and then turn toward me, his gray hair and beard fluttering in the wind.

He stands upright for a moment, arms open at my approach. And then I am within his embrace. "My daughter returns once more."

"And I will return until one of us is dead."

He leans back, smiling. The exchange has been our routine since my first solo venture into the forest and I returned alive. The first time he spoke those words, there were tears in his eyes—not everyone returns from the forest—but his confidence has grown over the years, and worry became pride.

He looks me over, eyes lingering on the wounds that are bleeding through my crude bandages. His confidence wavers some, but the smile remains. "There was a time when I was sure I would go first, but..."

"You'll still croak first, old man," Grace says, swatting his shoulder. "She's tougher than all the men of Essex." Her eyes widen. "Just...don't tell anyone I said so."

"Strength means little without the wisdom to guide it," he says, and the joy of my return drains away. He turns to enter his small dwelling, but I stop him with a question.

"What of my son?"

My father pauses, his weight bearing down on the canes. His lips crack open and a stillborn word hisses from between them. Then he shoves the skin hanging over the entrance aside and steps inside the hut. I glance at Grace, who looks sympathetic, but I'm not sure for whom.

"He has trouble standing for long," she says, motioning me to follow.

With a sigh, I enter the skin-wrapped hut. It smells of pipe smoke, animal hide, and the herbs that hang from the walls in bundles. The domed ceiling is open, allowing a cone of light to glow on the deer-skin floor. The space is tight, but dry and cozy in a way that reminds me I'm exhausted.

When my father lowers himself to his mat with a groan, crosses his legs, and motions for me to join him, I'm trans-ported through time. A child again, ready to hear another of my father's stories, I sit. But the illusion lasts only a moment.

Despite his age, my father picks up his already packed pipe and strikes a flint to the dry leaves. Such is his skill that a single hot ember the size of a sand granule is enough for him to get the contents burning. He breathes in deep, holds, and then turns his head to the ceiling exhaling toward the opening.

"That's going to get you killed," I warn. Like fires, smoking during the summer months is forbidden, especially some-thing as fragrant as Mary's Leaf.

He chuckles. "So few are my visitors that I would be forgotten during the next migration if Grace did not remind them I still lived. And there has never been an elder who carries the weight of all human knowledge, that was not, on occasion, soothed by the pipe." He smiles at Grace. "Or by a strong woman."

Grace bows her thanks at the compliment and then crouches beside me, opening a small medical chest with bandages, a sewing kit, tinctures, and oils. "You know how this goes, and I know you can handle the pain. So pretend I'm not here and get down to the business at hand."

We sit in silence, him puffing, me fuming, Grace dabbing, wiping, and sewing. But my father is a man who cannot be rushed. His words are well thought out and concise. When he speaks, there will be no mystery in his message, and no more efficient way to communicate the facts.

I wince as Grace tugs the thread through my thigh, closing up the puncture wound she's already disinfected with alcohol. The pain is nearly enough to erase the rest of my patience, but interrupting my father's train of thought would mean starting the process over again.

Then he speaks, just a single word.

"Plistim."

He now has my undivided attention. I stop feeling the curved needle sliding through my skin. I stop smelling the Mary's Leaf.

"He's been found," he says. "Salem, too. Forty Modernists, some of them known to us, some of them not. But all of them together."

There are layers of information in his simple words. Found, not killed. The Modernists operate in small cells, recruiting teenagers when they first venture into the forest, regaling them with stories of times long past and showing them trinkets that have survived the ages—like my knife, but far more unique. That they are together, in a group forty strong, means they are plotting something. It also means that action will be taken against them. A war party will be sent, and if Salem is with the Modernists, there will be no capturing or torturing. It will simply be a slaughter. But it will not be quick. Wounds will be designed for maximum pain, drawing out the end so that those who witness it will pass the story on, deterring generations of young people from the Modernists' path.

A prick of pain draws my eyes downward. Grace's wrinkled hands are shaking, but not from age. She's nervous. Rushing to finish before... "They're nearby," I say. "At the Divide."

My father shakes his head, slow, either buying Grace time to finish or because of the calming smoke curling from his nose, up and around his head.

"In Essex?"

His head continues to shake. I should have let him continue. He would have told me by now. But this is my son we are talking about, and while my family, and our tribe, might have disowned him, he is my life. He is the boy I failed to raise right, whose curiosity dug in and never let go. I should have seen myself mirrored in him, should have spent more time teaching him the law. I could have prevented his seduction.

"What will you do?" my father asks. "If you find him first?"

He knows me too well.

"I will give him the chance to renounce his ways and leave with me. To the North. Teach him to live off the land, and the importance of the Prime Law."

"You forget, Plistim was an elder. There is nothing of the law, and the time before, that you could teach your son that he does not already know."

"Then he will have to teach me."

My father smiles. "It will be a lonely life for both of you."

"No more than now."

My father dips his head. "Should you embark on this fool's errand, I will likely pass before, and if, you ever return, which I would not recommend."

The true reason for his delay becomes clear. When he relays my son's location, and I leave my father's hut, it will be the last time he sees me.

Grace ties a bandage around my leg, cinches it tight, and gives it a pat. "She's ready."

My father leans forward on his knees, reaching for me. I lean forward to meet him. His weathered hand on the back of my neck draws me closer until our foreheads are touching. "You are my most dear and cherished love," he says, and I nearly protest, because Grace is here with me, and I know what she means to him. But her hand on my back, rubbing slow circles, silences me. "Your mind is crisp. Your body hard. And your heart is pure. The Prime Law guides you in all things."

The words he is speaking to me are profound, not just because they are the final words of a father to a daughter, but because they mirror the words spoken from one elder to another at the time of transition. They are the same words spoken to Micha when he ascended into my father's position.

"I am sorry about the man your husband, our elder, turned out to be, but I am proud of the woman you became."

His words bring tears to my eyes and drill home that this is the last time I will see him.

My father's voice lowers to a gravelly whisper. "Be wary of the man to whom you are still wed. As I have known from the moment I first laid eyes on your son, Micha also knows he is not the father. His respect for me is the only reason you yet live, and that respect has been waning of late. Should he see you in the wild..."

My stomach clenches, not out of fear of my husband, but that the truth has been known, by my father of all people, all this time.

He gives my neck a pat. "You are not the only one with secrets." His free hand slides around my back. I feel his fingers interlock with Grace's, and I can't help but huff a laugh.

"I had hoped," I say, pausing to take a slow breath, preparing to say my goodbyes to them both, but then my father utters a single word, guaranteeing that I will never speak the words.

"Suffolk."

The small county is the only visible land south of Essex, separated by the great outflowing Karls River, once crossable, now miles wide and untold fathoms deep, part of it draining into the ocean, the rest roaring from a small fork into the Divide. It is unreachable, forbidden, and the only place in the known world where the great structures of the past still stand, their skeletal frames visible at sunset.

"They have ventured into the old city," he adds.

I push myself up, testing my legs. The expertly sewn wounds remain sealed. "How can we possibly know this? It is beyond our reach."

"A traitor in their midst. One who saw the error in what they plan to do. I believe he was one of Salem's friends."

"Where is he? I would have words with him."

"You know where he is," my father says.

Dead, I think. Tortured first, every secret expunged, and then slain.

"When did my husband set out?" I ask.

"This morning." My father points to the right of the entrance. "For you."

There is a fresh pack tied to a bed roll, no doubt full of food, water, and medical supplies. A spear is strapped on either side, their metal tips gleaming and sharp. And on the back, my father's ancient machete, a staple of my childhood, unused for decades.

I pick up the pack and slip it over my shoulders. This, along with the knife at my waist, is everything I will need, short of a way to cross the Karls River.

"I love you both," I say, looking them in the eyes, and then I slip out of the hut, beginning my journey south, to Suffolk county, where the city of Boston once stood.

I make it three steps down the hill before my father stops me. "Vee."

He stands framed by the small hut, Grace by his side. "If Salem does not agree to join you..."

My father is seeking assurance, to know he was right to tell me.

And I have no trouble giving it to him. "If Salem denies what I offer...I will kill him."

5

The journey to Suffolk is dangerous, but not because of the terrain. While the forest floor is rarely level, the hill atop which my father has made his home is more than twice the height of anything between the village and the coast. The forest is dense in places, but the machete makes short work of any plants barring my path. The number of times I am forced to employ the blade reveals my path is the one less followed. A venture to the south of Essex is normally made by traveling east to the coast, and then south along the shore. It is a circuitous route, but avoids traveling along the Divide. While the people of Essex do not fear proximity to the vast gorge, traveling along its unexplored edge is considered foolish. It's also a direct, southeasterly route that will shave a day from the journey and put me ahead of Micha and his war party.

I've seen no evidence of my husband or his men. They would do their best to mask their presence, as we all do, but fifty plus unwashed men, eating, drinking, pissing, and shitting, are easy to track by smell alone. If I can maintain my pace, I should beat them to Suffolk and have plenty of time to...

What?

Find a way across the largest river in all of New Inglan? I'm a good swimmer, but even if my leg wasn't hurt, crossing the Karls without being swept out to sea, or sucked into the Divide is impossible. People have tried. All have perished.

But the Modernists found a way across. For forty people.

The trees to my right thin out, revealing a sliver of light that draws my eyes.

I stop like a deer that has caught a predator's scent.

But the open maw facing me is miles wide and infinitely longer. I'd prefer the jaws of a mountain lion.

Distracted by thoughts of my son, my husband, and Suffolk, I wandered further west than intended. The Divide's edge is just four hundred feet away. I could reach its edge, at a full sprint, in twenty seconds.

I could look into the abyss.

Part of me is tempted by the idea. It's the same part of me that remembers cooked meat, who listened to my father's stories, and who snuck off to be impregnated by a man who was not my husband. But I am not a fool, and I will not be responsible for humanity's demise, simply to look at...

What?

No one knows.

I understand the Modernist's temptation. I have the same questions. About the world. About my place in it. About the point to it all. The Prime Law gives many answers about these things, but to those with the intelligence to see it, they are incomplete answers designed to dull interest in things beyond. The truth of the world is only meant for elders, who, in theory, are wise enough to retain the information without being corrupted by it. For the rest of us, a taste of knowledge leads to evil.

That is why my father raised me with a firm understanding of the law, ensuring that the knowledge I had gained from him at an early age did not cause me to falter. Salem had no knowledge of the world before, and my efforts were more relaxed as a result. If I must slay my son, it will be because I first failed him.

I walk along the tree line, ten feet back, listening to the rush of warm air rising from the Divide. Large hawks float in the warbling air, held aloft by great wings as they look for prey foolish enough to approach the precipice.

"What do you see?" I ask the bird before it tilts its body and soars out over the chasm, headed to the far side, beyond the orange-hued horizon.

The sun is falling, and as tempting as it is to walk through the night, even Micha and his men will stop to sleep. Better to rest and arrive with half a day to spare, than a full day and only half a mind.

Knowing a close proximity to the Divide is the fastest route, I keep the thin tree line in sight as I limp further southeast, moving until the sun is neatly divided by the horizon. Then begins the search for a suitable tree. Without a companion to keep watch, I will need to sleep in the branches. Although many predators hunt during the day, they still stalk the darkness aside those that are strictly nocturnal. Some will even climb to find prey—but not without making a lot of noise.

The oak tree I find growing along the tree line is ancient, hundreds of years old. Its long, sweeping branches are full of large green leaves that will keep me hidden. A quick run, and a push off the trunk, sends me high enough to catch the lowest branch. My leg aches from the effort, but I have no trouble hoisting myself up. As comfortable in the trees as I am on the ground, I head upward until I find a suitable crisscrossing of branches to support me. After unfurling and securing my bed roll, and attaching my pack to a branch, I have a small meal of dried meat and berries. Fed, but not completely satiated, the setting sun's orange light draws my eyes west. Cracks in the foliage shimmer with a warmth that makes me feel alive.

I stand and walk along the branch while holding on to a second. Weight flexes the limb downward, opening a passage through which I can see the setting sun, and the Divide it frames.

A hiccup of surprise escapes my mouth.

I'm forty feet up and now able to see the far side. I've never seen it this close before, and never framed by the setting sun. What looks like a silhouetted tree line is backlit by a wash of orange clouds at the horizon. Orange becomes red, and directly overhead, red becomes purple.

"It is beautiful," I say, intending the message for a son who cannot hear me. "I understand why you want to go there..."

And then I'm reminded why such a thing is impossible.

A shadow, projected upward by the setting sun, crawls along the sky, stretched out to impossible heights, bubbling over low-lying fluffy clouds, masking its identity.

The Golyat.

The hairs on my arms rise up in unison, as though pleading for mercy.

I'm gripped by a horror that's been instilled in me since birth, but the quiet voice of curiosity is never far behind.

"What are you?" I whisper.

A fast moving cloud, low to the ground, cuts the shadow in half. When it leaves, the shadow has shrunk.

For a moment, I think this is because the sun's angle has changed, but the further the sun sets, the longer the shadows get.

A smooth patch of wispy clouds becomes the shadow's canvas, and at that exact moment, the creature stands and reveals its true form.

I stumble back, losing my footing and nearly my grip. The sudden fall, and the rush of adrenaline that comes with it, clears my mind enough to return some sense of self-preservation. I climb atop the branch once more, and with shaking limbs, I find my way to the bed roll. My eyes are no longer drawn to the light, or to the shadow still moving about in it.

But I can still see its distinct shape, its human-like form as recognizable as my own shadow. Arms, legs, a smooth head.

But it's not human.

It can't be.

It's far too big.

While the measurements are not precise, both ends of the estimated size scale are daunting. At the low end, the Golyat stands seventy-five feet tall. At the high end, two hundred feet tall. Wise men and elders have attempted to calculate the exact height for generations, but the number is always changing. Most believe the creature's height to be somewhere in the middle.

No matter the size, human beings would be as grasshoppers in its sight.

And likely a food source.

The Golyat is real. Of that there is no doubt. And that is why any serious breach of the Prime Law cannot be tolerated. It is why those whose actions threaten to expose our presence to the monster must receive swift and harsh consequences.

And why I will either whisk my son away to the wildlands of Brunswick, or put my knife through his heart.

The idea of killing my son makes me ill, but the knowledge that his actions could lead to horrors beyond imagining makes it necessary. And while it is not required for mothers to kill errant sons, in this case, it will be merciful. While Micha would draw out the boy's killing, especially if he knows Salem is not his son, I will make his death quick.

The same cannot be said if I manage to get ahold of Plistim. The man is a warrior, hardened by a harsh land, but as a shepherd, I have faced far worse than any one man.

Sleep is impossible.

My thoughts are torn to shreds by combating worries. I lay still for several hours, and then give up. I gather my gear, leave the tree's safety, and set out through the night. Better to be a day early with half a brain than half a day early with half a brain.

I can sleep tomorrow night, I decide, skirting the forest's edge, where predators are less likely to lurk. Through the break in the trees I look up at the lunar ring, arching its way across the horizon. It's a pale rainbow of dust, all that remains of what was once called the moon. The ring is visible during the day, as a thin, white line, but it's spectacular at night.

It does little to soothe my racing thoughts. They carry me through the night and the following day, at the end of which I sleep—only to dream of the Golyat sitting atop my father's hill, Plistim in one giant hand, Salem in the other, all three of them laughing as I thrash and drown in a puddle.

Despite a solid night's sleep, the third day of travel finds me weary. I push onward, determined to outpace Micha, but my dreams have stolen all hope of saving Salem. As the sun begins to set on the third day, I realize my progress has been far slower than planned.

Defeated and bladder full, I stop to relieve myself. Pants down, squatted down where I stood, I listen to the steady stream of urine, studying its odor for any sign of illness. When my task is complete, the sound of rushing liquid continues, but distant, and far more vast than I can manage.

I reach the forest's edge at a run, nearly spilling out past the tree line, which would have been disastrous. The Divide is just twenty feet away. To the right, it stretches northwest to the horizon. To the left, a short, fast moving branch of the Karls River roars into the abyss. Beyond the waterfall is the rest of the Karls River, racing eastward, toward the sea and Suffolk.

And my son.

With no regard for the coming night, I follow the river east, leaving the Divide behind, and racing toward what I hope will be my son's salvation, but what I am certain will be his death.

And probably mine.

6

I smell them before I see them, their mix of scents spoiling the fragrant forest air, made sweeter by the roiling river. Micha's men are congregated by the water, debating in groups, no doubt wondering how to cross. I can't hear what they're saying, and don't really care. I'm too late. Micha and his men either traveled through the night, or took a less circuitous route than I believed. I wasn't sure how to cross the Karls before, but now...with the narrowest stretch of river occupied...it's a hopeless endeavor.

I shouldn't have stopped to sleep last night, I think, but I also know it's a foolish thought. After the previous day's journey, and my long search along the riverbank as the sun fell to the horizon, I was exhausted. And searching through the night was impossible. I rose with the sun's return and searched another hour before catching my first whiff of company.

Hidden high in a tree, I look up from the men, following the fast moving and very deep waters. The churning river flows into the ocean, glimmering in the morning sun, just a mile to the east. But this isn't what holds my interest. Near the horizon to the south is the island of Suffolk, the remains of its once towering structures point skyward.

How had such immense buildings been constructed? What materials had been used? Wood rots after a time. And stone mortar crumbles. It's hard to believe life was so different before the Golyat, but there's the evidence, beckoning to the young and foolish.

The group of men falls silent at Micha's return. He looks frustrated, but that's nothing new. The world around him is a constant disappointment, never measuring up to his lofty expectations. He addresses the men, but his voice is distorted by distance, his orders impossible to discern.

I need to get closer, I decide. If Micha and his men devise a way across, I will follow if I can. Suffolk is a large island. There's still a chance I can find Salem first.

I land on the ground without making a sound, but being quiet means little when you land a dozen feet from two men with spears. I spot them when I'm already dropping to the ground, far too late to avoid detection. The best I can do is hope they're fools.

My landing alerts the two men to my presence, but I don't look at either man. Instead, I recover my gear from a nearby bush and say, "Let Micha know that I haven't seen a way across, but I'll keep looking."

When I turn around, I'm greeted by spear tips aimed at my chest.

The two men, who I'm pretty sure are brothers named Zac and Bents, squint at me. Recognition leads to confusion, and Zac says, "Eight?"

"Lady Eight," I say with a smile.

Zac grins, but Bents, older by a good ten years, remains on guard. "Didn't realize you were with us."

"Wouldn't be a good tracker if you did."

"You're a shepherd," Bents says, knuckles paling as he tightens his grip.

"And I track animals all day. People aren't that different."

"It's Vee," Zac says to his brother, lowering his spear. I'm honestly moved by the sentiment, and that he used my prefer-red name. If I recall correctly, Zac is the second youngest of six children, the four eldest being brothers and the youngest being a daughter, making him the youngest son. "She's the elder's wife. She—"

"Isn't supposed to be here," Bents says, motioning for Zac to raise his spear again, which he does. "At best, she is neglecting her shepherding duties because her son is over there." He points toward Suffolk. "Or she is one of them, come to stop us, or she plans to warn the Modernists of our approach."

Zac grows more alert, his spear held at the ready once more.

Bents is no fool, and he's very well informed.

"You're wasting time," I say, sticking to the act. "I need to continue my search, and if you're unsure about whether or not I should be here, go ask Micha." It's a dangerous gamble, but the closer I get to the truth, the more believable it will be. "My father sent word that the Modernists had been found. I requested to join the war party so that I might kill Salem myself. You know who I am. Both of you. Though my station is low, my allegiance to the Prime Law, and to my *father*, is without question. As is my skill with a spear."

I'm not comfortable bringing my father into this, but it works. Bents is considering my words, the skin of his knuckles brown once more. It's not much, but his relaxed guard might give me the edge I need to subdue the brothers.

My oldest brother, the one killed by Micha in legal combat, taught me how to hunt and fight. While I have plenty of practice dealing with wild animals, men with weapons is a different problem. They're smarter, well trained, and I don't want to kill either of them, which means I'll be holding back, and they won't be.

But I have little choice. Surrendering means facing Micha, and if my father is right, my husband is counting the days until my demise. He knows my dedication to the law, and that I'd never associate with Modernists, but my presence is close enough to guilt that putting me to death would never be questioned.

While Bents has yet to decide my fate, I turn toward the river and let my eyes go wide, like I've just seen something astonishing. It's a hard sell because from the ground, the river is barely visible through the trees. My gaze remains locked on the water as I wait for them to notice my faux shock and look to the river.

Zac falls for it first, turning to look, but Bents doesn't even flinch. Then his brother comes to my rescue, saying, "Holy shit..."

Bents asks, "What?" a moment before I do.

"I...I think she found it," Zac says. "The way across."

Is he mocking me? Perhaps Zac is smarter than I thought, but only playing dumb?

Then I see it for myself and know that of the three of us, I am the biggest fool. The churning water, white with froth, does a decent job of hiding the thin white streak stretching out into the river. So much so that I didn't see it, probably because I was too busy pretending to see something.

Bents turns to look. "I don't see anything."

"In the river." Zac points. "A rope."

When Bents turns to face the river, I reach back and pull one of my two spears from behind my back. I hold the blunt end high and draw it back to strike.

"Maybe you were telling the—" Bents turns toward me as he speaks, fast enough to see my incoming strike, but not soon enough to fully avoid it. Wood strikes skull at an angle and glances off, but it still sends Bents to the ground.

Zac spins around, shock in his eyes, both from seeing his brother on the ground and the spear in my hands. He has a kind of 'I thought we were friends' wounded look about him that makes me feel guilty for what I'm about to do.

I jab the spear's blunt end toward his forehead. The solid strike should crumple him in on himself and allow me to focus on his older, larger, and more dangerous brother, whose angry grunts and shuffling feet reveal he's far from done.

The entire fight plays out in my head. I strike Zac, and while he's still falling, I spin and give Bents a few good whacks on the head, hopefully knocking him unconscious without killing him. What actually happens is a far cry from my vision.

Zac is younger, and faster. He parries the blow and leaps back out of range. There's a moment of naïve confusion and then it melts away, replaced by determination and an expert fighting stance that I recognize, but don't know. While Bents is no doubt a brawler, Zac has studied under a master. The fighting techniques used to be known by many names, but like the people of New Inglan, it has become an amalgam of styles known as Jutsu.

Bents picks himself up. "Eight the savage, wild in the woods, a dead animal in bed."

The personal taunt is meant to reveal just how much Micha has talked about me, not to mention humiliate and distract. But it's a far cry from the things I've imagined my husband saying, so it doesn't faze me. I turn sideways, looking at neither man so I can see them both in my periphery.

"Zac," Bents says. "She attacked us. No need to hold back."

Shit. Murder is against the Prime Law. Killing in self-defense is not.

I wait to see who will attack first, hoping to repeat the trick I used on the lion. But I'm still not trying to kill these two. They're not my enemies, even if they are now trying to kill me. And I am still bound by the law.

But they wait, and the delay is almost aggravating enough to make me strike first. But then I see movement to my left. It's subtle, but shifting at steady intervals. I figure it out, just before Bents lowers his last finger, completing the countdown.

I throw myself backward and down, rolling over and onto my feet as the two men stab their spears into the spot where I stood just a moment before. They strike with such force that they nearly impale each other. Before that surprise can wear off, I attack.

A wide, low swing connects with the back of Zac's knee. Bents might be bigger and meaner, but Zac is definitely the more dangerous of the two. The connection is solid, but the Jutsu-trained brother moves with the strike, reducing the damage done. A wince of pain is my only reward.

I spin in the other direction, swinging for Bents. With just inches between my spear shaft and his big head, Zac blocks the strike.

Okay...damn. I need a new plan.

I glance at the river and the line running across its depths, just a few inches beneath the surface. I doubt the pair would follow before reporting to Micha. One of them, maybe, but not both. The trouble with this plan is that it would require turning my back to run. As with the lion, turning my back on these two will be the very same moment I die. Unlike with the lion, I don't see facing them head on as having a very different outcome. The spear will pierce me front to back, rather than back to front. I'll be dead either way.

But there is little choice. The brothers press the attack, swinging and jabbing their weapons one at a time, keeping me on the defensive. I block, duck, and dodge, but never manage a return strike.

Zac spins his spear feigning a blow that tricks me into blocking empty air. He then reverses the spin and thrusts the weapon toward my side with enough force to punch through and out the far end of my gut. I twist my body and let my backpack get disemboweled. The strike pitches me forward onto my stomach. I try to roll onto my back, but the pack stops me. So I roll the other way, slipping out of the backpack, and relinquishing my spear as I do.

I'm not happy about losing the weapon until I see Bents yanking his spear out of the now twice-stabbed backpack. I draw my knife from the sheath on my hip, ready for the fight, but knowing I'm going to lose.

Zac holds off. "I respect your spirit. You fight with passion. I don't want to kill you."

"Screw that," Bents says, raising his spear to throw, and at this range, he won't miss. Just as his arm starts its forward arc, there's a thump followed by Bents's eyes rolling back and his body falling limp.

Zac spins fast, raising his spear in a defensive position, blocking two stones that come hurtling from the woods. The projectiles are followed by a man in loose-flowing garments, his face concealed by long strips of fabric, tied around his head.

The newcomer attacks with a staff, his strikes coming like a well-practiced dance. Zac blocks each strike like a good dance partner, but he lags behind by a fraction of a second, bringing each blow closer to connecting than the last, until wood finds skull and Zac drops to the ground.

Before I can run, or thank the man, he spins around, swinging the staff out in a wide arc. The knife in my hand pings as it's struck and flung away to the leafy forest floor.

The fighter sizes me up, looking me over. "You're married to the elder of Essex."

The man's actions and words tell me a lot. First, he's not with Micha. That much is obvious. Second, he's not from Essex. No one from our county would call Micha 'the elder of Essex.' He would just be 'the elder.' His rolling accent, adding syllables where there aren't any, tells me he's from one of the far north counties. And last, he recognizes me, which means he has status. He's attended a gathering of the elders or one of the solstice ceremonies. Either way, this is likely not the first time we have met.

When I fail to answer, he asks, "Why are you here?"

"Show me your face."

He takes a step closer, weapon ready to strike. "Answer me now, or join these men."

I look down at the still forms of Bents and Zac. Their chests rise and fall, unconscious, but not dead. Though this man clearly had the skill to slay both men, he let them live, following the Prime Law. Armed with this knowledge, I decide to tell the truth.

"I'm here to kill my son," I say, the words tasting horrible in my mouth, so I tack on the less horrible truth. "Or save him."

The man glances toward Suffolk. "He's with them?"

I nod.

"Why are you not with your husband?"

The truth, again, I decide, and I motion to the two brothers. "I think that is clear. I did not find myself a shepherd because I am beloved."

The man laughs. I can't be sure, but I think he is smiling behind that mask.

"Why are *you* here?" I ask.

"Our paths are aligned," he says. "I am here to kill my father."

He does not add on an 'or save him,' as I did. "Who is your father?"

The smile lines beside his eyes flatten out.

The staff lowers.

"Plistim."

7

"Easy," he says, as I side-step toward my impaled pack and the weapons it still holds. "You handled yourself well against them, but..."

He doesn't need to finish the sentence. We both know how a physical confrontation between us would end: with me either dead or unconscious. Neither option appeals, so I stand my ground and take a calming breath.

"Your name?" I ask.

"Shua," he says without hesitation. "You don't know it. I am one of fifty-three siblings."

"Fifty three?"

"Plistim had thirteen fertile wives when he left."

"And you?" I ask. "How many wives do you have?"

It's an odd question, I know, but experience has taught me that the more wives a man has, the poorer his character.

"I loved a woman once," he says, lost for a moment. "My father married her. Her three children, which should have been my sons, are now my siblings."

"That's...horrible." If true, it's no surprise that Shua wants to kill his father.

"The world is horrible," he says. "But a man need not be defined by it."

"Nor a woman," I say.

"Indeed."

I think he's smiling again, but it's hard to say. "Why do you hide your face?"

Shua goes rigid, his ear cocked to the side. He holds an open palm toward me, eyes closed, listening, or meditating. Then he speaks in a whisper. "They're separating into groups. Searching the river bank. It won't be long before they're discovered..." He motions to Zac and Bents, and then turns to the line running out into the water. "...and the way across is compromised. We need to go now."

"Together?" I'm a little taken aback by how quickly he has decided to trust me.

"Our purposes are aligned. My father will die, and if your son does not agree to leave with you, he will as well. I will not stand in your way. We will uphold the Prime Law together, and if possible, we will avoid your husband and his men."

"Not dying would be great, too."

"And we'll try not to die." The lines around his eyes appear again. A tiny smile. "Agreed?"

And now I'm surprised by how quickly I've decided to trust him. There's just something about him that is both familiar, and trustworthy. I hold out my right arm, offering a formal alliance, the way our fathers might when agreeing on a wedding.

Shua chuckles at the gesture, but then locks arms with me. "Agreed."

I collect my weapons and gear before chasing after Shua, who has already started toward the river's edge, breaking down his spear. The weapon comes apart into four segments that he clips onto his thighs. Other than that, and a few small pouches hanging from his belt, he carries no gear. He's crouched in the shallows when I arrive, already fighting the current despite the ten inch depth. "It's not a rope," he says. "It's metal. Cable. Bolted into a buried boulder."

Most people wouldn't know what cable is, but I'm aware. My father told me how the world was once powered, and energy ran through countless miles of metal cable, or wires. Like most ancient things that survived the centuries, the cables were collected over time, and stored in vast pits, or caves, hidden so that common people wouldn't question the world that is and once was. Plistim must have had access to one of these stores of ancient materials. I crouch beside Shua, looking at the cable. It's closer to a tightly braided mesh of metal strands than the insulated variety.

"It runs all the way across?" I ask, knowing full well that he doesn't know the answer.

"Only one way to find out." He steps deeper and nearly loses his footing. Trained in Justu or not, a man cannot resist the power of Karls River. We will be swept away from the cable long before reaching the far side.

"Wait." I put my pack on the ground and rifle through the supplies packed by my father and Grace. "I might have something." Finding the odd shaped metal devices, I pull them from my pack. "I don't know what they are, but—"

"Locking carabiners," Shua says, taking both and looking them over. "Stainless steel. Where did you get them?"

I don't reply. The devices, which are not one of the few ancient objects allowed under the Prime Law—like blades—could get my father in trouble.

"Very well," he says, handing one of the two carabiners back. He twists a thicker segment of metal, unscrewing it and sliding it down, allowing him to open the metal loop. He then hooks it onto his belt, and leans into the water. After hooking it around the metal cable, he lets the loop snap closed and screws it back in place. I follow each of his steps while fighting hard to not be swept away by the current. After just thirty seconds, I'm attached to the cable.

"It is convenient you had these," Shua says.

The implication is clear, and I respond with indignation. "I am *not* a Modernist."

"Mmm."

His brief reply is infuriating, not because he doubts me, but because he's right. Why would Father think to include such strange devices, knowing full well that I've never seen them before, but they are ideally suited for crossing the Karls? *A question for another time,* I decide, and I step deeper into the cool water. At any other time of year, this crossing would be impossibly frigid. But now, at the height of summer, it's almost refreshing.

When I'm waist deep, the current lifts my feet from the rocky river bed. For a moment, I'm at the river's mercy. Its endless water flows over me, dragging my body and my now waterlogged backpack down. But then the carabiner catches, and I'm able to reach out and grasp the cable. Pulling myself up means defying the river's power, and it takes everything I have.

Back on the surface, I sputter and cough until Shua's hand wraps around my mouth. It takes a few moments, but I manage to control my breathing again.

"Quiet," he whispers, but it's not possible. The water rushing around us is making enough noise to attract the attention of any-one on shore.

When I nod, he removes his hand and points to the riverbank behind us. I turn slowly and spot five men, a hundred feet back. They're moving slowly, searching the water's edge. They *will* find the cable, and if we're still here, us along with it.

"My pack is too heavy," I tell him. "See the machete?"

He looks back and nods.

"Can you take it?"

He draws the blade and sheath from the backpack and then I slip out of it. The pack, its contents, and the bedroll are luxuries I can do without. Food is everywhere, if you know where to look. The summer air provides all the warmth I need, and I've slept in far worse places than a tree without a bedroll. Only my father's machete, and the knife on my hip are irreplaceable.

I hold the backpack under the water, drowning it and the gifts it contains from my father. When bubbles stop roiling to the surface, I release it. The pack is swept away into the dark depths. While my heart is heavy at its loss, my body feels half the weight.

Shua hands me the sheathed machete and I slip it into my belt. Then, without a word, we set out along the taut cable. Hand over hand, our progress is slow and waterlogged. Each pull forward into deeper waters increases the pressure against my body. My arms ache as I resist a river said to be powerful and deep enough to wipe away the Golyat.

Deeper waters bring colder temperatures, and my muscles begin to shiver from cold and exertion. Despite being twice my size, Shua is faring no better. He pauses to look at me and glances back at shore. His determination falters, and when I look back, I see why.

My body says I've scaled a mountain, but we're only two hundred feet from shore, with many thousands left to go. Even worse, Micha's men have nearly reached the cable. When they find it, they'll follow its course out into the water and see our two chattering faces staring back.

Maybe this isn't how the Modernists crossed? I have trouble believing someone could resist the river's current all the way across, not to mention forty people.

I look at the cable, following it into the depths. It doesn't cut straight across the river. It's at an angle.

"We need to stop fighting it," I say, and when he shows no sign of understanding, I add, "We need to let go."

A little more of his face is revealed as the saturated wraps concealing him are tugged down. Something about him is familiar, but as an elder's son, that's not really surprising. I know what Plistim looks like, and Shua most likely resembles his father. What the lowered mask truly shows is his indignation. His words back up his expression. "That's insane."

"You're good at Jutsu," I say. "I'm good at insane. And not dying."

His eyes go wide with fright. A moment ago, I wouldn't have thought the man capable of fear, but the look in his eyes is unmistakable, and has nothing to do with my idea.

"What is it?"

"Something bumped me," he says.

"I bumped you," I say, as the river continues to thrash our bodies together.

"My feet," he says. "Hard."

His feet are a good eighteen inches beyond mine.

That's when I see it, cutting through the water.

A fin.

I point it out. "There."

The foot-tall fin hints at the shark's size. I can't identify the species based on a fin, but its size suggests a man-eater. The ocean and I aren't fast friends. I spend most of my time in the forest, and have never faced a shark. But I have seen the remains of unlucky fishermen, and I know a single shark can inflict far more damage in a single bite than a dozen mountain lions.

A vibration runs through the cable, tickling my fingers. Shua has let go, and as I'd hoped, the current has launched him away at an angle. I take one last look back at shore—the men are closing in—and I look at the shark, making a wide circle. Then I let go.

Water rushes over me for a moment, and then the carabiner slips over metal and I'm carried downstream and across the river at the water's full speed.

Which I now know is about half the speed the shark can manage when swimming with the current.

8

Shouts cascade from the shore. Short excited barks. Wild dogs with a fresh kill. Micha's men have found the cable. When the voices turn angry, I know Shua and I have been spotted. When anger turns to laughter, I know they've seen the shark, closing in.

I'm far enough from shore to not be recognized, so the men probably think we're with the Modernists, lookouts perhaps, going to warn the others. If we can survive the river.

"How do I stop it?" I shout, as the river whisks us further away from shore and downstream.

"I've only been to the ocean twice."

His words enrage me. How can a man who spent his life training to fight not learn how to fight against the things in this world that most frequently harm people? Murder is un-common. War is unheard of. We live on the fringe, and aside from the Modernists and the occasional legal combat, humanity is united.

While the current hurtles me along, I focus on the fin and try to keep my head above water. I draw the machete and hold it out in front of me the same way I would while facing a lion or bear. Predators are fierce killers, but like most living things, they're not fond of pain. Unless they're defending their young—or starving—a sharp poke is sometimes enough to make them think twice.

But this is a shark.

Are sharks even smart? I've always pictured them as mindless eating machines, or violent bullies. While some fishermen have been consumed, many more have been bitten and released. Some have lost limbs. I've never been able to think of a good reason for this behavior beyond, *sharks are assholes.*

I cough and sputter as churning water rolls over my head and down my throat. When I recover, the fin is gone.

The frothing dark water is impossible to see through, despite the late-morning sun blazing down upon it. I can see the blue sky reflected on its surface more than I can beneath it.

Machete still outstretched, I slip beneath the water, holding my breath. It's quieter beneath the surface. Almost peaceful. Beams of yellow light shimmer down from above, reminding me of the green aurora that sometimes decorates the sky. The moment's beauty is cut short when a long, sleek body slips through the beams of light, partially lit like an apparition. It maintains a steady speed with little effort, its course unwavering and unquestionably toward me.

Though I can now see my adversary, there's not much more I can do than hold the blade out and wait. The shark twitches and somehow cuts the distance between us in half. Its black eyes glare. Its body goes rigid. And then with another burst of speed, it comes.

Just as quickly as the creature attacked, it turns away, just a foot from the blade's tip. *It couldn't have seen the blade,* I think, the eyes had closed and gone white as it rushed in. But it seemed to sense the weapon and understand its purpose.

Out of air, I surface and take a deep breath.

We're nearly halfway across the river now. Micha's men, small dots on the shore, which might include Micha himself, rush toward the line's end.

How long will it be before they follow? *Minutes,* I decide.

Will the shark sighting deter them? *Unlikely.*

If Shua and I reach the far side with our limbs and lives intact, we'll need to keep moving. While I have a low opinion of Micha, he's smart enough to figure out how to use the cable, especially after his men watched us being whisked away by the water.

"Where is it?" Shua shouts. He's five feet ahead of me, face still covered, but the brave man who came to my rescue is now lost in a torrent of water and fear.

"Take out your weapon, and come under!" It's more of a command than a suggestion, and I don't wait to see if he obeys. With a gulp of air, I slip beneath the surface once more, ready to face our attacker and maybe a gruesome, thrashing death.

The shark is there, and easy to find, cutting an agitated circle around us, looking for the best angle of attack, which is going to be Shua, if he doesn't get his head underwater. My frightened partner announces his arrival with a bubbly shout. Despite the loud declaration of his fear, his hands work fast, freeing the various parts of his spear from his hips and assembling them. When he's done, the long spear will provide him far more protection from the shark than my machete, which is probably why the shark snaps its tail and returns to stare at me.

The predator moves back and forth, biding its time, perhaps waiting for me to surface again, which I'll have to do in a few seconds. Just as my chest begins to tighten, the shark swims deep, beyond the sun's reach.

Where are you?

My lungs burn.

Pressure builds in my head.

I have to fight to keep my mouth closed. If I open it, instinct will force me to breathe in.

I need to surface, but if I do—

The shark slips back into the light, its tail a flurry of motion, its body rocketing up toward me, triangle teeth bared, white throat gaping. I try to angle myself downward, but the carabiner and the swift river conspire against me. The best I can do is pull my legs up and hold the machete down.

When the shark is ten feet below me, a fraction of a second from striking, my body overrides my mind. Lips part. Water rushes in. My head breaks the surface, coughing and then gasping. Somewhere in the back of my mind, I register a swirl of water opposing the river's flow for just a moment, and then I gasp again.

Did the shark turn back? Was my leg's dismemberment so fast and precise that I have yet to feel it?

Though I have two deep breaths in me, my lungs are far from satiated. Despite this, I clamp my mouth shut and plunge beneath the surface again.

When the bubbles clear, Shua is revealed, still under, still clutching his spear, but struggling to hold on. The shark is impaled on the tip, wriggling back and forth. With a cloud of red, the shark yanks free and disappears into the dark with a burst of speed.

I don't think it will return, but with blood in the water, its brethren might come looking.

Shua and I rise together, both coughing, desperate for air, and dry land. Despite having saved my life again, there's nothing noble or brave left in the man. The part of me that was humiliated to need saving is glad to see this side of him. The rest of me wishes his brave countenance would return. There was comfort to be found in it.

Our rapid course across the river slows, taking my attention away from Shua. The water here is divided into strange, flat sheets that appear to defy the river's flow. And then, we're motionless, captured in one of the placid sheets. It takes me a moment to realize what's happening. I've seen it before, but only from a distance. "The river's current is fighting the incoming tide." I point to the river's far side. "Look, the current."

Despite the river's continuous flow, it's currently battling the ocean's mighty tide. The result is a seaward current behind us, and an inland current ahead. We're caught in the space between.

"Pull yourself forward," I shout.

Shua follows the command, but is slowed by the spear in his hand. While I quickly slip the machete into my belt, he'd have to waste time dismantling the spear. With sharks and blood in the water, I doubt he'd want to relinquish the spear anyway. So he pulls with one arm. At first, I think he's moving slowly, but then I realize he's matching my two-armed pace.

After a few hard pulls we reach the cable's end, where it is attached to a large stone rising nearly to the river's surface. Beside it is a second mounted cable, stretched tight across the river, following an upriver course. The design confuses me until I remember the incoming tide. The outflowing river and incoming tide have created a vortex, and we're in the middle of it. Had the tide been flowing out, we would have been stuck here until the waters reversed.

"We need to switch between the cables." I point to the second cable, just under the waterline. Shua grips my arm when I detach the carabiner and nearly slip away. A moment later, I'm attached to the second line. Shua repeats my actions with more grace, and we slip into deep water once more. The inland ocean current tugs us along, speeding us toward shore, completing a massive V through the river.

We remain vigilant throughout the remainder of our water journey, but the shark does not return, and if others have been drawn by the blood, they don't find us. If we're lucky, they'll head for the far shore, now out of sight, where Micha and his men have no doubt started crossing the river.

I shout in surprise when my feet strike something solid. Then I realize it's the rocky riverbed. A moment later, we're in waist deep water, fighting the rushing tide as we unclip the carabiners and scramble toward shore. Chilled through and exhausted, my walk becomes a crawl as I move onto dry land. Shua isn't faring much better, his strong body brought low by the journey.

Despite our condition, I can't help but smile. Part of me is thrilled to set foot on Suffolk's forbidden land. I glance up at the trees, a mostly leafy green with the occasional pine, identical to the land we left behind. Even smells the same. Of flowers. Of warm, damp rot. Of the ocean, and the river. This land is alive. And as far as I can tell, free of the Golyat's corruption.

"We should keep moving," I say, pushing myself up onto shaky legs. Each step is a challenge, and will continue to be until we rest. My preference would be to rest here, but it won't be long before Micha and his men arrive. They'll need to rest, too, but I doubt they'll want to share the beach.

Shua pushes himself up and stands a bit easier with the help of his spear.

I take the machete to a nearby tree, severing a fairly straight branch and then shaving it clean of twigs and leaves. With my weight supported by the staff, I step into the dense woods that, until the Modernists' arrival, had not been touched by mankind for five hundred years, and yet, will soon be covered in its blood.

9

With a half hour of hiking between us and the river, we come across a large flat stone at the center of a clearing and decide to stop for a rest, and a chance to dry out in the hot sun. Without a word, both Shua and I begin to shed our clothing, hanging them on branches to dry. Wet clothes are not only uncomfortable and cause chafing, but they restrict movement.

Shua's lack of shame matches my own, and we're soon both naked. His body, like mine, is fit, his lean muscles punctuated by scars. The difference between our scars is that mine are mostly jagged, from teeth, claws, branches, and stone, while his are almost all clean, straight lines—the kinds of wounds only a sharp blade can deliver.

While his scars tell the story of a man who has been trained in combat, and seen his fair share, his face remains a mystery, wrapped in a brown shroud. "I bare myself to you and you're not courteous enough to show me your face?"

He laughs at the joke, giving me a once over. "Nothing I haven't seen before."

While he finishes draping his loose clothing, which has absorbed significantly more water than my tight garb, I inspect the strange stone. Aside from a few damaged areas, its height is even. There are a few cracks where vegetation has sprouted, and a large hole from which a tree has grown. The surface and sides are pocked from weathering, but it's really just a big slab of porous stone. "I've never seen anything like this."

"They were destroyed in New Inglan hundreds of years ago," Shua explains. "Along with most other creations of the Time Before."

"This isn't natural?"

"Have you ever seen a perfectly flat and square stone before?"

Now that he's pointed it out, I feel foolish for asking. So I propel the conversation onward. "What is it?"

"A building foundation."

"People built huts on flat stones?"

"It's not really a stone," he explains. "It was something like a liquid, poured into a frame and allowed to harden. It formed a very strong base upon which tall structures could be built."

"Like in Boston."

He nods, and sounds a bit wistful when he says, "Buildings far larger than the Golyat."

He knows a lot about the Old World, which isn't surprising given his father's identity. While my father rambled about his knowledge to a daughter he didn't quite realize was paying attention, Plistim is known for telling the elder's sacred knowledge to anyone willing to listen.

Shua motions to my thigh, where the stitches Grace gave me are holding up. "Something bit you?"

"Mountain lion."

"You killed it?" There's a trace of dubious machismo in his voice.

"And ate its heart, before killing its mate."

He pales a little bit at that, but I don't think it's because I killed two lions. "It's true, isn't it?"

He looks away from the wounds. "What?"

"About Aroostook. You don't eat raw meat."

He turns. "Haven't for more than a hundred years."

"*What?*" I'm staggered. It's a gross violation of the Prime Law and puts Shua and all of Aroostook dangerously close to being Modernists. What would happen if an entire county was declared an enemy of the Prime Law? War? Mass murder?

He's still smiling under those wrappings. "Piscataquis, Penobscot, and Washington, too. And all of the wildlands and Brunswick, of course."

I'm beyond words, managing only a few strained grunts.

"All of the elders know," he says. "We are distant enough from the Divide and have been cooking food for a century without incident. It's safe."

"It's—"

"Against the Prime Law," he says with a nod. "The Prime Law was amended a hundred years ago, leaving several laws to the discretion of each elder. While most counties' elders opted to maintain the old laws, those furthest from the Divide loosened them."

"That's moronic."

He shrugs. "And yet, here we are. Free of the Golyat and still alive."

I concede the point mentally, but won't verbalize it. Just speaking the words would feel like a violation. "The amendments weren't enough for your father, then?"

"Not nearly. He believes that humanity can, and should, return to the ways of our ancestors. He embraces technology, and innovation, and freedom above all else."

"Even if it risks everything?" I ask.

"He doesn't believe the Golyat poses a true threat. There are whales in the ocean, a hundred feet long—"

"Really?"

"—and yet the waters of New Inglan still teem with life. Even if the Golyat consumed people, how could it devour our entire population, or that of the outside world before our time? In the same way our ancestors hunted whales with giant spears called harpoons, he intends to bring low the Golyat, slaying the creature and freeing mankind from its self-imposed slavery."

"You sound convinced."

"I've heard the speeches enough times to recite them with his inflections."

"Did you ever believe him?"

"For a time," he confesses. "When I was younger."

"And now?"

"I'm here to kill him. What do you think?"

"Right…"

A growl tickles my ear. It's barely there, but enough to raise the hairs on my neck. I pick up the machete and scan the forest for movement, searching for any aberration in the brush, tall grass, or trees.

"What is it?" Shua whispers.

"A growl."

The next sound I hear is snickering.

"What the hell is wrong with you? Quiet."

"The growl was me," he says, and when I turn to face him, he raises his hands, pleading mercy, but still laughing. He pats his belly. "I'm hungry."

"When did you last eat?" I ask.

"Yesterday," he says. "But I obey the laws of the counties I travel to. I haven't eaten meat since leaving the north."

"What have you eaten?"

"Berries. Roots."

I expect the list to go on, but that's where he stops. I can't help but shake my head at the man who is a natural with a weapon, but useless in the forest.

"If you don't eat something substantial, you won't last long."

"In case you forgot, you lost your pack, and all your food."

It's my turn to laugh, but not really in a kind way. "We are surrounded by food."

He scans the area, clearly spotting nothing edible. While we are surrounded by plants, mushrooms, insects, and fruit, all of which are edible, a man Shua's size needs calories—muscle and fat. I require far less, but just talking about food has awakened my hunger.

"We'll hunt," I say.

"I can't eat raw meat." He looks a little peaked.

"Can, and will, or you're no use to me."

"There isn't time," he argues. "Once our clothes are dry, we need to move. My father won't be idle."

"If you collapse from hunger and exhaustion, you'll never reach your father. Certainly not before Micha does." I bend down and pick up a rock the size of my fist. "And we'll be done eating long before our clothing dries."

The animals have been quiet since we've arrived. Despite being separated from people for five hundred years, they've maintained their fear of us. But I doubt they've grown any smarter. I spotted them when we first arrived in the clearing, high in the branches, nervous heads bobbing.

I reach my hand out to Shua. "Spear."

He hesitates a moment, but then hands his weapon to me. I heft it, feeling its weight. It's a little longer, heavier, and more flexible than I'm accustomed to—designed for fighting men, not killing animals—but it will work. I hurl the heavy stone toward the broad tree. The loud *thunk,* as it strikes, kicks off a panicked flurry. Plump turkeys burst from the leaves, lacking any clear sense of direction or grace. Some flutter into neighboring trees. Three of them take flight across the clearing, directly overhead.

The spear wobbles as it flies upward, but my aim is true. The pierced turkey rises with the weapon's impact, and then falls with it. I catch the spear and hold the already dead turkey out to Shua, who looks both impressed, and disappointed.

"Let's eat," I say.

"Don't you need to prepare the bird? Remove its feathers? Clean the meat?"

After removing the bird from the spear, I place it atop the flat stone and draw my knife. With a quick cut, I remove the head and hold the bird upside down by its feet, draining the blood until it slows to a trickle. Then I lay the turkey down again, slip my blade into its neck, facing up. I cut a line down its chest, over the sternum, and into its gut, mimicking my technique with the lion, but on a much smaller scale.

After exposing the ribs, I place the machete against the sternum and give the blade a hard whack. These ribs flex and crack far easier than the lion's did and soon we have access to the turkey's innards.

"You're depleted, so you can eat the organs. I'll eat the meat."

"Organs?"

"I'm trying hard to not mock you," I admit, "because I want you to know how serious I am when I say this. If your lack of food slows you down, I will leave you behind, and I cannot promise you if I come across your father, that I will be as merciful with his death as you will. Most of my days are spent in the forest. If you want to survive it, you'll do as I say."

With that, I reach into the bird's chest and tear out its heart. After shaving off the arteries, I carve the vital muscle into four, bloody, bite size segments. "You don't need to chew it. Just swallow it."

He takes the first bit of heart and after a moment's debate, tosses it in his mouth and swallows. He clenches his eyes and mouth for a moment, and then relaxes.

"Not bad, right?" I ask.

"Not good," he says. "But I'll live."

He eats everything I give him, while I peel raw muscle from bone and eat, chewing and relishing the flavor. Ten minutes later, my belly is full and little of the bird remains. I rub my hands in the dirt, and then together, drying and flaking away the blood. Shua does the same without question. Then we collect our mostly dry clothing, dress, and strike out again, heading toward the island's core, where the last remnants of the Old World still stand.

10

Walking through the quiet forest, I don't feel like I'm rushing toward a small army of Modernists, or being pursued by Micha and his men, who have no doubt set out from the river by now. Shua and I keep a brisk pace, not a word shared between us for thirty minutes. Our course is southeast until we hear the ocean's waves crashing against the shore. We redirect south, keeping the ocean on our left and avoiding the beaches. The open sand might make for faster travel, but it would expose us to both sides of this conflict, which we would like to avoid, save for two people. Neither of us have any illusions about fighting through the Modernist ranks. Stealth is paramount.

Our progress slows when we're forced to navigate a swamp, and then again when we reach a network of concrete foundations. Some are just small walls, rising from the soil, the structure filled in and reclaimed by the forest. Others loom eight feet high. Every single one feels like an adventure. I want to explore. I can't deny it. But such things are folly, so I squelch the childish emotions.

The concrete foundations are laid out in a grid, which is discernable, even though some foundations are missing.

"How tall were the buildings?" I ask. I've seen the towering remains from a distance, but have never really considered their size before time crumbled them.

"In Boston? Almost eight hundred feet." Shua speaks the unfathomable number with the confidence of someone who is not guessing. "In the world...I believe it was two-thousand, seven hundred feet, plus a few. In a place called Dubai."

The number stops me in my tracks. "That's...not possible."

"A lot of impossible things were once possible." He pauses to admire a row of foundations, interspersed with tall trees. "People inhabited the whole planet. Traveled to the moon, before it was destroyed. Built machines that looked like people and could think on their own."

"What is a planet?" I ask.

He looks a little stunned. "You know about the moon?"

I nod.

"What it looked like?"

"Round," I say. "Like the sun. Like a ball."

"A sphere." He points at the ground. "Our...world is a sphere, too. Like a ball. It's why the horizon falls away instead of stretching out forever." He crouches down, collecting a handful of rocks. He places a large one down. "This is the sun."

He places a smaller rock a foot away from the sun. "A planet is a sphere that circles the sun."

His finger cuts a circle into the soil around the large stone. He moves the planet stone along the course, and then places a pebble beside it. "A moon revolves around a planet."

"Until it's destroyed."

He nods and asks, "You know of the Red Star and the Bright Star?"

"Of course." I'm a bit offended by the question, but try not to show it, as I'm positive my knowledge of the stars is about to be torn asunder.

"Neither are stars." He places two more stones on the ground, one closer to the sun, one further away. He points to the closer. "Venus." And then to the further. "Mars. Both are planets. Like Earth. But where nothing lives. There are other planets, too. In our solar system, and around other stars."

I have no idea what a solar system is, but I sense the grandeur and immensity of what he's telling me. For a moment, I feel small and afraid, but my curiosity has been piqued. "Our planet is Earth?"

He smiles. "Your father taught you a lot, but not every-thing, huh?"

"My father knows all of this?"

"Perhaps not all," he says. "He doesn't have access to the libraries."

"Libraries?"

"A place where books are kept."

I may not know as much as my father, or Shua, but I know what a book is. My father had one, when I was young, full of words I couldn't read and images I had trouble comprehending. "How many books?"

His eyes crinkle, that hidden smile returning. "Thousands."

"And you can *read* them?"

"Everyone in my family can," he says. "But I wish they couldn't. We wouldn't be here if they were ignorant of the past."

The question on my tongue is forbidden. To speak it incurs painful punishment. But Shua and I have already broken laws punishable by death, so I ask, "Do you know what happened? In the Time Before? What the Golyat is? Where it came from?"

He shakes his head. "Those things are not in the libraries." Then he reveals a staggering truth that I only doubt for a moment. "No one knows what happened. Not my father, not yours, and not your husband. All we know is that what once was, is no more, and that the Golyat is to blame."

He stands. "And if my father is not stopped, those dark times could very well return."

With that, we set out again, our pace even faster, to make up for the time lost speaking, and because the knowledge garnered has reignited my sense of urgency.

The foundations disappear when we reach a hill and start climbing. Near the top of the hill, Shua stops and takes a slow step back, sliding behind a tree. His body language is easy to read: he's spotted someone.

I slip beside him and whisper, "Who is it?"

"I don't know," he says. "His clothing is...odd. But he's carrying a sword."

I lower myself to the ground and roll my head out around the tree so slowly that not even a mountain lion would notice. I stop when I see the man, standing sentinel, sword at the ready, as though expecting us. For a moment, I think he's in shadow, but I can see the sun's rays gleaming off his strange, wide hat. His clothing is black, with splotches of green, his fighting stance unusual, but steady.

Behind him is a solid gray wall. *Another foundation,* I think, the top of it obscured by the large trees behind the man.

I roll back and stand. "We go back down, separate, and flank him."

"Why not avoid him altogether?"

"He's not with Micha," I explain, "which means he's a Modernist. I don't know about you, but I'd rather be told where to find your father, than search the whole island for him."

"Mmm," he says, and starts back down the hill. When the man is no longer visible, we split up, heading in opposite directions and then back up. I move swiftly, comfortable in the forest, able to move with little or no sound. If the deer cannot hear my approach, neither will the man with the funny hat.

When I spot him again, I slow, approaching low to the ground, a cat on the hunt. I can't see Shua yet, but I'm sure he's there.

The man maintains his post with perfect stillness, revealing a discipline the likes of which I have never seen. His drawn weapon tells me he's expecting a fight, and won't have a chat without first being subdued. I wait a moment longer, giving Shua time to close in. Then I slip behind the man and draw my knife.

I creep to within ten feet of the man, my eyes locked on target. When I'm close enough to strike, I do.

The knife leaves my hand as I charge.

Part of my mind registers Shua saying, "Davina, wait," but I'm committed.

Around the same time my thrown blade strikes the man's thigh with a metal on metal ping that tells me he's wearing armor beneath his clothes, I bring the machete down on his sword. The plan is to either disarm him, or knock his sword downward, giving me a chance to place my blade against his throat.

That's not what happens. Instead, he resists my downward swing. A vibration moves through my arms, numbing them, and I nearly drop the weapon.

What kind of man possesses such strength? I wonder, looking up into his eyes, which is the very same moment I realize he is not a man at all. "What..."

"It's called a statue," Shua says, approaching from the side, weapon lowered. "It's made out of metal. I've never seen one before, but they were once common. Not too far south from where we are now, there stood a statue of a woman that stood taller than..." His eyes widen and turn up. "Taller than that, but...wow."

I turn around and look up. What I had taken for another foundation is nothing of the sort. Constructed from layers of granite blocks, the stone structure rises into the air like an oversized needle, at least two hundred feet tall.

"What is it?"

"I don't know," he says, his voice oozing a sense of wonder that I'm feeling, too.

This is dangerous.

With every discovery I feel myself becoming more and more intrigued by the past. "Doesn't matter. Best if we try to forget it."

"Agreed," he says, but he doesn't sound any more convinced than I did a moment ago.

We round the tall building and are faced by the stone ruins of another. Neither of us give it a second glance as we walk by, though I secretly hope our return route will bring us past it again.

Old World ruins fill the forest, now part of it. Ancient buildings, long since crumbled, have become hills lined with both trees and beams of rusting metal. We pass more statues, and metal poles, and the five-story framework of a building that Shua says was once much larger.

I try to imagine what it all would have looked like, buildings intact, trees gone, but I can't see it. I have no frame of reference aside from the ruins I'm seeing for the first time.

As the sun passes by overhead, we start up another hill. Looking up, where there should be trees, I see blue sky. The forest either ends on the far side, or there's a steep drop off. Near the top, we slow our ascent, unsure of what we'll find. When I peek my head up over the crest, I feel like I'm back in the river, breathless and near to drowning.

My strength is sucked away.

I fall to my knees. And despite everything I've been taught about the Time Before, about what is permissible, and what is not, about how even thinking about such things is forbidden, tears fall from my eyes from the raw power and beauty of what once was.

11

Tall rectangles rise from the forest, stretching skyward. These are the monstrous buildings I've seen from a distance. But I was only seeing a small fraction of the city's actual size. It's beyond comprehension. Like a dream. Or a nightmare. Could human beings have actually built this? It doesn't seem possible.

Many of the structures have crumbled, and a few lie on their sides, like decomposing corpses. But a dozen still stretch toward the sky. Of those, some are gutted, revealing their internal framework. Others are heavily damaged from fire and something violent, but they still have thick walls lined with grids of empty rectangular holes. Three of the buildings, one of them the tallest of the bunch, look almost intact.

"Why are there holes?" I ask. As impressive as the buildings are, I can't think of a good reason why such megalithic structures would be built in a way where someone could fall to their doom with ease.

"They're windows," Shua says. "They had glass in them."

"What's glass?"

"It's solid, like metal, but far more fragile, and clear. Like perfectly frozen ice that isn't cold and doesn't melt."

"A transparent wall."

"Exactly." His eyes squint. I think he's smiling. "You have a decent vocabulary for a shepherd."

"I had a good accidental teacher. My father rambled a lot. About the world. About the Law. He didn't know I was taking it all in."

Shua lets out a subtle laugh, but it strikes me like a hammer. "What?"

"Have you ever considered that he did?" Shua asked.

"Did what?"

"Know," he says. "That you were listening? That you were learning?"

The possibility has tickled my thoughts on occasion, but to speak it would be to suggest a violation of the Law that would have resulted in my father losing his position. Possibly worse. But out here, with Shua, whose father has violated every law within the Law, I'm free to ponder the notion, and speak my mind.

With a smile, I say, "He knew."

"Why? Do you think? If you'd said something—"

"Because he loved me," I say. "And he wanted more for me."

"Is that why he allowed Micha to marry you?" He speaks the words with disdain, either disapproving of the concept of arranged marriage, or revealing his feelings for my husband, who we would be wise to remember is not far behind us.

"We make mistakes with the people we love the most," I say. "That's why we're both here, isn't it? To correct our mistakes. I failed to raise my son with enough respect for the law."

"And me?" he asks. "How did I fail my father?"

I stand and start down the steep hill leading toward the city. "You didn't kill him sooner."

My words must have some kind of effect on Shua because he falls silent. I don't know if he's saddened by the truth of my words, angry for suggesting he failed, or more determined because he agrees. His face remains hidden from me, and I don't bother looking back to read his eyes. He can feel however he wants. It changes nothing.

I walk with my head turned up. The closer we get to the ancient buildings, the bigger they seem.

Why would people live in a place like this? The structures' colossal sizes are imposing. I've faced down every predator known to man, aside from the Golyat, and have never felt quite so intimidated...though the shark was a close second. And it's not just their size.

Looking at these buildings, I have no trouble envisioning the kinds of horrors people with that much knowledge and ability could inflict.

Limited to swords and spears, I've seen mankind's dark heart on occasion. But if our ancestors had the ability to build, and destroy, entire cities like Boston...

Why would anyone want to claim that kind of self-destructive power?

Until peoples' hearts change, we will find a way to turn innovation into suffering. The anguish of some might be reduced, but on the backs of many more. That's the way of the world now, with so little. How much more so was it then, or will it become if the Modernists bring technology to the world once more...and the Golyat with it?

We walk through what Shua tells me were once streets, hard flat paths made from a kind of hot, almost liquefied stone laid out between the buildings. Moving things, with wheels, rolled along them, under their own power, carrying people from one spot to another. The journey from my father's hill in Essex to Boston might have once taken less than an hour. I understand the concept of a wheel—we have carts for the migration, but *we* move *them*, not the other way around.

I try to look straight ahead when my neck grows sore from staring up. The forest between the buildings, and inside the cores of many of them, is thick and wild. Vines climb the sides of buildings, stretching more than a hundred feet up, taller than the trees, maybe even helping hold the structures together.

With no sign of the Modernists on the ground, and no real idea of where to go, I focus on what I can hear. The wind coos as it moves through the empty buildings, like a giant, sad bird. The leaves shift and rustle, tapping out a beat to accompany the bird songs and squawking gulls. If we're still and silent, the distant sound of crashing waves echoes through the city.

But there are no voices.

No human smells.

No trace of the Modernists.

"How do we know they even came to the city?" I ask.

"We don't," he admits, "but I can't think of another reason to visit Suffolk."

"Perhaps the water on the island's far side is easier to cross?" My eyes drift upward again. The building looming above us appears mostly intact. "Perhaps, Suffolk isn't an island at all?"

The question, spoken without much thought, staggers me to a stop. It's not impossible. No one has been to Suffolk in five hundred years. Who's to say the ebb and flow of the water around its shores hasn't changed? Even if the water isn't missing completely, perhaps only a stream remains, or an average-sized river, which the tribes are adept at crossing.

"We can't find them from down here," I say, still staring up.

Shua stops beside me, following my gaze. "You want to... Up there?"

"We could wander this island for days and find nothing. At the very least, we need to study the landscape. It could give us an idea of where to check first. Or maybe we'll get lucky and spot one of your father's meat cooking fires."

I meant the last remark as a jab toward his father, but he offers a convinced nod instead of a laugh. As we head toward the behemoth of a building, part of me wishes Shua had dismissed the idea of entering, and climbing it. Being surrounded by this ancient civilization feels akin to strolling through a bear's den. But walking through the ruin's doors is like putting my head in the bear's jaws.

The building looks much older than those I've seen so far. Its gray brick façade looks almost noble, despite being overgrown by vines. Nesting birds flit in and out of the vines, many of them in the refuge created by the row of large, arched windows along the second floor. I'm about to move on when I spot letters above the arches. There are entire words, and I can't help but feel fascinated by this message from the past. Shua has seen and read books, but these are the first written words I've ever seen in my life.

"What does it say?" I ask, knowing Shua might have trouble reading the words. Some have crumbled. Others are overgrown with vines.

He cranes his head up, mouthing words to himself as he scans the line of text running from one end of the building to the other. Then he says, "The commonwealth requires the education of the people as the safeguard of order and liberty."

I'm not sure what a 'commonwealth' is, but I suspect it's some kind of ruling authority. That's the only part of the sentence that makes sense to me. In New Inglan, under the Prime Law, keeping the people from being educated protects us from freedom, which might otherwise lead to our mutual demise. "Were they really that different from us?"

"You think they were different?"

I motion to the inscription I can't read. "They valued freedom, education, and liberty above all else, and it led to their demise."

"That's not entirely accurate," he says. "Most of the world before lived in poverty, as slaves, or under the rule of a cruel dictator. And while freedom was a governing principle to the people who founded Boston, and the country in which it was once a part, the generations that followed willingly gave up that freedom for the illusion of it."

"But why? Freedom is death."

I expect this ancient truth to ring true with Shua. Those three words have ended many an argument about the Law.

Freedom *is* death.

Instead, Shua is amused.

His condescending laugh irks me, and I bark, "What?"

"Freedom is death..." He pauses long enough to tamp down his smile. "It's a bastardization of the original, which meant something closer to 'Freedom *or* death. The actual words are, "Live Free or Die: death is not the worst of evils."

My mouth opens to speak an argument or mock the words, but the second half—'death is not the worst of evils'—rings true. I know from experience.

What I manage to say is, "Huh..."

"The words were spoken by General John Stark, who fought to free New Hampshire from the people who ruled it."

"New Hampshire is..."

"What you know as Rockingham, Strafford, Belknap, Carroll, Grafton and Coos, plus a few more counties that were lost during the Divide's creation. 'Live free or die' was their motto, and there was a time when the concept guided far more people than the Prime Law does now."

"You sound...enamored," I say.

He shrugs. "A craving for freedom is one of humanity's most primal desires."

His words are traitorous, but I don't say so.

"It was a different time," he says. "And as much as I agree with the heart of those words, I also live in a world where freedom is death. Had the founding fathers of that country, which no longer exists, had the foreknowledge of where their undefended liberties would lead, I doubt they would have pursued it so thoroughly, or, at the very least, they would have noticed when their freedom was plucked away bit by bit. Bad men, when left unchecked by good, become evil."

"You sound like them," I say, looking up at the inscription. His words have a noble poetry about them, on occasion.

"Another bastardization," he says. "The original sentiment was, 'the only thing necessary for the triumph of evil is for good men to do nothing.' That's why we're here."

"You're calling me a good man?"

"Good is still up for debate. Man?" He shakes his head. "I've seen you naked."

"True," I say, "But for the record, I'm nothing like them."

Even *I* hear the hollow sound of my words, but I can't *not* say them. An admission of understanding is to admit doubting the Prime Law. And if I'm to carry out my mission, my faith in the guiding principles of *my* forefathers needs to be unshakable ...even when it's shaken.

"You're the daughter and wife of two different elders, and yet you find yourself a shepherd, alone in the forest, surrounded by dangers. A woman with your family connections, even as the eighth daughter and eighth wife, does not end up in your low position unless she also values her freedom above all else."

I sigh, take one last look at the inscription, and then strike out toward the towering building that will be our lookout. "I think I've had enough talk of freedom for one day. And you would be wise to control your tongue, and possibly your heart's desires."

"Why is that?" Shua asks, following behind.

"It's enough that I might have to kill my son, and you your father," I tell him. "I would hate to have to kill you as well."

I don't hear him laugh, but I'm sure he's smiling. Then again, maybe he's deciding whether or not to kill me, too. His revelations about the ancient world might simply be a test of my loyalties. As we approach the crumbling building, I step aside and motion for Shua to take the lead. If he decides I'm a Modernist, I'd rather not make it easy for him to kill me by standing in front of a several-hundred-foot drop. Then again, a quick death at the hands of gravity might be less painful than at the tip of his spear.

Knowing Shua could kill me at any time, regardless of our location, I follow him up a slope leading to a window. The building's entrance has long since been buried and perhaps several floors underground. He steps through the hollowed out window. I step through after him and immediately regret it.

12

While the exterior of the building stands mostly intact, the interior is hollowed out all the way to the roof, giving us a clear view of the sky high above. The vast height and towering walls disorient me. Dizziness forces my eyes back down, feeling a bit embarrassed by my weakness. But then I see Shua stretching and rubbing his eyes, and I know he's feeling the same thing.

"That's, ahh...that's... I don't know." He smiles.

"Like your brain hurts?"

"That sounds right."

I look up again, but not toward the ceiling. The walls are thick, but they look fragile, too. Every hand and foot hold will be suspect. "We can climb this."

"Climb it?" Shua sounds both aghast and impressed. "You were planning to climb the walls?"

"How else would we get up there?" I motion toward the non-existent ceiling without looking.

He points across the open space, which is layered with decay and small saplings struggling to grow tall with the limited amount of sunlight they receive. "I was going to take the stairs."

I'm vaguely familiar with the concept of steps, though they are forbidden. There are mountains in the North, where steps were carved into the granite in the Time Before. But I've never seen a staircase like this, zigzagging up through the building, supported by thick metal beams. The steps are pocked with decay, but there appear to be metal rods woven through the concrete. "Will it hold us?"

When Shua shrugs, I realize he does that a lot. As much as he knows about the Old World, he doesn't know everything.

"We can always scale the walls back down." He takes the first flight of stairs and jumps up and down on the landing without incident.

I take another look at the walls, which look about ready to cave in, and find no comfort in his words. How many more years will this ancient structure resist decay? A hundred? Or maybe just one? For all we know, today could be the day the building shudders and falls in on itself.

"This was your idea," Shua says, taking the second set of steps. At least they seem solid enough.

I follow him up the stairs, eyes down, wary for weak spots. There are a few gaps, and the occasional missing step, but for the most part, the staircase is intact. Ten minutes into our vertical hike, I need to stop for a rest. The tops of my thighs are burning. I've climbed the tallest hills in Essex and scaled untold trees, but I've never used my muscles like this. The repetitive motion is taking a toll on them.

A flight above me, Shua pauses, looking equally out of breath. He stretches with a groan.

"This is how people moved through these buildings?" I ask.

"Just in emergencies," he says. "They mostly used boxes hung from cables that could move up and down through buildings. Bottom to top in seconds."

"Like cars," I say.

"But with less freedom. Up and down. That's it. And they were communal. Shared by everyone. They called them 'elevators.'"

"Elevator," I say, enunciating each syllable. "That's a horrible word."

"Grating," he says. "But somehow appropriate for all this." He motions to the crumbling building around us, at its jagged edges and hard surfaces.

We start upward again, bolstered by our mutual distrust for the building. "So they moved from one location to another, in cars, and then up and down in elevators. Did they have to walk at all? Between the cars and elevators?"

"They did," he says, "but there were ways they could avoid that, too. Mostly, they sat. Not everyone, but most. My father used to joke that when the Golyat emerged, people were too fat to run away."

"That's horrible," I say.

"And probably true. 'Fatted cattle for the slaughter,' he called them."

"They needed a shepherd to keep them moving," I say, getting a winded laugh out of him.

Shua pauses, one flight above me. "I think this is high enough."

"Why?" I ask, despite desperately wanting him to be right. "We can't be more than halfway up."

"Which is still far above the forest," he says, and as I climb the steps to join him, he motions to the next flight and adds, "Also, this."

The staircase has crumbled, leaving a gap between us and the next floor. The railings are intact, but they are rusted and untrustworthy.

For the first time since starting our ascent, I look over the edge.

"Don't," Shua says, but his warning comes too late. Looking down into the building-turned-pit is even more disorienting than looking up. I step back from the edge, gripping the rail for balance, and it crumbles. I lose my footing, but just for a moment. Shua grasps my arm and steadies me. "Told you."

I tug my arm free without offering my thanks. I've survived long enough without help. I don't need it now, and not from a man who still doesn't trust me enough to reveal his face. As much as we have in common—our upbringing, heritage, and current goals—he is still a stranger to me.

A quick scan reveals the situation. The staircase has no windows, but the surrounding floors do. From inside the building, I can see out the far side, but much of the view is blocked. I'm not sure it matters, as most of that view is dominated by the ocean. I'm fairly certain the Modernists aren't attempting an ocean voyage. Building a boat would take a lot of time, manpower, and raw materials. They had to at least know there was a chance they'd be found out and pursued. Whatever they're doing here, it won't take long.

The adjacent floor is largely missing, but there are metal rods protruding from the walls, marking where the floor had been. The beams are bent downward and are coated with rust, but they appear thick and strong. The nearest window is just ten feet away, and from this angle, I can't see through it.

To get a clear view to the west, we're going to have to climb over to the window.

"I'll go first," Shua says, either following my eyes and discerning my conclusion or coming to the same on his own.

I wave him off and step toward the staircase landing's open edge. "You're twice my weight." I regret my decision, fueled more by bravado than logic, when I step onto the first metal rod. It vibrates beneath my foot, but remains intact. It's not the footing that bothers me; it's the clear view of the three-hundred-foot drop beneath me.

"Hey," Shua says. When I glance back, he's extending the base of his spear toward me. "For balance." Between the spear's length and Shua's arm, it gives me something to hold on to nearly the whole way across. I clutch the staff harder than I would ever admit and slide along the wall, feeling it crumble behind my back as I slide across. I'm just two feet from the window when I'm forced to let go of the spear. I feel exposed and laid bare, at the mercy of gravity and the skill of whatever long-dead worker built this portion of the building.

A deep breath, and then I lunge the remaining distance, throwing myself into the open window, clutching the thick wall...which turns to gravel under my weight and begins sifting through the metal beams. I shout in surprise and fright as the concrete supporting me melts away.

"Vee!" Shua says, and somewhere in the back of my mind, I'm aware that he's using my familiar name, rather than my formal name.

My slow descent comes to a stop when the loose concrete slides away to reveal the metal framework holding it together, like roots in the earth. "I'm okay." The words are as much to convince myself as Shua, and they're proved accurate when I don't plummet to my death.

While scrambling to find a better grip, my eyes drift upward. The view outside my window is expansive, further than I've ever been able to see. The city is laid out before me, intercut by the forest, which stretches out to the river that splits and surrounds the island. As wide and perilous as the river crossing to Suffolk was, the water on this side is a raging torrent of water, impassable by any means of which I can conceive.

Distracted by the view, I forget about the window, and lean further out, turning my gaze north. Essex is laid out before me, stretching into the distance, and I know that I am in one of the buildings that I have looked upon in the past, and tried not to think about.

But it's not the tallest building. That honor belongs to the impossibly tall structure to the east. It's not far away, but the library conspired with the forest to block my full view of the megalithic structure.

"What was the name of that building?" I ask.

"Which building?"

"The tallest in Boston. You never told me its name."

"John Hancock Tower."

"They named a building after a person?"

"He played a large part in setting the people free several hundred years before skyscrapers, cars, and elevators existed. He was one of fifty-six men who signed a document declaring the land independent from the people who had ruled it."

"Sounds important," I say, wondering what John Hancock would have thought about the building bearing his name.

"He inspired people," Shua says, sounding despondent. "A lot of men did back then. Their words *still* inspire men."

I tear my eyes away from the view. "What do you mean?"

"My father carries a copy of the document. The 'Declaration of Independence,' they called it. Its words support his view. They are, perhaps, even the foundation of his views, and they are in stark contrast to the Prime Law."

His revelation reminds me of why we're here. I turn my eyes outward again and my body locks up.

"What is it?" Shua asks.

I can't answer him. I'm frozen, like prey, waiting for the killer bite on the back of my neck.

The Divide lies to the northwest. I can't see its end, or its bottom, but for the first time in my life, I can really see the far side. It looks remarkably like Essex, covered in old growth forest. But the forest is alive. A path of movement slides through the tall trees, shaking branches, bending trunks, sending birds flitting toward the sky.

I can't see it, but I know what's creating it.

"Vee," Shua hisses. "What is it?"

"The Golyat," I whisper.

"You can see it?"

I shake my head. "It's hidden. In the trees." I turn toward him, eyes wide. "Approaching the Divide."

"You're sure?" he asks. "Why would it? After all this time?"

"It must see something," I say, my stomach churning with anxiety at the idea that we might be witnessing the Golyat's return to New Inglan. When I turn back to the window, motion pulls my eyes skyward, and I know exactly what has attracted the Golyat's attention.

"There's something in the sky."

"Describe it."

"It's round...like a pouch, but upside down, and big. Really big. There's a basket hanging from the bottom. And..." *What the hell?* "...part of it is on fire. I think there are people in the basket."

"It's a balloon," he says. "A hot air balloon."

I don't really care what it's called. It's currently riding the ocean's breeze, carrying people toward the Divide's far side. I'm about to head back to the stairs when I see a second balloon grow, like a fast-blooming flower, at the top of the John Hancock building.

"Next door!" I shout. "They're next door!"

As I turn to leave, I spot something else. Another aberration. This time on the ground. Men. A lot of them. Moving through the forest.

Micha is here. But has he seen the balloons? Did he hear me shouting?

None of it matters, I decide. If the Modernists aren't stopped, the Golyat will return.

John Stark was wrong after all. Freedom *is* death.

It's a lesson I relearn when I free my hands from the window's edge, and take a fast step on a rusted, metal beam that crumbles beneath my weight and sends me plummeting.

13

Metal beams bend, groan, and crumble beneath my weight as I fall atop what should have been my path back to the staircase. I can feel the old metal giving way, revealing just how fragile this timeworn building has become.

"Vee!" Shua says, holding his spear out for me to grasp.

I take hold of the outstretched weapon, but say, "I'm too heavy to—"

"Swing," he shouts, motioning down with his head, toward the landing on the floor below.

It's a horrible plan, and I'm about to complain when the metal beams decide to release me. How many corpses litter this city? I see a carpet of dead in my mind's eye, too plentiful for the scavengers to consume. The dead were the forest's fertilizer.

And I'm about to join them.

Perhaps the saplings below will grow taller from my blood, I think as gravity pulls me downward.

Then there's a tug as my fingers grip the spear's shaft. My fall becomes a swing, careening me toward the landing below.

A grunt of pain from above is followed by gravity's swift return, but even it can't stop my forward momentum. I'm flung back into the stairwell, crashing to the floor. I roll in a chaotic heap, across the jagged floor, and then down the next flight of steps. During the tumult, I spot the next landing below. Without a wall at the end, I'll plummet to my death despite Shua's rescue. As I'm beaten by the rotting steps, my instinct is to remain curled in a protective ball, but that will do nothing to slow me down. I unfurl my body and wind up lying flat, arms and legs splayed wide.

The steps dig into my belly, grind against my ribs, and scrape my breasts. But they also stop me short of falling over the edge. I come to a complete stop when my chin whacks against a step, driving my teeth into my lip. Pummeled, but alive, I unleash a string of curses as I pick myself back up. I'm not totally aware of what I'm saying, but the look on Shua's face as he rounds the landing above—a mix of worry and amused shock—says they're not words typically utilized by a Lady of Essex.

"Are you—"

"Alive?" I say. "Yes. Okay, not really."

He crouches beside me. "You're hurt?"

"What? Yes. But who cares? The Modernists are above us, headed across the Divide in..."

"Balloons."

"...balloons. And my husband is below us, possibly tracking us instead of your father." I push myself up, aware of the stinging beneath my clothing and the warm trickle of blood from several wounds.

"Meaning..."

"We're too late to spare my son or your father from their fates. If Micha doesn't know where the Modernists are, we need to show him."

"He might kill us on sight," Shua says, and he's right.

"Then we won't stand still," I say, and I notice Shua's spear is missing. "Your weapon?"

He motions to the floor far below. "Down there."

"Which is where we need to be." I vault down the next flight of steps, hand clutching the rusting rail as I round the bend and careen down the next flight. My descent is a barely controlled plummet dependent on the antique stairwell's structural integrity. The stairs shake with each landing, sometimes loosening beneath my feet, sometimes crumbling above my head, but it holds together as Shua and I spiral downward.

We reach the bottom at a run, out of breath, but with no time to rest. Shua's spear is buried, blade down, in the soil at the base of the stairs. He snatches it from the ground as we pass and head for the window.

I squint in the bright sun as I emerge, unaware of Micha's men until one of them shouts, "There!"

When my eyes adjust, I see a mob of men at the bottom of the hill, just inside the tree line. I recognize most of them, and they no doubt recognize me, which might be why they haven't shot an arrow into my chest yet.

I glance back and find myself alone. Shua has stopped short of the window, hanging back in the shadows, out of sight.

"Davina?" Micha's voice is just as deep and threatening as I remember it, but there is also a tinge of hurt in it. He's actually wounded by my apparent betrayal.

Micha steps to the front of his men, axe in hand, cloaked in fur despite the summer heat. His long hair is tied back, his beard braided. Beneath the grime, and hair, and furs, he's a handsome man. But he prefers to project a fierce exterior. Believes that power—rather than intelligence—garners respect. "I didn't want to believe it. My own wife, a Modernist. But here you are. I should have known the hardships of a shepherd's life would drive you to betray the Prime Law. You've always been weak."

"Micha, please, listen to me. The Modernists are—"

"Liars and thieves whose only future is death. I will not listen to your words any more than I would listen to Plistim's...or your bastard son's." I barely have time to register his sudden movement, and the axe spinning toward my head, but I manage to move my head to the side just enough to keep it from being split in two. The heavy axe strikes the weathered concrete wall behind me and buries itself five inches deep.

"Micha," I plead, but my husband is beyond words.

"Kill her!" he shouts, and I'm chased back inside the building by fifty men and a shower of hurled and shot projectiles.

When I don't see Shua, I think he's abandoned me and left me to fend off, or escape from, fifty men. He proves me wrong when he says, "Over here," and waves to me from the far side of the building, waiting by a hollowed-out window.

He slips through without waiting. If I can make it through the gap before Micha and his men enter the building, they might waste time searching for me.

Chased by the shouts of men who are not my enemies, but who want to kill me, I sprint through the sapling forest populating the ground level. Without slowing down, I dive out the window through which Shua fled. And once again, I nearly fall to my death. Shua's hand snatches my clothing as I sail out over a twenty foot drop. The hill rising up to the building's side is much shorter here.

My outward leap becomes a downward circle guided by Shua's strong arm. It ends with me being slammed into the solid exterior wall. The impact jars Shua's hand free, and I fall—but only a foot before I find a handhold. Though my body is wracked by pain, I climb down the wall with something close to reckless abandon. There's no way to know if Micha and his men saw my escape, but I doubt it will take them long to figure out where we've gone. Shua follows me, sliding as much as climbing.

We hit the ground at a run, following the building around to the left, away from Micha, but toward the towering John Hancock building. Despite its size, it's once again concealed by the forest's thick canopy.

It's not long before the sounds of pursuit continue. Our mad dash through the forest is leaving an easy trail to follow. But we've got a decent lead and will reach the tallest building in Boston, then and now, without being slain. I'm not sure what will happen when we arrive, but I'm certain it will include violence and death.

Shua takes the lead, scurrying through the trees, the forest under-growth, root tangles, exposed stones, and ancient debris with impressive agility, never slowing and without altering course.

A break in the trees reveals the John Hancock building looming above, its façade a mesh of metal, and tendrils of debris hanging from the exposed side like entrails. A childhood friend comes to mind in that moment. *Dyer would love this,* I think, looking up at the building. She had a strange fascination with entrails. I never understood why.

And then we're back in the forest again, closing in on the building. I'm about to ask if he has any ideas about how to locate the entrance, when I spot a woman up ahead. She's a stranger, dressed in brown and camouflaged with foliage. I only spot her because the moment she sees us, she's on her feet and running toward the building.

She slips through a hole in the wall that looks like it was created through violent means.

Shua redirects toward the woman, and we reach the door a moment later. I draw my machete as I pass through the gap, expecting a fight. But there is none to be found. Instead, there's a staircase rising up through the skeletal tower.

"Fuck," I grumble, looking up. The woman is already four flights up and moving fast. After our previous climb, our crazed descent, and the mad dash, my legs are weary.

Shouts echo from outside.

Micha is just a hundred feet back, closer than I expected, his men in tow.

"Fuuuuck," I say and start up the stairs, taking two at a time.

Thirty flights up, we're forced to slow our pace, as does the woman we're chasing.

Micha is closing in from below, the weight of his men rumbling through the stairwell. But they will soon tire as well. Not even a stalwart belief in the Prime Law can push a person beyond the limits of what is human.

We start running again, forcing the woman ahead of us to resume her faster pace as well. And all the while, Micha closes in. By the time we reach forty stories, the sound of pursuit is closer than ever. If they don't slow to rest, they're going to catch us before we reach the top. I know my husband, lost in rage, will never believe my words, but if he sees us killing Modernists, there is a chance he will spare our lives. That's assuming we will survive the encounter with the Modernists, who will be warned of our approach, and not be exhausted from the climb.

I feel ready to collapse when I see the stairwell's end, three stories above. The ceiling is mostly missing, but a patchwork of thick metal beams remain. There are more balloons visible through the gaps. Some are airborne, and two rest atop what's left of the roof. Great flames billow into partially inflated balloons, their heat tangible from here.

How long will it be before they're carried skyward by the hot air, and guided inland by the ocean's winds?

How long do we have to stop them?

With so many already floating away, are we too late?

All questions without answers.

We pause near the top, catching our breath. While my lungs start to feel better, my legs feel barely capable of supporting me. The approaching fight needs to start and end quickly, or I'll be useless.

Shua looks me in the eyes, asking 'Ready?' without uttering a word. I give him a nod and we charge up together.

I'm expecting an immediate assault, but that's not what happens.

One of the two remaining balloons is drifting skyward. Looking over the side of the large basket is a familiar face that wounds me far deeper than any weapon could.

Salem.

He's older and unkempt, and he has facial hair now, but his eyes are the same. And he's not looking at me with surprise or sorrow or anger. Instead, he looks...pleased. Maybe even relieved.

"You made it," A deep voice says, pulling my gaze to the one remaining balloon. Plistim himself stands beside the basket, smiling. His gray hair is cut short and his face clean shaven. He looks almost polished. Not at all the wild man I expected. Without hesitation, I hurl my machete toward his chest. He leans to the side, dodging the blade, which clatters inside the empty basket.

Plistim laughs. "I can see why you like her."

I draw my knife, never questioning who he is speaking to. "I'm going to kill you, and every Modernist following you."

"I'm afraid you've misread the situation," Plistim says, as I stalk toward him on shaky legs. He points to the trail of balloons floating east. "This voyage was inspired by the Modernist movement, but it is not for Modernists. The people you see up there, are family."

I grip the knife tighter, eyes on his chest.

"You are here, because your son asked for you. I thought it a foolish endeavor, but we wouldn't be here without his keen mind."

I point the knife at him, as I get close to striking distance.

"My son is not your family!"

Plistim smiles. "That is where you are wrong. That boy is my grandson."

This stops me in my tracks.

"I'm sorry, Vee," Shua says. I glance back to find him unwrapping his face. When he's done, I'm staring at the face of the man who fathered my son: Shua, son of Plistim, enemy of humanity.

In that moment, I realize what a fool I have been. This is the price of not following the law, and not honoring my wedding vows. My indiscretions, justified or not, have provided the means for Plistim to bring about humanity's final end.

In the next moment, I feel a thump of pain, followed by darkness.

14

I shiver and wonder why I'm so cold. It's summer, but the air feels raw. And thin. Like I've climbed a mountain, which the pain in my legs seems to confirm. My head pounds, the pain holding my eyes shut.

What happened?

All I know at the moment is that I'm hurt.

As I wake, my senses reach out to the world around me. Despite my shut eyes, I know I'm someplace unfamiliar. The only scents I can detect are hints of wood, rope, and smoke. But mostly I smell nothing at all, which is strange. I hear even less, just the wind swishing against a variety of surfaces. It's what I can feel that confuses me most.

I'm lying on my side, curled up, hands and feet together. The floor beneath me and the wall behind me are solid, but somehow flexible. What confuses me is that I feel like I'm wrapped in a mother's arms, being rocked back and forth, the wind a comforting whisper, the air crisp.

It's almost enough to lull me to sleep.

And then someone speaks. "Stoke it hotter, but watch the flame's height."

A repetitive shush of air is followed by a wave of heat—from above.

Where the hell...

"Good," the deep voice says, the familiarity of it pricking my numbed memory. I heard that voice, before I fell asleep.

Before I was knocked unconscious.

My memory returns with a second voice, this one instantly familiar, generating a mix of emotions starting with relief and ending in outrage. "She's awake."

I open my eyes to see Shua leaning over me. He looks concerned and a little bit apologetic, but not nearly enough to alter how I feel.

"Now I have to kill two men I care about," I say, and I instantly regret speaking. My quasi-delirious state has weakened the safeguards that keep me from thinking and saying stupid things.

How could I care about Shua? I've known him for a very short amount of time, and hadn't seen his face...

But that's not true. I had seen his face before. All those years ago. Both of us so young. After years of marriage to a brutal man like Micha, Shua had treated me with a tenderness I had not experienced before. In truth, I had thought of him, and that single night, many times since, and had been pleased that such a man was the father of my son.

But now that man, elevated by the memory of a young, desperate woman, had proven himself to be treacherous and violent.

Shua smiles. "She's okay."

"I am pleased," Plistim says, standing above his son, looking down at me and winking. I struggle to stand, ready to throttle the man, and then his son—my son's grandfather and father—but moving is next to impossible. My hands and feet are bound.

"For your own safety," Shua says.

"And yours," I say.

He smiles again, and nods. Shua is a handsome man, like I remember, though he bears more scars now. Salem is a clear mix of Shua and his father, the son of two elder families, after all.

Then Shua stands, letting me see our surroundings for the first time, and triggering the rest of my memories.

Billowing above is a massive balloon built from a thin fabric I've never seen before. At the base is a metal basket in which a fire burns bright and hot, its flames licking up toward the balloon, but never spreading higher. A young woman stands beside the flames holding a bellows for stoking the fire.

She notes my attention and nods. "I'm Shoba. I am pleased to finally meet my cousin's mother."

I push myself up so I'm seated against the basket wall.

"She is my sister's daughter. Her father was not known," Shua says.

"Never married?"

"A lack of marriage did not prevent *us* from having a child," he says.

"*We* did not have a child," I say. "I had him. Alone."

"You had a husband."

"You're right," I say. "Alone would have been better."

"She reminds me of your mother," Plistim says to Shua, standing at the basket's wall, looking out...at what? "A spirited woman makes a poor wife, but a good lover."

"Father," Shua says, a warning in his tone.

"And where is your mother?" I ask Shoba. When the girl looks at me, I'm shaken by her face. "In another balloon? Tied up? Or is she now married to your grandfather?"

Plistim huffs a laugh. "Told her that, did you?"

Shua says nothing, but doesn't look thrilled.

Nor does Shoba. "She's dead."

Before I can apologize, more out of learned etiquette than actually feeling sorry, she adds a detail that does make me feel sorry.

"In the Cull," Shoba says, and she returns to her duty, stoking the fire.

The Cull was the most successful of the few raids that have been carried out on the elusive Modernists. Thirty-seven people were killed. Men, women, and children. Most were tortured, horribly, and not one of them revealed the location of other Modernists. My father called it the 'darkest moment in mankind's history since the Time Before.' Harsh words from a man who swore to uphold and protect the Prime Law at all costs. The worst part about this revelation is that Micha led that raid.

Actually, that's not the worst part.

What's worse is that I was fully willing to take part in a similar raid. Though Micha meant to kill me as well, I was happy to lead him and his men to the Modernists in the John Hancock tower. I went there to kill my own son. Though the Cull is regarded as a dark time in our recent past, I was willing to repeat it, and take part.

And Shua knows that.

But there's no anger directed toward me, perhaps because he deceived me and knocked me unconscious. I remember that now, too.

Despite the Cull's tragic results and the brutality with which it was carried out, the cause was just, and it still is. The Prime Law protects all people from the evils created by our forefathers. Breaking the law would bring untold suffering to *all* people, not just the few who fell for the romantic teachings of Modernist propaganda.

And that's exactly what's happening today.

I'm sorry that a girl like Shoba lost her mother, but what I regret most about today is not arriving in time to stop Plistim, kill my son, and ensure that my family's name isn't forever associated with betrayal, and the Golyat's return. Of course, if the Golyat finds a way to New Inglan, there won't be anyone left to curse my name.

Shoba goes rigid, and for a moment, I think she's angry at me for not responding to her revelation about the Cull. Then I notice her eyes, staring out and down over the basket's side. Her fore-head pinches at the middle, her eyes widening, terrified by something below.

She's not my blood. But I can't stop myself from feeling a kinship with her. "What is it?"

Shua and Plistim both turn toward the girl. Then they follow her gaze downward. While both men are far more skilled at controlling and hiding their emotions, their complete lack of reaction says just as much.

"Can it see us?" Shua asks.

Plistim shakes his head. "The trees are too thick."

"We're not ready to face it," Shua says. "Not yet."

Face it? I think, having little doubt about what lurks below. *They actually intend to fight the Golyat? The monster that laid waste to the Old World and left humanity on the brink of extinction?*

"Let me see it," I say.

"Not a chance," Shua says.

"What do you think will happen? I'll shout down and alert it to our passage? That I'll compromise the safety of New Inglan? Only a fool would do that. Or a pair of fools."

"She's not including me in her insults," Shoba says, her fear replaced by disrespect and indignation.

"Naïveté is forgivable," I say. "In a few more years, you'll be a fool, too. Or dead, along with the rest of humanity."

"Is that what you were going to do with Salem?" Shoba asks. "Forgive him?" She rolls her eyes, looks back, and pales anew.

"Please," I say to Shua. "Just let me see."

Shua looks to Plistim, who shrugs. Now I know where Shua picked up the habit.

Shua crouches beside me. "Please don't do anything stupid. You're here because Salem asked, and we all approved. Your father is highly respected by the Modernists, and our son—"

"My son," I grumble.

"We wouldn't be here without him." Shua slips his arms beneath mine and lifts. We're unsteady for a moment, and I'm forced to lean against his chest for balance.

"What does that mean?" I ask. "How did Salem help you?"

Shua looks up at the balloon. "These were his creation."

"He *invented* them?"

"He read about them in books," Shua says, "but he figured out a way to build them. You could say he re-invented them."

I nearly ask, 'Salem can read?' but the answer is clear. It's not a skill he learned during his time with me.

I feel a similar wave of disorientation when I look away from Shua. I stare into the distance, further than I've ever been able to see before. The horizon is even further away than it was atop the John Hancock building.

How high are we? I wonder, remembering that the balloons had been flying up, just as much as away.

"Ready?" Shua asks, and when I nod he lifts me up and carries me to the side. Feet bound, my balance is precarious, but I hold onto the basket wall and manage to stand on my own. My balance is momentary, faltering the moment my eyes turn downward. I'm not entirely certain how high we are, but far to the right is Boston. The massive towers look short from my vantage point. And directly beneath us is the Divide, the bottom of which is cloaked in steam generated by the Karls River falls.

I want to drink in the view. I can probably see all of Essex, and the ocean beyond. I could study this image of the Divide for days.

And to the left, the Old World stretches far beyond the limit of my eyes' ability to focus.

That's where I spot it—the Golyat. Its location is revealed, once again, by the motion of trees from its passing. The path leads directly toward us, but not on an intercept course. The wind will soon carry us out of its path. Assuming the forest canopy remains thick, and the Golyat doesn't look up, it might not notice us.

But who can say for sure. We have no idea how well it sees, or hears, or smells. It might have heard our conversation. It might have seen the balloons lift off in Boston, and be rushing for a closer look. I find our shadow a half mile ahead, rolling over the tree tops. Had the Golyat been a little faster, the shadow would have crossed its path, and I have little doubt we'd have been detected.

That's when my gaze lifts, and I see other balloons in the sky, some not too far away, others miles to the north and south. There are ten in all, carrying Plistim's family, which could be fifty people, or more. After the Cull, smaller raids, and natural mortality rates, who's to say how many wives, children, and grandchildren the man has left? Clearly a lot. Micha and his men might have even been outmatched if the Modernists had stopped to fight.

"What do you think?" Plistim asks, a smile on his face.

"That I won't need to kill anyone," I say. "You're going to take care of that, all on your own."

I can see he's about to laugh, but a dry, husky chattering—like an oversized woodpecker—rises from below. The hairs on my arms stand on end. I've never heard the sound before, but some part of my instinctual brain understands its meaning.

Whether or not we've been seen, the Golyat is hunting us.

15

"How do we move faster?" I ask.

"We don't," Plistim says. "We are at the wind's mercy. We can ascend and descend as long as we have fuel for the fire."

"And how much fuel is left?" I scan the basket, seeing four backpacks, one of which holds my machete and knife, along with two fresh spears. They really were planning on my joining them. But how could they have known when I was coming? There's no way they could have known for sure, but my father made a big effort to summon me. Did they know about his runners?

Plistim smiles in a way that says, 'none.' "We brought enough to cross the Divide. More and we would have been too heavy. Our journey was always meant to be on foot."

"Journey to where?"

"I have ideas, but without knowing what we're going to find, fate will determine our destination...or your son, whose intelligence can overcome fate."

I can't help but laugh. Salem, my son, is smart, and curious, but he's no mastermind.

"You scoff at the accomplishments of your own blood?" Plistim asked. "I am a capable leader. Commanding."

"Arrogant."

He nods. "But Salem? He's our guiding force. We did not know it before, but without him, we were aimless. Ships without rudders."

I'm not sure what a rudder is, but I understand the point he's making. I just have trouble believing it.

"Your son will determine our course, and when we find it, our new home, free of the Prime Law. Free to become what we want."

"And what is it you want to be?" I'm not really interested, and I'm pretty sure the tone of my voice communicates that, but his reply is earnest.

"A painter."

When I have no response for that, he explains, "Paint is a medium for creating images. Like charcoal on a flat stone."

I remember spending entire days of my youth drawing animals on a large stone, washing it clean, and starting again. "You wish to be a child again?"

He chuckles and asks, "Don't you?"

No wonder the Modernists appeal to the youth so easily. Not only do they pursue the forbidden and taboo, but they also indulge in the mindless expressions of the young, who have no understanding of the world, or the law. For a boy like Salem, on the cusp of leaving such childish things behind, about to step into the painful reality that is manhood, these ideas must have tasted like honey.

My anger toward my son fades a bit. What child could resist such temptations? Had I been approached at his age, charcoal in hand, I might have been corrupted as well. "Where is he?"

Plistim turns south and points. "There."

The balloon is a mile away, on a solitary path, guided by the wind. The rest of the modernist balloons float to the east and north of us. "Who is with him?"

"My brother," Shua says, "And his wife. A few others. Our best hunters. They'll keep him safe."

"How will we find them?" I ask, trying to block out the sound of snapping branches rising from far below.

"Do you see the red spot?" Plistim asks, pointing at Salem's balloon again. The dark red spot is closer to brown, and I have little doubt it was created using blood. "That identifies his balloon. All the sons and daughters of Plistim can see it. And upon descending, we'll head toward it. Right now the course is clear for all: south. Salem and those guarding him will wait for our arrival."

"This is a big land," I say. "You can't—"

"Fire and smoke will be our guide," Shoba says.

"Are you insane?" I say, loud enough to make my fellow passengers tense. Shua leans over the basket's side, watching the Golyat's path. I haven't worked up the courage to look again. In a quieter voice, I say, "Do you intend to feed your people to the Golyat?"

"I intend to kill it," Plistim says.

"How can you do that, when our ancestors—who could build cities beyond imagining—could not?"

"Did you know our ancestors traveled to the moon?" Plistim asks. "Before it was reduced to dust. They also built devices capable of destroying entire cities. Entire counties. They had conquered disease and sickness to a point where nearly all babies born lived long lives. Even the unhealthiest of them could live seventy years, sustained by their technology."

"That's all impressive, and hard to believe, but you're actually proving my point."

"What they did not have, was your son."

I close my eyes, and control my emotions. I want to scream at the man, to remind him that my son is just a boy. He's not a warrior, or a hunter, and as smart as he might be, he cannot conceive of a way to kill something he has never seen—certainly not something that survived the might of our ancestors, whose technology was powerful enough to create the Divide.

It's not worth arguing, I decide. "Untie me."

"You have clearly stated your desire to kill me," Plistim says.

"More than once," Shua adds.

They're right, and as much as I would like revenge for the twisting of my son's mind, and the deception that led me here, things have changed. "Your deaths are no longer my goal."

Plistim narrows his eyes at me. "Explain."

"I cannot kill you all, and simply littering the land with your corpses would do no good. The Golyat would find them. The only way I can uphold the Prime Law and protect the people of New Inglan is to help hide you...even if that means keeping you alive."

Plistim smiles. "I am pleased to see Jesse's logical mind was inherited by his daughter."

"Fuck you."

"And his penchant for profanity."

"Don't speak about my father. You know nothing of him."

His smile widens. "Your father was my friend."

"Bullshit."

"As youth, we were inseparable. You see, I was raised in Essex. Because of my interest in the Old World, and the library my father protected, I was sent as far south as possible, to be looked after by the elder of Essex until age, and the wisdom that comes with it, cured me of my infatuations. That was when your father and I became friends, and when I taught him all I had learned from the library, some of which he taught you."

I don't want to believe a word of it, but I had already begun to suspect my father's collusion with the Modernists. The four runners were sent to ensure I would arrive in Boston on time. That I returned to him wounded was a coincidence. Had I not, I might not be here. And I'm not sure how I feel about that. While this is truly the last place I want to be—within the Golyat's reach—my presence means that there is at least one person among the Modernists who hasn't lost touch with reality. I'm not sure I can prevent the Golyat from discovering them, but I can at least try.

"My father was a Modernist," I say.

"He...was sympathetic to our cause. And helped when he could, especially after the Cull. Future bloodshed was avoided, mostly thanks to the warnings he sent. But he also believed in the Prime Law and feared what would happen if it was broken. When Salem explained our plan—"

"My father *saw* Salem?" This revelation feels like a bigger betrayal than my father secretly aiding the Modernists.

"Once," Plistim says. "Two weeks ago. He asked for Jesse's help. To get you here. When he explained his plan, Jesse agreed. Begrudgingly, mind you. But he agreed. I believe his words were, 'A mother should be with her son, even if it means leaving her father.' But I also think he understood the truth."

"And that is?"

"That life beyond the Divide, with us, holds more promise of a life worth living, for you."

That's when I understand. As well as Plistim thinks he knows my father, no one knows him like me, except maybe Grace. While unwilling to kill his grandson, his old friend, and people whose beliefs he understood, he would have seen that they needed guidance. That out here in the world beyond the Divide, they would need a shepherd to direct their path away from folly.

That's why he sent me. That's why I'm here.

Plistim might be in charge.

Salem might be their inspiration.

But *I'm* going to lead them. And like the deer, they won't even know I'm doing it.

I hold my bound hands out toward Plistim, leaning on the basket's wall to stay upright. "You have my word, I will not attempt to harm you, or any member of your family. Instead, I will do all that I can to ensure that you remain undetected, and safe."

It's Shua who takes my hands, places a blade between them and then cuts me free. "I believe her." He crouches and frees my feet next.

"Are you sure?" Plistim asks, staring at Shua, who's now staring me in the eyes.

"She is opposed to most of what we believe, but she is not a liar," Shua says. "Before, she would have killed us. And our son. But not now."

I tense at the word 'our,' but say nothing.

Shua turns the blade around, placing the point against his chest, and leaving the handle for me to take.

Plistim takes a step to intervene, but Shua holds out a hand, stopping him. Then he speaks to me. "I give you my life, to take or to spare."

I take the knife in my hand, looking him in the eyes. "You're a brave man. Stupid. But brave."

I give the knife a push. The blade sinks through fabric and skin. There's a flash of fear in Shua's eyes as the pain reaches his mind, along with the realization that he might have made a grave mistake.

When I pull the blade back, his fingers go to his chest, feeling the shallow wound.

I offer him a merciless smile. "I didn't want you to forget the moment I could have killed you but didn't."

Plistim laughs and claps his son on the shoulder. "You've always had a wounded heart. Now there will be a scar to match it."

I turn the knife around and hand it back to Shua, a red spot appearing on his light brown, loose-fitting garb.

I have another verbal jab drawn from my mental quiver and nocked on the bow that is my tongue, but it's cut short by a high-pitched gasp.

"Shoba," Plistim chides, his voice an angry whisper, but then he notices her attention is not on Shua's wound, and her gasp was not out of fear for his safety, but for the safety of them all.

Distracted by my freedom, no one paid the fire any heed, and did not notice as it ignited the balloon. With the flames spreading upward, the balloon descends. I lean over the basket's wall, looking down.

The shaking forest revealing the Golyat's presence is a good mile behind us now, still moving south.

I feel a moment of relief that quickly turns to dread when the shaking stops. A loud thumping pounds through the air, like the chattering of a cold child's teeth, and then the path turns west, pursuing our balloon as it plummets toward the forest and the horrible unknown.

16

"What do we do?" I ask, watching the flames lick higher, freeing the hot air from the balloon's girth.

"Hold on," Plistim says, doing just that.

I prefer to be actively involved in navigating life's challenges, but right now, Plistim is right. With no way to combat the flames, and the inability to sprout wings and fly away, holding on is the best any of us can manage.

But that's not entirely true. If we survive our uncontrolled descent, the current one-step plan will help no one. Gripping the basket's side, I take one last look and mark the Golyat's progress. It's still moving in our general direction, but it's not gaining. Thankful for the ocean's westward wind, I turn my eyes straight down. *Two thousand feet,* I guess. After watching our rate of descent for a moment, I estimate the time it will take for us to reach the ground. *One minute.* A quick glance back at the Golyat, and I think, *two minutes.*

I let go of the basket and stumble across toward the other side, as a gust of wind punches into the side of our deflating balloon.

Shua catches me by the arm. "What are you doing?"

"We need to hit the ground moving," I say, picking up the backpack holding my weapons, and slipping it over my shoulders. When he looks unconvinced, I say, "It's following us!"

Shua's eyes widen. He hadn't noted the Golyat's course change. He takes a moment to stand tall, looking back to confirm what I've told him. Then he crouches down, separating the three remaining packs.

"Father." Shua tosses a pack to Plistim, who struggles to put it on.

He pushes the other to Shoba, but she just glances at the pack and doesn't move, her fingers locked onto the basket's edge.

Shua moves to help his father, and I crouch walk to Shoba, thinking, *thirty seconds.*

"We can't waste a moment," I tell her, and I hold an arm strap open for her. "One arm at a time. You can hold on while you do it."

Shoba looks at me with the petrified eyes of a girl who believed life beyond the Divide would be easy, or noble, or anything other than plummeting from the sky while being pursued by the one thing in the world we were all taught to avoid. As obsessed with the past as the Modernists are, even *they* understand that the Golyat is a threat.

I've never had much patience with the idiocy of youth, including my own, so I shake the bag at her. "Now!"

When she doesn't move, I pry one of her hands away from the basket and force the strap around her arm. I slide around her body and repeat the process with her other arm, but this time she helps.

"See," I tell her. "You can—"

An impact jars the basket from below, but my eyes move upward. Half the balloon is missing and the thick ropes holding what's left together, which attach the basket to it, are burning bright.

A second impact is punctuated by a dead branch punching through the basket's side in the small space between Shoba and me. As the flaming balloon is carried past us, I can see what's about to happen: the balloon will pull the basket up and over, dumping us into the forest below. Still more than a hundred feet up, we will either be torn apart by branches as we fall, or die upon impact with the ground.

"Back!" I shout to Shoba, drawing my machete. Just as the still-burning ropes go taut, I bring the blade down. The basket begins to flip, but the branch falls away, and instead of being flipped over, we're spun around.

Our descent through the forest canopy is still violent, but the brunt of every impact is absorbed by the thick basket.

And then, all at once, we're still. I take two breaths while looking at the others, each of them frightened and bruised, but alive. The balloon is above us still, snagged in a pine tree that is starting to smolder. The scent is marvelous, and reminds me of childhood winters, snuggled in furs, warmed by the fire, listening to my father. But then the basket lurches down as a fiery band of rope snaps.

We're not on the ground.

I inch my way up to the basket's edge and look down at a fifty foot drop.

"We made it," Plistim says, smiling, unaware of the danger.

"Not even close." I point at the fire above. "We have maybe thirty seconds before the ropes give way and we fall to our deaths. And another thirty seconds beyond that before the Golyat arrives."

Another downward lurch and the sound of distant snapping limbs conspire to support my assessment.

"We can't—" Shoba is looking over the basket. "How—"

I grip her shoulder hard enough to make sure she forgets everything but my voice. "The trunk is narrow. Hug it tight, then loosen to descend."

"But—"

"Did you not teach your people how to survive in the wild?" I snap at Plistim, and then I redirect my glare at Shua. "Perhaps a little less time spent learning how to kill people and a little more time preparing for—"

"If our lives were not constantly at risk, we might have been able to—"

A tree snaps, creaks, and crashes to the forest floor. It's still too far away to see, but there is no doubt: the Golyat is approaching. The fiery beacon above us and the pungent smoke are easy to follow.

Shua slides out of the basket, wrapping his arms and legs around the tree, clinging to it like a bear cub to its mother. "Like this," he says to Shoba with far more patience. Shua slides down and pauses, waving the girl on. I'm tempted to pitch her over the side, but she begins moving, trusting Shua's demonstration far more than my words.

When they're both sliding down the tree's rough bark, I motion for Plistim to follow. He squints at me, suspicious.

"I'll be right behind you," I say. "Nowhere else to go but down."

He climbs onto the tree, looking nearly as uncomfortable as Shoba. I pause to watch their descent, hiss a quick, "Faster!" and then turn my eyes up. The tightest of the ropes, the one bearing most of the basket's weight, is burning just a few feet overhead.

Machete in one hand, I slip out of the basket, and onto the tree, gripping with both legs and one arm. I could do this with just my legs, but I'm not going down.

Not yet.

With a quick swing, I sever the rope at the basket, which lurches down. The sudden tug is too much for the burning ropes to support. Free of flames, the basket falls, drawing a shout from Shoba and wary glances from Shua and Plistim. With the still flame-free severed rope in hand, I scale up the tree several feet, reach out with the machete and cut away a six foot length, three of those feet burning.

Fifteen seconds, I think, and I loosen my grip on the tree. The bark's rough surface scrapes against me, and the effort puts Grace's stitches to the test. If the skin had not already begun to heal, the wounds would have torn back open. Even if that was the case, I would not have slowed. A thousand such wounds would be preferable to even laying eyes on the Golyat.

I hit the ground just a second after Plistim, who eyes the rope hanging from my hand, like a flaming whip.

I point uphill and whisper, "Go! Now!"

Without waiting to see if they comply, I drag the rope over the forest floor of orange, dry pine needles. Unlike the lush green tree tops that are more likely to smolder and smoke, the forest floor ignites with just the briefest touch, flames and smoke rising into the air. I pause by the basket, setting it ablaze, too. Then I drag the rope across the ground, creating a wall of fire between the Golyat's approach and the direction I told the others to run.

It's a minor barrier. I don't expect it to stop the Golyat, only to mask our presence. If we're lucky, the flames will conceal all traces of anything human—the basket, our footprints, our scents—and the chase will end before it truly begins.

When I stop, an unimpressive wall of fire is sending up a curtain of smoke thick enough to conceal the forest on the far side. The basket crackles and snaps as its tightly woven fibers burn hot and high.

That will do it, my conscious mind says, at the same moment my unconscious mind declares, *one second.*

Time is up.

Breaking branches lock me in place. The sound came from just beyond the wall of smoke.

The ground shudders.

An earthquake?

Two more rumbles roll beneath my feet, equally timed.

Footsteps.

The Golyat is as massive as we feared.

I crouch down low, each movement slight and measured. If a shifting breeze, or the Golyat's own movement, thins the smoke, swift motion could make me easy to detect. Right now, since I'm still alive, I think the wall is working.

A deep rumbling chatter, like trees snapping, thumps through the forest loud enough to quiver the smoke and send my hands to my ears. The sound is primal, communicating raw, frenzied hunger.

It's followed by a deep huffing, like the way a dog tastes the air in quick bursts before puffing it back out.

Once again, the smoke is concealing my proximity, but the Golyat is not fooled. It knows the fire isn't natural.

I'm assigning intelligence to something for which I still have no direct observation, but I have trouble believing a completely mindless force of nature could push the human race toward extinction. Then again, the Golyat seems to have been stymied by a vast gorge, and a deep, swift-moving river that I managed to cross, and now again by a wall of smoke.

Intelligent, maybe, but not very.

Then what is it? What made this creature so dangerous?

A flare of orange light, fifty feet up and behind the wall of smoke reveals a second tree has caught fire. The blaze might very well spread into a forest fire stretching hundreds of miles. I feel a pinch of sorrow for the destruction that could ensue, but if the Golyat remains on the inferno's far side, I will feel grateful.

The orange light grows brighter, cutting through the curling smoke.

And then, it moves closer.

That's not a fire, I think, taking a slow step back.

The luminous glow expands, following a winding path back and forth, like a bright snake emerging from its den. Just as something of a form begins to emerge, the ear-splitting chatter thumps through the forest, and at this range it's nearly enough to make me shout in pain.

Sensing the Golyat is about to push past my smoke wall, I have no choice but to drop the fiery rope and make a mad dash behind a foliage-cloaked tree just thirty feet away which, if the stories are true, is still within arm's reach. I want to dive, or slide out of sight as fast as possible, but I force myself to tip-toe and crouch, each movement a whisper.

The Golyat is a predator, I tell myself, taking a moment to look for the others. With no sign of Shua, Plistim, or Shoba, there are no deer to protect. I can remain hidden. I peek between a shield of leaves, watching as the orange light moves back, the ground thumping.

Is it leaving? I wonder—and hope. The ground shakes again, closer, two impacts so close together they feel like one.

What's it doing?

When the smoke wall bulges outward, I know.

And then, I see it.

17

The shape emerging from the smoke, has been colored by it. The dry black surface resembles a dark stone, if stone were made from stretched canvas. The gnarled shape slopes down, coming to a jagged end, below which are two holes, each twice the size of my head. As smoke rolls up and over a large, still-concealed form, the oversized dog huffing repeats. Smoke is pulled into the twin holes in quick repetitive bursts.

It's a nose, I realize. A nose that is larger than my whole body. But it's also deformed.

It's the nose of a corpse left to dry in the sun. The tight skin has pulled back against the bone structure. Sheets of blackened husk curl up where the too-dry layers have begun to separate.

Is the Golyat suffering from some disease? A kind of leprosy?

Curls of smoke spiral into the nostrils. A lung full of the brush fire smoke would cause even a regular pipe smoker like Jesse to cough, but the monster simply exhales from its unseen mouth, the sound of it dry and ragged. The breathed-on flames glow brighter, the inferno spreading outward, my wall growing thicker.

Did it smell us?

Does it know we're here?

The nose pulls back, the wall sealing itself with fresh smoke.

Heavy thumps shake the earth. The creature is on the move once more.

When the landscape falls still, I know it has stopped. Slithering along the ground, I move around the tree, still concealed with brush, hoping for another look.

But when I get it, I wish I hadn't bothered.

Though my view is obscured by forest, there is a clear sliver of space between myself and the burning balloon basket.

Four black fingers—bones wrapped in stretched, cracking flesh—each of them six feet long, poke through the smoke and grasp the fiery basket. Paying the hot flames no heed, the hand draws back, taking the remains of our transportation with it.

Though I haven't seen much of the monster beyond the smoke, what little I have seen provides enough for my imagination to paint a horrible picture, one that I hope to never see in completion. That, combined with the fact that the monster is inspecting our crash site, demonstrating signs of intelligence beyond that of the average predator, makes me slink back and plot my escape.

If I move without making a sound and am always careful to keep a tree, or a dozen, between myself and the monster, I should be able to escape undetected...assuming the Golyat remains behind the smoke wall.

And since I have no reason to believe it will, the sooner I leave, the better. I move on my hands and feet, like a true creature of the woods, distributing my weight between three limbs at all time. When I've put fifty more feet between myself and the monster, I get to my feet and creep away, careful to avoid dry twigs and brush that might scrape against my body.

The Golyat's exterior might be deformed and desiccated, but the way it used its nose to inspect the smoke resembled a hunter accustomed to tracking with all its senses.

A chattering so loud and frenetic that it causes me to stumble rips through the air. I catch myself against a tree and hold my breath. In the absolute silence that follows, I can hear the blood rushing past my ears.

Maybe it can, too.

The ground shakes twice.

Silence.

The chattering repeats and I can't help but exhale.

Once again, silence settles over the forest. Even the wind, which has fallen still, seems to fear the Golyat's wrath.

Two more quakes and I find myself looking back. Aside from a sea of trees ending at my wall of smoke, I see nothing.

Did it leave?

I look back and forth for any sign of it stepping around the sooty barrier, but the forest is clear.

Did it give up?

An orange glow, subtle at first, but then pulsing, reveals the monster's presence. The glow is much lower to the ground now than it had been.

It's crouching, I think, picturing something like a human form, arms and legs, a torso and head.

The orange blob of light trails downward again, racing back and forth, following a lumpy course that, when it stops growing and intensifies, I recognize as surely as I did its fingers.

Intestines.

A stomach.

The thing's digestive track is burning up.

Hungry.

And just like before, my view of this horrible reality is head on.

Which means...

It knows I'm here.

I take a step away from the tree. It might not be able to see me, but it knows I'm nearby. And when it figures out where...

I take two steps and am sucker-punched by another round of the chattering. My eyes clench shut and my foot comes down on a root. I know how to take a fall without injury, and without a lot of noise, but I'm disoriented by the monstrous noise. I fall flat on my stomach with an, "oof" that's accompanied by a crunch of dry leaves.

In the silence that follows, I remain still, hoping that the dry clapping sound drowned out my tumble.

The ground shakes from a footfall.

And then another.

By the third, I'm sure the Golyat knows where I am. I confirm it by glancing back as I push myself up. Through the vertical slits between the maze of trees, I can see a dark leg pushing through the smoke. While most of it is lost in the gray haze, the black, gaunt foot large enough to crush an elder's hut is unmistakably human...in a long-dead kind of way. The thick, striated nails peel back in layers, like mica.

And that's all I see, because my only hope now is to give up on stealth and try to outmaneuver or outwit the beast. In the open, I doubt it would take more than a few long strides for it to close the distance between us. Here, in the forest, while I can run through trees and ground cover with relative ease, the Golyat has to trailblaze a new path.

Trees crack and topple behind me, thumping against the earth, joining the cacophony of the monster's pursuit.

Despite my sore and wounded legs, I've never run so fast in my life. The part of my mind that registers pain, exhaustion, and the need for more air is switched off. The primal part of my brain—what my father called the 'fight or flight' instinct, present in all animals, including people—has taken over. It's numbed me to anything beyond running.

The rapid *tap, tap, tap,* of my feet over the dried forest floor is joined by the deep rumbling thud of the Golyat's feet. For every ten taps there is one thud, and a half dozen cracks as trees are felled or cleared of their branches.

When I notice I'm running uphill, a direction that will ultimately lead to me collapsing a little sooner, I turn right and run along the grade, weaving back and forth, the way I've seen deer do a thousand times. A herd of deer, moving as one, often evades a predator. But as soon as one, such as me, finds itself exposed and alone...

I get angry, as that thought was dangerously close to resignation.

From the Golyat's perspective, it is chasing something small and living. I doubt it's seen enough of me to recognize me as human. If I can escape it, perhaps there is still a hope of hiding humanity's presence.

Wishful thinking, I'm sure, but it's the best motivation I can conjure.

And then I see Salem's small face and wide eyes, age seven, listening as I related one of my father's stories.

Salem is here because of me, and he brought the Modernists with him. This is my responsibility, and I *will* see it through.

Noble thoughts and intentions, but ultimately not nearly enough.

I glance back and see a confusing wall of black rushing toward me. When I see the horizontal gaps, I see the wall for what it is—a hand. The fingers have already begun to curl, just a second away from grasping me.

A hard turn, back uphill, puts a tree between myself and the hand, which wraps around the trunk and lifts. Roots tear from the ground with an explosion of soil that sends me sprawling. As dirt rains down into my eyes and mouth, I hear my name, "Vee!"

"Shua?"

"Over here," he says. I can't see him through the falling dirt, but I can hear him.

I run for the sound of his voice, blinded by the mud in my eyes.

"Hurry!" he says, closer now.

A roar pursues me, followed by another round of chattering that draws an uncommon scream from my mouth.

The Golyat is dismantling me, body and soul, tenderizing its meal.

The shush of leaves that slides through a forest when a tree is felled grows louder behind me. In my mind, I can see the tree toppling through the air toward me. Its weight will smear me into the ground, its jagged bark shredding away my clothing and skin. I can almost feel it against me.

And then I do, but not from behind. The blow comes from in front.

And it's the last thing I feel.

18

"She's a lot like your son," are the first words I hear upon waking, and I don't recognize the speaker as Plistim, until Shua replies. "Impulsive?"

"Smart," Plistim says. "And impulsive. The second without the first leads to folly, but she appears to possess equal parts of both, making her—"

"Dangerous." I attempt to sit up, but the pain in my head keeps me laid out. Light trickling in reveals our hiding place. To call it a cave would be an overstatement. It's a hollow beneath a tree, perhaps dug out by bears. Roots hang from the ceiling, just five feet overhead, like stalactites. The air is thick with dirt-flavored dust, already tickling my nose.

"I was going to say, 'an asset,'" Plistim says. "But both are accurate."

"A compliment from the great Plistim." The words come out sounding a bit slurred, but adequately express my sarcastic contempt. "I'm thrilled."

Shua, Plistim, and Shoba are seated in a small half circle, all of them facing me. They're huddled together, gear stowed behind them, giving me space to lay sprawled. There is barely room for the four of us.

My instinct is to further taunt Plistim, but my distaste for the Modernist leader is dwarfed by my fear of the Golyat. "What happened?"

When Plistim smiles, my annoyance returns. When Shua smiles, I cringe and close my eyes. "I ran into a tree, didn't I?"

"Straight into it," Shua says, gently slapping one hand into the other, pantomiming the event that robbed me of consciousness for the second time in a day.

Burying my pride in a hole far deeper than the one hiding us, I say, "Thank you, for recovering me."

"Wasn't me," Shua says, nodding toward Shoba.

"Then, thank you," I tell the girl.

She nods and says, "You're heavier than you look."

A laugh coughs from my mouth before I have time to reign it in. I'm among the worst enemies of humanity, short of the Golyat. I should not be laughing. That, and the pain bursting behind my eyes, makes the laugh short-lived.

In the silence that follows, a heavy weight falls over the group. We're huddled below ground, deep in dangerous territory. We have no idea where we are, and other than 'south to Salem,' no clear destination. And there is no hope of convincing Plistim and his family to return to New Inglan. It would be a death sentence. For me, too.

If I could kill them all myself, I would. But that's unlikely, partly because their large number is scattered, and because defeating Shua is equally unlikely. My only option is to help keep these people hidden from the Golyat and hope they all manage to fall off a cliff together.

Shua slides closer to me and reaches out for my head.

I flinch back. "The hell are you doing?"

He smiles—he's always smiling—and says, "Checking your bandage. Running into a tree has consequences."

The trouble with wishing the Modernists would collectively fall off a cliff is that they're all so damn nice. Despite my intentions being well known, not one of them has treated me poorly. And now they've saved my life. Even Plistim, whose reputation is of a ruthless, fringe leader of fanatics, seems like a kind old man who is simply doing what he believes is best for his rather large family.

Misguided, yes. But, evil?

Shua peels a bandage away from my forehead. It sounds slick and squishy. When the open air hits my wounded skin, the throbbing pain in my head is joined by a sharp sting.

"It will be an attractive scar," Shua says.

Micha's other wives would shriek at the very hint of a scar, but those of us who live in the wild tend to wear them like badges. Scars add character, and tell stories. A lack of scars reveals a lack of living. Really living.

I graze my fingers across my forehead, feeling an array of small, open wounds, and then a longer stitched up gash. The stitches are tight and strong, worthy of Grace's capable skills.

"Thank you again," I say to Shoba, and the girl tries hard not to laugh.

She points to Shua. "That was him."

A deep breath and a sigh marks my resignation to stop assuming the Modernists fit preconceived notions about the roles of men and women. After all, I am an elder's wife *and* a shepherd. I'm as much a social oddity as any of them.

I close my eyes, focusing on the world beyond our hiding place, as my blood-soaked forehead grows tacky in the summer heat. A breeze sifts through the treetops, the sound relaxing. Birds sing, their melodies pleasant. The ground is still. I detect no hints of smoke. Our hole smells of earthy decay, which reminds me of childhood.

"Well?" I open my eyes, looking at Shua, who has yet to take his eyes off me.

"What?" he says.

"Where is it?"

Shua sags back a bit. "Gone. It searched for you, and when it did not find you, it vented its frustration on the forest. Then it left."

"In which direction? And don't you dare shrug."

He stops mid-shrug. "We haven't left since pulling you in."

I'm about to ask why, but the answer is clear. The Golyat isn't smart, but it's not dumb, either. Who's to say it didn't feign its departure and is sitting out there, waiting for me to emerge? It wouldn't be the first predator to prepare an ambush outside its prey's den.

I feel it's unlikely, but caution when facing the unknown is prudent.

Then again, Salem is out there in this horrible place, perhaps injured, and afraid. Motherly instincts I've been suppressing for years flare to life. I had been prepared to kill my son, but now that the act would serve no greater purpose, I find my hard heart softening. I had planned a swift death in loving hands for the boy.

But out here, his life could be ended by the Golyat. And I wouldn't wish that on my enemies.

When I push myself up again, I manage to rise into a sitting position. I pause, as the pain in my head becomes unbearable, and then ebbs with each beat of my heart. "If none of you is brave enough to take a look, I—"

Shua places his hand on my arm, as though tempting me to swat it away. Strangely, I don't. "The day is nearly over. Better to rest. And *if* the Golyat remains, perhaps it will give up during the night."

I concede the point by lying back down. When the resurgence of pain fades, I ask, "What did you bring to eat?"

"Nothing still bleeding," Shua says, making me smile again. "Sorry to disappoint."

He slides away for a moment and returns with dried fruit. When I frown, he holds up a strip of what I can best describe as petrified meat. "What...is this?"

"Our ancestors called it 'jerky.' The meat is marinated in brine and herbs, and then dried. It requires no cooking and the meat remains unspoiled for two years."

"*Two years?* But—"

"Why isn't the process used among all the tribes?" Plistim finishes, and then answers, "Because the drying process sometimes requires a small flame. The elders believed one taste of jerky would lead to outright cooking among all the tribes. To maintain control, the practice was outlawed. In Aroostook, we perfected it." He motions to the dried meat in my hand. "Try it."

I take a hesitant bite and chew twice before the flavor hits me. The cooked meat I had as a child, and all the raw meat I've consumed over the course of my life tasted like warm shit compared to this. It's almost enough to bring tears to my eyes, somehow both sweet and salty. It's like nothing I've ever tasted.

"This is how they got fat," I say, and I take another bite. Then another.

"Who got fat?" Shoba asks.

"In the world before." The words, spoken with a full mouth, are hard to understand.

"In the world before," Plistim says, "the food was far better than this."

Such a thing, like the Golyat, is beyond my ability to imagine. I eat all the meat, followed by the fruit. When I'm done, Shoba offers me a drink of water. I thank her, lie back, and fall asleep.

I dream of my son.

Running.

Screaming.

He's snatched from the ground by a black hand. Long fingernails dig into his skin as he writhes and falls away.

Salem hits the ground running, and I note that he looks like he did when he was ten, long hair flowing behind him. As the ground shakes, his course takes him alongside a deep swamp.

I yell to him, but he doesn't hear me.

He's showing off now, oblivious to the danger.

The hand reaches out again, but misses.

Relief is my companion for a moment, but then Salem trips and careens into the black water.

And then, I'm there, standing where the black hand had been. I look down at myself, skin charred like the Golyat.

"He can't swim," I whisper, charging toward the water. "He can't swim!"

I dive into the deep, fighting lily pads and tangles of aquatic plants. The water is dark and murky, impossible to see in.

My son is gone.

Drowned, because I drove him away.

I awake, sitting up fast, instantly aware of my surroundings and the sharp pain of my wounds. I swat and kick the others. "Get up. All of you."

"What's happening?" Shoba asks, fear shaking her whispered voice. "Is it back?"

I point to the bars of roots shielding us from the outside world. The rising sun cuts through the open spaces. "It's time to go." With that, I gather my bag, fight against weary muscles and mending skin, and push my way out of the earthen alcove.

Lying on my back, eyes to the sky, I half expect to see the Golyat standing above me. But the sky is clear. I roll to my feet with a grunt and scan the forest, much of which has been decimated by the Golyat's temper tantrum. The monster is nowhere to be seen, or smelled.

"It's safe," I say, looking back at the hiding spot, which was created when a tree was partially toppled, probably during a wet storm, tearing some of its roots from the ground. It landed against a second tree, and remained living, its hanging roots stretching down to the ground, creating a natural lean-to.

While the others slide out of the earth, I get my bearings and then note the Golyat's path. "It's headed north." The words relieve me, but not Plistim.

"It's going for the others," he says, his frown deep.

While Salem landed south of our position, the rest of Plistim's family descended to the north.

I expect Plistim to follow in the giant's footsteps, but he turns away from the monster's clear path and strikes out south. "Let's go. Salem will need us."

When everyone follows without debate, I realize those four words—'Salem will need us'—is the common ground that unites us. Without him, this temporary alliance would come to a sudden, and likely violent, end.

19

I set the pace and am pleased when everyone manages to keep up. Then I realize that might be because the pain in my legs and head keep me from running. In a moment of determination, I move at a sprint, hopping over roots, fallen trees, and clumps of rocks. Ten seconds into the run, I'm forced to stop completely.

Head in hands, I lean against a tree, teeth clenched. It's all I can do to not scream in frustration.

I flinch back when a hand touches my shoulder. When I reel around to declare "I'm fine," I'm expecting to see Shua and his always-caring eyes. Instead I find Plistim and *his* caring eyes, which only enrages me further.

"I can give you something for the pain," he says.

"We don't have time to brew a tea," I grumble. During the winter, when fires are allowed, tea can be quickly brewed over a flame. While the Modernists could enjoy hot tea all year round, the rest of us had to make sun tea, or cold tea, which takes a long time and lacks the healing properties of hot tea.

"Not tea," he says, digging into his backpack. His hand emerges clutching something brown and shiny. He notes my confused look and says, "We found them in the library basement."

"What is it?"

"A bottle," he says. "It's glass."

I think back to the missing windows in Boston. "Glass was brown?"

He shakes his head. "Normally it was clear, but it could be any color. Our ancestors once had enormous images, which they called art, made entirely from colored glass. And when the sun shone through it…" He smiles, eyes drifting like he can see what he's talking about. With a shake of his head, he returns. "But it's not the glass bottle that's important. It's what's inside."

Plistim pulls a wooden cork from the bottle that was clearly not part of the original design. He places the open end against his finger and shakes it back and forth. Then he rubs his dampened digit against the back of my neck.

I grimace and pull away, but he persists, saying, "It will help the pain, which will keep you from slowing us down."

Anger swells—not because he's insulted me, but because he's right. If he can help the pain, I need to let him.

He repeats the process of wetting his finger and then rubbing the liquid into my skin. When he moves to my temples, the back of my neck begins to burn. I'm about to mention it when a strong scent of mint strikes my nose. I grasp his wrist, stopping him from applying more. "What is that?"

"Peppermint oil," he says.

"Everything in the forest will be able to smell me."

"Maybe so," he says, "But have you ever seen an animal, predator or prey, eating peppermint?"

I have not, but don't say so.

"What you won't smell like, is food," he adds.

I release his wrist and allow him to finish. He's gentle, the way Grace would be, careful to not rub the oil into my wounds. Then he steps back. "How do you feel?"

My eyes blink water from the peppermint fumes, but the strength dissipates as the oil is absorbed. I'm about to complain about the discomfort, and the burning, when I notice the pain in my head has dulled. I roll my neck back and forth. "Better."

I take two steps, ready to continue our trek at a faster pace. I pause long enough to say, "Thank you," and then run, as much toward my son as away from my gratitude. I'm not sure why I thanked him. He brought me and my son to a hellish place and might very well have doomed all of New Inglan. But his simple kindness and careful ministrations could not be overlooked. Plistim is not the violent rebel we were all told about. He is more like my father than I would like to admit.

The journey south continues at an acceptable pace. The forest is unending, carved by the occasional river and grassy clearing. I look for signs of ancient cities, but I manage only to spot a few vine-laden walls, which might have once been something, or nothing. I don't stop to inspect.

After two hours, I slow to a walk. "We've gone far enough." While I have no real way to know how far Salem's balloon traveled before descending, my gut says we're close. But the land here is so vast, we could search these woods for weeks without spotting any sign of Salem, or his balloon.

That's why they'll use fire and smoke, I realize. It's dangerous, but necessary. How else could they find each other in an unfamiliar land?

"When will they light a fire?" I ask.

Shua stops beside me, eyes on what little of the sky can be seen through the trees. "Should have already. Also, in case something happens and we're separated, we won't find them at the fire. They'll leave a trail, at least a mile long, for us to follow."

"That...makes sense," I admit. "But how are we supposed to spot smoke from here?" I motion at the trees concealing the sky.

"We didn't even know if there would be trees," Plistim said. "This is a new world. We planned as best we could."

"I can climb," Shoba says, looking up at the trees.

I shake my head. "The branches will be too thin to support your weight long before you're high enough to pierce the canopy."

"But—"

"I've climbed more trees than any one of you, probably than all of you combined. I've spent the last two years of my life eating, sleeping, living, and shitting in trees. We're not going to waste time so you can prove to me what I already know."

Shoba looks at Plistim with a 'do I really have to listen to her' expression, and to my surprise, he responds, "Davina is right. We would be better served by finding a hill, or a clearing."

"Then we should head that way," Shoba says, pointing east.

I'd been so intent on following a southward course that I hadn't spent much time looking east or west. Once I do, I know the girl is right. Yellow sunlight glows through the trees, revealing a spot of land where nothing grows. It could be rocky terrain, a natural clearing, or even the remains of a concrete foundation, preventing any new growth for hundreds of years.

I strike out toward the clearing, resuming my quick pace and then speeding up as we draw nearer. At first, my run is fueled by anticipation. At spotting smoke. At finding Salem. And then, it's fear that drives me. The nearer I get to the clearing, the more I'm positive it's not natural or some consequence of ancient construction.

Fallen trees litter the forest floor, some toppled with their roots upturned, others shattered. The smell of pine and sap is thick in the air.

Entering the clearing, I leap from tree to tree until I'm standing in the center. The clearing is only twenty feet across, but it stretches out of sight in either direction.

This isn't a clearing.

It's a path.

I note a large footprint, where green leaves have been crushed into the muddy soil.

"You said the Golyat headed north." Once again, my anger is barely contained. I don't look back at the others. I'm speaking to all of them.

"It must have circled back," Shua says.

"Why would it do that?" Shoba asks.

I lock eyes with Shua. He knows as well as I do that a predator wouldn't change course so drastically, and with such destructive fervor, without a reason. We saw the Golyat from the balloon, moving through the forest without destroying everything in its path. It didn't decimate the landscape until it detected me.

"It's hunting them," Plistim says, despair creeping into his voice.

"Or," I guess, "It saw their fire."

"There have been natural fires over the course of the past five hundred years that didn't signify prey," Plistim says. "Why would it—"

"Because *we* taught it differently," I say.

I move back to the forest, where the sky is blotted out, but the ground is clear of fallen trees. Then, in direct disobedience to the Prime Law and everything I've been taught, and believe, I follow the Golyat's path.

The trail of destruction leads us through miles of terrain, some of it rough, some of it level. We traverse it all, never slowing and in complete silence. I would run like this day and night until we find Salem...or what's left of him.

It's not until I hear the distant chatter of the hungry Golyat that I slow. The thumping was distant, and muffled by the forest, but it still sets me on edge. We're getting close. My stomach churns, in part from the sound's effect, but also from the knowledge that I might not like what we find.

Favoring stealth over speed now, I creep onward, spending a half hour covering the next mile in silence. The others follow my lead, stepping where I step, and never speaking. Modernists are good sheep, which I imagine is why they agreed to follow Plistim across the Divide en masse.

The cleared path widens ahead, revealing a broad circle of destruction similar to what we saw upon leaving our den this morning.

This is where they came down, I think, looking for the balloon, but spotting nothing more than fallen trees. I stop short of the clearing, hidden behind a tree. I let my other senses see what my eyes can't.

The forest is lush with leafy decay and pollen. There is a trace of wood smoke, but not enough to signify a fire. But it could be the remnants of the flames that had held another balloon aloft.

Then I smell something else. Another kind of decay, but mixed with something pungent and acidic. Like bile. And blood. And shit. And piss. As a hunter, these are all scents I'm accustomed to, but not when they're distinctly human. I'm not sure if the Golyat remains nearby, but I know for certain that people died in the clearing ahead.

I make it one step before Shua catches my arm and mouths the word, "Wait."

With a hard yank, I'm free and running. I enter the clearing, unsure of what to expect, and totally unprepared for what I find. If not for the severed arm at my feet, I'm not sure I could have identified the swirl of humanity scattered on the ground, and across the trees, reaching thirty feet up.

I fall to my knees, tears in my eyes, and retch into the blood-stained ground, adding my fresh bile to the mix of foul odors.

20

I'm not alone on my knees. Plistim falls with a groan of anguish. The dead are his family, too. Despite all the horrible things I've been taught about the Modernist leader, he's still just a man. A father. A grandfather. As his body shakes, bare hands gripping the blood-soaked ground, I have little doubt that he loves his family, which includes my son.

Shua moves through the carnage with a hand to his mouth and tears in his eyes, but he hasn't come undone. Shoba stands still and quiet, her brown skin pale. Her face triggers my maternal instincts.

I push up from the ground and keep my eyes on the girl. She glances my way, and when we make eye contact, she nearly cracks. Tears flow down her cheeks. A tremble starts in her fingertips and runs up her arms.

"I—I—I..." Shoba's lips quiver.

When I reach for her, she sobs and falls into my arms. I barely know the girl, but I give her all the comfort I can muster, holding her close, stroking her back, kissing her head.

"I've got you," I tell her. "I've got you."

"I—I've never seen anything like this." Shoba's voice is muffled by my chest, which is good because the high pitch would be audible from a distance. But I don't have the strength to shush her.

"No one has," I tell her.

"I have," Shua says, making eye contact with me. It's the first time I've seen anything like displeasure from him, directed toward me. I'm about to ask him what he's talking about when he adds, "The Cull was meant to be a message. To the Modernists. But the savagery of it..."

"It gave us resolve," Plistim says. "It was the moment we knew the people of New Inglan would never accept us, or our ideas. To stay was to suffer, and to live under the constant threat of a violence that we now know mirrors the Golyat's brutality."

I have nothing to say.

What *can* I say?

I have always believed the Cull to be a horrible thing, but also a necessary thing. Hell, I was nearly a willing participant in a recreation of the event. While I was unaware that the Cull was so...revolting in its execution, dead is dead. What Shoba, Plistim, Shua, and I are feeling now—the despair, revulsion, and desperation? This is what they would have suffered back then, but at the hands of their fellow man, not a monster.

While Shoba weeps into my chest, I watch Shua work his way through the scene. *What's he doing?* When he crouches down, picks up an arm severed at the elbow, and inspects it, I cringe. Then he places the limb down, delicately, like he could damage it further. He extends two fingers on his left hand.

He moves through the carnage, inspecting bits and pieces, extending two more fingers.

He's identifying the dead, I realize, *and counting them.*

Shoba stops weeping, wipes her eyes, and steps back like she's just switched off the part of her that feels. "Did you find them all?"

Shua stops his search, hands on his hips, looking desperate to leave. He shakes his head. "Not everyone."

"Who's missing?" Plistim asks.

"Del, Holland, and his wife," he says, but then he looks in my eyes, unashamed of the tears wetting his cheeks. "And Salem."

Emotion overwhelms me, a mix of desperate hope and fear. "Don't say that if you're not sure. Don't you dare say that."

"They're not among the dead," Shua says. "Whether or not they still live..."

That there is a chance Salem is still alive is enough to pull me from the emotional brink. I work my way through the dead, taking note of the various body parts still recognizable as human. While I can't identify those that I see, I'm sure none of them is Salem.

I pause at the clearing's core, where Shua crouches atop a blood-free, fallen tree trunk.

I wince when I see what he's looking at, not because I know what it is, but because of how it smells.

"I'd appreciate it if you didn't react," he whispers.

"To the smell?" I say, now trying hard to keep my nose from crinkling.

"When you figure out what it is."

The ominous words make me forget all about the odor, and the death surrounding us.

I stare at the dark gray, semi-liquid mass that appears to be spreading into various states of viscosity. The middle is somewhat solid, swirling up to a flaccid cone. Toward the outside edge, the mass is soupy, and lumpy. The outer edge is a clear liquid that's oozing into the forest floor, and... I lean a little closer...dissolving it. *What the hell?*

It's my nose that ultimately solves the riddle. The scent wafting up is something like shit. Charred shit. The smell of digested meat is masked, but unmistakable. It's Golyat shit.

As I begin to process that, hiding my shock and revulsion becomes nearly impossible. This isn't just Golyat waste, it's what's left of their family members, who were not only killed and strewn about, but eaten and hastily passed back to the earth.

"I think we should go," I say, trying to sound calm. I stand and survey the area, as though trying to determine which way to proceed, but I'm really just trying not to look back down.

Shua stands with me. "We just need to find their trail. They are not adept at covering their tracks."

"Or surviving in the wild," Shoba adds, with the voice of a girl on the fringe of giving up.

I leave what can be best described as a circle of death and decay, happy to return to the forest, which feels alive and fresh in comparison, where just a tinge of hope still remains. When the others join me, I say, "Salem is smart. He wouldn't just hope that we'd find their trail, he'd leave one for us."

Plistim nods, already scanning the area.

"*If* they left on foot, and not in the Golyat's hands," Shoba says.

"Enough of that," Plistim snaps.

"Let's split up," I say, and I point to Shua and Plistim. "You two head around that way." I motion to the left. "I'll take Shoba around the other way. If they left a trail, we'll find it."

Shua looks to Plistim, unsure. I'm sensing my normal assertiveness might be as unappreciated here as it was in New Inglan. Plistim has been the Modernist leader since their inception. They're probably not accustomed to someone else—not to mention an outsider who had planned to kill them—taking the lead. So I justify the decision with, "Shoba lacks experience, and Plistim—no offense—has aging eyes."

Plistim is nodding before I finish. "A sound plan." He turns and starts walking away, waving for Shua to follow him.

I start in the other direction without a word. Shoba isn't exactly a light foot. I know she's following without looking back.

With each step I sweep the area, looking for any sign of passage. It doesn't take long to spot a broken branch. I bend to inspect it.

"Is that..." Shoba looks at the branch, the break fresh and partial.

"It was them," I say, "but not on their way out." I bend the branch, revealing a break that could have only happened by someone entering the clearing.

"You're sure?"

I hate to crush the flicker of hope in her voice, but there's no doubt. I point to the footprint a few feet away, toes pointed toward the clearing. "There's no heel print. They were running."

I stand and move on, stopping when I reach signs of a very different path. The signs are almost too big to notice, and Shoba misses it. "What do you see?"

"Up there," I say, pointing to the trunk of a tall pine. Thirty feet up, the bark has been sheared off. Then I point to the ground around us. The foliage is compact, and the saplings dotting the forest floor stand at an angle, still trying to right themselves after being crushed. "We're standing in a footprint."

To our right are more signs of the Golyat's passage, slower and more careful after satiating itself on Shoba's family. "The Golyat went this way, which means..."

"Salem and the rest went the other way," Shoba finishes, and she's right.

I look across the clearing. Shua and Plistim are moving at a slower pace, having a heated and hushed conversation. They haven't found anything yet, but I suspect they'll be the ones to spot Salem's path.

When I start moving again, I walk a bit faster and spend less time searching for signs of passage. We're too close to the Golyat's trail. Shoba stays close and quiet, never questioning our new pace.

"Who is Del?" I ask. "Another one of Plistim's many descendants?"

"She is family," Shoba says, "but like you, not a blood relative."

"Oh?"

"She's...a wife."

I'm gripped with fresh sadness. Had Del seen her husband and children slain and consumed by the Golyat? "Married to one of Plistim's sons?"

"No," Shoba says, offering me a sympathetic smile. "To yours."

"To my what?"

"To your son," she says. I'm still confused, but her next words make everything clear. "Del is Salem's wife."

The news locks me in place. "My son...is married. But he's just a boy. A child."

"Less of a child than when you knew him," Shoba says, and before I can complain anew, she adds, "Don't be harsh on Plistim for marrying them. Salem loves her. Adores her. But crossing the Divide...it was just for family. For her to come, they had to be wed."

"When did this happen?" I ask, feeling more sorrow at having missed this part of my son's life, than anger at Plistim for allowing the union.

"A week ago."

A bird call flutters across the clearing. It's convincing, but also unlike any bird in the forest. Shua waves at us from across the clearing. In my haste, I nearly decide to cross through the gore, but I decide against it, not as a mercy to myself, but to Shoba.

We hurry around the clearing, no longer looking for signs of passage. As we close in on Shua and Plistim, I see it before Shua points it out. A symbol is carved into the bark of a maple tree, the wound still fresh. I place my hand on the carved symbol and whisper, "Salem."

"You recognize this symbol?" Plistim asks.

"I don't know what it means," I tell him, "but I know Salem carved it for me."

"For you?" Shua sounds slightly offended.

But then I put the matter to rest by drawing my blade and showing him the edge. Near the handle of what my father said was once called a KA-BAR knife, a symbol has been etched, and it's unmistakable.

While I have no idea what the symbol once stood for—and apparently neither does Plistim—I know what it means now: Salem is alive, and he's left a trail for me to follow.

21

A second symbol on a tree, ten feet away from the first, gives us a direction. While I want to sprint in pursuit of my son, moving through the forest in a straight line is impossible. Even the Golyat would have a hard time maneuvering through the number of obstacles in our way without being driven off course. So we move at a steady clip, spread out in a line, twenty feet apart, with the hopes that Salem won't stray beyond our combined line of sight.

The quiet hike reminds me of home, of stalking and guiding deer, of time spent with a younger Salem. The birds keep us company, their songs the same as though in New Inglan, the species no different on this side of the Divide.

Part of me expected the whole world to be corrupted, but life, it seems, has continued undaunted by the Golyat.

Then again, we have yet to see a single mammal larger than squirrels, which skitter in the trees, twitching their tails and chirping as we pass. While squirrels populate all of New Inglan, there aren't nearly as many here.

There's nothing to eat them here, I think. But since there is little else to hunt, and our supplies won't last forever, the squirrel population will soon take a hit, albeit a minor one... and only if we survive long enough to run out of food.

Two chipmunks scurry past, one chasing the other, both squeaking as they partake in a battle for territory, or mating rights. I follow their course up a tree, and stop as they climb past another symbol carved by Salem.

"Here," I say, placing my hand on the fresh carving, feeling my son's closeness. Then I move on, searching for another marking.

"Over here," Shua says, standing by a marked tree to my left. The new markings turn us forty-five degrees to the right, heading west. We've already been walking for miles. I'm not sure why Salem hasn't stopped, or why he'd head west, but there must be a reason.

"Too bad he didn't think to carve a note into the tree," Shoba says.

We're all wondering the same thing. *Where is he going?*

"Look," Plistim says, pointing ahead. Just fifty feet away, due west, is another symbol. Further still, another. "His balloon was the furthest south. He knew everyone would come to him. With the Golyat stalking the area, fire isn't an option. So he's creating a net. Everyone moving south will come across his carvings. He's trying to unite us."

The theory is sound enough, so I don't bother questioning it. All that really matters to me is that we now have an easy trail to follow. If we move fast, we might even catch up. While Salem and Del might be running, too, they have to stop long enough to carve the symbol every fifty feet. Spread out any more than that, there's a good chance it will be missed.

I set the pace, which turns out to be too ambitious once more. It will take a few days of rest for my legs and head to feel normal again. Since being mauled by a mountain lion, I've spent the majority of every day on the move. Happily, for my pride's sake, it's Plistim who calls for a rest first.

"As much as I would like to find the boy, I'm not as spry as you three." Plistim stops by a tree carved with the ancient symbol. He looks older now. Tired. But I can still sense his strength underneath. Like my father, the power of his convictions are enough to fuel his body.

After a drink of water and a bite of jerky, Plistim restarts the journey, though much slower than before.

We walk in single file now, with Plistim in the lead, Shoba with me, and Shua in the back.

"Do you know him well?" I ask Shoba.

"My cousin?"

I smile and nod. While I'm displeased about everything that's transpired since returning to my father's hut, I am secretly happy that my son has another relative whose bloodline does not trace back to Micha. As much as I would like to throttle Shua, he is a better man than my husband, in character—and if my memory of that night is trustworthy, in bed.

"I spent nearly every day with him since he arrived, though there were times when he and Del snuck off to..."

When her cheeks turn red, I say, "I was young once, too. I know what they were doing."

Shoba clears her throat. "When we met, and he learned I was his cousin, he hugged me in a way that said he would never let go. Family is important to him, you know. It's why you're here. Why grandfather agreed to risk everything to get you here."

I nearly say, 'I wish he hadn't,' but that's not true. The Modernists couldn't have been stopped—by me, or Micha. My being here with them is the best case scenario. And now that I know them, and the truth about the Cull and how it affected them, I could never take part in such a thing.

"If you're wondering if he missed you," Shoba says, and I do my best to hide my anxiety over the sudden, and insightful, shift in topic, "he did. He spoke of you often, and never negatively. He asked Plistim to recruit you on several occasions."

"I'm assuming Plistim said *no*?"

"You *did* follow us to Boston with the intention of killing us." Shoba gives me a nervous smile that says she's still worried about the possibility.

"I wish you no harm, child," I tell her. "I still don't agree with all this. I think it's the epitome of stupid. But you are my son's cousin. I'm not sure what that makes us, but—"

"Why not auntie?" Shoba says.

"I'm not married to your uncle," I point out.

"I see the way he watches you," she says. "My uncle."

"He's simply making sure I don't slit your throats."

Shoba manages a laugh at my dark humor. "Is that what he was doing when my cousin was conceived?"

It's my turn to laugh. "He was drunk."

"He wasn't," she says. "He told us. He knew what he was doing and who you were. He fancied you then. Still does."

"And the woman he loved, whom your grandfather married?"

Shoba giggles this time. "A fiction meant to gain your trust. Honestly, I think the story was inspired by you, if you switch Plistim for Micha."

I roll my eyes. "How could such a thing be true? We only spent a few hours together."

"In the time before, it was called 'love at first sight.'" Shoba is beaming. A romantic. "They wrote books about it." She gives me a sideways glance that says she knows more, and then quickly can't stand the anticipation. "You knew him before. As a child."

"I knew a lot of children." As the daughter of an elder, I was either stowed away, learning from my father, or attending social events held by one of the many elders' families. Four gatherings per year were required, all during the spring, summer, and fall months, but many more occurred in plentiful years.

"You knew him as 'Bear.'"

The revelation staggers me, and I need to catch myself on a tree. I glance back at Shua, reexamining his face again, looking for similarities. Could he really be the same boy? Bear was...chubby. And for a series of summers, he was my closest friend. Intelligent and funny, we would spend entire days walking together, me showing off, him making me laugh.

When the Modernist movement became public, I never saw him again. Or perhaps I did, but I didn't recognize the man as the boy I once knew.

"Please don't tell him I told you," she says.

"I suppose I'll just have to 'recognize' him." I glance at Shua, who's now walking backward. I nearly move on when I see that he's slowly assembling his spear.

I take a step toward him, but am stopped by Shoba's worried voice. "Wait, now?"

"Not now," I tell her. "Something's wrong. Catch up with your grandfather."

Shoba takes a look around the forest, no doubt worried that the Golyat is about to storm through the trees and gobble us up. It's not an unfounded concern, so I don't bother trying to put her at ease. The girl's fear will help keep her alive.

Instead of hurrying back to Shua, I simply hold my ground and wait for him to reach me. Watching him move, I search for any signs that he is, in fact, my old friend. But nothing about the man resembles the boy. Not the way he moves, with confidence and strength. Not the way he looks, rough and handsome. He is a different person, but is that really surprising? He became a man in Aroostook, which is a hard enough life, but then he joined, or was dragged into life on the run as a Modernist. But that did not happen until after Salem was conceived. The only true explanation is that at some point, the boy whose physique garnered the nickname Bear, had decided to become a lion.

"What is it?" I whisper to him as he approaches.

"A smell," he says. "Just a momentary whiff."

He doesn't need to say more. We're moving uphill, the air flowing down carrying our scents with it. That he smelled anything out of the ordinary means whatever the odor's origin might be, it was close. And since the rest of us did not pick it up, it was coming from behind, or to the side, rather than from ahead.

"You're the expert," he says. "Thoughts?"

I turn my head uphill. Shoba has just reached Plistim, who is looking back at us. The hill's crest is just a hundred feet beyond. "If we can crest the hill, we'll be downwind of it. If something is stalking us, we'll smell it coming."

"If it doesn't attack first," he says.

"Predators are patient. If its plan is to ambush, it will approach with stealth." When he starts moving uphill, about to charge, I grasp his arm. "*Unless* we run. But we do need to group up. Being together will buy us time."

"And then?"

"If it attacks, it will try to separate us, driving the healthy away from the weak." I ponder the scenario for a moment, and then add. "It will try to eat your father, because he's old, or me, because I'm wounded."

"Animals are smart enough to tell the difference?"

"They can *smell* the difference, and instinct drives them." I start up the hill, motioning for Plistim to wait for us. "But until we know what's out there, we need to be prepared for anything. Predators beyond the Divide, in Golyat territory, might be nothing like what we're accustomed to. Their instincts and hunting styles could be entirely different."

"And here I thought you'd just get us all killed," he says with a smile. "Maybe you're actually here to save us."

And that's when I see it. The crinkle of skin around his eyes. The joy he finds in his own humor. This *is* Bear. The realization nearly makes me laugh and weep. The father of my son is *Bear*. As children, we would have both found this immensely funny. But now...

I shake my head. The boy Shua once was is nothing like the dangerous man he became. I can't let our past cloud my judgement of who he is now, and whether or not I will allow him to continue being a father to my son.

When we reach Plistim and Shoba, a series of silent hand gestures gets them moving again. Atop the hill, I whisper, "When we start down the far side, run for ten seconds, and then stop. That should give us a little distance."

"From what?" Shoba asks.

Shua shrugs, and even that now seems familiar.

"Are you able to run?" I ask Plistim.

"I am rested enough," he says.

I step ahead of the others and say, "Stop when I do. No talking."

The moment we step beyond the hill's crest, invisible to anything still climbing behind us, I sprint. Running hard, and downhill, we cover two hundred feet in ten seconds. I slide to a stop beside a thick oak bearing Salem's carved symbol.

The others follow suit, crashing to a noisy stop in the leaf litter.

Then, aside from our rapid breathing, the forest is silent again. Totally silent.

The bird songs have stopped.

The chipmunks and squirrels have hidden.

And despite the quiet, I don't hear the animal stalking us.

I *smell* it.

The scent is new to me, but I have no trouble identifying its origin.

It's the Golyat...somehow moving without a sound, and thus far without being seen. But now that I know where it is, I lean out from behind the tree and peer uphill.

When it steps into view, a disturbing realization presents itself.

The Golyat is not an *it* or a *he*...

It's a *them.*

22

"You go ahead," I whisper to Plistim and Shoba. "Get to Salem. If I don't make it, tell him we tried. Tell him I love him."

The pair hesitates. "What do you intend to do?" Plistim asks.

"Slow it down," I say. I have no illusions about killing a Golyat, even if this one is not much bigger than me. The creature at the top of the hill shares the same stretched, black skin and withered form as the monstrous creature that attacked earlier. If not for the orange-tinged illumination emanating from the creature's insides, I'm not sure I would have identified it as a Golyat, though. Despite the size difference, they do appear to be similar. "Draw it away."

"Can you not do that on your own?" Plistim asks, revealing his concern is more for his son than for me.

"I assumed your son would not leave," I say, giving Shua a glance. Knowing he is Bear, I feel more confident in his loyalty to me. Bear would have never left me. If Shua remains, perhaps that boy I once trusted with my life is still part of the man?

"I would not," he says, and I'm glad for it. "If neither of us follow, tell Salem his parents died fighting together."

"I'm sure that will be of great comfort to him," Plistim says, voice oozing sarcasm.

"*I* will tell him," Shoba says, backing away.

"Go," Shua says, urging Plistim away, and then he attempts to reassure his father with, "We *will* follow."

With a sigh, Plistim turns and follows Shoba down the hill-side, following Salem's path.

"How do you want to handle this?" Shua asks, when Plistim and Shoba are out of earshot.

"Heck if I know."

He tries not to laugh. "What I thought."

A chattering locks us in place. It's close, and loud, a sharper version of the big Golyat's ear-shattering thump.

This is closer to a woodpecker.

Shua and I lean in separate directions, peeking around opposite sides of the tree that hides us from the creature. It's just one hundred feet away, squatting atop a slab of granite, its blackened body lit by the sun, as though on display.

Head upturned, the thing sniffs at the air, tracking us by scent. It squats on its hind legs. Its forelimbs and broad, clawed paws are raised for balance. Its eyes, like its body, are black, but the most disconcerting feature is its skin. The black flesh is tight and separated into layers, stretched tight over bone. A few patches of black fur cling to the sides of its face, like mutton chops. It looks like a living corpse, emaciated by time, dried in the sun, its skin cracked apart and pulled tight.

It takes a long drag of air through its nose and then goes rigid. A gurgling churns in its gut, as the orange light there flares brighter. The illumination spreads, twisting down, following the path of its intestines.

I have felt intense hunger before. I know the sound of a stomach so starved it would eat itself. I understand the pain that goes with it, and I remember what I did to satiate that all-consuming pang.

The Golyat isn't just a predator, it is a creature of intense hunger so great that it seems to literally burn within the creature, like a liquid furnace.

When its eyes drift toward us, Shua and I roll back behind the tree.

"It's a bear," he whispers, catching me off guard.

"What?"

"Ten summers ago, the bears in Aroostook were struck by mange. Lost all their hair." He points toward the creature now hidden behind the tree. "That's what they looked like. Well, the dead ones. But those that survived didn't look much better. Except for the glowing. I don't know what that is."

How can something be both Golyat and bear?

I don't have an answer for that, and there isn't time to debate the matter.

A repetitive, dry huff coinciding with a crunch of leaves announces the beast's charge.

"Don't move until it passes," I say, and before Shua can agree or complain, I leap up and sprint away at an angle. Fully exposed, I run, doing nothing to cloak my presence.

I glance back at the hairless, former bear, sliding through the leaf litter, attempting to alter its downhill course. Its claws scrabble across the ground and then catch, propelling the monster toward me. Its jaws tremble with frenetic energy, its teeth snapping together.

Finally knowing what the sound is doesn't take away its power. Somehow, as I remember the resounding chatter from the larger Golyat, knowing the sound came from ravenous jaws makes it worse.

Arm hair standing on end, I focus on running, and on coming up with a plan. If this was a normal bear, the tactic used on the mountain lion would be my first choice. Let the monster's own weight and force fuel its demise. But this isn't a normal bear. It's a Golyat. A destroyer of mankind.

But what do I really know about them?

What does anyone know about them?

Rumors.

Imaginings.

Even the Prime Law is silent about the Golyat. About where they come from. How and why they kill. And how, or if, they can be killed in return. I'd guess our ancestors knew the answers to most of those questions, except maybe how to kill the Golyat.

I doubt my small collection of primitive weapons will be much more effective against the creature than the Old World's power, but I'm not about to run myself to exhaustion and die without a fight.

My knife is not an option. Nor is the machete. The Golyat has the sharp claws and teeth of a bear, and though it looks gaunt and severely malnourished, I suspect it retains all its strength. A quick look back reveals the creature hasn't been slowed by its deformities. In a few seconds, the thing will be upon me.

Rounding a tree, I make a sharp turn to the right. I don't see it, but I hear the Golyat bear slide past as it tries to make the corner. I pump my legs, but I'm spun around as something tugs on my backpack.

The bear's hooked claws are buried in the backpack's skin. Another few inches and it would have been mine. Rather than allow myself to be carried along by the monster, and flung downhill, I let my arms go slack. As the pack is torn away, I catch hold of one of the two spears and manage to free it.

Spear in hand, backpack lost, I run once more. Free of the pack's weight, I'm a little faster, but not nearly fast enough.

The creature's ragged breathing grows louder, marking its approach, and warning me that I have just seconds. Out of options, I run in a straight line, making for a thick pine with rough bark. I slide to a stop, position myself in front of the sturdy tree and plant the spear's base against it. Unlike the mountain lion, the Golyat doesn't view the spear as a potential danger. It's jaws open up, revealing a dull orange light from its gullet, and the creature consumes the spear tip.

As the bear jams the spear down its own throat, I leap down and to the side, rolling to my feet and spinning around to watch the creature die.

But that's not what happens.

The bear groans and gags, acting as any wounded animal might. It staggers back, confused about the wooden pole extending from its mouth, and the pain caused by the metal tip in its gut.

The Golyat heaves, and for a moment, I think the blow might actually be fatal. But then its stomach glows brighter. Tendrils of luminous orange drool dangle from the creature's mouth, coating the spear shaft, which is now steaming. The liquid dripping on the ground consumes the leaves, turning them to sludge.

Run, I think. *Get away.*

But I am rooted. Anything I can learn about the Golyat is more than I knew ten minutes ago.

The bear's torso begins to bend and flex, like it's about to vomit. Its inflexible skin cracks and grinds, puffing black bits of skin into the air, revealed by beams of sunlight filtering through the trees.

The foot-and-a-half of spear still protruding from the creature's mouth tips toward the ground, as if the wood has become soft. Then it stretches and breaks. The wood that hits the ground is solid. The wood that remains dissolves into more of the steaming slurry, some of it oozing from the monster's mouth, some of it sliding down the creature's throat.

When the gray goo's scent reaches my nose, I realize I've seen it before, back at the balloon's crash sight. The dead weren't just slaughtered and scattered, they were consumed and digested on the spot.

The orange in the creature's gut flares brighter still, and for the first time since impaling itself, the beast turns its black-eyed attention back toward me.

"Vee!" Shua shouts. He's a hundred feet back, my backpack clutched in his hand. "What are you doing?"

What *am* I doing?

I take one step and am stopped by a retching sound. The Golyat's gut convulses. I've seen a dog throw up enough times in my life to know what's coming next.

Instead of running, I leap and climb, scurrying up the pine with all the dexterity of a squirrel. There's a wet pop from below, and a splash of liquid. Ten feet above the ground, I look down. The tree, and the ground around it, are covered in a steaming gray sludge mixed with streaks of liquid orange. The tree's base is steaming now, being digested, just as I would have been, had I not fled.

The Golyat turns its head upwards. A shudder shakes through its body, and then it violently shits a stream of gray, orange, and silver. The fluid splashes onto the ground, smoldering everything it touches. Once again, I'm locked in place by what I'm seeing. Streaks of silver, glistening in the sunlight, are all that's left of the spear tip shoved down the beast's throat and into its bowels. Rather than killing the creature, the weapon has been broken down and expelled in seconds.

That helps answer the how. A Golyat could eat an endless stream of people, digesting them and passing them just as quickly as it can swallow them down.

The insatiable bear leaps onto the tree, its claws raking the bark until they catch. Beneath it, the trunk slowly liquefies. With a heave, the beast leaps two feet closer, and that's all I need to get moving.

Moving vertically, I outpace the bear, but I'm also running out of space. Fifteen feet from the top, I feel the trunk bending from my weight. If the trees here were closer, I might try to leap from one to the next. I don't think the bear would make the leap. But I think it might survive the fall if it tried, leaving me in the same position in which I now find myself.

The tree bends again, but this time it has nothing to do with me, or the Golyat.

The tree isn't bending, I realize. *It's tipping!*

The tree's trunk, covered in lava-like digestive juice, is giving way.

The entire tree is going to fall, I think.

And then it does.

23

When a tree falls, there is usually a groan as the fibers stretch, followed by a loud snap as the wood gives way. This tree falls in relative silence, as the liquefied base slides off the trunk. It's not until the branches strike nearby trees, shushing and breaking, that the familiar sound of falling timber fills the forest.

Death reaches out for me, from below where my body will be broken, and from all around, where branches threaten to impale me. Both options are preferable to being devoured and shat out by the Golyat, so I consider letting myself fall.

Then I spot an opening, a break in the branches of a neighboring tree. Pushing off hard with my legs, reaching out with my arms, I leap into the air. Eighty-five feet above the ground, I arc through the air, descending ten feet before reaching salvation. My reception is harsh. The smaller tree's rough bark scours layers of skin from my arms and forehead as I wrap around the trunk like a desperate baby. My legs slam down on thin limbs, halting my fall with painful suddenness. But if the branches were any thicker, and harder, my legs would have likely broken.

Despite being free from the falling tree, I have yet to reach safety. The thin pine trunk to which I've fled bends under my weight, threatening to fling me free, or break under my weight. Before it can bend far enough to dislodge me, I slide free of the branches and down the trunk with no regard to the gouges being worn into my hands.

When the bending stops and I find myself safely stowed on a thick bough, I pause to inspect the scene, which has gone prematurely quiet. The falling tree has yet to hit the ground, which means...

It's stuck.

The branches are intertwined with those of the surrounding trees.

"Vee!" Shua shouts from below. When I spot him, he points toward the falling tree. I follow his finger and spot the Golyat, still huffing and clawing its way upward. It doesn't look built for leaping, but it will eventually reach a point where it can move from one tree to the other.

A sudden, jarring shift quakes through the conflagration of limbs. The steaming, melted base is sliding downhill, exerting more force on the branches. They'll give way eventually, and I don't want to be here when they do.

"Get out of there!" Shua says.

I shake my head. "It will follow!"

He stabs his spear into the ground and takes my second from the backpack. Then he aims the tip upward, nearly at me, and hurls it. The spear passes beneath me. A dry tearing sound and a hard thump punctuates the spear striking both Golyat and tree, pinning the creature in place.

The bear tugs itself up with its forelimbs, but its hind legs hang useless now. Shua managed to pin the creature and sever its spine. But will such a wound kill the beast?

I don't know, and I don't want to be here to find out.

Hands and feet move without thought, whisking me toward the forest floor.

When I'm halfway down, gravity wins the battle, propelling the tree to the ground, shaving branches as it goes.

Pummeled by broken limbs and a cloud of falling pine needles, I work my way around and down the maze of branches until I reach the clear trunk. I slide the rest of the way down, further abusing my skin, but reaching the ground with just enough time to leap away from the falling tree. The ground shakes with a thunderous boom that makes me cringe. As bad as the Golyat bear might be, there is far worse stalking these woods, and the sound might draw it—or them—straight toward us.

I take two steps away from the scene as Shua waves me on, and then I stop upon hearing a groan.

The Golyat bear is pinned beneath the fallen tree, its head and arms extending almost comically. Despite the groan, I see no pain reflected in its black eyes. It turns toward me and chatters, desperate to consume me, even while pinned.

"Vee, what the hell?" Shua takes me by the arm, pulling me back. "Let's go!"

When the tree atop the Golyat, and the ground around it, begin to steam, I turn and flee.

It takes just a minute to find Salem's symbols again, and we're back on track. The Golyat bear isn't dead, and I think it will eventually be freed from its prison. But maybe its hind legs will remain useless?

Then again, maybe not. For all we know, the beast is already freed, healed, and hunting us down.

The image of it spurs me on faster and keeps me numb to the wounds covering my body. It's not until ten minutes later, when Shua says, "Hold up," that I slow down just long enough to shake my head.

When he catches my arm and tugs me to a stop, I reel around on him. I want to shout, but I haven't forgotten there are things in the forest that can hear us. As a result, my, "What is it?" comes out sounding feral.

"You're cut," he says, looking me over.

"I'm fine." Even as I say it, the sting starts to set in.

"You're covered in blood."

"I said. I'm. Fine." Along with the sting, I now feel the stiffening tackiness of drying blood, all over my body.

His patience leaves with the speed of a lightning bolt. He leans in close, speaking just a few inches from my face, his voice matching my own near-growl. "You. Smell. Like. Blood."

Those four words undo my anger, and in addition to the stinging and sticky sensations, I can now smell myself.

"If that thing is tracking us again, there is nowhere we will be able to go that it can't follow. And if there're any more Golyats wandering around, they're going to smell you next time a stiff breeze rolls past. Now, listen." He stands still, holding his breath.

I do the same and have no trouble hearing the sound of water flowing over rocks.

"We need to wash and bandage your wounds," he says. "Get rid of anything covered in blood. Until we do that, we can't follow my father and Shoba, and we can't go find Salem."

He's right. We'd lead every monster tracking us, now or several days from now, straight to them. The scent of my blood will likely linger until the next rain.

I respond by striking out again, this time leaving the marked trail and heading toward the sound of rushing water.

"We need to do this fast," Shua says, spear in hand, eyes scanning the woods.

"You're just trying to get my clothes off again."

"In my experience, it's not difficult."

His sense of humor's return gets a smile out of me. It's short-lived, but only because the flexing skin pulls open a gash on my chin. Cool air rushes into the wound, and I wince at the sting. But it's nothing compared to what I'm going to feel in the water.

The stream is just two feet across, but deep enough to lie down in.

Shua motions to my clothing, as I shed my backpack. "Everything with blood on it stays here."

"I know," I grumble, shedding clothing until I'm standing in just leather undergarments. During the summer months, many women in Essex dress like this, myself included, but not while trekking through the forest and fighting wild things.

Leaving a pile of bloodied clothing behind, I step into the cold stream. Goosebumps rise over my body. I make a slow circle expecting to find Shua watching me, but his eyes are on the trees around us.

"Fast," he says. "Once your blood is in the water..."

He doesn't need to finish the thought. My scent will be carried downstream. Anything lurking near the water will pick it up, and if it's a Golyat, I have little doubt it will come running.

Water flows around me as I sit. The cold and stinging water steals my breath for a moment. Then I lie back and let the water envelop me. The frigid stream numbs me to much of the sting, allowing me to run my hands over the wounds on each arm, my hands themselves, and my face. After thirty seconds of rapid scrubbing, I sit up and then stand.

Shua steps into the stream with me, his shirt removed. He tears a strip off the loose, brown fabric and balls it up, dabbing it on my wounds. "Looked worse than they are, but some are still bleeding."

He leans to his pack and digs inside, returning with a small container. He twists off the cap to reveal beeswax. After dabbing away the blood again, he dips his finger inside and then smooths the wax over my still-open wounds. It stings just for a moment, but then fades. After repeating the process with three more wounds, he tears what was his shirt into several more strips, which he ties around the sealed cuts. When he's done, he leans back, and says, "It's not pretty, but it will keep you from filling the forest with your stink."

"You've always been a charmer," I say.

Shua turns back to his pack, returning the beeswax, but then stops moving. For a moment, I worry he's heard or smelled something, but then he says, "Always?"

I climb out of the stream, picking up my pack. "Fast, remember."

"There's time," he says.

I'm not sure why I'm dodging the truth. I suppose I'm not ready to have that conversation, half naked, wounded, tired, and maybe being pursued by a monster that will eat us, digest us, and pass us in the time it takes for me to say, "For what?"

"You know?"

"Yes," I say, and when I see his slowly spreading smile, and what might be dampness in his eyes, I step back into the stream and face my old friend, turned momentary lover, turned father of my son, turned abductor, turned...what? Ally? Friend once more? "I know it's you, Bear."

The transformation in his face both breaks and warms my heart. Though we've been together in the past, and for many days now, this feels like a reunion. In that moment, I see Shua for the friend I once had. While his body has changed, his smile and eyes are the same, as is his kindness toward me and toward others...even if he did knock me unconscious and lie to me. He believed he was doing the right thing, and now that I'm here, I don't disagree.

Moved by a flood of memories, I embrace him as the boy I knew, but then I feel him as the man he has become. He returns the hug, leans back, and says, "Okay, now we can run like hell."

Then the ground shakes, and so do we.

24

With miles between us and the stream, it's clear we're not being pursued, at least not by whatever shook the ground. The bear could still be back there, dragging itself along after us, or perhaps back to full strength. Our run tapers to a jog, and when we can no longer sustain that pace, a walk.

And once again, everything seems normal. The birds have returned. The squirrels and chipmunks, too. A snake slithers past. Cicadas buzz in the summer heat. Warm leaf litter fills the air with the scent of earthy decay, and the promise of new life. This is summer in the forest as I've experienced it my entire life.

What's missing are larger mammals: deer, rabbits, racoons, skunks, and porcupines. While these creatures avoid people the same way we might a Golyat, it's not uncommon to cross paths with one or two during a day in the forest.

"This feels familiar," Shua says, as though reading my mind.

"Like home."

"That's not what I meant," he says, and he points a finger back and forth between us. "This. Us."

"Us?"

"Walking together."

I picture Shua two feet shorter, and a lot softer, walking beside me, talking about the weather, the tribal gossip, the things he'd seen and done while traveling. I would laugh at the stories, which seemed to have no end, tell far fewer of my own, and we would pass the days while our fathers focused on county issues. Looking back at my life, those days were some of the best.

I wish I could say the same right now.

But I can't.

"Familiar," I agree. "But not the same."

"Maybe someday."

"I doubt it," I say, and I sense his disappointment. "You'd have to gain a lot of weight."

I smile at him as he chuckles, and then I tense when he stops and turns up his ear.

Voices. Male and female. They're barely audible, but not far ahead.

I draw my machete and Shua assembles the four segments of his spear faster and quieter than I would have thought possible. We stalk forward side-by-side, no longer mimicking the casual walk of youth, but the dangerous creep of two killers.

A wall of pocked gray covered in moss and mushroom growth blocks our path. An ancient wall, still standing. We must be entering the fringes of what once was a city. I search the area for other foundations, or hints of previous construction, but I see nothing. Perhaps this one structure is all that remains.

We pause behind the wall, listening.

"I don't think they're safe," the man says.

"How can we know if we never try it?" the younger woman asks.

"Our supplies are not sufficiently depleted enough to warrant taking the risk."

Shua and I lock eyes, relieved. The arguing pair are Plistim and Shoba.

"Shoba," Shua says, drawing a gasp from the girl on the wall's far side. "Listen to your grandfather."

The sound of running feet fades and then grows louder as Shoba rounds the wall's far end and throws herself into her uncle's arms. "I wasn't sure I'd see you again."

"I would not let a Golyat keep me from my family." Shua kisses her forehead.

When he releases her from the embrace, I'm surprised when Shoba redirects her affection toward me, squeezing me in an embrace. When

I stiffen, she lets go, but misunderstands my discomfort. "Sorry. You're wounded." She looks me up and down. "Like, everywhere."

Shoba scowls at her uncle. "You made her do all the fighting?"

Shua shrugs. "My theory is that she smelled more like food."

"Come," Shoba says, leading us around the wall, giving me a moment to ponder the girl's affection. It wasn't really the hug that caught me off guard, it was that I enjoyed it. That I welcomed it. Felt buoyed by it. Just days previous I would have killed these people, and now...I'm starting to feel like I've always been one of them.

The paranoid part of me says that's their plan, to woo me with affection and turn me against the New Inglan counties. But why? We have left that place behind and move further away with each mile we walk. The Golyats have already discovered and eaten some of the Modernists. If they were smart enough to figure out where the modernists came from, and I'm not convinced they are, then the damage has already been done.

Shoba's affection is real, and my appreciation for it, is too.

We circle the wall and enter what remains of the foundation. While one wall has mostly crumbled and been overgrown, three still stand nearly eight feet tall. The floor is covered in earth, leaves, and pine cones, indistinguishable from the surrounding forest.

"Ahh!" Plistim says, arms open, smiling wide. "The hunters return victorious." He claps Shua's shoulder with one hand and leaves the other extended for me.

I stop short, happy to accept Shoba's affection, but not quite ready to receive Plistim's. He smiles at me and lowers his hand to Shua's other shoulder.

"Victorious is a gross exaggeration," Shua says.

"You are alive," Plistim says. "Is that not a victory?"

"Victory would have been killing the beast." I note the small campsite erected in what's left of a building's foundation. Shoba and Plistim were planning to spend the night here. A collection of mushrooms sits between their discarded backpacks.

"How *did* you escape it?" Plistim asks.

I crouch beside their small camp, inspecting the mushrooms. "I put a spear down its throat, your son put a second through its back, severing its spine and pinning it to a tree, which then fell atop it."

When I glance back, Plistim and Shoba stare down at me with wide eyes.

"And it *still* lives?" Shoba asks.

"We left it under the tree, but it was alive," Shua says.

"Then the danger was addressed?"

"Temporarily," Shua says, and Plistim's eyes widen further.

"The Golyats can..." I pause for a moment, thinking of how best to explain it. "...digest anything. The spear stabbed into its throat was dissolved in seconds and evacuated from both mouth and ass. The metal had been melted."

"The digestive fluids turned everything they struck into steaming sludge," Shua adds. "It's what felled the tree, and when we left, was already working its way through the Golyat's prison."

"We should assume it survived," I say, "But we took steps to make sure we weren't tracked by scent." I motion at my scantily clad and bandaged body.

Shoba seems to notice my lack of clothing for the first time and digs into her backpack. She removes a folded lump of dark green fabric as loose and flowing as Shua's. "It's not much," she says, holding the clothing out to me, "but it will help with the insects, and won't overheat you."

I unfurl the fabric to reveal what looks like a seamless, hooded winter garment, but the fabric is so thin it's nearly transparent. I slide into the odd clothing and let the fabric fall around me. It almost feels like I'm wearing nothing, but the color will help camouflage me, and the fabric will keep out the mosquitoes and black flies, so, "It's perfect. Thank you."

Embarrassed by my own gratitude, I turn my attention back to the mushrooms. "Now, three of these species are edible. The fourth will have you seeing rainbow-eyed, dancing Golyats where there are none." I pick through the mushrooms, separating food from hallucinogen. I leave the food on the ground and stow the inedible mushrooms in a pouch on my belt.

"Why did you keep them?" Shoba asks.

"They cannot be eaten," I tell her, "but that doesn't mean they are without use."

Shua chuckles. "I'm sure."

After a meal of dried meat, berries, and mushrooms, night falls and we settle in, lying against the tallest wall, where concrete meets the floor. Shoba lies beneath a dark skin, and the rest of us are mostly covered in leaves. I suggested sleeping in the trees, but only Shua had done so before, and Plistim pointed out that given the first Golyat's height, the ground might be safer than the tree tops. Having survived two monsters of different sizes, I'm confident that nowhere this side of the Divide is safe.

I've spent a good portion of my life sleeping in discomfort, surrounded by danger, so I settle in with no complaints. I've always thought that being killed in my sleep would be preferable. Were it sudden enough, I might never be aware of the pain or terror that comes with life's end.

While Shoba whispers concerns to Shua and Plistim, I drift away.

When I open my eyes again, the great ring is visible in the sky, framed by countless stars, their ambient light filtering down to the forest. I listen to a breeze move through the trees, leaves scratching, trunks creaking. Night insects chirp a tune, joining the chorus.

It's peaceful, and nearly lulls me back to sleep.

When the insects stop, my eyes open wide.

Aside from the silence, the night remains unchanged. Silhouetted trees shift direction with the wind, and that's when I smell it. A Golyat.

Its offensive odor, of living decay, makes it easy to identify. But is it the bear, or the giant?

The ground shivers. It's not violent, or loud.

A gentle shush of leaves draws my attention to Shua. I see his open eyes, and when he sees me, I give my head a slow shake. Our best strategy is concealment. Shua ducks beneath his dark fur, fully concealed. Plistim and Shoba remain asleep, which is good, as neither of them is breathing loudly, or worse, snoring.

Dust falls onto my face as another vibration moves through the foundation. It tickles my nose, threatening a sneeze. I hold my breath, preventing the dust from irritating me further.

Four black fingers slide over the top of the wall above me. One by one, they close, gripping old concrete, dropping more dust into my face and eyes. Blinking tears to remove the grit without the use of my hands, I watch as a dark shape looms over me. Though it's dark, I can make out the form of a gaunt man, perhaps fifteen feet tall. His limbs look long and frail, but I sense power emanating from the thing.

It leans out over the wall, sniffing.

Nobody move, I will the others. *Nobody breathe.*

And then, it's me who makes a noise, instinct driving me to push a short breath through my nose, fighting off the urge to sneeze.

The creature's head snaps down. I can't see its black eyes, but I'm sure it's looking straight at me.

The creature's teeth chatter gently, and I cringe, not just because of the sound's effect on me, but because it could wake up the others. If Shoba opened her eyes now, I have little doubt she would scream. And that would likely lead to all of our deaths. Right now, it's just me in danger.

The beast leans a little closer. I can smell its tangy breath, and I feel the warmth of it on my face, tasting it in my mouth.

When its jaws grind open, I close my eyes and wish I were asleep for what happens next.

25

A scream tears through the night. At first, I fear it's mine, but my lips are still pursed, clamped down by my teeth, drawing blood from the force. Then my fear moves to Shoba, but the sound isn't loud enough to be her. Heart pounding, breath held, my entire body seizes with tension.

The Golyat's attention snaps up. Its slender body rises into the moonlight, exposing a human silhouette, deformed by emaciation with bones that seem to have grown out of proportion. Its arms and fingers are long, its shoulders jutting out. Human, but not.

Orange light flares in its stomach when the scream repeats, its hunger igniting—perhaps literally. A twisting, high-pitched gurgle roils from the creature's gut. And then it rises up another five feet and steps over the wall and into the foundation. The Golyat's long, slender legs carry it across the leafy floor and past the crumbled wall in two long steps.

My eyes strain in the darkness, trying to discern details beyond its general shape. The creature slips into the total darkness of the forest and disappears. Well, not completely. Catching my breath, I watch the still spreading brightness of its gut slide through the dark like an apparition.

"Hey," Shua whispers.

"I'm okay."

"Thank God."

His genuine concern is appreciated, but mine lies with the woman whose scream pulled its attention away. The Golyat was following our trail, of that, I have no doubt. Covered in leaves, my muted scent must have just seemed like a continuation of the trail that had led it to us.

But it had looked right at me.

"They can't see well," I say, and then add, "In the dark."

"Should we travel at night?" Plistim's voice catches me off guard. Has he been awake for the whole encounter?

"Well, we can't see very well at night, either," I point out. "We'd have a hard time following Salem's trail, and would make too much noise, like whoever that was out there."

"Do you think it was Penn?" Shoba asks, revealing that she, too, is awake. Since she's not asking questions about what happened, it's safe to assume she was awake for that, as well. She's tougher than I thought. "It sounded like Penn."

"Could have been a fox," I say. "Or a goat." Having seen neither species, not to mention anything larger than a squirrel this side of the Divide, it sounds like the bullshit it is.

"There's no way to know who it was," Plistim says, "or how they are faring. What it means is that the others are nearby and closing in. They'll find Salem's trail. Some of them likely already have. Our priority is reaching them alive."

"Is there a plan in there," I say, "or just a declaration of intent?"

I see Shua smile in the ring-light. I can't see Plistim.

"We'll leave at first light and won't stop until we reach Salem, or the night returns."

"Sounds like a plan," I say, but I don't feel it. Between the balloons, the fires, the screaming, the death, and falling trees, the return of humanity to this side of the Divide has not been quiet. And as we congregate to a single location, each group potentially being tracked or outright hunted by a Golyat—or two, or three—the forest is going to grow more and more dangerous with every passing hour.

A true survivor would head in the opposite direction.

But I can't leave Salem any more than they can leave their family, which also includes Salem. If we can reach him, and they can reunite with the members of their still living extended family, perhaps the best we can hope for is to die together.

There are no more screams during the night.

No more Golyat callers.

I know because I did not sleep.

When the sky shifts from black to purple, I nudge Shoba awake and roll from my bed of leaves. We pack in silence as Plistim hands out sticks of meat. Three minutes after rising, we locate Salem's symbol, spot a second fifty feet away, and then strike out west.

Where are you leading us, Salem?

I've considered the possibility that Salem is simply running in a straight line, doing his best to assemble the Modernists, but lacking a destination. If this is true, his attempt to help could simply turn his new-found family into a Golyat buffet.

"Is there a better word for you?" I ask, after two hours of hiking. "All of you? Than Modernists."

Plistim laughs. "Your husband coined that term, long before he was an elder, but shortly after he set his eyes on the prize. He conjured an enemy for people to fear, exaggerated and distorted what we believed."

"I'm not trying to argue the point," I say, and then motion to the forest around us. "But..."

"An educated risk," Plistim says. "Everything you believe about our ancestors and what lies on this side of the Divide was filtered through elders whose primary goal was to maintain control through fear."

"So far, everything I've been taught seems pretty accurate."

"The Golyat is not a single all-powerful deity. There are many of them—"

"Not an improvement," I say.

"—and they are far from intelligent, or perfect hunters. Last night, we escaped certain death simply by staying still in the dark. Do you really think creatures such as these, would see our balloons, and the people in them, and come to the conclusion that there were many more people on the Divide's far side? That takes intelligence and reasoning, two qualities which the Golyats do not possess."

He's not wrong, but his reasoning is flawed. "How could you have known that before? It was a foolish risk, and not your decision to make alone."

"I didn't make it alone," he says. "I made it with my family. With your son. And with your father."

He lets that sink in for a bit, and then says, "The Golyats were present at the Divide's creation. Humanity was already in ruins. You don't think they would have noticed the fracture in the Earth and understood that their prey had hidden on the far side? Even a creature of instinct would understand such a thing until distracted. And yet, there are no Golyats in New Inglan."

He pauses to look me in the eyes. "But there were.

"Our ancestors created the Divide, and then cleared the land. Our ancestors were warriors, who fought for humanity, who believed in freedom."

"They created the Prime Law," I argue.

"They did," he says. "But it was never intended to be permanent."

"How can you know that?"

"Have you *read* the Prime Law?" Plistim asks. "The original document?"

I shake my head. Despite my father's casual ramblings about the Law, I've never actually seen a physical copy of it.

"During its first years, New Inglan went by a different name. Kingsland. It was one of five 'safe zones' meant for humanity to begin again. The Prime Law uses the word 'reboot.'"

I intended to hike right on past Plistim and continue on my way, but the revelation staggers me. "Wait...there are other people? Beyond the Divide?"

He nods. "Somewhere, yes."

"And if you find them?" I ask.

"We will follow in the footsteps of our ancestors, and theirs before them. We will fight for our freedom, or die in its pursuit."

"Live free or die," I say, using Shua's version of the ancient quote.

"Precisely."

It's an inspirational idea, but I'm not sure it will ever be more than that. It's been five hundred years since the Divide's creation.

We're armed with spears, knives, and assorted longer blades. The Golyats can *eat* our weapons. Whatever uprising the founders of Kingsland had hoped for, that time has surely passed. After all, what kind of person would concoct a plan that would take centuries to see through?

A boom rolls through the forest, silencing the birds and insects.

"That wasn't a footstep," Shua says. "We would have felt it. In the ground."

I point in the direction from which the sound came. It's the same direction Salem's symbols lead. "It wasn't far."

A deep, resounding chatter claps through the forest from far behind us.

A second string of higher pitched snaps follows from the north.

The sound was heard by hungry ears, drawing very unwelcome attention straight toward us.

When a vibration rolls through the ground, we run.

The vibrations increase in frequency and strength.

Despite our head start, the Golyats are closing in.

"Hurry," Shua says, taking the lead with longer strides. I scramble up a hillside behind him, lowering myself to all fours for a moment to tackle the steep grade. At the top we pause, overlooking a valley.

There is a clearing below, covered in long grass. It has a curved lump in the ground so perfect and symmetrical that I know it's not natural.

Another boom draws my eyes to the front of the strange lump, where the ground is carved straight down, as though by a knife. From our angle, above and to the side, it looks like a cave. Then I see a door open, thick and metal.

A person steps into view, dirty, wearing unfamiliar clothes, hair wild and out of sorts, but I recognize my son, and his voice.

"It won't close!" he shouts.

"Try again," an unseen girl replies.

The door swings shut, but clangs once more, ringing the dinner bell.

The ground behind us shakes, propelling us down the hill, into the valley, where my son awaits.

On the far side of the valley, trees part.

The first of the Golyats have arrived.

"Faster," I shout, sprinting down the hill toward the open door. "Don't stop! We just need to get there first."

My voice catches Salem's attention. His eyes widen upon seeing our group, and then again, when he sees me. He smiles briefly, until the Golyat at the valley's far side chatters its teeth, and its gut flares to life.

26

My legs move as fast as I can manage, hindered by exhaustion and wounds, but aided by the slope. I'm hyper aware of my surroundings, of Shua ahead of me, of Shoba and Plistim behind me, of Salem waving us on, and of the Golyat stretching to its full fifty foot height.

Like the bear, the monster's flesh is desiccated and stretched. Layers of black skin flex and grind with each movement, ancient and living at the same time. Unlike the bear, this Golyat is more human in appearance. It stands upright, with a kind of twitchy limp, its ligaments too tight. It's emaciated—stomach sucked in, oversized ribs nearly tearing through the skin, long, nearly exposed muscles twitching. Overgrown bones protrude from its elbows, the deformities hooking out like weapons. Its wide hips give it a distinctly feminine form, but its face, sunken and charred, is sexless. The black eyes are devoid of conscience. Despite its ravenous hunger, the creature seems like an empty vessel; a shell of what it might have once been. Or perhaps it always looked like that.

I'm detached somehow, like I'm watching it all happen to someone else, whose fate I'm not totally invested in. The world takes on a dreamlike quality, moving slower despite everyone, and everything, moving as fast as they can.

The ground rumbles out of time with the approaching Golyat, reminding me that a second monster is approaching from behind, and shaking me back into my body. The world comes into clarity again. Loud chattering fills the air, almost drowning out the sound of screaming, but not quite.

And then, to the left, movement. In the haze of fear and impending carnage, I think the newcomers are more human-sized Golyats, but when I focus on them, I see two men and two women running into the valley, headed straight for Salem. They're closer to the open hatch, but also half the distance to the Golyat, who sees them at the same time I do.

When the monster adjusts its course, screams turn to shouts, urging them to run faster.

The very selfish part of me, which I believe exists in everyone— whether they admit it or not—is grateful for their appearance. The Golyat will reach them first, and be slowed when it does. I wasn't sure we would make it before, but now...

The ground quakes again. Another footfall from behind. The massive weight of it chills me. *It's the big one,* I think. *The one that ravaged the forest when it couldn't find us.*

The next ground-shaking impact stumbles me. Gravity tugs me further and I fall, but I'm no stranger to turning a tumble into a graceful roll. My hands reach the ground first, before I tuck in and flip. The backpack makes it uncomfortable, but I perform the roll without losing much speed. What I do lose, is heart. Eyes open as I roll, and I see the forest behind us shatter.

A massive arm sweeps through the trees, long fingers hooked. Some trees break. Others are uprooted. All are flung into the air as the massive Golyat clears the obstacles.

I don't see it step into the valley, and don't bother looking back. If I'm about to be crushed or eaten, I don't want to see it coming.

Don't let it happen, I think, trying to run faster. *Don't die in front of Salem.*

Screams pull my attention back to the smaller, feminine Golyat. The creature has grasped one of the four people in hand, the long, slender fingers squeezing tighter. The woman's scream becomes shrill, and between the rumbling, shouting, and abject chaos, I think I hear a crack. The woman falls silent and limp, fluid dripping from between the Golyat's fingers. And then, jaws spread wide, head turned up, the monster consumes her. Two grinding chews and a swallow is all it takes.

Then the feminine Golyat turns its attention to a man who has fallen, wailing in despair. I'm not sure who they are, but there is no mistaking the anguish that comes with watching someone you love die horribly.

As the feminine Golyat's hand reaches down for the man, he draws a knife. For a moment, I think he's a fool for attempting to fight the beast with a simple blade. Then he plunges the knife into his own chest, and I realize it was the perfect tool for the job. He's dead before the Golyat picks him up.

An angry roar tears through the air behind us. I don't look back, but I hope that the larger Golyat, seeing its smaller counter-part consume a meal, is enraged.

The feminine Golyat seems to register the larger creature's presence for the first time. I see what looks like surprise, and then it hurries to scarf down the man. Her glowing stomach flares, gurgling loudly, and then with a hiss, she sprays what's left of her quickly consumed and digested meal from her bony ass. The valley floor behind her steams, digested by the liquified remains of what had been, just seconds ago, two people.

But they were more than people—they were Plistim's, Shua's, Shoba's, and Salem's family. People they knew. People they loved.

When a shadow falls over us, I cringe, ducking down like it will help.

Thinking I'm about to be plucked up, I draw my knife, prepared to repeat the man's suicidal act of self-mercy. But the shadow continues past me. A massive black foot, the skin cracked and sucked in around bone, crashes down just ahead of Shua. He dives to the side, narrowly avoiding crashing into the foot.

I pause long enough to yank him to his feet, and then we're off and running around the giant foot, closing in on the open door, where Salem still stands. My son, equal parts hopeful and fearful just a moment ago, looks pale and numb, his eyes locked on the feminine Golyat that consumed and excreted two people.

He's in shock, I think, now just twenty feet away and closing in.

The man and woman who survived the feminine Golyat's assault make it to the open door first, rushing past Salem. I catch a glimpse of the woman's face, and I'm struck with a sense of recognition, and then they're in the tunnel's darkness.

A chattering mixed with a high-pitched shriek draws my attention back up. The feminine Golyat is backing away, shuffling through its own steaming waste, as the larger creature closes in. I catch a glimpse of the thing's leg, which is taller than the fifty foot monster, and then notice I'm about to crash into Shua's back.

I come to a hard stop behind Shua and find myself face to face with Salem, who's being squeezed by his father's embrace. Tears flow down my boy's face as he looks at me. I can't tell if they're from the horror he's just witnessed, or from a sense of joy at our reunion. But I know my own tears are for him alone, and they blur my vision when he reaches out and takes my hand.

"Inside," Salem says, as Shua lets him go. He waves Shoba and Plistim on as they approach the door. "Hurry!"

Being a shepherd, I step aside to make sure everyone gets past. Shua and Salem waste no time entering. They're followed by Shoba, who sprints inside without slowing. Plistim hurries up next to me, but then stops to turn around, both mortified and fascinated by what's happening.

One hand on the door, I stand beside the man who was once my enemy and my father's friend, head craning upward.

I follow the large Golyat's legs upward. They're flexing and powerful, despite their slenderness. Its hips protrude, but nothing like the smaller creature. *This one is male,* I think, and I look for evidence of this between its legs. I see a hint of something shriveled and probably not functional, but it's enough. Male and female. The Golyats, like people, are a species.

But do they procreate?

Are they even capable?

I look higher still. A long arm the size of a towering tree creates eddies of wind as it swings past. The slender, taut stomach burns with orange light from the inside, brighter where the skin is cracked open. And then the ribs, lumpy and huge, heaving with massive breaths. Everything above that is lost in the sun, but I put the creature's height at a hundred and fifty feet. It turns slightly, revealing its back, where long protrusions grow out from its spine, some of them nearly as big as the female.

The feminine Golyat, still cowering and backing away, shifts its eyes toward Plistim and me. Her orange belly glows brighter, setting her teeth chattering once more. Then her attention shifts back to the big male, and it lunges.

Her deformed elbows dig into the male's lower ribcage, hooking the monster in place while its slender feet and toes pummel his torso, punching holes in the withered flesh.

The male bellows, forcing my hands to my ears.

His long arms come up, gnarled fingers grasping at the smaller, more aggressive female. He pulls, but the elbow hooks keep her locked in place. With a second angry roar, he pulls harder. The female's arms stretch, her feet now kicking at open air.

There's a tearing sound, dry at first, and then wet. Flakes of black skin burst from the female's shoulders. She shrieks as the massive bones pop loose. Tendrils of slick flesh hidden inside the creature stretch and then snap, as both arms come free. Black, clear, and brown liquid sprays from the vacant shoulders as the unhinged arms fall to hang from the male's ribcage.

"Oh god," Plistim says. "Oh my god..."

I share his revulsion, but find no voice for it. I simply stand in shock, watching as the male lifts the now whimpering female, grasping both her thighs and ribs.

Then, the beast pulls.

The female's eyes and mouth go wide with pain, or shock, or some kind of monstrous realization that this is the end of her life—if a Golyat can think and feel such things.

Several loud pops issue from inside the creature. And then all at once, it comes apart at the midsection.

A wave of gray and orange explodes from its gut, splashing against the male's body and arcing out in all directions. Including mine. I spin around, hooking an arm around Plistim's waist and the other around the door's handle. I dive inside the hallway beyond, throwing Plistim ahead of me and slamming the door shut as hard as I can. The heavy door closes with a resounding boom, followed by a dull slosh of liquid against its far side.

I take three deep breaths and then look into the darkness. Freed from the mesmerizing sight of the two Golyats fighting, there is only one thing on my mind. "Salem? Where is Salem?"

27

Before my question can be answered, the ground shakes. Dry grit falls on my face, grinding against my eyes, forcing blinks and tears. Worried voices mingle in the total darkness, each wondering what do to. Where to go.

The ground shakes again, but this time it's from an angry, chattering roar that I recognize. The big Golyat, twice denied its human meal, is venting once again.

A hand grasps my arm in the dark, someone seeking a companion and the comfort of another. Searching fingers move down my arm, find my hand, and grab hold. I squeeze back, confused, disoriented, and fairly certain we're all about to be buried alive.

And then, a light. The flame is small, but it eradicates the absolute darkness, and reveals my son's face. He holds a small torch, no bigger than a chicken leg on a stick. Bathed in light, he can't see those of us back in the shadows, but I can see him.

His once curly hair is cut short, like Plistim's. The beginning of a beard is growing in on his face. It's patchy, but it suits him. His tan skin is made darker by layers of dirt and dried blood. His journey hasn't been easy. He's taller than I remember, which is to be expected, but I had always imagined he would grow into a bulky man, like Micha. Instead, he's slender, but toned, like his actual father. When he left, I stood five inches taller than him, but now he could probably rest his chin atop my head.

"Follow me," Salem says, between angry rumbles. He slips further into the hallway, holding the flame high to light the way. At the back of the group, I shuffle along, and only now do I think to look at the person whose hand I'm holding. Shoba meets my eyes when I look at her, her eyes nervous, her smile sheepish and forced. Between what we just witnessed and the decaying state of this tunnel, now taking a beating from above, I'm surprised she's not worse off. I feel on the fringe of tears myself. I squeeze her hand, and she returns the gesture, both afraid, both trying to comfort the other.

A resounding boom shakes the tunnel, knocking more dust free. The group doubles its pace. A muffled roar chases us, but fades as the tunnel stretches inward, and downward.

The air cools as we descend into the earth, and with every degree lost, I relax a little more.

After five straight minutes of hurrying through the metal and concrete hallway, which is strangely free of earthy scents common in subterranean spaces, the slope levels out. Vibrations still slide through the floor, but they're subtle, and the sound is diminished. I don't know where we are, but it's clear the Golyat can't reach us here.

The tunnel walls around Salem disappear as he steps into a wider space where the flame's light can't reach the walls. Our footsteps echo off a high ceiling as we follow.

"We arrived here yesterday," Salem says, coming to a stop. He reaches, the torch out, lighting a second and then a third, both mounted atop stands made of long, straight sticks. "We should be safe here. The structure was designed to defy extreme forces, and time."

"Where is *here*?" Plistim asks.

"I'm sorry, grandfather. Your questions will have to wait." He looks around Plistim, scanning the group. "Mother?"

Emotions surge faster than I'm prepared for and something like a bark escapes my mouth. I let go of Shoba's hand, step around Shua, and stand before my son for the first time in two years.

His eyes, like mine, are wet. But he stands his ground. "You intended to kill me?"

"Yes," I say, knowing he already knows the truth. "If I could not convince you to flee with me. But intention and ability are not always aligned. Standing before you now..." The tears break free, rolling down my cheeks. "I could have never..."

My words are cut short when my son's arms wrap around me. Despite the facial hair and height, I can still feel my baby's still frail body, held in my arms, nursing at my breast, protected from the world by myself alone. What mother could kill her own son?

"I missed you," he whispers.

I find speaking impossible and respond by holding him tighter.

"You know about my father?" he asks, voice still quiet, but no doubt audible to the group.

I nod against his chest and reply, "He's an ugly, lying asshole who fornicates with pigs."

Salem tenses. Turns his head toward Plistim. "You didn't—"

"She was talking about me," Shua says, smiling as he pats my son—his son—on the shoulder. "And for the record, the pig thing only happened once."

Salem snorts a laugh. "I'm glad—about the two of you. Not the pig."

Laughter is a strange thing, and I've learned that Plistim and his family are capable of finding humor even in dire circumstances. Despite all the death and the horrors of life on this side of the Divide, they still take time to find joy.

Trying not to smile, I say, "There is no 'two' of us."

"Then I will take him for myself," says the woman who seemed vaguely familiar. She's smiling, joining in the banter, standing with a man who looks disappointed by her proclamation. "Not that I want to come between Vee and her Bear, but let's face it, you've had plenty of time to—"

"Dyer?" The name comes out of my mouth before I'm totally certain it's her. Like my son, and Shua, age and time have transformed the small girl I knew into a woman. I look her up and down. She's dressed like Shua, a segmented spear broken down and attached to her thighs. She's a foot taller than me, hair tied back tightly, and she's nearly as muscular as Shua. She's not just a woman now; she's a warrior.

"I'd like to say you grew up," Dyer says, looking down at me. "But…" With that she clasps my shoulders and gives me a firm squeeze. It's an awkward kind of greeting. More than a handshake. Less than a hug. In addition to her weird obsession with entrails, she always was a bit off socially. She ends her dual shoulder grasp with, "Welcome to the family."

Family. The word catches me off guard. Like Shua and myself, Dyer was the child of an elder, of Strafford county. That she's here means... I look at the small man standing beside Dyer. He's no taller than me, and not quite as strong. While Dyer carries a large sword on her back, the man appears to be unarmed.

I offer my hand to the man, but he just looks at it. I was so distracted by his size that I failed to notice the scowl beneath his bushy beard.

"Holland," Dyer backhands the man's shoulder.

He lifts his hand, and I think it's to shake mine, but he points at me instead. "She shouldn't be here. She has no right!" He glares at me and then walks away to the torch-light's edge.

Despite Dyer's toughness, she looks wounded. "Forgive my husband. His first wife and children were caught in the Cull."

My stomach twists. Micha's brutal legacy is chasing me, even across the Divide.

"Which Davina did not participate in," Plistim says, looking stern. "And her father gave us more than her husband took away. I will talk to him." He gives me a nod and heads for Holland.

"Shua," Dyer says, reaching her right arm out toward him. They lock arms and thump their foreheads together. Dyer smiles and turns to me. "I tried to lay this one, but after you he had eyes for no one else." She nods her head toward Holland. "So I married his brother."

"*Brother?*" My surprise is impossible to hide.

"That's what I said when I found out." Dyer chuckles. "Different mother, of course, but they're similar enough...where it counts."

I give her a wide-eyed stare, dipping my head toward Salem, Shoba, and...a young woman to whom I have not yet been introduced.

"They've heard far worse from my mouth," Dyer says, but I barely hear her.

My son's young wife is short-haired, dirty, and armed with a bow—a quiver of arrows hanging from her hip—a hand-axe, and three knives. She's also stunning. Despite her rugged appearance, she looks nervous at my attention.

"You must be Del," I say, stepping closer.

She tries to smile, but it doesn't look comfortable. "Yes...mother."

Dyer snorts a laugh, and I try hard not to smile.

"Vee," I say. Newly married women generally refer to their mother-in-law as either 'mother' or 'ma'am.' It's not until later in life, when they have children of their own, that they are allowed to use less formal terms. That I've told her to call me not just by my first name, but by my nickname is technically an honor, but more because I loathe the tradition. "Please."

She nods, still worried.

"You love my son?" I ask her.

Her nod speeds up.

"And you her?" I ask my son.

"Of course," he says, like I'm supposed to know this, either based on what Plistim and Shua have told me, or on my knowledge of my son's character, which is currently limited.

"Good enough for me," I say, and I reach for the girl. Everything about this is a breach of tradition and protocol. While Plistim and his family are all about breaking laws—pretty much all of them—they must have been worried that I would have objected to the marriage.

"Really?" Salem blurts, confirming my suspicions.

"You're the bastard son of the shepherd called Eight, and a man called Bear, who is the son of the most reviled villain in New Inglan." I smile at my son. "It would have been stranger for you to follow tradition. Though I must confess my sadness at missing the ceremony. I'm sure it was beautiful."

"It was raining," Dyer says.

"I was covered in mud," Shoba adds. "Fell in a puddle."

"We were both ill," Salem adds, growing more comfortable.

Del's smile looks more authentic now.

"You shoot?" I motion to the quiver and bow.

"I *hunt,*" the girl says, adding confidence to her grin.

"Can you eat what you kill?" I ask. "Without the flame?"

"How else does a predator eat?"

With that, I give in and step toward the girl. She meets me halfway and we embrace as mother and daughter.

"Well, this is frikkin' adorable," Dyer says, "but the floor is still shaking. Since I don't want to be buried alive, or eaten outside, how about you tell us where the hell we are and what we're doing next."

I nearly respond, but it's my son everyone is looking to for an answer.

"C'mon," he says, stepping toward the darkness. "I have something to show you all."

"Did you find something?" Shua asks, the first one to follow.

"I'm not certain yet," Salem says. "But I think it's a message. From our ancestors."

28

The ancient ruins, which look neither ancient nor ruined, are revealed in flickering orange light, one torch after another. Unlike the other Old World structures I've seen—or what remains of them—this place was clearly designed to defy time itself. The concrete walls are intact, showing no signs of degradation. The rough surface has been covered in a smooth, tan substance Shua tells me was once called paint, similar to dyes, but thick enough to color solid objects.

We're in a central room, fifty feet across and several hundred long. The walls are thick, the doors metal, and the feeling ominous. The ceiling is arched, perhaps twenty feet tall at the apex. I would have had trouble imagining a space so large and solidly built just a few days ago, but I've now seen Boston. This cavernous room is small in comparison to those megalithic buildings.

There are rooms to each side, their doors propped open. Closed hallways are at either end. We entered through the hall to our rear, but the hallway ahead has yet to be explored. Salem spent most of the previous night and day going through the large central area, trying to make sense of everything. He'd intended to search the entire structure, but got distracted by whatever it is he's taking us to see.

"What is this place?" Shoba asks, as we're led across the room, inspecting signs we can't read and equipment for which even Shua and Salem can't guess the purpose.

"It was the headquarters for an organization called FEMA. It's an acronym for Federal Emergency Management Agency."

"Anyone else understand less than fifty percent of that?" Dyer says.

"Less," I grumble, feeling a little intimidated by my son's command of a language I thought I spoke fluently.

"Their job was to provide emergency relief. Like if a storm destroyed a town, they would provide temporary shelter, water, or food. There used to be buildings above us, too, but they're long since gone. This..." Salem motions to the broad space around us, his voice echoing off the solid walls, "...was a bunker designed to survive far worse than natural disasters."

"Like the Golyats," Shoba says.

"Not the Golyats," Salem says, looking solemn. "But just as bad, if not worse."

"What could be worse?" I ask. Having many of my fears about the giant destroyers of humanity confirmed, I can't imagine anything more fearsome.

"They had weapons..." Salem shakes his head, and looks around the room, eyeing the ancient, now dormant technologies around us with disdain. "They could have destroyed the world. The whole planet could have burned in toxic fire."

"They were used against the Golyats?" I ask.

"No one knows," Plistim says. "But they weren't created to use against the Golyats. They were created to use against other people, in other countries, on other continents. They moved around the world faster than we can move around a single county. Wars spanned the globe, and when they used their weapons, their bombs, hundreds of thousands of people could die faster than you could thrust a sword through an enemy's chest."

The group falls silent. I've never heard of such nightmarish things.

"Actually," Salem says, "They used the bombs against the Golyats, too. And they worked, but they also killed people and poisoned the earth. But the Golyats spread too far, too fast. To kill them all would be killing everything, and everyone."

"How do you know this?" Plistim asks, more excited by the information than horrified.

"It's all here," Salem says, approaching a door. The room ahead juts out into the large space, walling off a portion of it. Unlike the walls all around us, these walls have a large, shiny rectangle embedded in them. I glance toward the flat surface and flinch when I see someone staring back.

Dyer catches me, "C'mon, you're not *that* funny looking."

In the flickering light, I see the person looking back is myself. It's like a pond has been frozen vertically. I place my hand against the smooth surface. "Is this...glass?"

Shua knocks his knuckles against the clear wall. It bongs with each strike, the sound not entirely unpleasant. "Glass windows. Now picture this covering all of the open spaces in those Boston buildings."

"How is it made?" I ask.

Shua shrugs.

Salem stops in the doorway. "Melted sand."

I rub my hand over the surface. Even after all this time, it is smooth to the point of being flawless. "This is sand?"

"Our ancestors had many achievements," Plistim says. "Many of them are marvels beyond our comprehension. They could have been great if they were not also fools."

Plistim's contempt confuses me. I thought the Modernists all but worshiped the Old World and the people who had built it. But it seems his admiration for their greatest works is tempered by revolt at their most heinous. Having lived among people my whole life, I'm not convinced humanity would do much better with a second technological golden age. Self-destruction is part of who we are. Since the Cull, Plistim and his family should know that better than most.

We filter through the door into a room with limited space. There are three chairs along the back wall, facing a table, behind which is another, larger chair. A map covers the back wall. I've only seen a few very crude maps. This one is massive, and detailed. Given the size of the text I can't read, I think the land it covers is vast.

The desk holds several hard objects with unnaturally smooth surfaces, curves, and textures. I touch it all, trying to feel a connection with our ancestors and guess at what these things would have been used for, but they resemble no tool I've seen.

Salem sits behind the table and picks up something that makes a little more sense. "This is a journal. It was left behind by a man named Lew. I don't understand some of it, but I understand enough." He flips through the pages revealing handwritten text and crude sketches. "While Lew had nothing to do with the Golyats' creation, he was part of a group that tried to save humanity from them. We know how that turned out, but for him, it was all in process. A lot of it is vague, though, written from the perspective of someone who knows more than we do. Listen…"

He flips through the pages, finds what he's looking for, and reads, "'Fi spent the last week creating the Divide. She's exhausted, but the job is done. We held the line, and Kingsland is secure. Fi is now en route to Alaska where S and Z await. I think she's being pushed too hard, but desperate times…'" Salem looks up from the page. "The tools used to create the Divide are never revealed, but someone named Fi oversaw the project. I think we have her to thank for New England's continued existence."

"New England?" I say. I understand he's saying *New Inglan*, but he's pronouncing it strangely.

"That's how our ancestors said the words," Salem says. He stands and moves to the large map. He points to a small section, tracing his finger in a circle. "This is New England." He draws his finger in a straight line, carving the circle in half. "This is where the Divide is." He taps to the right of the Divide. "This is Essex." He taps to the left, barely moving his finger. "This is where we are now."

My eyes shift left, following the map across a vast and forgotten land, ending at another ocean. We've traveled so far over the past few days, but according to the map, we have barely moved at all. The Earth, our planet, is far more vast than I had thought.

I can feel my mouth opening in astonishment, but clamp it shut. Since I'm the only one asking questions, I assume this is common knowledge to the others. But I can't keep myself from asking more questions. "And the other land Lew wrote about? Alaska?"

Plistim steps up to the map, raising his finger far to the left and as high as he can reach. "Here."

"That would take a summer to reach," I say.

"Years," Shua corrects.

"Alaska is not our destination," Salem says with the uncompromising confidence of a leader. He turns the book a few more pages, close to the end, and reads, "'We're leaving today, for Pinckney. We'll work on a way to stop the Golyats for as long as it takes. God willing, we'll take the planet back. If not, at least we've got the five safe havens protected.'"

"Pinckney," Plistim says, taking a seat. "Is there any mention of where? Specifically?"

Salem scans the page, turns it, and then stops. "He mentions a Fletcher Mountain."

"You know where it is," I say. "don't you?"

Plistim looks on the verge of tears, or rage. He dips his head, and I'm not sure if it's a nod or not, but then he says, "I do."

"Then that's where we'll go," Shua says. "Perhaps the solution we've been looking for will be there."

"The solution we sought was within reach all along," Plistim says. "But no longer."

"I don't understand, Father," Shua says, crouching down in front of the man, who appears to have aged ten years in the past few seconds. "Why can we not go to Fletcher Mountain?"

"Pinckney was once a town," Plistim says, "in Grafton."

A kind of weighted silence descends over the room and everyone in it.

Grafton county is one of five counties that border the Divide, located in the mountains. It is hard to reach for much of the year, and from this side of the Divide...impossible.

"We came all this way, sacrificed so much, and so many, only to discover we should have never left." Plistim lifts his head and looks to each member of his family. "I'm sorry I brought you here, to this horrible place." His eyes meet mine. "I should have left you behind."

In an odd-feeling act of compassion, I place my hand on Plistim's shoulder. "I'm glad you didn't."

"Then you're a fool like the rest of us," he says.

"No one here is a fool," Salem says. "We made it this far, we can make it back."

"How?" Shoba says.

Salem mimics his father's shrug and then his mother's way with words. "I have no fucking idea."

29

Since the discovery that the answers to the world's Golyat problem lie in our unreachable homeland, the group has dispersed throughout the firelit 'facility,' a word Shua taught me. We're all sifting through ancient relics, trying to decipher a use or meaning that might help us figure out our next step. For those of us who can't read, the task is doubly hard.

Despite Salem's confident proclamation, and the group's subsequent decision to at least attempt a return trip, not one of us believes it is possible, at least not any time soon. Our best bet is to recover one of the balloons and repair it, but there are several problems with that plan. First, most of the balloons would have caught fire or been damaged upon landing. Without animals to hunt, we'd lack furs. Without a knowledge of the land, and what grows where, other natural resources will be hard to collect. Winter is just months away. If we cannot cross before then, we'll need to have stores of food to last the winter. While the FEMA bunker provides shelter, we'll need to find edible plants and make a lot of squirrel jerky if we're going to survive the cold.

No one wants to be here that long, though I have yet to point out that we will be hunted upon our return to New Inglan. Without a true home to return to, winter in the mountains of Grafton will be harsh. But at least there will be animals to hunt, and furs to keep us warm. Surviving in either location means taking action now.

Which is why I'm feeling frustrated by going through a box of unrecognizable junk. Several of the facility's rooms are filled with metal boxes. Some of those boxes hold endless amounts of fragile paper. Some, like mine, hold objects that might have served a purpose five hundred years ago, but have no place in the present age. I suppose if we can uncover some ancient technology or knowledge, perhaps it will help, but I'm not holding out much hope.

The object in my hand is solid, and constructed from metal. Its two halves come together in a joint that moves when I squeeze it. But one metal side just taps against the other and nothing happens. "Stupid..."

Shua sits on a box next to me. The grin on his face says he knows what I'm holding. He digs through a nearby box and slides out two pieces of paper. He looks over the pages, reading their contents. "We're not interested in the work schedules of people who have been dead for five hundred years, right?"

I shake my head, but I am interested.

So is Shua. "Looks like eight hour days, five days a week."

"Five days a week? Eight hours?" I'm incredulous. "What did they do for the other hundred twenty-eight hours each week? Sit?"

"Most of them did that while working," Shua says. "And they were able to get a lot more done in a lot less time. They had machines capable of doing jobs for them."

"What's a machine?" I ask. "A slave?"

"A non-living slave, perhaps." Shua holds out his hand, asking for the strange object I'm holding. I give it to him and he holds it up. "Like this."

"That's a machine?"

He hands two pieces of paper to me. "Can you attach these to each other?"

I fiddle with the pages, trying to fold them, and then lick them together. But I cannot devise a way to join them with what I have on hand. "I would sew them. Like skins."

"Or..." He slips the two pages inside the ancient object's open end. Then he squeezes. The two metal sides *clack* together. Shua squeezes a little harder and one side compresses with a *click*. When he moves the device away, a thin grey line is left on the pages, which are now held together. He moves down the paper, squeezing again and again. It takes just two seconds for him to fully join the two pages.

He hands the paper to me. "It was called a stapler."

I inspect the seam. "Less work, but more completed..."

"Right," he says. "They had machines that could sew seams even faster and with more skill than a person could achieve. There were devices that could freeze and preserve food, even in the summer months. They even had things called toilets. They would defecate into them—"

"Inside?"

"Yeah, but they would push a lever and water would carry it away."

"Where?"

He shrugs, and this time I don't mind. "Someplace we never want to discover would be my guess."

I squint at Shua. "You seem...upbeat. And aren't you sup-posed to be up there?" I nod toward the ceiling, which in this long, rectangular room is flat and gray. I'm surrounded by metal shelves and metal boxes. Everything in this place seems designed to survive the ravages of time, but for no good purpose. Even the stapler.

"Dyer just started her watch. Yours begins in six hours. You should probably get some sleep."

Since dozens of family members are still unaccounted for, we decided that one person would keep watch. It took an hour for us to risk opening the door, but the large Golyat was nowhere to be found. The female was very dead, torn asunder, scattered about and, where its digestive fluids spilled, lying in a puddle of fetid gray sludge.

As disturbing as her mutilated corpse is, I still see it as a victory. She is proof that a Golyat can be killed, and that there is no allegiance between the beasts, at least not while they are ravenous, which appears to be all the time. My thoughts drift to the charred bear with its glowing stomach. It was smaller, and not human in form, but it was a Golyat, and Shua and I might have very well killed it after all.

Despite what we've learned, I feel discouraged by it. If our ancestors had enough power to destroy the world, how could they have failed to defeat the Golyats? There is still much to learn about the monsters. That is for certain. Knowing they can be killed is a start, but learning how to kill them *all* is the key.

Shua hands the stapler back to me. When I take it, my hand lingers on his for a moment, triggering memories of his gentle touch. I twitch back, dropping the ancient device to the concrete floor where it snaps open, spewing tiny metal strands.

"Sorry." He quickly bends to pick up the stapler, cleaning up the mess no one would care about.

"My fault." I watch him, feeling an uncomfortable affection for my once long-time friend, one-time lover, and now...what? My discomfort grows to the point where the part of me that is fierce can't stand it anymore. "What are we?"

When Shua looks up at me, confused, I point back and forth between the two of us. "This. You. What do you want?"

"What do *you* want?" he asks, and I can't tell if the question is meant to be earnest or playful.

A vibration tickles my feet, and as I ponder the answer to Shua's question, I almost miss it. "Did you feel that?"

Shua blinks. Looks down. "Feel what? Did you touch me?"

"The floor shook." I stand, pluck my torch from its makeshift stand and hurry for the door.

In the large, arched space we run into Shoba, who looks relieved at our arrival, and Holland, who looks like he wants to slit my throat.

"What was that?" Shoba asks.

Before I can reply, the floor shakes again. This time the vibration is coupled with a distant gong from the hallway we have yet to explore.

"Plistim went down there," Holland says. "With Salem and Del."

I'm moving at the mention of Salem's name. Shoba and Shua, too. Holland remains behind. I'm not sure what his relationship with the others is like, but his affection for Dyer is unquestionable. Whatever is happening down here, his concern is with her, exposed to the Golyats.

The hallway is long, straight, and featureless. Our rapid footsteps echo around us. Then the floor slopes up, headed toward the surface.

Did they go outside? Was the shaking a Golyat?

A door that fills the hallway's end intimidates me into a full stop, not because it looks dangerous, but because I'm afraid of what I'll find on the other side.

Shua steps around me and tests the door's lock. When the handle turns with a clunk, he swings the door open. The large slab of metal swivels without a sound, moving faster than Shua is ready for. He steps back as the door slams into the concrete wall with a resounding gong that shakes the floor.

When we pull our hands from our ears, Shoba says, "Well, now we know what shook the floor."

Shua steps toward the opening. "The second shake must have come when the door was closed."

The revelation relieves me, but my positive emotions are held in check by darkness beyond the open door.

"Hello?" Shua shouts into the open space, as I lean in with the torch.

"Hey!" Salem's sudden appearance in the circle of firelight startles Shua, Shoba, and me, all three of us stumbling back, hands going for weapons. Salem doesn't notice. He's lost in the excitement of discovery. "Come see this!"

We step into the space beyond and find a chamber even larger than the one behind us. A vaulted ceiling is thirty feet above us, the chamber's walls beyond the torch's reach. There also appear to be several large, solid objects between us and the far wall, along with rows of shelves, like those in the rooms behind us, but holding larger cases.

"Ugh," Shoba says, putting a hand to her nose.

The room is full of offensive scents, like nothing I've ever smelled before. Shua looks equally displeased. "You know what that is?"

"No," he says, and he follows Salem without another word. I hurry to keep up, being the group's only source of illumination. After working our way through a maze of I-don't-know-what, we reach a clearing of sorts, where Plistim is revealed, down on one knee, inspecting a length of what I think is rope.

"This could work," Plistim says.

"Why are you in the dark?" Shua asks.

"The door closed on its own," Salem says. "It startled me, and..." He bends down, picking up his extinguished torch. "Dropped it." He holds the torch against Shua's, lighting it anew.

"You're lucky we came," Shua says, sounding a bit disappointed in both Salem and Plistim. "It could have taken hours for you to find the door in the dark."

"I memorized the path back," Salem says, and when his father's look of disapproval does not waver, he adds, "but we should have been more careful."

The father-son moment catches me off guard, but I don't disapprove. Shua is the kind of influence Salem grew up without. After the past few days with Shua, I have no doubt he was a strong and steady guiding hand for my son during the past two years.

The father my son deserved.

Shoba loses interest in Salem's mishap, crouching down beside Plistim. "What is all this? She tugs the rope revealing what seems to be a never-ending, bright orange line.

"Rope," Plistim says. "Enough to reach the Divide's bottom." He looks up, his earlier defeat now missing. "And back up again."

30

"We've waited long enough." I feel horrible saying it, but someone has to. After three days of waiting for new arrivals, not one more member of Plistim's family has followed Salem's path to our doorstep. Shua, Dyer, and I have kept watch topside, from the trees. There have been no signs of life. No rising smoke, no shouts...or screams...no lingering scents, and no Golyats. The large beast moved on, perhaps sensing easier prey nearby, or just waiting patiently for the moles to leave their den as a group.

"I don't think I can say that to him." Shua sits across from me, hands clasped on the branch he's straddling. We're fifty feet up in a pine tree, wrapped in a blanket that's been coated in sap and covered with pine needles. According to Salem, we look and smell more like a pine tree than a pine tree does. If a Golyat shows up, we'll find out just how astute they are.

"We've been ready to leave since yesterday," I say. "Every day we wait brings winter closer. There is no way to guess how long the journey, the crossing, or the search for Mount Fletcher will take."

"It could be days," he says, feigning hope. "Weeks at the most."

"Years at the most," I correct. "Months if we're lucky. Weeks if a Golyat decides to toss us across."

"Have I told you how pessimistic you are?" His question nearly triggers an aggressive response, but then I see his smile and know he's teasing.

"Better to be a successful pessimist, than a shat-out, steaming pile of positive thinking."

I'm expecting a broader smile, so I'm caught off guard when he frowns. It doesn't take long for me to figure out why. I've just callously described the fate of several family members, people we witnessed being slain in the most horrible way, people whose slippery, gray remains have been slowly drying out in the summer sun. I glance down at the field where the dead Golyat remains, laying in a dried out pool of its insides. "Sorry."

"You meant no disrespect," he says. I find his forgiving nature unfamiliar, unexpected, and at times, unwelcome. He should hate me. Not long ago I would have killed him for his beliefs.

A part of me doubts that. I try to put myself back in time, imagine what I would have done if I'd known what Shua had planned. I would have tried to kill him. I doubt I would have succeeded. But if I'd known who he really was, if I had known he was Bear?

I replay the story in my head. I can't even imagine killing him now.

I would have betrayed the Prime Law to spare Bear's life. And now that he's a good father to my son... I think, for the first time, I understand Plistim. Growing up as the youngest in a large family, in a culture that didn't value me, I was never very close to anyone aside from my father. But Plistim feels that way toward everyone in his family, and they return that affection.

In some ways, I envy the man. Despite the hardship he's endured, when he dies, he will have given and received more love in a single year of his life than I will have during the past twenty.

What I do not envy is the pain that comes with such deep attachments. With every passing day, Plistim has fallen into a deeper depression. As our plan to reach Mount Fletcher progressed to the point where even I thought it might be possible, he has been more focused on his family's fate. With each day it seems more and more likely that the rest of the people he led across the Divide are dead. Or will be before they can find us.

"And you're right," Shua says. "I need to tell him. He will hear it from no one else." He slides toward the trunk, freeing himself of the protective blanket.

I grasp his hand, squeezing.

When he turns to face me, I sense hope in his eyes.

Then I crush it, by raising my hand and giving him a stern look. For a moment he's confused, maybe even hurt, but then he understands. He goes still, unmoving, not breathing.

The sound is faint. A gentle shushing of leaves. I close my eyes, giving image to the repetitive sound. The cadence suggests walking. Two feet. Not large. Despite the noise, I feel no vibrations.

I flinch when a second, louder noise rings out below. It's Holland, leaving the bunker. He's flung the door open. The small man, who lacks even a hint of Shua's forgiving nature, looks around and up, but never spots us. Then he heads for the Golyat's remains.

"What's he doing?" I ask, irritated enough that I've already determined to give the man a slap when I see him next. Dyer might not like it, but he's putting everyone at risk. We've all been a little more relaxed after not detecting even a trace of a living Golyat for days, but this...

Shua shakes his head and puts a finger to his mouth.

We sit and listen. Following the gong of Holland's exit, the forest has gone silent. The birds are quiet. The insects, too.

The distant shushing has stopped. Who-, or *what*ever is out there heard Holland. If he's quiet, maybe it won't—

A sneeze cuts through the forest. Holland wipes his nose as he nears the drying puddle of Golyat insides and digested meals.

The repeating shush of leaves grows a little louder and a whole lot faster. But there is something about the sound that my imagination has yet to flesh out. I focus on the sound once more, seeing the feet sliding through leaves...

No, *over* leaves. But nothing with feet moves like that, not unless, "It's dragging something."

Holland is oblivious to the danger. I'm not sure what Dyer sees in the man. Perhaps she just needs someone to take care of. Whatever the reason, I can't let him die because he's an idiot.

Shua's eyes widen in time with mine. We know what's coming.

"The bear," Shua whispers.

I imagine the Golyat bear with limp hind legs, dragging itself through the leaf litter. The sound fits.

"Go," I say, and I follow him to the trunk, leaving the blanket behind.

As we scrape our way down, trying to move fast and quiet, I keep track of Holland. If he wanders any further, I'm going to have to shout to him, which could inspire the Golyat to move faster, and help it home in on our location.

Holland remains crouched by the remains.

The hell is he doing?

He reaches out a hand.

I want to yell at him. Why would anyone touch that shit?

Shua reaches the ground first, stepping aside as I land and spin around. Two steps into my sprint, Holland pokes a fingertip into the gray. Even from here, I can see a dry film bend under his finger. He lifts his hand, rubbing his fingers together.

When we're close enough that I think he should have heard us coming, he reaches for the puddle again, this time pushing his finger harder. The skin bends, and then, snaps. His finger punches through, dips inside and then is yanked back.

Holland's face morphs from surprise, to concern, to fear, and finally to abject pain over the course of a single second. Then he opens his mouth to scream.

"Stop!" I hiss. "It will hear you."

Holland manages to contain the scream, but I can already see his effort won't last long. It's not just because of the pain; it's because of the horror that his finger has become. Starting where the gray touched his finger, his flesh is all but melting away to reveal bone, which liquifies a moment later. In seconds, the effect will move to his hand, and his arm.

His agonized face beseeches me for help, so I grant it.

"Hold up your finger," I tell him. "I know how to stop it!"

He obeys, believing my lie. While I suspect there is a way to stop it, I'm not certain it will work. When he clutches his eyes shut in pain, struggling to contain that scream, I draw my knife and swing it through the air. Holland's digesting digit falls away, shrinking to nothing as it hits the ground.

Holland gasps, looking relieved for a moment before opening his eyes and seeing the stub that remains where his finger had been.

The pain of having a finger removed by a sharp blade appears to be far less than having it melted, but the sight of it is more than the man can handle.

Holland's scream bursts from his lips faster than Shua can clamp a hand over the man's mouth. It lasts several seconds and is loud enough that I worry more than just the bear-thing will hear it.

Despite his mouth being covered and my, "Shut-up, you idiot," Holland sucks a lung full of air through his nose, preparing to let out another cry. When a fervent chatter replies to his first scream, the second croaks to a stop in his throat.

"What's happening?" Dyer says, storming from the open tunnel, sword drawn. Del is with her, bow in hand, arrow nocked.

"She cut off my finger," Holland says, somehow already forgetting that he's all but summoned a Golyat.

I'm about to shove him toward Dyer when I see the very real menace in her eyes, directed toward me.

Shua steps between us. "Holland put his finger in the Golyat's remains. It was digesting him. Vee took his finger to save his hand, and perhaps his life."

"And..." I say, my voice a warning.

"A Golyat is coming," Shua says.

That takes Dyer's full attention away from me and puts it squarely on the forest around us. The shushing leaves are loud enough to hear without focusing now.

"Was it you?" she asks Holland.

The man is too busy wrapping his bloodied hand to answer, but I have no qualms about assigning blame. "His scream drew it faster, but his sneeze caught its attention."

"Idiot," Dyer mumbles, and then to me. "Sorry for my misdirected anger. Husbands are..." She shakes her head with an eyes-closed sigh. Then she turns to Holland. "Inside. Now."

"W-what are you going to do?" he asks, already retreating toward the door.

Dyer looks toward me, asking the question without saying a word.

I nod.

She bares her teeth like an angry wolf. "We're going to kill it."

31

The Golyat bear drags itself into the clearing, a hundred feet away. For not having hind limbs, it's still moving at a good clip. Despite that, and the fact that it could still devour all of us, I don't feel afraid. The monster looks more pitiful than horrifying.

Dyer chuckles. "This is the Golyat you spoke of? The one that nearly killed you?"

"It had four legs when we faced it," Shua says in my defense, but it's not necessary. Dyer's smile fades the moment the beast chatters at us, its manic jaws spraying froth into the air. The creature's dried out and stretched hide, shattered in the middle, sheds black flakes with each surge of its two operable legs.

The closer it gets, the less comical it becomes.

"Del," I say, "stand closer to the door. Be ready to open and close it should we need to retrea—"

"I will not stand down from a fight simply because I'm younger than—"

"Do it!" I snap. "And show me how good your aim is. Take out its eyes."

Del hesitates, no doubt trying to figure out if I'm keeping her away from the fight, or trying to put her in the best position for it. The truth is both. While I would opt to protect my son's young bride, her skill with a bow could help us not die. Putting her at a safe distance, but still within arrow-range is the best of both worlds.

"Go!" I shout, drawing my machete.

Del backs away, drawstring pulled back, already tracking the Golyat.

"Wait for it to stop," I tell her, "and then—"

The bow twangs.

An arrow flies. There's a dry chop, like a small axe against wood, and then an angry roar.

Despite having an arrow embedded in one eye, the Golyat doesn't lose stride, heading straight for me. While it's probably chance that out of the three of us, the monster has decided to pursue me, I'm not certain. What if it remembers me? What if the Golyats lock in on a prey until they've caught it?

My stomach churns. That would mean the big one is still nearby, too.

"How are we going to handle this?" Dyer asks.

The Golyat bear is just fifty feet away. The arrow falls away, melted from inside the creature's head.

"Move back," I say, waving Dyer back, and then Shua.

"Like hell." Dyer digs in her heels.

"Flank it, damn it!" Either my anger or the strategy puts the pair in motion. As the one-eyed Golyat closes in, they move away and then out to either side. The monster turns its head toward each of them, but doesn't alter its trajectory.

I hear the bow string *twang* behind me, and then an arrow whistles past. I don't see it until it's buried in the creature's forehead. Any other animal would have dropped from the shot, but the Golyat isn't guided by a mind. It's driven by instinct and hunger.

"Shit," Del whispers behind me. She'd been aiming for the other eye. Had she hit it, I'd already be moving.

Though Del and Shoba are close in age, they are night and day in a fight—Shoba the kindhearted soul, Del the arrow-tipped fighter. And yet, I find myself growing equally fond of them both.

As the arrow melts away, I aim my father's machete and stand my ground.

When the Golyat is five feet away, I shout, "Now!"

Shua lunges, stabbing his long spear into the Golyat's back. The blade punches through the creature, and then the soil beneath it, locking it in place. The monster begins to thrash, so I stab with the machete, putting the broad blade through its dried-out forehead. It tries to twist, but between Shua's spear and my machete, it's stuck.

And then, with a hard chop from Dyer's sword, the creature's horrible life comes to an end. Shua and I withdraw our weapons from the corpse. Shua's spear comes out without a blade, the wood dripping. When I see the machete's blade starting to drip, I throw the weapon beside the now-still body.

"Shitty cupcakes," Dyer says, staring at her long sword as the blade bends in the middle, where she cut through the Golyat's neck. Then she tosses the weapon to the ground and we hurry back toward the bunker door, where Del waits for us.

"What's a...cupcake?" I ask.

"A sweet baked bread of a sort," Dyer says. "Sweeter than anything we've tasted. Holland read a book about them to me."

"They had time to write books about sweet bread?" I ask.

"They even wrote books about nothing at all. Stories they imagined."

"The more I learn about our ancestors, the less impressed I am."

She gives a nod. "But cupcakes? C'mon. I've been working on a recipe to make them now."

With that, she enters the tunnel followed by Shua.

I pause to put a hand on Del's shoulder. "You did well. I'm proud to have you as a daughter." While she beams at the compliment, I motion for her to go ahead. I linger by the door, listening for a shift in the wind, a distant rumble, or a chatter. I hear nothing, and then the forest sounds return.

Safe for the moment, but not for long, and certainly not forever.

I close the door behind me and head down the dark slope. I navigate the darkness, hand on a wall, until I see an orange light ahead. It flares brighter and then separates as one torch is used to light a second. While one continues down the other hurries back toward me.

As the light grows brighter, I see the torchbearer is Salem.

"Holland told us a Golyat was attacking." My son looks me over. "Are you okay? Are you hurt?"

"I'm fine," I say, and I'm caught off guard when my son wraps me in a tight, one-armed hug, his free hand holding the torch away from us. Despite being larger than me, he feels small in my arms again.

"I was worried," he says. "I have *been* worried. You were a shepherd for so long."

I want to tell him he could have visited, but that's not true. Back then, guided by the Prime Law, I would have likely tracked him and alerted the counties to the Modernist's hiding spot.

"It was good for me," I tell him.

"To be alone, in the forest, for years? I heard about your lion bites. And your scars."

I don't remember telling anyone about my vast collection of scars, but then I remember standing naked in front of Shua, back on Suffolk island. I'm going to have to talk to him about telling his son when he sees me naked.

If he sees me naked. At the time, I was unburdened by caring what Shua thought, but now...

I give my son a pat and move back. "My father taught me an old saying once. He said that when a person survives tragedies and trials, it gives them a thick skin."

"That's the definition of a scar," Salem says.

"The saying is a metaphor, stupid."

I'm happy to see my son smile. "Then we'll all have thick skin soon."

"Probably," I say, but think, *I hope not.* No mother wants her children's lives to be surrounded by death and pain. Life in New Inglan is hard, sometimes violent, and often life threatening, but I have never witnessed death more crude and pointless as those who fell to the Golyats.

"Your wife fought well," I say, hoping to change the subject.

"She fought?" He sounds appropriately mortified. Del must have kept that detail from him when they met below.

"From a distance. Blinded the Golyat in one eye." I put an arm around his waist and guide him down the hall. "Try not to make her angry."

I'm expecting a laugh, but he grows serious instead. "Mother..."

I wait in silence. He's working toward something.

"Do you think..." Salem twists his lips for a moment. "I was wondering if you and...my father—"

"Did he put you up to this?" I blurt.

Salem squints at me. "You sound nervous."

"Angry."

"I was going to ask if you thought you would be friends again," he says, "like when you were children."

Shit.

"But now I'm thinking I should have asked—"

"Don't say it." I squeeze his side, making him flinch. "Don't even think it."

His smile broadens with each step downward.

Seeing his happiness at even the potential of a future between his father and me, I lower my defenses. This might be the last chance in a long time, perhaps ever, to bond with my son. "You know I'm married, right?"

"The Modernists don't recognize county marriages," Salem says. "Dyer was married to an ogre of a man before joining us."

"How about this...when this is all over, the Golyats are dead, we are free, and my husband is not trying to kill us, ask me again. Until then, let's focus on trying to stay alive."

We keep walking, and Salem keeps smiling, but the air between us grows heavy.

"We need to leave," he says. The admission pains him.

"We do," I agree. "No one else is coming."

"Do you think they're all dead?" Shoba asks, suddenly crouching between Salem and me. The girl, who generally walks through the forest with all the grace and silence of a rutting moose, has managed to sneak up on us. Hiding my surprise at her silent arrival takes more effort than I'd care to admit.

"If they are, they died pursuing freedom." I try to inject a little feeling into the words, but I don't entirely agree with the sentiment. I'm not sure any cause is worth a death in a Golyat's fiery gut. "Live free or die."

"Well put," says a voice from the darkness ahead. It's Plistim. "And reason enough for me to relent. We have stayed here long enough. All that's left is to determine a time for our departure."

Armed with the suspicion that the large Golyat has yet to give up the hunt, I consider the question of timing. We need to put as much distance between us and the beast as possible. If it locks onto our trail, there will be no outrunning it. "Tonight. Under the cover of darkness. And we're not resting until the sun sets again."

To my surprise, Plistim nods his agreement and then raises a finger. "But first...a surprise."

"I don't like surprises," I tell him.

"I think you will like this one," he says. "I heard you lost your weapons."

32

"Weapons," I say, looking down at an assortment of weapons laid out on the ground. There are machetes, hatchets, knives, a strange looking bow, and a set of arrows. Despite the haul, I'm disappointed.

"A lot of weapons," Dyer says, helping herself to a replacement sword. It's smaller than her previous blade, but its curved, shiny surface looks new, and deadly.

"But nothing...powerful," I complain, picking up a machete. It feels a lot like my father's, before it melted inside a Golyat's head. "Nothing unique."

"Actually," Plistim says, "there are many such weapons here."

Dyer's head snaps up, a look of excitement in her eyes. "Then let's use 'em."

"While the machinery is intact, the elements used to power the devices are long since fouled. They would be less useful against the Golyat than these blades."

Dyer nudges me with her elbow. "This would be an appropriate time to use 'shitty cupcakes.' As an expression, I mean. Not to eat. Because we're disappointed, but..." She motions to the spread of weapons. "Could be worse."

"Thanks for the lesson," I say, only half paying attention, while I inspect the blades, looking for a symbol that matches the one on my KA-BAR. While there are several of the big knives on the floor, none of them bear the marking.

"Wow," Del says, picking up the bow.

"Thought you would like that," Salem says. "Took a long time to find the string, which is actually more of a wire, and get it strung."

"Have you tried it?" Del asks.

"You'll be the first."

Del takes her time, replacing the arrows in her quiver with the longer, harder and sharper collection laid out before her. When she's done, she nocks an arrow and pulls on the string. It bends just a little.

"This is really...hard." Del grits her teeth and pulls harder. The bow bends more and then the several small wheels turn. The string comes back and Del's eyes go wide in time with her smile. "I can feel how strong this thing is."

She turns the bow toward the wall.

"Wait," I say. "It could—"

The bow releases. There's a quick hiss of air, and then a single *ping* of metal on stone. Shua holds his torch higher, lighting the concrete wall, where the arrow is embedded.

"Well, damn," Dyer says.

"Everyone take what you want, and then what you can carry along with the rest of your gear, and not be slowed down." When everyone helps themselves to the assortment of weapons—even Shoba, Plistim, and Salem—Shua points at Holland. "You, too."

Holland holds up his wrapped hand. "Can't hold a sword."

"You can carry one," Shua says, tossing a sheathed machete to Holland, who catches it in his left hand.

"It's burning like a bastard," Holland says, as he slips the weapon over his left arm.

"That's what happens when you cauterize a wound, dear," Dyer says. She did the job herself, thirty minutes ago, while Plistim, Shoba, and Salem laid out the cache of weapons. His bleeding had stopped. He will live. But he has yet to stop complaining or blaming me for his woes. Dyer keeps him in line, though, so I feel no need to engage.

Our new weapons serve as a nice distraction, holding our interest throughout the remainder of the day. By the time Shua returns from the bunker entrance and announces the sun is setting, we're all anxious to leave. The journey ahead will mark our collective end, or the beginning of a new life. No one has discussed the odds of the latter coming to fruition, likely because we all know the numbers would be discouraging.

We set out when the sky is still purple, aiming to head northeast as fast and as quiet as we can manage until nightfall. During that time, there will be no talking, no breaks, and no slowing down. We carry the bundles of rope on two stretchers—there will be no running to the Divide—everyone taking a turn. The bright orange ropes are covered by blankets coated in sap, leaves, and pine needles. It looks like we're carrying two mounds of earth. As we travel, we repeat Salem's path of carved symbols, this time including arrows to help guide any stragglers. By the time night falls completely, we've covered a good five miles without incident or even a hint of danger. In the darkness, we slow to watch our step and check the stars, but we continue on through the night without cease.

Seven hours into our trek, we hear the distant chatter of a hungry Golyat, but when it repeats, it's further away.

Two hours later, with the sun just thirty minutes away, a stink.

Shua holds up his hand and everyone stops moving, and we lower the two stretchers of ropes to the ground.

A dry huffing sound, deep and resonant, filters through the trees to our right.

It repeats and is then followed by a dull, orange glow, ten feet off the ground. The orange light reflects off the nearby tree and reveals a dry-skinned man with dead, black eyes. The Golyat is only twenty feet tall, but that's still too big to handle with our weapons, and still plenty big enough to eat us.

It can't see us, but it can smell us, and now that it's waking up, it will hear us if we make a run for it. And running would mean abandoning the rope, which would mean abandoning our mission.

I tense when Del crouches, drawing an arrow back, aiming it toward the Golyat. I wave my hands and shake my head. She sees the gestures. Looks right at me. And then takes aim again.

Shit.

The bow string snaps tight.

The Golyat grunts, turning its eyes toward us, as Del ducks back behind a tree. Then there is a loud *thunk* far beyond the monster.

Del wasn't aiming for the Golyat, she was aiming at a tree.

Despite the distance, the *thunk* of the arrow finding its mark is far louder than the *shush* of her bow string.

The Golyat spins around. Its chattering teeth cut through the night. Then it's up and running toward the sound, moving away from us.

I'm hopeful for a moment, but then a second set of chattering sounds out to our left.

"Around the trees!" I whisper, and follow my own command, exposing myself to the first Golyat, which is still running away.

The ground shakes with the rhythm generated by two sets of large, running feet. I curl up behind the tree, as do the others, one to a tree. The bundles of rope are exposed, but they look like two lumps in the ground. Orange light fills the forest. The long, straight shadows of trees bend back and forth as the creature runs toward, and then past us. In the glow of its digestive system, we would have been easy to spot, but the forty foot tall, feminine form doesn't look down, or back.

When both monsters chatter again, I stand and motion for the others to recover the ropes and move out. We haul ass as a group, chased by the sounds of two hungry, and angry Golyats. I can't tell if they're fighting, or just tearing the forest apart looking for us, but the sound fades away as we awkwardly walk-run with the stretchers until the light of day.

With the sun's arrival, we slow our pace. Had we come across the pair of Golyats now, both monsters would have spotted us. We'll need to find any more of them first. But since their legs resemble the hard, dry surface of tree bark, that's not a simple task. So we let caution guide us forward, and through each task performed on the way.

There's a debate the first time we stop for a true meal. Should we eat on the move, dissipating the scent of our food over a large distance? Or should we stop and risk attracting immediate attention? Fearing a long trail of jerky scent could put a predator, Golyat or not, on our path, we opt for stopping. When we're done eating, Shua digs a three foot deep pit, which we take turns squatting over. When everyone is done, Shua fills in the hole, sealing the odor in the soil.

If anything with a nose comes through here in the next few days, it will smell us, but it won't be drawn from far away, and it won't have a path to follow.

Before setting out, we roll in the dirt, decaying leaves, and drying pine needles, letting the earth's scents mask our own. Then we set out again, northeast, over rolling hills of endless trees. We're joined by bird song and buzzing bugs irate at the day's heat.

When the sun starts to set again, I make a proposal. "We could go through the night again. Sleep a few hours in the morning and then make another full day's walk."

Following deer through the woods of New Inglan, this would not be an unusual schedule to keep. The group's reaction reminds me that I'm the only shepherd in the group. All but Del, who looks tired, but eager to please her mother-in-law, collapse at the suggestion, as if the words actually added to their burden.

"I can't," Holland says. He's panting and saturated in sweat. All of us are, but his face is red. He looks sunburned, but the hue is common in men with weak hearts. Not everyone is built for a life on the run.

Dyer sits beside her husband, leaning back against a tree. "For once...I agree...with my cupcake of a husband." She gives Holland a nudge. "I'm serious, there is no end to that word's versatility."

Holland starts to unwrap his jerky.

"If you open that," I say, making no effort to hide my irritation, "we're going to get up and move five more miles before stopping."

"I'm so hungry."

"You'll be hungry in the morning, too," I tell him. "You can eat before we set out."

Holland grunts, lies in the tree's shade, closes his eyes, and falls asleep. I've never seen anyone nod off that fast, but then, I haven't seen many people as weak. In some ways I'm amazed he survived into adulthood. Perhaps his first wife was also a warrior, protecting him when others would have fallen prey to my father's 'survival of the fittest' theory. While he didn't originate the theory—an ancestor did—he was a proponent of it.

Protected by a ring of boulders, trees, and raised terrain, the group actually managed to collapse in a decent area to spend the night. I sit upon a rock, take a drag of water from a skin, and say, "No food until morning. No talking louder than a whisper, or not at all if you can avoid it. I'll take first watch. Shua, you're second. Dyer, you're third."

The group looks to Plistim, who nods his agreement.

"How about this," I say, annoyed by their reaction. "When we're in the forest, trying to survive while predators might be hunting us down, *I'm* in charge. When making decisions about the big picture..." I motion to Plistim. "There won't always be time to get approval."

"Sounds like you're one of us now," Plistim says.

The words I utter next redefine my entire life. "You know I am."

He smiles and nods. "It's a good idea. As is sleep." He lies back, head on backpack and closes his eyes.

While the others settle in for the night, I head up into the trees. I keep watch until it's been dark for two hours. A gentle bird call summons me to the ground. It's Shua, waiting for his shift.

"Anything?" he asks.

"Nothing."

We share a smile in the dark and part ways. While he scales the tree, I take his spot on the ground, conscious of his lingering smell and how I fall asleep with a smile on my face. When I wake, it's not because the sun has come up. The night is still dark, but it's not quiet.

It takes a moment to get my bearings in the unfamiliar, star-lit surroundings. *It's Holland,* I think, crouch-walking toward the sound. He's twitching around in the leaves, his body rigid.

While the sound sleepers around us are oblivious to the noise, the gentle scrape of feet on tree announces Shua's approach. We arrive beside Holland at the same time.

When Shua reaches for him, I catch his arm. Something feels wrong.

"He's shivering," Shua says. "The wound must be infected."

He gives Holland's shoulder a shake and whispers, "Holland. Wake up."

When he gets no reply, Shua pushes the man onto his back. He's shivering so violently that his teeth clack together. The sound sends a chill down my back.

"I don't think he's shivering," I say, as his face comes into focus. His red skin is now gray, the color of death, but living. And then with a gurgle that startles me, an orange glow ignites beneath his clothing, flaring bright enough to reveal the horror on Shua's face.

33

"Golyat," I whisper, stepping back from Holland. "How is that possible?"

The idea that Holland has always been a Golyat, but intelligent and in disguise, crosses my mind. The idea is as revolting as it is nonsensical. Nothing about it fits.

"His finger," Shua says. "It got inside him. It's *changing* him."

"Making him a Golyat." And there it is; the missing knowledge that reveals why our ancestors weren't able to kill all the Golyats. They *were* the Golyats. Or became them. Some survived, but if the Earth was really populated by billions of people, the Golyat numbers must have spread around the globe. Separation was the only means of survival.

That there aren't more Golyats is a testament to just how many were killed in that ancient war. Unless...there are more somewhere else.

What really matters is that there is one more of them now, and unlike the rest, this one has a name, a past, and loved ones.

"We need to kill it," I whisper.

"But...that's Holland."

"Is it?"

The Holland-Golyat claws at itself, tearing away clothing as though it were rotted and weak. Black eyes snap open, locking onto me, and then Shua. The orange in his gut flares brighter. He spasms in pain, clutching his stomach and turning away.

I draw one of my three new machetes, and Shua his new sword.

"Kill him," I say, aware that I'm asking Shua to do what I can't bring myself to do. Holland's disgust for me is well known. If I kill him, it could look like I decided to take his life out of spite, rather than self-defense, or even mercy.

And when I hear Dyer's voice, I know that's exactly how it will be taken. "What in the name of the ancestors are you doing?" The question is followed up by the slow pull of a sword from its sheath.

She can't see him, I realize. Shua and I are in the way.

"Step away from my husband."

"It's not Holland," Shua says. "Not anymore."

"Step. Away." Sensing that Dyer is close to raising her voice, which could summon even more trouble, I take a slow step to the side.

Shua does the same, catching my eye as he moves. There is a threat in front of us now, and a threat behind. One of them needs to be killed, the other simply disarmed. Shua has the skill for both jobs, but we both know I could never defeat Dyer in combat.

But Holland. I could take his head.

When Shua taps his own chest, angles his thumb toward Dyer, and then points at me and Holland, I nod. He's come to the same conclusion.

But maybe such action won't be necessary. If Dyer can just see.

"Look at him," I say. "It's not Holland."

The man who used to be Dyer's husband twitches, his back to us. His body convulses as he stands.

"What did you do to him?"

"He's changing," Shua says. "Into one of them."

"Holland," Dyer says, but her husband's only reaction is to stand up, tearing away the last of his clothing. "Holland!"

The shout catches the newborn Golyat's attention. It swivels around, eyeing Dyer. As much as it is no longer Holland, some vestiges of the man remain. It's enough to draw Dyer a little closer, though her sword is still drawn and no longer held toward Shua.

"Holland..." Dyer's sword lowers, the anger leached out of her.

She stares into his black eyes, and for a moment, I think I see sadness pulling Holland's eyebrows together. But then he lurches forward and staggers back.

The orange flares brighter still, drawing a high-pitched squeal from Holland. As his body convulses, his face sinks in, transforming from a look of new death, to ancient decay. His skin blackens and dries, the outer layers cracking and curling. The effect moves down, charring him, sucking the muscle and fat downward, toward the blazing gut, leaving dry, desiccated flesh behind. His legs shrink in as well, the meat moving up with slug-like undulations.

His stomach swells with his own insides, fuel to the flame.

Teeth chatter.

Roiling fluids gurgle.

Skin stretches, full of liquified insides.

Dyer raises her sword, ready to end her husband, but then Holland's squeal becomes a shriek. Every last vestige of the man disappears as he roars at his wife, bending forward, arms open to grasp, fingers hooked.

"Back!" Shua shouts. "He's going to burst!"

And then he does, but not how any of us envisioned.

As the skin of Holland's stomach blackens, hardens, and constricts, there's a wet pop and then a frantic spray vents from his back side. A foul scent like nothing I've ever experienced wafts through the air as Holland shits himself out.

I stagger away from the stench, which is growing worse now that the forest behind him is being liquified, too. When the stream begins to spatter in a wide arc, I back up faster. "Don't get any on you! It's what changed him."

What happens next goes beyond strange and right into impossible. As the last of his insides drain out, his body grows. Arms and legs lengthen. Skin stretches and cracks, sheets of it falling away. In seconds, he's a foot taller and a little more intimidating, though he is still shorter than both Shua and Dyer.

A fuller understanding of the Golyats burrows into me. When they eat, they grow. A lot.

How many people has that big one consumed? I wonder. *Hundreds? Thousands? More? How big can they get?*

My fuller understanding has left me with more questions to which there are no answers.

"What's happening?" Plistim asks, staggering as he awakens.

"Golyat!" Del says from somewhere behind me. Her voice is followed by a grunt and then the snap of a bowstring.

The arrow strikes Holland with enough force to punch through his head before being embedded in a tree. The shot puts a neat hole in one side of his head, and a large hole in the other, taking a good portion of his brain with it.

The mortal wound doesn't drop Holland, but it does stagger him.

If not for the growing puddle of waste around him, he'd make an easy target.

Whatever damage was done by having a portion of his brain removed is short-lived. Body hollowed out, dried, and darkened, Holland turns his eyes on us once more, moving from one to the next, perhaps sensing the world as fully Golyat for the first time.

A second arrow punches through Holland, this time puncturing his neck. The blow has even less effect, but that's because she missed her mark. She was aiming for his spine. Had she struck it, Holland's new torturous existence would have been brought to a swift end.

"It's hard to see," Del complains. The light from above, from the stars and the dust ring, is enough to see by, but not see well.

A torch flares to life in Salem's shaking hand. "There!" The forest is filled with a flickering orange glow and dancing shadows that are sure to draw the attention of anything looking in this direction. Since I haven't heard a response to our shouts, I don't spend long worrying about it. Holland is enough to worry about for the moment.

"Stop," Dyer shouts, holding a hand out to Del, who has already nocked another arrow. "It should be me."

As wounded as Dyer must be, she's expressing it with anger and resolution.

Del holds her fire, while the rest of us back away, granting her wish.

As we fade into the trees, Holland's focus shifts to the woman standing her ground. He looks her up and down like he might have upon their first meeting, but his black eyes are full of a different kind of hunger. His stomach growls and flares, warning of an attack.

Dyer takes a defensive stance, ready to swing, but unable to close the distance between herself and her husband without stepping in steaming Golyat waste.

So she waits.

But not long. Tendrils of smoking fluid drip from his teeth as he bares them, cracking lips and cheeks apart.

His body flexes, stretching out its new form, ribs snapping apart, expanding within his chest, making him look even more malnourished, despite just having made a meal of himself.

Holland takes an unsteady step, nearly slipping as the gray soup around him oozes up between his gnarled toes. He recovers, taking another step, and then another.

"C'mon, Love," Dyer says, moving back, matching Holland's pace. She has tears in her eyes, but doesn't falter. Holland is already dead. The monster that is left needs to be dealt with before she can mourn him.

As I watch the pair moving through what had been our campsite, I do a quick mental count of our group and come up short. Where is Shoba? I'm about to ask aloud, when I find her, sound asleep at the base of a tree just a few feet away from Holland. Exhaustion made her immune to the sound, but the fire light is making her stir. I want to warn her, to tell her to stay quiet, but in her drowsy state she's likely to question my order.

When Holland pauses his advance, what's left of his nostrils twitching, I know it's too late. His black eyes shift toward her curled up form, now stretching open, almost welcoming.

"Shoba!" I shout, lunging toward the girl, hoping to yank her away.

Her eyes snap open just as Holland reaches for her.

We both catch her by an arm, but he doesn't need to pull her away, just a little closer.

"No," Dyer shouts, rushing in, but we're both too late. As Shoba lets out a scream, Holland's mouth opens wider than should be possible, and clamps down on Shoba's face.

I see flashes of the sweet girl. Her smile. Her comforting presence. In a world of conflict and harsh living, her soul is a rare one. *Was* a rare one. Despite her heart still beating, despite there still being air in her lungs, her life has just come to an end. She cannot survive this, so I decide to end her suffering.

My anguished scream blocks out the sound of metal severing flesh and bone.

Confused when Shoba's body falls away from her head, Holland spits her crushed head from his mouth and refocuses on Dyer.

Holland lunges, reaching out for his wife, mouth open to bite.

Dyer swings the sword in an arc that robs Holland of both arms from the elbows down. She rolls to the side avoiding his jaws.

Holland staggers, but doesn't fall. As he turns around to face her, his arms drain a mixture of fluids, all of them eating up the earth.

"Recover your gear," I tell the others, fighting back sobs and tears. I can't help but feel like I killed Shoba. I know everyone will understand, that my actions we merciful, but that doesn't change the fact that her blood now stains my blade. *Her human blood,* I remind myself. Had Holland not consumed her, Shoba would have become Golyat, too. Like Holland. Even the smallest exposure to his blood could lead to one of us being transformed into a monster. Should his insides strike anything, it will become useless to us—like Dyer's now steaming sword.

I watch while the others yank our gear away from the scene, but I remain rooted in place, ready to help my old friend kill her once-husband. But she doesn't need my help.

Holland charges again, this time reaching out with stubs.

Dyer angles her steaming sword up into his ribs. The blade slips through his body, locking in place between his bones. She pivots and twists, spinning Holland around and using his own momentum to pin him against a tree.

"Live free or die," Dyer says to her husband. "It's time for you to be free."

Dyer withdraws the blade, spinning around and swinging hard.

I duck as a spritz of sizzling liquid arcs out from the sword, which has cut through dried skin, taut flesh, and thickened bone.

Dyer lets go of the sword and stumbles back, sickened by what she's done and what's become of her husband, who despite having obvious flaws, she loved.

Holland's husk of a head falls away, rolling to the ground. His body scrapes down the tree, leaving a trail of smoldering wood in its wake. The sword bends at the middle and falls apart.

I relax my stance, fall to my knees, and weep for Shoba. But before my first tear can reach the ground Salem says, "Dyer! Your sleeve!"

All eyes turn to Dyer's arm. Just above the elbow, her clothing is wet and steaming, the digestive fluid eating through the garment, seeking out her flesh.

34

"Shit, shit, shit," Dyer says, trying to shed the clothing without touching the affected area. When she can't manage it, she draws a knife, cuts the fabric up the middle and slides out. The loose garment falls to the ground, revealing Dyer's powerful form. While her shape is all woman, she has more muscle mass than Shua.

I close in while Dyer inspects the rest of her clothing, quickly checking one fold after another. "See anything?"

I'm about to say I don't, when I do. And it's not on her clothing. A small dot the size of a tick is smoldering on the back of her arm. I take the limb and lift it closer to my face.

Dyer hisses through her teeth. "What did you do? That hurts."

"Don't move," I say, but she starts to twist. "I said, don't move!"

My shout locks her in place.

"What is it?" she asks.

My answer is swift and without voice. The knife in my hand is so sharp, and the cut so fast, that it takes a moment for her to feel the pain. But she feels it at the same moment the small fillet of her arm falls into the leaf litter at her feet.

She reels away, clutching the wound, blood squeezing between her fingers. "Fuck did you do to me?"

"Bandage," I shout to Shua, who retrieves a clean wrap of cloth from his bag and tosses it to me. He then draws a knife and holds it in the flame of Salem's torch, which we need to extinguish soon.

I approach Dyer, bandage in hand, but she eyes me warily.

"Let me bandage it."

"Tell me," she says.

"Your hands are dirty," I tell her. "You're going to get an infection."

"Vee, damn it, we just cut off the heads of two people we love. I can take whatever shit you have to say."

"You had some on your arm," I tell her. "Just a drop. So I cut it away. And deep. We'll need to cauterize it."

"Wasn't enough to take my husband's finger, you needed a piece of my arm, too?" Her anger melts into regret. "I'm not blaming you. I just...that didn't work either. We'd be better off increasing the head count to three."

"We don't know how it works," I say. "He dipped his finger in it. You barely felt the drop before I cut it away."

"She's right," Plistim says, sliding into his backpack. Salem and Del are already prepped to move. "We don't know enough to make any kind of determination."

"But you will if you don't kill me. You can track how long it takes me to change." Dyer dips her head toward Salem. "I'm guessing you already worked out the time between when Holland lost his finger and now."

The discomfort on Salem's face says that he has.

"You just want to study me," Dyer says. "I would rather die now."

I'm about to come to Plistim's, and Salem's defenses, when the elder says, "You're not wrong. Knowing how communicable the... transformation is, not to mention how long it needs to take root, and turn you into...well. All of that knowledge would be beneficial to all of us. But to be honest, I hope the only thing we learn is that it cannot be spread by a single drop that's been cut away. Holland was your husband, but we are your family. All of us."

Plistim's words are spoken with calm determination, but I can see he's struggling, and not because of Holland. Shoba's death is weighing heavily on all of us, but no doubt heaviest on her grandfather, who brought her on this insane journey. With so many of his people lost or dead, the burden he carries must be immense. That Shoba's death didn't break him speaks to the man's indominable fortitude.

Dyer's defenses sag, but she says nothing.

Shua steps in front of Dyer. "If the time comes, when the pain is too great, I will free you from it." He glances at me, nodding what I think is thanks and a silent communication that I will not have to take another friend's head.

Dyer offers a sad smile and leans her head forward. Shua places his forehead against hers.

"Until then," he says. "I expect you to fight. Now...hold your tongue."

Dyer's eyes go wide. "What—"

Her voice is cut off by the sizzle of burning flesh. She grunts in pain from the scalding, but manages to keep her mouth shut. Shua holds his knife to the wound longer than seems necessary, and then pulls it away.

"Asshole," Dyer says.

"Balm and a bandage," Shua says.

I supply him with the bandage he'd given me, and take the balm offered by Plistim. Shua dips his fingers in the herbal concoction and smears it over the wound. Dyer winces, but doesn't make a sound.

A minute later, the wound is sealed, treated, and bandaged.

"Try not to use the arm for a few days," Shua says.

I'm sure Dyer heard him, but she says nothing. She just turns to her husband's remains and stares.

A distant chatter puts a chill in the air.

Salem extinguishes the torch.

"It is time," Plistim says. "The smell will draw attention."

The observation puts the stench back on the forefront of my mind, and I nearly vomit in revulsion. While Del and Salem move away, finding our direction with the stars, I whisper a goodbye and an apology to Shoba's body. Shua stands by my side, sniffing back his own tears. "She was as close to a daughter as I've ever known."

Damnit, I think, when his words draw a sob from me. He places his hand on my shoulder, squeezing. "Thank you. For what you did. I'm not sure I could have done it, but it needed to happen. You quieted her suffering. Kept her from becoming a monster."

"I failed to save her," I point out.

"We all did," he says, carving up the responsibility between himself and the others.

"They'll eat her," I say, pointing out the horrible truth that will haunt me.

"What made her Shoba is already gone," he says, hinting at his beliefs in a higher power and an afterlife. A discussion for another day. He squeezes again, wiping his tears away and straightening his posture, ever the warrior in control of his emotions. "We need to go, before the Golyat arrive and no one can be saved."

I stand and wipe my own tears, before Shua and I tiptoe out of the small battlefield, careful to avoid the ground where even the smallest wisp of steam rises.

"Take a minute," Shua says to Dyer, standing still, eyes on her desiccated husband's Golyat corpse, "but that is all."

He follows me away, giving Dyer privacy, but not losing sight of her. We stop short of Plistim, Salem, and Del.

"Perhaps we are lucky to have never found a love so intense," I say. "Losing it exaggerates the pain of death."

"What of your son, and your father?" Shua asks.

"They are blood," I say. "Loved out of nature."

"That sounds cold."

"The mother of a murderer loves her son, even if she hates the man he has become," I say.

"As you did Salem when you set out to kill him."

The observation bites, and I nearly bite back, but he's not trying to insult me. And, he's right. "Yes. But when you choose to love someone...when you take someone who is not blood and surrender your heart to them... That is a different kind of love. To lose it like this... To take the head of the man you love... I cannot imagine such a thing, but I know I wish to never experience it."

"I think," Shua says, head heavy, "you are trying to dull the pain of Shoba's passing by denying you already have a keen understanding of what that feels like."

I want to defend myself, to tell him he's wrong, to cuss him out, but in my heart I know I'd come to love the girl, blood relative or not. She didn't deserve to die, not by my hand or anyone else's. "The sting is a good reminder. Love has no place in our world."

Dyer turns away from her deceased husband and starts toward us. I take her approach as my cue to end the conversation I'd rather not continue. Not because I'd change my mind, but because I can tell my words have stung. Shua has feelings for me. It was easy to see when we were young. It is even easier now. And why not? We are attracted to each other. We have common history. We enjoy each other's company. And, we have a son.

The trouble is not that we have all those things, it's that they—like Shoba and Holland—will likely be taken away from us over the coming days. The only way to survive is to close off the heart, fight, and if others die—even Shua or Salem—the rest must continue on. The same holds true if I die.

My father taught me something he called a catchphrase, a saying passed down through generations of my family. I repeat it now. "The mission comes first."

"Without love," Shua says, looking disappointed, "there would be no mission." He walks away without looking back, joining the others. They strike out together, carrying the stretchers of rope, knowing Dyer and I will follow.

"Give me that," I say to Dyer, reaching out for her backpack.

"I don't need your pity," she says.

"Your arm."

"I have two." She slings the pack over her good shoulder and carries on past me. When I catch up, she asks, "What did you say to make him pouty?"

Knowing she'll see through a lie, I tell her the truth. "I told him our mission comes first. That love has no place in our world."

"Harsh," she says. "But true."

I feel a trace of justification. Dyer knows what I'm talking about first hand.

"But it's also bullshit," she says.

"Bullshit?"

"What I'm feeling..." She clutches her chest. "It hurts all the way to my soul." She motions to her arm. "Even if this turns me into a Golyat, it will not compare. Losing *my* life is nothing compared to losing my *life*."

It takes me a moment to hear the subtle difference in inflection, but then I get it. Somehow, Holland was more important to her than her own existence. Some old part of me understands, but it's been a long time since I felt a connection like that. My husband is a beast, my son left me, I was separated from my father as a shepherd, and shunned by everyone who knew me as Eight.

"The difference between the pain of death, and the death of a loved one is that the first ends you. The second, if you allow it, sets your course and makes you stronger." She looks me in the eye. "No matter what becomes of me, I will see this through until my death, whether it be at the hands of a Golyat, falling into the Divide, or Shua's blade taking my head. I will do that because Holland died doing the same."

We walk in silence, and I don't think it's because she's run out of things to say. She's just letting it sink in.

"I'm like you," she says. "An outsider married into the broad family of Plistim."

"I'm not mar—"

"I know," she grumbles. "But you're a part of this family now, as is your son, and the man, whether you've got the balls to admit it or not, you have feelings for. The point is, you would do well to remember that the pain I have suffered tonight has already been suffered by all of them." She motions to the four walking ahead of us. "They have lost countless loved ones over the past few days, including Holland and Shoba. My husband was Plistim's son. Shua's brother. Salem's uncle. And whether you admit it or not, Shoba had become like family to you. Since the Cull, it is not customary for Modernists to linger about the bodies of their loved ones. Instead, we move on; we continue to live, and fight for our right to live free, to honor the dead. You might think they're fine because they've trekked off into the dark without a word, but they are weeping for Holland and Shoba, even now."

I look at the group with new eyes, and see Shua wiping his sleeve across his face. Del and Salem walk side by side, both at the front end of a stretcher. Del closes the distance between them and puts her head on Salem's shoulder for a step. It's not much, but it says, 'I'm with you.' Plistim has his head hung low. The stretcher looks heavy in his hands. Their pain is palpable from here.

"They're carrying on despite the pain," I say.

"No," Dyer says. "Because of it. I know you had no pleasant feelings for my husband, but when one of us dies," she motions to the others and to herself, "this is a lesson you should attempt to put into practice."

She quickens her pace and leaves me alone with my thoughts, none of which are good company. My imagination drifts, showing me images of Shua being eaten, of Salem transforming into a Golyat. Then I relive the moment of Shoba's passing, the feel of my blade passing through her neck, the sudden silencing of her scream. It doesn't take long to bring tears to my own eyes. After wiping them away, I catch up to the others, fueled not by our recent losses, but by a determination to prevent the deaths of those I love. I look at the back of five heads.

At the people I love.

A distant chatter speeds us along as the rising sun turns the sky pink. A second chatter responds, and the ground starts shaking. The beasts must have detected the scent of Holland's and Shoba's deaths.

How long will it be before they track us down?

How long until someone else dies?

Not long enough, I think as we continue our journey through a land long ago claimed by people-turned-monsters, who exist only to consume.

35

Seven days. Seven quiet days. No Golyats. No screaming. No running. Dyer is still alive, and human. We've fallen into a steady pace and routine, covering an impressive amount of ground despite the heavy burdens we carry with us. I thought we would be easily tracked, but being absolutely saturated by the forest smells, and careful with our own, the only trail we're leaving is the one carved into the trees every fifty feet.

It seems like a futile effort to me, but I keep that to myself. If it gives the others hope, so be it.

Our supply of jerky ran out two days ago. Del and I have had no trouble supplying squirrel meat, but Plistim and Shua have struggled to consume the raw flesh. Dyer, Del, and myself, being women raised outside Plistim's family have no trouble with the still warm meat. And I'm happy to see that Salem has not lost his taste for it either. After some mocking, courtesy of Dyer, the two men forced down their first meal and have had less trouble with each subsequent meal since.

The noonday sun is nearly above us when we reach a grassy slope leading to a tall crest, upon which a lone oak stands. Its wide branches shade the hill's top, but the path to the hilltop will leave us exposed.

Shua had insisted upon being the scout, but when it comes to stealth, my skills are undisputed. Shua might be good at sneaking up on people, but deer are far more skittish and have heightened senses of smell and hearing. If you can creep up on a deer unnoticed, there isn't much in the world that could sense you.

I hope.

That's the argument that landed me on the hillside, crawling my way through tall grass like a snake, invisible to anything at ground level. From above, a bird would have no trouble spotting me. The same holds true for a tall Golyat, but we haven't seen or heard one of the monsters in days. The closer to the Divide we get, the less populated the world becomes.

Plistim and Salem agree that we're no more than a day's journey from the Divide, but they also both admit they could be off by a week. Or more. The terrain is foreign to all of us, and the segment of map, removed from the bunker wall, does little to help us judge distance. While Salem had plotted and planned the journey to the FEMA facility, the route back to the Divide has been unexpected, and chaotic. Walking in a straight line through a land of hills, trees, cliffs, lakes, and rivers, wasn't easy. But we maintained a steady pace for as long as the sun was in the sky, and covered a lot of ground.

I slow near the hill's crest, where the grass grows shorter in the tree's shade. I close my eyes and listen. The breeze ahead is loud. Dry leaves scrape. The sound is pleasant and continuous. If not for the day's heat and the possibility of being eaten alive, the sound would lull me to sleep. I test the air with my nose, sniffing like a dog. It's sweet. My memory recognizes the odor, but cannot put an image to it.

Detecting no smells or sounds associated with danger—normal or Golyat—I slide up onto the hill's crest, where a twisting mat of roots and deep shade have conspired to prevent grass from growing. I rise into a crouch and move to the hill's far side, peeking over the tan grass.

A vast green clearing stretches for miles ahead, and to either side. It looks like grass, but it's taller than me, and thick. Wind slides through the field, shifting stalks and filling the air with a leafy static.

I'm not sure what it is, but there are no Golyats visible. While the occasional tree dots the landscape, there are very few spots for anything taller than Dyer to hide.

Feeling safe, I stand so the others can see me from the bottom of the hill, and I wave them up. They come single file, carrying the heavy ropes.

Dyer leads the way, still only carrying her own backpack. While she hasn't transformed into a Golyat, the wound is red and hot. At the end of every day, she struggles with fever and night sweats.

Despite their efforts to not leave a trail, it's impossible for five people carrying two heavy stretchers to move through the tall grass without leaving their mark. While waiting, I draw my blade and carve the ancient symbol into the tree's bark. I'll add an arrow when I'm told where we're headed from here.

"What is it?" Dyer asks upon reaching the top and looking at the tall, green field beyond.

Plistim and Shua lower their stretcher to the ground and join us.

"Corn," Plistim says after just a moment. "An ancient crop. A sweet vegetable."

That's why I don't recognize it. Crops have been outlawed for five hundred years with most ancient farms long since destroyed.

"I've eaten it, I think." I try to recall when, but the memory evades me. But my subconscious remembers it and sets my mouth to watering.

When my stomach growls, the group tenses. I raise my hand. "Me."

"It grows wild in parts of New England," Plistim says. "It's likely your father had it served."

One of the perks of being an elder is first choice of meat and foraged foods. If something like wild corn was gathered, it wouldn't be uncommon for an elder to keep it all. The only other people likely to have eaten it are those who collect it and are wise enough to partake before returning to the village.

"We should eat," Shua says, opening his pack where the day-old remains of three squirrels are wrapped.

With the corn so close, I'm in no mood for meat, but I know I'll need the sustenance. I would need to eat a field of vegetation to substitute meat. But I'm still craving the flavor.

We eat in silence, enjoying the view, the smell, and the sounds. After the long journey and the horrible events that preceded it, I really just want to stay beneath this tree and sleep for days. But until we're across the Divide and either prepared for winter, or at our destination, we need to keep moving.

When I stand, and all but Plistim groans, I know I'm not the only one feeling weary. When the elder stands with me, the others rise.

"What are you thinking?" Plistim asks.

Over the past days we've fallen into a comfortable dual leadership position. It now feels natural for me to decide our next steps. I think, because we haven't run into any trouble since Holland's changing, they believe in my skills. But what I know, and won't tell them, is that I think we've just been lucky.

I point across the field of corn. "See the odd shaped hill?"

"It looks more like a giant stone," Plistim says.

He's right. The jagged surface is more stone-like than soil, but the large patches of green growing on its surface means at least some soil is present.

"A hill once," Salem says. "Eroded now. I wonder how much more of it is underground."

"It's a rock," Dyer says, stretching her wounded arm and wincing.

"For all we know, it's the top of a glacial valley that's been filled in," Salem adds. "Landscapes change over time."

"A big rock, or a really big rock, it's still just a rock." Dyer motions to the stretchers. "I want to go. My arm needs to be tested."

"I'd like to look at it first," Plistim says.

"I changed the bandage this morning," she says. "I'm good."

"Still infected?" Plistim asks.

"A bit."

"So, yes."

"I'm tired of only carrying my own weight," Dyer says. "I don't like to be coddled, or mothered."

"Shua, you're with Dyer. Plistim with Del." I nod to my son. "Salem, with me." I turn to Plistim. "I'll scuff a path in the dirt. If nothing goes wrong, we'll break beneath that tree—" I point to the only tree between us and the rock. "—and then the rock."

Plistim nods, and I set off with Salem. We crouch walk down the far side of the hill. Having looked for miles in every direction and seeing no sign of a Golyat, I'm less concerned about leaving a small trail through the grass, and more concerned about entering the corn, where we will become all but invisible to anything hunting us, but also to each other.

The cornstalks are taller and sturdier than I was expecting, stretching twelve feet tall. I step inside the field and despite having to push my way through, the plants simply bend away and spring back up. As long as we're in the corn, there will be nothing to mark our passage save for the gouges I'm making with my toes.

I take a moment to breathe, surrounded by the strong scent of the corn, still familiar, and still stirring my hunger. The smell is so powerful that detecting anything else would be difficult, which is a benefit, and a risk. I give Salem a nod, and he waves the others along before following me into the field.

Large buds grow from the stalks, each the size of my forearm. They assault me as I walk past, far heavier than I would have thought the plants could support.

After several minutes of silent walking, I ask, "So...you are fond of rocks?"

Salem laughs. "Not rocks, but what they tell us."

"So you study rocks to learn about...what?"

"It's called geology. An ancient science."

"You've studied the ancient sciences?" While I understand the concept of science, the practice of it beyond applications that improve the nomadic life, are strictly forbidden. While I'm not surprised a Modernist would be interested in such things, I did not expect my son to have acquired some kind of expertise in them.

"Biology, chemistry, astronomy, genetics. I've read about them all, but put little of what I've learned into actual practice."

"What is genetics?" I ask.

"It's what makes us, us," he says, which makes absolutely no sense. He must realize this, because he adds, "We're made up of tiny little bits that we can't see, and all of those little bits contain information. It's called DNA. If you change our DNA just a little, you might end up with a deer instead of a person. When a child is conceived, the baby is composed of both the mother's DNA, and the father's. They work together to form someone that is both, but new. It's why I look like you *and* dad."

"And why, when you're angry, you look like my father," I say.

Salem is silent for a moment. "Is he well? Grandfather?"

"Last I saw him," I say, though I am concerned for what might have befallen him if my husband concluded the Modernists had his help. "He and Grace are together."

"You didn't know?" Salem says.

"You did?"

He smiles. "I caught them once. In the woods. When I was ten." His smile becomes a laugh, and then an uncomfortable scrunch of his lips. "I promised not to tell."

Since I'd rather not picture my father buck naked and humping sweet Grace in the forest, I reverse course a bit. "So...when a Golyat's... juices gets in our blood, maybe it changes our DNA? Makes us into something else?"

"That's one theory," he says. "Of mine. Since Holland. No one would have ever guessed that the Golyats had been human once. Hell, we thought there was just one of them. Our ancestors used to say 'ignorance is bliss', but I don't think so. Ignorance leads to death, or enslavement to a person, or a system."

"You Modernists... All conversations lead to freedom," I say. "The concept, at least."

Salem smiles in a different sort of way, like he's proud of me. "I didn't even realize that's what we were talking about, but yes. Ignorance binds people as easily as chains."

"Or a Divide."

He nods.

"Is that why you crossed?" My raised hand stops him from answering. I crouch and wave him up beside me. Then I point to the ground, where a lump of corn has been peeled open and chewed.

"We're not alone," Salem whispers, a statement I agree with by drawing my machete.

36

We creep closer to the shredded corn. There are small yellow nuggets scattered on the ground, along with the peeled leaves and what looks like hair. But most of the yellow has been gnawed away. After this quick examination, I relax. "Tell me what you see."

"Three ears of corn," Salem says. "All eaten."

"Ears?"

He picks up one of the forearm sized corn pieces. "This is an 'ear' of corn. When you peel the leaves away, what's left is a 'cob.'"

I look around at all the intact ears around us. I'm about to complain that there isn't a creature with ears like that, but then I remember the lynx native to New Inglan. The cat has similarly shaped ears, including little tufts of hair at the top.

"What else?"

"I don't see anything else," he says.

"What don't you see?"

"Tracks."

"And?"

When he doesn't answer, I say, "Shit. You don't see shit."

"You've spent too much time with Dyer."

"I was being literal," I say.

His eyes widen a touch. "Oh." Now he's looking. Really looking. "No tracks either."

"Which means either a bird did this," I say, "or an animal light enough to not leave tracks." The ground is covered with centuries worth of decaying corn crops from countless previous summers. In the dry heat, the mixture of packed down decay and plant fibers makes a strong surface. Even I have to dig my foot in to leave a trail for the others.

"Find the stalks missing ears," I say, and I set about searching. I find the first. Salem locates the other two. "Not a bird," I say.

"How can you tell?"

"The missing ears are all lower to the ground. A bird wouldn't care about height, but an animal on the ground, whose neck only stretches so high, would."

"Why wouldn't they just tear the plant down?" he asks.

"Same reason we're not," I say. "Either way, I don't think we have anything to worry about."

"Unless mountain lions eat corn," he jokes, but it's not a bad point. Cats don't leave a lot of tracks, especially on terrain like this, and it's not unheard of for them to munch on vegetation when food is scarce. Out here, a meal larger than a squirrel might be impossible to find.

I keep my machete in hand as we strike out again, not as tense, but still ready. If a cat *is* nearby, I have no doubt it's already stalking us.

Stalks rattle to our right. I tense and listen. Something is moving through the field, in roughly the same direction, and not in a hurry.

We press on, despite the noise. I'm more curious than fearful now. A predator would have never revealed itself in such a careless way, and I have no doubt the creature is aware of us. We're nearly to the tree when I spot an aberration on the ground.

When I see the dark lumps for what they are, I relax and sheath my machete.

"What is it?" Salem asks.

I wave him up, and take a handful of the dark lumps. "Still warm." I hold my hand out to him.

Nose scrunched in revolt, he says, "Is that...shit?"

I nod and raise the nuggets to my nose, breathing deeply. "Deer shit."

"Deer?" He looks around like he might actually be able to see something through the endless maze of stalks.

I drag my foot through the dirt, continuing our trail, and then move toward the tree. "Slow and quiet."

As we near the tree, the corn thins. I pause when I spot a break in the field ahead. I slip out of my backpack and draw my machete again. The corn made me hungry, but the thought of a deer kill makes me ravenous. I part the last stalks of corn and peer through, ready to attack.

Deer, dozens of them, react to my appearance by looking up, gazing at me and then lying down. They're smaller than deer in New Inglan, their feet wide and perfect for distributing their weight to not leaving tracks. The males have small sets of antlers, curved in over their noses in a way that would prevent them from catching on cornstalks. All of the animals have what looks like green moss, or mold, growing on their backs. From above, they would be disguised from birds, or from Golyats.

"What are they doing?" Salem whispers.

"I have no idea." I slip out of the corn and the deer don't react. I stand to my full height. Still nothing.

"These aren't normal deer," he says, and he's right, both in action and how they look. "I've studied books about animals in the world before. These deer aren't in them."

"Their DNA has been changed," I guess.

He smiles and nods. "Natural selection."

"What is that?"

"You remember what survival of the fittest is?"

I roll my eyes.

"Right. So, over the past five hundred years, all the deer with antlers pointing outward, or with fur not appropriate for the growth of what I think is algae, or so big that they were easy to spot, were killed and never had babies. Their DNA was never passed down to their children. But those that survived, possibly because of a fluke of nature, reproduced. Over generations the changes would become more dramatic until we have a whole new species of deer."

"That also don't fear people," I say, stepping further into the clearing beneath the tree. A few of the deer watch me. Most go back to resting in the shade.

"Mom," Salem says, as I approach the nearest deer, machete in hand. "Don't."

"What?" I ask, struggling to resist my instinct to kill and eat the animal on the spot. "Why not?"

Salem moves past me, to the deer I intended to slay, and puts his hand on its neck. The creature sniffs, and then closes its eyes when Salem starts petting it. "These animals have lived on this side of the Divide for five hundred years. They have no fear of us because there haven't been people here during all that time. To them, we're just fellow survivors, hiding from the sun and the Golyats. You have to respect them for that."

"We also need to eat," I point out.

"We can eat the corn. And squirrels. But let's leave the deer in peace. I just...eating them makes me feel a little bit like a Golyat."

His words sour my stomach, not because thinking about the Golyats disgusts me, but because I can see his point. "Or like the Cull."

"Exactly."

I use the machete to lop off a few ears of corn and hand a few to Salem. We find seats against the tree, surrounded by deer who are far more interested in us now that we've got corn in our hands. Unsure of how to eat the plant, I tear away the leaves and hair, exposing the bright yellow insides that had been eaten by the deer. Then I take a bite and taste a flavor that surprises me with its intensity. "Oh," I say. "Oh, that's good."

Ignoring the juice running over my chin, I take three more bites and chew, while Salem digs into his. When a young deer approaches me, I hold out the corn and let it take a nibble before taking a few more bites. Some of the other deer, seeing an easy meal, stand and join their friend. Soon we're sur-rounded by the small animals, partaking in our meal and making me smile. A few minutes earlier, I would have killed and eaten them. But now they are kin.

"Holy hellcakes," Dyer says from the edge of the clearing. "What's this?"

"We made friends," Salem says.

As the others file into the clearing and deposit the stretchers of rope on the ground, they look at the deer with a mixture of hunger, and delight.

I point my thoroughly chewed corncob at Dyer, who's drawing a knife. "We're not eating them, by the way."

"Why the hell not?" she asks.

"We don't eat our friends," I say, feeding the nearest deer and getting a laugh out of Salem. "There is plenty of corn, and it tastes better."

Shua cuts an ear of corn from a stalk and tries biting it, leaves and all, which makes Salem laugh harder. The sound transports me through time for a moment, sitting by a lake as Salem threw large stones into the water, laughing with each kerplunk.

"Peel it first, Father," Salem says.

Shua listens to the instructions as Del and Dyer gather their own ears and start eating. Soon, all but Plistim are seated with the deer, enjoying a feast. While Plistim seems relaxed, a long respite was not planned for. With daylight still with us, we should be moving. But this is the first truly pleasant experience we've had since arriving in this land. The corn will sustain our bodies for a time, but the memory of this moment will sustain our morale far longer. So I say nothing as everyone, including the deer, share a meal.

I peel a corncob and hold it toward Plistim. "Hey."

When he looks, I toss the corn to him. He catches it, nods his thanks, and takes a bite. He seems to relax a little more with each bite, wandering around the tree trunk. When he stops, his jaws tight, his body locked in place, our group and all the deer tense.

"Did you not search the whole clearing?" Plistim asks.

I did, I think, but then not where he is looking. I'd inspected every bit of the clearing, but not the tree itself. I've only looked at the side where we sat down.

We move slowly to keep from startling the deer, and gather on the tree's far side, staring down at words carved into the bark. The cut isn't fresh, but neither is it old. Within the past few years. I reach my hand out, touching the text, trying to connect with whoever wrote it. "What does it say?"

"Queensland," Salem says. "The rest is numbers. Two. Five. Three. Two."

37

"Queensland?" Dyer says. "Is that like Kingsland?"

Salem nods. "One of the five safe zones established by our ancestors. In Alaska. There are notes about them in Lew's journal, but not many details about their founders. I think they worked together. Like a team."

"Like us," Del says.

"But far more powerful," Salem says. "Powerful enough to create the Divide."

"But not stop the Golyats," Dyer says.

Then what chance do we have? That's the next logical question someone should ask. No one does. Just thinking it is hard enough. Giving it voice...making it real... The answer would undo all the positive morale provided by our small friends. The answer—*no chance at all*—would become prophetic the moment it was uttered.

Salem takes it in the other direction, spinning hope into his words. "I haven't finished reading yet, but Lew hints at possible solutions in the works. Said they would take decades to perfect. Perhaps, over time, they were simply forgotten?"

"The Prime Law would have prevented anyone outside their inner circle from knowing the truth. If they found a way to defeat the Golyats, they died before sharing it." Plistim's words are sobering, but he puts a positive spin on them, saying, "Which means the knowledge is still out there, waiting for us to find it, and utilize it."

"What are the numbers?" Dyer asks.

"Two. Five. Three. Two." Shua reads the numbers and guesses, "Directions of some kind. What did they call them? Coordinates?"

"Not the right kinds of numbers, and there are no decimals," Salem says.

And just like that, I'm lost. Coordinates? Decimals? They're speaking another language. A forgotten language.

"It's the year," Plistim says. "Two thousand five hundred and thirty two."

"The year is five hundred and thirty four," I point out.

Plistim shakes his head. "When the Prime Law was put into place, the yearly calendar was reset so people would feel less of a connection to their past. We consider the year to be 534 P.D. That's Post Divide."

He says that last bit to me.

"I know," I grumble, but most people in New Inglan wouldn't.

"By the ancestors' calendar," Plistim says, "we would be in the year 2534."

"This was carved two years ago," Salem says, his voice reverent. "There are people beyond the Divide. People from Queensland! And they've traveled all this way."

"But why?" Del asks. "Why come here if they had their own protected land?"

"To be free," Plistim says. "To find us. Perhaps to free us. Despite the time and distance, they are still our kin."

"Or," Shua says, his jaw tense. No one's going to like what he says next, and he knows it. "Their own lands were overrun, so they fled, and went out in search of new lands. Human history from the time before, is essentially one war after another, each side defending or claiming land. For resources. For food. For the simple loathing of their neighbors. We don't know the people of Queensland. They might not even have a Prime Law." He motions to the carving on the tree. "For all we know, they're as much of a threat as the Golyats."

"I refuse to believe that," Plistim says.

"That humanity can be violent, envious, and self-destructive?" Shua plants his fists on his hips. "You of all people know that these evils did not die with our ancestors. And they won't, even if we succeed. We need to be cautious."

"This is two years old," I say. Even if Shua's paranoid theory is correct, whoever carved the tree's bark is long gone, and I'm not a fan of paranoia. "Salem, you said the deer here weren't afraid of us because they hadn't been hunted by people in five hundred years."

"Yeah," my son says.

"Which means that whoever carved this tree, like us, had the mind and heart to not kill these animals." I turn to Salem. "Just like you. And if the people who did this are anything like Salem, I would like to meet them."

"Perhaps," Plistim says, "after reaching our goal, and achieving our great end, we will search for our brothers and sisters scattered across the continent and help set them free as well."

Everyone but Shua is pleased with the idea. Before we can dream up theories about the people of Queensland, and before Shua can turn them bleak, Plistim says, "But we will achieve nothing if we do not stay the course. If the deer can eat in the cornfield without fear, so can we. Have your fill while we walk, but take none with you when the field ends. Its smell will stand out once we're back in the forest."

When we set out again a few minutes later, after scarfing down several more ears or corn, I am now the last in line, carrying a stretcher with Shua. In front of him are Salem and Del, also carrying a stretcher. Plistim and Dyer are in the lead, which given the field's relative safety and lack of Golyats, I'm okay with.

"Why so pessimistic?" I ask after a few minutes of walking. The small deer keep me company, strolling through the field beside me, sniffing the ground. The little creatures make me happy, and in some ways remind me of how Plistim's family has accepted me.

"Realistic," Shua says. "It's easy to get caught up, thinking like my father, seeing opportunity and hope everywhere, but without a dose of realism, the dream can become a nightmare."

He's talking about the Cull. Or the deaths of all the people who followed Plistim across the Divide and disappeared. Including his brother and his niece.

"What about 'freedom or death?'" I ask.

"There has to be a point where the price is too steep," Shua says. "I don't know what I would do if I lost you or Salem."

My inclusion in that statement nearly trips me up. *It's because I'm who he's talking to*, I decide, and let it go.

"But I know none of this will be worthwhile if I do. Even if, in the end, we succeed." He looks back over his shoulder. "And yes, Vee, I meant to include you."

Despite the dire words pre-empting his last, Shua smiles and turns forward again, leaving me to stew in his pot of emotional turmoil. When verbalization beyond a few stutters escapes me, I say, "Asshole," which gets a laugh out of Shua and extinguishes the smoldering worry that's been eating him up.

"I can live with that," he says, plugging along, strong hands on the stretcher, maintaining the swift pace set by Plistim. "Could have been worse. A skunk's taint. A Golyat's shriveled scrotum."

I snort, then I'm embarrassed by it, and laughing along with Shua over the course of a few seconds. "Don't listen to him," I say to the deer, looking down. But where I expected to see small, half-interested eyes looking back at me, I find only empty ground and cornstalks.

"Hold up," I say, coming to a stop and tugging Shua back.

"We should at least wait until its dark," Shua says, his mood still light. "Also, if I remember correctly, you're a little loud when you—"

Shua's quip trails off when he sees what I already have. The deer—all of them—have stopped. They form a neat line, stretching out into the field, as though held back by an invisible barrier.

"What are they doing?" Shua asks.

I've never seen animal behavior like this. It's like they're afraid of something, but not enough to run away, only to keep a rigid distance.

I lower the stretcher to the ground, forcing Shua to do the same.

"We should keep moving," he says. "Forget the deer."

Ignoring him, I cut an ear of corn, peel it quickly and crouch. The deer snuff at the air, their eyes on the corncob just a few feet out of reach. It's an easy meal. Several of the deer stretch their necks out toward me, but won't step forward.

I toss the cob to the deer and stand up, scanning the area, but I see only corn. "They're afraid of something, but there's nothing out here to—"

My eyes lock on to the huge, jagged stone, which is coated in green growth. We're just fifty feet away. By now, the others are crossing by it. I can see grasses, moss, and even saplings rising from the hard surface. But there's something wrong with the stone.

It's moving.

Fluttering.

It's not stone, I realize. *It's skin.* Old, dry, sun-bleached skin, peeling away in sheets to reveal the darkness underneath. If not for the stiff breeze bending both corn and loose flesh, I would have never seen it for anything but a rock.

The formation was never a hill, the tip of a covered glacial valley, or just some oversized rock. "It's a Golyat," I whisper.

Shua whips around, staring at the rock. "But there're plants growing from it."

"It's been there for a long time," I say. "Maybe hundreds of years. Long enough to collect soil and seeds on its body. Long enough for saplings to grow as tall as me."

"Then it must be dead," he says.

"We still need to get past it." I bend and pick up the stretcher. "Quick as we can, without making a sound."

Shua nods, hoists up his side, and heads out. We reach something close to a jog. Moving quickly with a stretcher is a challenge. Running needs to be perfectly coordinated. Charging through a field of cornstalks without making a lot of noise is nearly impossible.

When we reach the massive figure lying on the ground, we slow until we're silent. The others have already moved past without trouble. We can do the same.

I watch the colossal form as we pass, trying to determine what its head, body, and limbs must look like, but it is too covered in growth for me to discern its bends and folds.

Halfway past the once-human, now geological formation, something changes. It's just a feeling at first, unseen, but it slows me to a stop, and Shua with me.

Shua makes a gentle clicking sound at me, the message clear, 'Move your ass.'

But I can't look away.

I need to see if I'm right.

And then I do.

Deep within the black, white, and green form, an orange light blooms to life.

The Golyat isn't just alive.

It's awake.

38

Shua and I fall into a natural kind of sync, our legs working in tandem despite the difference in gait. No longer concerned about making noise or disturbing the corn, we slide through the field like an arrow through grass, barreling through every stalk in our path.

Our retreat isn't stealthy, but right now, I think we have time. While the thing we mistook for strange geology is a Golyat, it's been there for a very long time. Its joints will be stiff, and the roots covering its body might bind it for a time.

I'm even feeling hopeful that we'll be able to clear the field and re-enter the forest by the time the thing actually manages to rise. But then Shua trips. As he falls forward, he lets go of the stretcher to catch himself. He hits hard, rolling through several stalks of corn, but he doesn't get the worst of it.

I do.

The stretcher arms hit the ground, dig in, and come to an immediate stop. I, on the other hand, do not. I careen into the stretcher, my left thigh smashing into the handle before I'm tossed up and over onto the bundles of strapped-down rope. I land hard on my back, coughing and gasping.

And if all the noise wasn't enough to stir the beast, the smell of blood, so bitter compared to the permeating scent of corn, wafts into the air.

Shua is hurt, is my first thought. Then I sit up, wince, and realize that the scent of blood is coming from me. The stretcher handle struck my mostly healed, mountain lion bite, separating new skin and old stitches. A spot of blood oozes from my leg. The wound will need tending, the blood cleaned away, and the stitches redone, but not here, and not any time soon.

"Up," I groan, rolling off the ropes and pushing myself to my feet. My back and leg scream at me, begging me to sit, but I bend down for the stretcher handles instead. "And watch your damn step."

While Shua picks up his side, a breeze rolls over me, pulling my attention back. I watch the cornstalks bend, revealing the wind's course, stopping only when the breeze reaches the mound.

The orange light flares brighter.

A gurgle like a stream over rocks fills the air. And then, a single chomp of unseen teeth. The sound resonates through my body, draws a yelp from my lips, and sets Shua and me running again.

We've only made it fifteen feet when a second chomp rolls across the landscape, no doubt sending the deer running to the field's far side. They might not be afraid of people, but their aversion to the long-slumbering Golyat reveals they knew exactly how far away to stay.

The chomps come a few seconds apart, speeding up into a bona fide chatter, that, as usual, stand my hair on end.

I flinch when I spot Salem running beside me, carrying a stretcher with Del. On the surface, they know what's happening—we're running from a Golyat—but they haven't figured out where it is yet.

"That rock." I motion behind us with my head. "Not a rock!"

Salem glances back and nearly trips like Shua did.

"Don't look," I shout, and then I disregard my own advice when the ground shakes. The formless mass rises and peels itself with all the quickness of a flower blooming in the morning.

It looks slow because it's big, I chide myself. What looks like a few feet from this distance could be closer to twenty.

When we catch up to Plistim and Dyer, I know we've reached our peak speed. No one is going to get left behind, even if it means we all run a little slower.

"Straight ahead," I shout to them. "We need the trees!"

I don't think the trees will stop or even slow it down, but I suspect its size will put it above the canopy. If we can reach the shade, it might not be able to see us.

We're chased by the sounds of a waking behemoth. Its old joints pop like thunderclaps, snapping back into place. When it chatters again, this time somehow even louder, the pace approaching frenetic, I can't stop myself from looking back.

None of us can, and as a group, we slow.

Great sheets of old flesh are caught in the wind and yanked away. Roots stretch and snap. Blankets of moss fall to the ground, while others cling to the monster's flesh. As the Golyat unfurls, the long spires of its spine—those at the crest of its back stretching forty feet long—separate and flex open.

Massive legs push off the ground. Arms unfold, unleashing a torrent of collected dirt. The monster rises higher and higher, shedding more of itself and its collected growth, until all at once the day grows darker, the sun blotted out by the creature's head.

Staring up at the Golyat's back, I know that this is the true monster of legend. The destroyer of men. Nearly twice the size of the largest Golyat we've seen, this creature could make a meal of hundreds of men and hunger for more a few seconds later. *How many did it eat to reach such a size?* And how long has it been since its last meal?

The more important question is: *How long until its next meal?*

Hoping the answer is, 'Not any time soon,' I nudge the stretcher into Shua and urge the others faster, whispering, "Go, go, go!"

When the ground rumbles again, I alone look back. The Golyat is shifting, turning its body, torso first and then legs, grinding the earth beneath its wide, weight-bearing feet. With much of the old skin shredded away, I'm given a clear view of its slender form. Not only is its skin stretched and tight, but so are its insides. Between its ribs and hips, there are gaps in the flesh, all the way through the body, where organs would have once been contained. But they have long since been digested by its own internal combustion.

The Golyat brings its arms forward, stretching out the last of its kinks. Ribs pop apart, the giant rib cage expanding. A breath, like howling wind, is sucked down deep.

Up in the sun, the face turns toward us, sunken in, coated in crumbling greenery, and covered in cracks and gaps. Its black teeth are exposed and clenched tight. The two black eyes snap open, blink twice, and turn down.

While the creature's expression remains locked in place, the sudden flare of light from its gut reveals that we have been spotted.

Head turned toward the clouds, it looks big enough to reach up and touch them. The Golyat unleashes a ravenous roar that staggers all of us to a stop, stretchers dropped, hands clutched to ears, our own shouts of pain making a chorus.

While screaming and holding my head, I look forward. The tree line is just a quarter mile ahead.

"We need to move!" I scream, but not even I can hear my voice, nor can I remove my hands from my ears.

When the roar is finished, my whole body registers the shift. Shaking corn stalks go still. And for a moment, there is peace.

"We need to move," I say again, the words barely leaving my throat, but this time everyone hears and everyone obeys.

The first thunderous footfall shakes the ground just as we get started, stretchers retrieved.

Ahead of us, the Golyat's shadow reaches the tree line first, rising up as it takes a second step.

I don't have to look back to know it's gaining on us.

"We should drop the stretchers!" Del shouts.

"We will die without them," Plistim replies, out of breath, but pushing through it.

"We could circle back," Del says, lacking conviction.

"We either escape this together, or we die together," Plistim's declaration falls under the purview of his leadership. Mine is to make decisions that keep us alive. Plistim's is to make bold, sweeping guidelines to which we all adhere. In this case, we'll either live as a group, or die as one.

On the surface, it sounds foolish—the words of an elder who's lived a long life and outlived most of the people he loved. But I have no argument to make. We either make the trees with the ropes and survive, or we die here and now. Losing the ropes means giving up on crossing the Divide, and that means we'd all die out here eventually.

Queensland.

The carved word flits through my mind.

Someone survived out here, and for who knows how long. Perhaps years. Maybe even generations. If deer can adapt to life beyond the Divide, why not people?

The third impact shakes the ground so violently that I stumble. Shua slows for a step and keeps me from falling. Then we're back to full speed, but a stretcher-length behind the others.

A quick look over my shoulder reveals a foot and leg, fifty feet back.

Teeth smash together far overhead, finally reaching the staccato rhythm of the smaller Golyats. It senses the kill.

I don't have to look back to know it's reaching for me, its hand large enough to engulf both Shua and myself, not to mention dozens more.

A second chatter cuts through the air, slamming into my body, but not from above. This time the sound came from... ahead.

"There's another one!" I shout, and I'm a little surprised when I sound hopeful. "Keep going! Straight ahead. Don't stop for anything!"

The trees ahead explode apart, giving birth to a hundred-foot-tall Golyat. Like the rest, its black skin is sucked inward in sheets of stretched out and parched flesh. But its bone structure is different. Like most Golyats we've seen, its bones have lengthened and thickened, sometimes in dramatic ways, like the spines rising from their backs. But the newcomer's ribs have grown spikes, some a few feet in length, others closer to fifteen feet, and all of them punching through the dried skin.

Its black eyes find us first, and then its competition.

While its stomach flares, the creature charges into the cornfield. Even though it's smaller than the gigantic Golyat to our back, it is far less decayed, free of tangling roots, and much faster. Despite the distraction, the larger of the pair remains on task, which I only know because its fingers, each ten feet long, slide up beside us in the cornfield and begin to curl shut.

39

"Left!" I shout.

Shua angles away from the Golyat's hand, which we have no hope of outrunning. The fingers slap through the corn, sending ears sailing through the air, slapping against us as we flee.

The fingers start to close, and I shout again. "Down!"

Working in unison, Shua and I fall to the ground. I land hard on my stomach, making no effort to slow my fall with my hands. My ribs, stomach, and head take the brunt of the impact. Air coughs from my lungs, but instead of feeling breathless, I feel momentary relief.

The hand scours the field around and above me, grasping hold of several dozen cornstalks but missing me and Shua. The bottom of the creature's hand clips the stretcher, yanking it up. The stretcher flips through the air, coming down twenty feet away, still intact, the bundles of rope still bound in place.

"Move!" I shout, climbing back to my feet.

This time, Shua argues by tackling me and repeating my earlier order. "Down!"

I'm struck from the side by what feels like a Golyat's back-hand, but it's just Shua and his heavy backpack. I hit the ground again, this time battering my back. But I don't complain. Above me is the smaller, spikey-chested Golyat. Its foot crashes down just ten feet away, and then it's airborne, throwing itself at the larger creature pursuing us.

Shua stands, grabs my backpack, and lifts me up beside him. My instinct is to complain that I could have done it myself, but I just run for the stretcher. Shua resumes his position at the front, and while the two titans grapple, their bones clacking together like stones in a rockslide, we strike out for the forest once more.

An impact shakes the ground, and I can't help but look back. The cornfield obstructs everything at head level, but the Golyats are impossible to miss. The smaller of the battling pair has been thrown to the side. It's down, but already pushing itself up and looking no more haggard than it did when it first exploded from the trees.

Despite that, the recently awakened behemoth turns its head skyward once more. I know what's coming and shout, "Ears!"

Shua and I stop together, dropping the stretcher and clasping hands over our ears just in time to muffle the bellow. The ragged, baritone roar hurts, and not just my ears. Standing this close to the source, it feels like we're back in the Karls River again, facing the raging current.

When it stops, the monster chatters, eyes back on us.

The fallen Golyat chatters, too, announcing its hunger to challenge the first. But the larger of the two ignores it again, reaching for us, a quick meal its only true concern.

When a third chatter knocks through the air, the monster pauses. When the ground shakes behind it, the Golyat actually stops to look. A third Golyat rises up over a distant hill. In fact, it is the same hill we first descended into the cornfield. And when the creature rises up over it, I recognize it. The two hooked arms hanging from its ribcage are impossible to mistake.

It's been tracking us. All this time.

And that means any Golyat that walks away from this encounter will do the same if we manage to survive.

When a fourth chattering sound, this one equally powerful to the one standing above us, tears through the air from the distance, Shua and I recover the stretcher. We keep a good pace, but we avoid making a spectacle of ourselves.

As the ancient Golyat turns to face the new challenger, who is the smallest of the three, the fallen creature pushes itself back up, squaring off. The ground rumbles as something even more distant charges toward the open field, its hunger awakened.

Further still, more chatters cut through the air. And then more roars. The shaking impacts become a constant quake.

Have we managed to wake them all?

While we have encountered a number of roaming, hunting Golyats, how many more were in some kind of hibernation?

Not wanting to find out, I focus on the path ahead.

Ten seconds of running and we're in the trees, hidden from all the Golyats. But they're not paying us any attention. Despite their ravenous appetites, they face off to claim their prize, even as it runs away.

With more Golyats closing in, we don't linger to see how the fight plays out. I don't have to watch to know it will be sickening, violent, and fuel for the nightmares that will no doubt haunt me when this is over.

Do the dead dream? I wonder, and I hope not.

Running through the forest is both easier—trees are easier to run between than cornstalks—and harder. The ground is shaking. Leaves and pinecones fall around us as trees sway. A roar from ahead announces the approach of yet another Golyat.

Plistim and Dyer duck behind the largest trees they can find. Shua and I follow Dyer, while Salem and Del move in behind Plistim. We fall in against the trees, waiting as the impacts grows louder and closer. I dig into the ground, yank out a clump of decaying leaves, and pat it down on my bloody leg, hoping to conceal the scent.

The new Golyat pushes through the trees between the others and us. The fifty-foot-tall creature lunges past, barreling through the smallest trees, while being knocked about by the larger, sturdier ones. It doesn't stand a chance against the others, but it shows no fear as it heads for the clearing and the sounds of its much larger brethren.

As it shoves away from a pine, the trunk bends, exposing a slice of sky. Only I don't see sky. The behemoth is there, arms reaching over its head where a smaller Golyat clings to the spines jutting out of its back.

Roars cascade through the forest. If we're as close to the Divide as Plistim and Salem think, it's possible the people on the far side can hear the raging battle.

Though it's hard to hear anything, the forest ahead appears to be open. We strike out together, but we can't run. Unlike the level field, the forest is full of obstacles that require navigation. The terrain is uneven, riddled with roots, rocks, and shrubs. But we make good time. The sounds of unimaginable battle start to fade behind us, but our urgency remains.

Whichever Golyat stands victorious will come hunt us down. Persistence is usually an admirable quality, but it's one I wish the Golyats did not possess. The monsters would probably follow us around the entire planet.

"Up ahead," Del says, her keen vision spotting a change in the forest before the rest of us see it.

But when I do, there's no mistaking what it means. Light glows behind the trees a half mile ahead. The forest comes to an end. It could be another field, or rocky terrain, or a path carved by a passing Golyat, but there's something about it...something familiar.

It's the air. The way it flows. The scent of it.

"That's the Divide," I say.

"I think she's right," Shua says.

"We'll need to scout the edge," Plistim adds. "Find the best way down."

"No time," Dyer says.

"If we don't—"

Dyer points to our left. "No time!"

Two hundred feet away, a monster matches our pace. It's identifiable as a Golyat thanks to its blackened and stretched skin, its sunken form, and its exaggerated bone structure. But it resembles nothing else we have seen thus far. It stands twelve feet tall, running on two long legs, with sword-like talons that tip the ends of its three toes. I do not see a pair of arms, just two flailing stubs. The head atop its long neck bobs forward and back with each step. A black beak snaps open and closed, the chattering sharp, but also subtle compared to its toothed brethren.

I'm not sure what species, but this Golyat was once a bird. It's not nearly as big as the brawling humanoid things behind us, but since it started out as something much smaller, its size is still impressive, and more than enough to tear us to shreds.

"It looks like a dinosaur," Salem says. I have no idea what a dinosaur is, but the look of terror in his eyes means it's not a good thing.

"You all keep going," Dyer says, starting to veer toward the dinosaur-Golyat.

"What are you doing?" I shout at her. "It will kill you!"

"I'm already dead," she says, and for a moment I think she's being a romantic. Then she tears the bandage away from her arm to reveal blackened and dried flesh. "Spreads a little every day. I've been waiting for a good way to go out. This is it."

Dyer draws two swords and unleashes a battle cry as she angles toward the raptor. The giant once-a-bird squawks and rushes to meet her, its gut vibrant, nearly yellow.

"Bullshit," I grumble.

"Del!" I shout. When the still-running girl glances back at me, I nod toward the bird. "Help her! Plistim, take the stretcher!"

We pause for a moment, to make the exchange. Del doesn't hesitate, handing her load to Plistim and nocking an arrow on her bow.

"Do what you can," I tell her, "and catch up. Let's go!"

Salem looks mortified, and about to argue.

"Now!" I shout, and I give the stretcher a shove, bumping it into Shua.

We leave Del behind as she draws her bowstring back, takes aim, and lets the arrow fly. There's a whack, an angry squawk, and then Dyer roaring like the Golyat she is slowly becoming.

I glance over in time to see Dyer leap through the air, swords raised and aimed toward the Golyat, which has an arrow in one eye. As impressive as the attack is, the monster swings its head, colliding with Dyer and slamming her to the ground.

Instead of stopping to consume its meal, the chattering thing keeps running—straight for Del. As a second arrow flies, striking the bird's forehead, I lose sight of Del, the Golyat, and Dyer, convinced I've just sentenced my daughter-in-law—my son's precious wife—to her death.

40

My eyes squint as the gaps between the trees grow larger, allowing the day's bright light to filter into the forest. Despite nearing the end of our journey to the Divide, my heart aches as chattering, angry squawks, and inhuman war cries rise up from the forest behind us.

Del and Dyer are giving the beast hell, but can they stop it? And if not, will their sacrifice give us enough time to escape over the edge?

Plistim exits the tree line first. His feet grind over solid stone as he comes to a sudden stop. Salem, eyes wet with tears, fails to react in time, bumping into his grandfather from behind.

Plistim's arms flail as he teeters on the Divide's edge. Shua drops the stretcher and lunges for his father, grasping his belt and yanking him back. Plistim falls atop the stretcher of ropes he'd been carrying. Rather than complaining, expressing fear, or anger at Salem for nearly killing him, he is simply concerned for my son.

"It's okay," Plistim says to Salem. "It was an accident. It's—"

But Salem, who's now glaring at me, isn't hearing him.

"You left her!" Salem stabs a finger at me. "You. Left. My. Wife!"

When he storms in my direction, I'm sure he's going to strike me. I have to fight against my instincts to not raise my hands, not in defense, but counter attack. If he hits me, I'll live. He's right to be angry at me, but he's also angry with Del, who chose to listen, and maybe sacrifice herself.

Maybe is what Salem needs to remember.

"She's strong," I tell him. "And smart. Give her a chance."

"And when you're done with that," Shua says, digging climbing gear out of his pack, "help me figure this shit out."

Salem swallows his rage, wipes his tears, and hurries to help his father. While they prepare for a journey to a land below the land, where no living man has set foot, I close my eyes and listen.

The distant battle between Golyats still trembles the earth and fills the air with the sounds of a great storm, but Del and Dyer's struggle has gone silent.

"Please," I whisper to no one, who somehow feels like some-one. "Let them survive."

"Almost ready," Plistim announces, throwing a bundle of bright orange rope over the side, and watching it fall and unravel.

Shua approaches me holding what looks like a tangle of belts that have, for some reason, been stitched together and decorated with metal clips and carabiners. "Put this on."

"I don't even know what it is."

"It's called a harness," he says, holding a hole open. "Take off your pack."

I slide out of the backpack, still not hearing any action from the woods.

"One leg at a time." Shua slides a strap up my thigh, carefully avoiding the bloody, reopened wound. We repeat the process with the other leg. Then he wraps and binds a second strap around my waist, then over each shoulder. When he's done, he cinches everything tight. "They're uncomfortable, but will keep you from falling."

Then he leaves me again, to continue prepping. He shoves several small metal devices into a crack, letting them snap open inside. "What are those?"

"Camalots, or 'cams' for short," Salem says, clipping the rope into carabiners attached to loops at the end of each device. "They'll hold the rope."

"And us?" I say.

"Each one can hold upwards of three thousand pounds," Salem explains. "We're using four, just in case."

"In case a Golyat wants to climb down after us?" I joke.

No one laughs. Salem glances toward the quiet forest, and then returns to his work. When they're done with the rope, the three men slide into their harnesses.

We're ready to go.

I turn toward the forest, resisting the urge to go back. The four of us can complete the mission and, if we're lucky, end the Golyats' reign. Then I remember Shua's words about love. The desire for freedom can't exist without love, and it is not the result of success, it is what propels us toward it.

I take a single step back into the forest and stop.

Heavy footfalls are approaching, oblivious to the crunch of leaves and twigs underfoot.

"Shua," I say, drawing my machete.

When he steps beside me, weapon drawn, I shake my head. "I don't want your help. I want you to go. The three of you."

"No," Salem says, overhearing. "Not you, too."

"You don't need me from here." I give Shua a shove. "Go! Now!"

Shua looks as wounded as Salem, but he steps back. He reaches out for his son and leads him to the edge, where Plistim has already started preparing to descend, attaching a heavy bundle of rope to a carabiner on his harness. He attaches a second rope to Salem, and then shoves the second stretcher of ropes—already attached to the line, over the side. He slides over the edge behind the falling ropes and out of view, holding something attached to the rope. Salem gives me a last, sad look and follows him. Shua clips himself to the rope and then holds the device up so I can see.

"This is a rope grip. You clip it on, like this." He demonstrates the action. "Squeeze it to stop. Loosen your grip to descend. If you let go completely, it will catch and stop you from falling, but only if your carabiner is attached."

I nod my understanding, and he pauses. "Vee..."

"Just go," I tell him. Whatever he's got to say will distract me from what I need to do. The time for talk has passed. The time for action is nearly upon me. I turn away from him and crouch behind a red-berried bush, machete ready to swing.

"I have the last of the rope," he says. "All you need to bring is yourself."

His rope grip hums as he descends. When I think he's out of sight, I look back to confirm it and feel a sudden and profound loss. The three men I've just sent along have all taken me off guard, with their knowledge, understanding, and compassion. As much as I loved Salem before, I now feel like I really know him for the first time. My son is brilliant, and brave in ways I did not know—perhaps he has enough of both to save humanity, five hundred years after it nearly destroyed itself.

The heavy footsteps grow louder, nearly upon me. I grip the machete tighter, my muscles tensing before the strike.

I glance through an opening in the bush, peering through tangled branches and leaves, and I see a flash of brown.

Not black.

"Del?"

"I'm not as pretty," Dyer says, entering the clearing, "but you'd never know in the dark."

While I'm thrilled to see Dyer alive, even if she is bleeding from several fresh wounds, I'm mortified that she's not Del.

Then Del enters the clearing, out of breath, only five arrows left in her quiver. There's not a single injury on her.

Before I realize what I'm doing, I pull the young woman into a hug. She's rigid for a moment, but then returns the embrace.

"You killed it?" I ask, stepping back.

"I wouldn't say 'killed' it," Dyer says. "But she put ten arrows in its head, I cut off its beak, slit its throat, and put two swords in its gut. All melted, of course, but—"

"It's still alive?" I ask. "Still hunting us?"

"Oh, right," Dyer says. "I also cut off its leg. So unless it's going to hop after us—"

A repetitive thump sounds out from the forest.

Dyer sinks in on herself, rolling her eyes and sighing. "Shitty cupcakes."

Del hurries to the climbing gear. "What do we do with this?"

"Wait..." Dyer scans the area. "They left?"

I nod to the rope that's wiggling as the three men descend.

"Typical," Dyer says.

"Put these on," I say, holding up the harnesses. When they both look at me like I've lost my mind, I help both climb into the awkward garments, careful to avoid touching Dyer's blackened triceps.

Dyer stretches her legs and does a squat, tugging at the tight straps. "I can't tell if I like or hate this."

I take the three remaining rope grips and attach them. Then I clip a line between them and the carabiners on Dyer's and Del's harnesses. I show them the grip, keenly aware that the thumping is growing louder. "Squeeze to slow down. Loosen to descend. If you let go, it will stop. Now go!"

Del goes first, moving slow as she hangs out over the ledge, eyeing the strange devices holding all her weight. But when Salem's excited voice rises up from below, "Del!" she leaps down, buzzing out of view.

"What happened to dying today?" I ask Dyer, as she heads toward the edge.

She shrugs. "What can I say? The thing was a chicken."

I clip myself to the rope. "It was afraid of you?"

"No, literally a chicken. I've feathered and roasted enough to know what a burned chicken looks like. Being a Golyat made it bigger, uglier, and more dangerous, but that didn't teach it to fight."

The same can't be said for the human Golyats, which fight with brutal, headstrong tactics.

"The problem with chickens," Dyer says, "is that they keep on running, even after you cut off their heads. Or, I guess, legs."

With that, she drops over the side, falling from sight.

"Squeeze to go slow!"

The line snaps tight, the cams holding fast. There's a thump, followed by a, "Fuck!" and then the sound of a buzzing rope grip sliding down.

I sheath my machete, finish clipping myself on and move to the edge, grip in one hand. The thumping is joined by a papery hiss, and I see the large black bird hopping toward me on one leg, the other missing at the knee. Its mouth is now a beakless hole, its head decorated with arrows, points jutting from one side, feathers out the other.

I lower myself part way over the edge.

The bird lunges for me.

Then I leap out over the abyss and loosen my grip.

The chicken-Golyat flies out over the Divide's vast open space, and without the wings it was born with, it plummets.

"Incoming!" I shout down to the others who pause to watch the creature sail past. I watch it for a moment and then look down. My head spins at the depth, but I can see the bottom. A river runs through the valley far below, concealed partly by mist. There are patches of green, black, and specks of white dotting the land below.

I'm about to look away from the dizzying view when I really see what lies below. There *is* water, and plants, but the segments of black crisscrossing the bottom aren't stones. Just like the moss-covered behemoth still fighting for its right to consume us, the massive formations below are bodies.

Golyat bodies.

Thousands of them.

41

With living and hungry Golyats still out for blood on the land above, there is no choice but to descend. I don't know if the others have figured out that the land far below is riddled with sprawled Golyat bodies or not. They're either ignorant to it or determined there is no choice, which is correct, so I don't bring it up. I just focus on descending, which is far easier than I would have guessed.

The rope grips allow us to push off the wall, descending in great leaps, covering vertical terrain in seconds rather than minutes, and in minutes rather than hours. My forearm is a little sore from holding the device. And my legs ache from pushing, but more from injuries. Otherwise, our journey into the Divide is easier than our trek across the land was.

Despite dangling from a thin rope held in place by small metal clips, all of it bearing the weight of six adults and even more rope, I feel safer here than I did up above. The occasional vibration buzzes through the rope, hinting at a dramatic battle above still being waged by who knows how many Golyats, but a howling wind rising up from below, not to mention the wall of stone we're climbing down, prevents us from hearing anything.

With each shove and drop, we leave the Old World horrors behind—I glance down at the huge, black bodies—maybe.

Hopefully.

Hope is a strange thing for me. Possibly a new thing. But I'm feeling it now, my thoughts on the future and seeing the good that might be, rather than just on the bad and how to subvert it.

"Switching," Dyer says from below.

I squeeze the grip and come to a stop. Dyer is at a break in the rope, where Shua inserted more cams and started a new line down. When we reach the breaks, we have to lock ourselves into the first rope, switch the grip to the new rope and then leave the first behind. If we ever need to make a return trip, great fiery balloons might not be necessary—for as long as the rope will last while exposed to the elements.

A chill runs through my body. I've just passed out of the sun's reach and into a layer of mist that glistens on my skin. Despite the chill, I smile. It's cleansing. All traces of the monsters above have faded. We are unable to hear or feel the Golyats in the depths.

Moving faster than we could on land, we complete the descent in an hour. Shua catches me as I make the final drop onto a jumble of large stones that slopes away from the vertical wall. After detaching from the line and securing my grip in a belt pouch, I look up. The Divide's height is dizzying.

Shua holds me again as I stumble and I don't yank away like I normally might. I'm happy for the help, and that he's alive.

"Look at it," Salem says, jaw hanging wide, eyes upturned. "All the strata. It's like looking back through time."

"What are strata?" Del asks.

"See the layers of stone?" Salem points to the large bands running through the valley wall. "The different colors represent different times on Earth, most of it long before there were people, or even life of any kind. It's not just the history of humanity, but of our planet."

"A history?" Dyer says. "You can read it?"

"In a way," Salem says, pointing high. "See that dark band, way up there? That was probably created during a time of volcanic activity, or even a meteor crash."

It's all very interesting, and I enjoy hearing Salem explain things, but the planet's history isn't going to help us cross the Divide or scale the far side. I sit down on a flat stone and give Shua a swat. "You want to get my pants off. Well, now's your chance." When I start tugging down my clothing, Shua blanches.

"To stitch me up," I add.

Dyer stands behind Shua, a kind of shocked smile on her face. "Too many jokes. There's just..."

She shakes her head and sits down beside me. "Better clean me up, too. We don't want all those bastards out there getting a whiff of us. They'd react like we're a couple of bitches in heat, and we both know only one of us is." Dyer nudges me with her elbow.

I'm about to tell her to stop when I see Shua's face turning red and decide I'm enjoying her banter. He's digging supplies out of his pack—bandages, needle and thread, ointments—trying not to look either of us in the eyes.

"Just leave the arm," Dyer says, glancing down at the wounded, blackened flesh. "It stinks, but like them. Could help mask us."

It's a horrific, but good, idea.

"Does it hurt?" I ask.

"Actually..." She bends her arm, then taps the wound with her hands. "Can't feel a thing."

"Okay," Shua says. "Who wants to let me poke them with a needle first?"

Dyer quickly derails Shua's attempt at a verbal jab with, "I'm glad you're up front about your size." She nods toward his crotch. "Otherwise, she'd be disappointed."

"There's no surprises down there," Shua says, and it's my turn to be embarrassed.

And Salem's. He's ten feet away, sitting with Del, still looking up. "Seriously. I'm right here."

Dyer chuckles. "Don't act like you and Del haven't—"

Del raises her hands. "No! Don't. Nope. Leave me out of this."

I'm smiling when Shua slips the needle into my leg, but it's gone by the time he's finished.

Dyer inspects the stitching. "Word to the wise, don't let a sexually frustrated man stick his needle in you. That's going to scar." Dyer lifts her shirt, revealing a tight stomach and a long cut. Only the middle of it is deep enough to require stitches, but it soaked her clothes in blood. We'll both need to change and leave our garments behind.

Shua leans down with a needle and thread, but Plistim grasps his arm. "Stop!"

When all eyes turn to him, he says, "We don't know if...this—" He points to the black wound. "—is in her blood. She needs to stitch and clean herself."

Dyer looks down at her stomach. "I've never stitched skin in my life, let alone my own stomach."

When no one poses an alternative, Plistim deflates a bit. "Then I will do it."

"Father," Shua says, but he's stopped by a raised hand.

"My life has been long. My children are grown. I will accept the risk."

"You realize that you're talking about not becoming like me, right?" Dyer says, still joking. "And that 'like me' means a slow painful transformation into a Golyat unless someone takes your head off."

"Apologies," Plistim says, taking the needle and thread from Shua. "It will also let us know if the effect is transferable before a person has become fully Golyat."

"Hurrah for learning," Dyer says. "Now stick your tiny needle in me and let's get the hell through this death valley."

"I'm confused," Salem says.

Dyer winces when Plistim pokes the needle into her skin, but manages to say, "That's a first."

"You both keep talking like the Golyats are still with us, but—" He points to the dizzying heights above. "They're up there, where they've been for five hundred years. We're safe down here."

"Umm." Dyer looks at me. "I'll let you take this."

I'm a bit surprised when Salem, Del, Shua, and Plistim turn to me, waiting for my answer. "Did *none* of you look down?"

"'Don't look down,'" Salem says. "That's what you told me when I was young and you wanted me to climb trees. So I didn't, and I don't."

I turn to Shua, my eyes asking, 'you too?' and his response is a classic Shua shrug. I motion to the valley beyond us, irritated. "Well, look now!"

We're still a good hundred feet above the valley floor, needing to descend the hill of stone before reaching it, but the giant shapes of

Golyats aren't hard to make out. What I can see from here, that I couldn't see from above is that many of them are partially embedded in the ground, either sinking in over time or falling from above.

"Oh," Plistim says. "Oh my..."

"Those are all Golyats?" Del asks. "There must be hundreds of them."

"Thousands," I say. "It looked like this for as far as I could see in either direction."

"Do you think they're..." Del looks down at her quiver of five arrows. She knows as well as I do that if even one of them is alive, there won't be anything we can do.

"Doesn't matter," Dyer says. "That's where we're going. No sense in getting worked up about it. Now..." She pats her injured stomach. "Finish stitching me up, let's do something about our stink, and move out. The sun might have already set in the Divide, but the sky will be blue for a while yet."

"We can reach the far side by nightfall," Shua says, trying to sound positive. "Start our ascent in the morning."

Not one of us wants to spend the night *in* the Divide, surrounded by Golyats that might or might not be dead, but scaling the far side, in the dark is impossible.

Plistim goes back to work on the stitches, and fifteen minutes later, Dyer and I are clean and dressed in the fresh, loose-fitting fabrics of the Modernists. Our wounds have been covered in ointment and bandages that mask the scent of blood. Since both of us are wounded, we're not required to carry gear, or the one remaining stretcher of rope.

Despite my painful wounds, walking without carrying a heavy load is a welcome reprieve. We descend the stone hill without incident and step onto the hard-packed, almost desert-like valley floor. Rock dust from the cliffs have filled the valley, wrapping around the great bodies that fill it.

We slow as we pass by the first Golyat. Its body lies in a twisted manner, likely where it landed. While its flesh and bone remain, the spines on its back jut out in two different directions, revealing a break. The creature's arms are mostly buried, as is the side of its face. Sand fills its open mouth, its black eyes covered in grit.

Who were you? I wonder. *Were you a man or a woman? What did you do? How did you live? How did you become this?*

Where I normally feel horror upon seeing a Golyat, I now feel sorrow. To die at the hands of a Golyat is...unimaginable. To become one, knowing you'll kill and devour everyone around you...that's worse.

I glance at Dyer's arm, protruding from a thin shirt she called a 'tank-top.' The black has spread beyond the bandage.

How much longer does she have?

Before I can guess, a slice of white amidst the Golyat's black flesh catches my attention. It only takes a moment to recognize the very human-sized, sun bleached bones scattered atop the Golyat. *That's what the white speckles were,* I realize, remembering the view from above.

I scan the area around us, eyes open for more than just giants, and spot the dead scattered all around.

"Shit-stained cupcakes," Dyer whispers, looking around.

The group grows tense, as one by one, we all see the human dead.

"They must have fallen," Shua says. "Or jumped. The Golyats followed them in."

The idea of all these people leaping into the Divide with the intention of luring Golyats in after them shifts my opinion of our ancestors a bit. Maybe they weren't all mindless, placid, do-nothings? Maybe some of them were brave, and bold, and sacrificial. I look at all the dead around us. Not just some... many.

"But they cover the Divide," Salem says. "Both sides. Not even a Golyat could jump across."

The observation triggers an epiphany. "This is how New Inglan was cleared. They didn't just seal the counties off from the Golyats' advance, they sealed it off and then purged the creatures. They would have fallen from up there," I point to the New Inglan side. "And there." I point to the cliff behind us, and freeze.

The orange line is barely visible now. If it weren't for the lone figure sliding down, I would have never seen it. I lower my finger toward the fast moving person.

"Who...is that?"

42

"No one we know," Del says, eyes squinted.

I'm pretty sure that if the eagle-eyed Del can't identify the distant figure descending the cliff with what looks like reckless abandon, none of us can.

"Should we go back?" Shua asks. "Or wait here? Our tracks shouldn't be hard to follow."

He's right. While walking through the valley of death, we've kept quiet and masked our scent, but haven't bothered to hide our footprints. Why would we? We've been leaving a visual trail since landing.

"Or I can wait," Del says. "And you all go ahead. Reach the far side and set up camp before it's dark. I'll catch up with...whoever that is." Del eyes the cliff. "I think it's a woman."

I'm not sure how she could even tell that from here. Whether or not she's right, her plan has merit.

"We're not leaving you behind," Salem says, crouched by his backpack, searching through its contents.

"I know," Del says, a little annoyed. She motions at the valley around us. "Because there's nowhere for you to go that I can't follow. And if a Golyat wakes up it will be because of you all, not me."

I smile at her confidence, but lose it when Salem pulls an odd-shaped device from his backpack. I recognize the two black cylinders, attached at the middle, as being from the bunker, but I don't understand its function any more now than I did then.

"We can use these," Salem says. "To see who it is."

"What is it?" Dyer asks, snagging the device, looking it over.

"They're called binoculars," Salem say. "They let you see over great distances."

Dyer holds the binoculars up to her eyes. "Can't see shit."

She nearly tosses them, but Salem says, "Whoa, whoa, whoa," takes them back, and plucks a black circle away from each end of the two cylinders. "You have to take the caps off."

Salem raises the binoculars to his eyes, and I see round glass embedded in the middle of the larger side. "You're looking *through* them?"

"The glass lenses bend light, magnifying everything." Salem twists a knob on the top and then slowly scans the distant cliff. He's smiling now. I don't know what he's seeing, but the device must be working. He wouldn't be smiling otherwise. Then he freezes. "I see her. It is a woman... but..." He lifts his eyes from the binoculars for a moment, and then looks through them again. "...I'm not sure who."

"Then you can't see her well after all?" Plistim asks.

"I can see her fine," Salem says, his smile gone. "I just don't know who she is."

Before anyone can ask for elaboration, or ask for a turn, I emulate Dyer, taking the binoculars from my son and raising them to my eyes. I stumble back, momentarily disoriented by the dramatic shift in perspective.

"Find the top of the cliff," Salem suggests. "Then the rope, and work your way down."

His advice, not surprisingly, is sound. I scan up until I find the top of the cliff and the forest. Despite the great distance, I can see the texture of bark on trees and even a squirrel leaping from one to another. Keeping the cliff in view, I move slowly left and have no trouble spotting the bright orange line. Then I shift down, following the path.

Then I spot her. The first thing that strikes me is how fast she's moving. Instead of pushing off the wall and sliding down in big leaps, she's all but running down the cliff. One arm is stretched back, holding the rope, the other is tucked under her waist, which I can't see because she's descending face-first, but no doubt also holding the rope. Her hands are covered in black gloves that match the rest of her tight-fitting black garb.

Why is she dressed in all black, in the summer? I think, and then I answer the question without asking it aloud. *Because she travels at night.*

In the darkness of night, the only part of her that would be easy to spot is her hair, even more than her speed, and that's what catches my eye and holds my attention. I've never seen hair like it. The yellow, almost-white color is spectacular. A few shades lighter than a mountain lion's coat, but long, flowing and wavy. Everyone in New Inglan has tan skin and black hair. On rare occasion, there might be a child with brown hair, but it conforms by adulthood. And while hair can be brushed out straight, it never really moves like this woman's. Where my hair is stiff, hers appears to bounce and dance in the wind.

It's the hair alone that fuels my next statement. "None of us knows her."

Plistim grunts, waving a hand at me, asking for the binoculars. "We knew everyone who came with us."

I take my eyes away from the glass. "You're missing the point." I hold the binoculars out to him. "She didn't *come* with us."

Salem's eyes widen. He'd seen her, and didn't recognize her, but hadn't considered the possibility.

Plistim peers through the binoculars, repeating the same steps that led me to the woman. When he stops, it takes just a moment for him to drop his jaw. "She is a stranger to me." He lowers the binoculars. "She is from beyond the Divide."

"We should go," Shua says, ever cautious. "After crossing the river, we can cover our tracks, conceal ourselves in the rocks overnight, and head up in the morning."

"Puss," Dyer says. "Why hide?"

"We don't know her intentions," he says.

"I don't know if you've noticed," Dyer says. "But we're pretty bad ass. Between the six of us..." She turns to Salem. "Well, five of us, we've killed just about every living creature that walks the land, including a frikkin' Golyat bear. So if she's following us with anything other than good intentions, she'll regret it."

It's a good point, but not without risk.

"I'll stay behind with Dyer," I say. "Neither of us is needed to complete the mission."

"I should stay," Shua says.

"We're both injured," I remind him. "And one of us has to climb all that—" I point to the cliff ahead of us. "—without the help of a rope. That's you, big guy."

"Agreed," Plistim says, returning the binoculars to Salem. "Dyer and Vee will stay behind to determine the woman's intentions. If you detect even a trace of deceit, savagery, or Golyat influence—"

"I'll take off her head," Dyer says. "Just as soon as someone gives me a weapon."

I glance at the others. Each carries just one blade, and Del her bow with five arrows. They might not need the weapons down here in the valley, but heading back into New Inglan without weapons would be foolish.

"Take this." I draw and hand my machete to Dyer. When Shua is about to object, I draw my ancient KA-BAR knife and spin it in my hand to show my familiarity with the blade.

He closes his mouth, sighs, and says, "Just be careful."

"When am I not careful?" Dyer says with a grin.

"That was a joke, right?" Shua says, sliding into his backpack. "It's hard to tell with you sometimes."

"Meh," Dyer says with a shrug. "We'll see."

Shua taps Del's shoulder. "Take the lead. Salem behind you. Then Father. I'll follow. Let's go."

Del nods and starts off. Salem hesitates a moment and then follows.

"We know nothing of the people beyond the Divide," Plistim says. "Caution is paramount."

Dyer doesn't joke this time. She just nods and faces the cliff behind us.

As Plistim heads away, Shua approaches. He looks about ready to lecture me, or add another word of warning to Plistim's. When he's just a few steps away, I halt him with a raised hand. "I know what I'm doing. I don't need advice, and I don't—"

Shua catches me off guard, covering the distance between us in a final step, wrapping his hand behind my head and placing his lips against mine. The kiss is awkward and stiff until I realize what's happening and relax. In that moment, I realize that his lips were the last mine touched, all those years ago when Salem was conceived. Feeling them again now transports me to that night, to the raw affection I felt. I know now that his passion wasn't fueled by alcohol, but by the knowledge of who I was and what I meant to him.

And now that I know who he was, and who he became, I am able to return his affection with my own. I push against him, pulling him tighter, long dormant desires waking.

"Holy fuckcakes." Dyer looks back, smiling as we separate. She's unimpressed by our affection, focusing instead on her colorful language. "Mixing things up. What do you think?"

"Did you actually see something?" Shua asks.

"Well, yeah. That kind of language doesn't work out of context."

Shua takes a deep breath, calming himself, more from the kiss than impatience. "Then what did you see?"

Dyer points to the valley's far side. "She's at the bottom."

"Already?" I say, spinning around. I find it hard to believe, but the yellow-haired woman is easy to see, leaping her way down the rocky slope toward the dusty floor below.

"Go ahead," I tell Shua. "We'll be fine."

He pauses just a moment, and then gives a nod before heading off.

I watch the woman with Dyer, both of us silent for several minutes. Then she looks back, as though checking to make sure we're alone. "So," she says. "You're going to ride that, right?"

A groan signifies my displeasure with the question as I turn forward again, watching the woman. But then I can't help myself. "You know I am."

Dyer gives me a whack on the back, knocking a smile onto my face. "Atta girl. Hey—" She steps on her toes, searching. "Where'd she go?"

We search for several minutes, but the woman has disappeared.

"People don't hide when they're nice," Dyer says, standing a little more vigilant. "We're not hiding."

"But we are armed," I point out.

"So what's the plan, then?"

"If she maintains her pace, and follows our trail, she'll reach us in thirty minutes. If she's not here, or doesn't show herself within two hours, we'll leave."

Dyer nods and grunts her agreement.

We stand sentinel, but our wait is far less than expected. Twenty minutes into our vigil, Dyer goes rigid beside me. "Umm, Vee?"

I turn toward her and spot a blade tip pushed up against her back.

A feminine, but gruff voice says, "I am Bake of Queensland, descendant of the great Tremble. Drop your weapons, or I will gut you both where you stand."

43

"Call me crazy," Dyer says, "but I already like her."

The woman is far enough behind me that I can't see her face without turning around, and I suspect my action will only lead to conflict.

"Drop. Your. Weapons." The woman pokes the tip of her sword into Dyer's back.

Dyer winces and hisses, but absorbs the pain and speaks through clenched teeth. "Not going to happen."

"Then you will die where you—"

Dyer spins around slapping machete against sword. Unprepared for Dyer's speed and strength, the woman named Bake loses her sword. The weapon falls too far for her to reach without me, or Dyer, cutting her down.

Bake leaps back, taking up a fighting stance I've never seen before. She looks unperturbed by the loss of her blade. "The women of Queensland are more dangerous with their hands than any—"

"Are the women of Queensland also trained to be drama queens?" Dyer asks. "Because holy cupcakes, you are—"

A kind of righteous rage flows into the woman. She charges Dyer, showing no fear of the blade already cutting toward her. And Dyer isn't holding back. If she lands the blow, it will be deadly.

But she doesn't land the blow.

Doesn't even come close.

Bake dives to the ground, rolling beneath the machete. When she comes up, Dyer is overextended. She gets a fist to her exposed side, and when she doubles over forward, the rest of her body is flung backward when Bake swipes out her legs with a low, spinning kick. She fights with the fluidity and ease of Shua, but faster.

With Dyer on the ground and momentarily subdued, Bake turns to face me as I charge. She could have gone for her weapon. She's fast enough to have reached it after dropping Dyer, but she just makes two fists and waits.

KA-BAR gripped in my right hand, the blade turned down, I throw a punch with my left. Unlike Dyer, I'm not going for a killing blow. I want answers, not blood.

Bake ducks the punch, as I knew she would, and attempts a counterstrike, just as she had with Dyer. Her fist connects with my ribs at the same time my true punch impacts the side of her head.

We both stumble back, recovering. I give my ribs a push. Bruised, not broken. But the pain awakens the wounds I've worked so hard to ignore. My body is covered in bruises, scrapes, cuts, and punctures. At my best, this woman might be enough to undo me, but now?

I caught her off guard once. I don't think that will happen again.

She goes on the offensive, moving back and forth, throwing me off balance. And then she strikes with a series of punches and kicks. I dodge some, block others, but generally take a beating.

She's wearing me down. No one blow is enough to impair me, but collectively, they're taking a toll. A solid kick strikes my shoulder, bringing a shout of pain from my mouth.

Bake smiles. Anyone could see that I'm just about done.

And that's exactly what I want her to see.

She leaps at me, open hands outstretched to grapple. Once I'm in her strong arms, the fight will be over. What I should do is lean back to avoid her. What I actually do is lunge forward, into her arms, slamming my forehead into hers.

A kind of vibration moves through my head. Lights, like fireflies, dance in my vision, blinking in and out. As bad as it is, Bake got it worse. She stumbles back and drops to one knee, staggered but not out.

I stumble-run and tackle Bake onto her back, holding my knife over her throat, ready to plunge it in. Instead of speaking, I just catch my breath. I'm halfway to passing out, and I'd rather her not know that. The knife does all the talking for me.

"You fight well," Bake says. "Dying by your hand is honorable."

"I'd rather not kill you at all," I say.

"Your friend—"

"Had a sword tip in her back." I glance at Dyer, who's picking herself up. She's angry and embarrassed but no closer to death's door than she has been for the last week. Of, course, her arm is covered. There's no way to tell how far the Golyat infection has progressed.

Bake looks ready to argue, but her eyes lock onto my blade and then slowly widen. I glance down at my knife. She's looking at the symbol.

"You carved the trees," she says, no doubt talking about the path we left, that apparently led her straight to us. "Who are you?"

"Davina," I say, and when she waits for more, I try to match her introduction. "Davina of Kingsland." It feels strange using the name, but also right. New Inglan, I now know, is a bastardization of New England, the name given to this part of the world by people long since dead. "Descendent of..." I have to reach back in my memory, to the few times my father spoke of our family's ancestors. He always seemed proud of our lineage, but never really gave a good reason why. "...of Sig."

The woman's already white skin turns even more pale, and for the first time, I really see the blueness of her eyes. Her capacity for violence is matched by her striking beauty.

"I am sorry," she says. "I would not have attacked had I known you were a king."

"A what-now?" Dyer says. She's recovered my machete and Bake's sword.

"A king," Bake says.

Dyer chuckles. "Vee is a lot of things, but she's not in charge of anything in Kingsland, and doesn't have anything swinging between her legs."

"As a descendant of Sig, you are granted the title, king," Bake says. "Just as I am a queen."

"In Kingsland," Dyer says, "She's called an 'eight,' and it's not a compliment."

Bake looks aghast. "You are disrespected despite your heritage?"

Growing weary of holding a knife to Bake's throat, I ask, "If I move, are you going to—"

"I would never," she says. "Though we have not met before today, we are bonded through time by those who came before us."

When I lift the knife away, she doesn't move. I slip away and sit. She does the same. Dyer stays standing, holding the two weapons, still ready for a fight.

"I am the eighth child of an elder and eighth wife of another elder," I explain.

She doesn't seem to understand the significance of either, though she asks, with an appropriate level of disgust, "Men take more than one wife?"

"The Prime Law says that elders can."

"You *still* live under the Prime Law?"

"Well..." Dyer points to the cliffs above us. "*We* don't, but everyone else up there does."

"The Prime Law was created to restore a natural balance to humanity, to return us to a more simple way of living, and to ensure that the Golyats did not discover the people hidden in the five purged territories. It was meant to be eliminated after a period of one hundred years, at which point the Second Law came into effect."

"And what is the purpose of that law?" I ask.

"Reunification," Bake says. "But...it was not meant to be. Our ancestors had no way of knowing the Golyats would resist time's assaults. There was to be a conclave four hundred years ago. Only representatives of Queensland arrived at the location specified in the Second Law. To reach the conclave, we exposed ourselves to the Golyats and were forced to defend against periodic attacks for four hundred years. And then, they got through. After the Golyats destroyed our homes, we fled into the wild, dispersed over a great distance. As a queen, I led my people here, in search of...well, in search of you. But the Divide was too great a barrier to surmount. Or was, until you left that rope."

"Where are your people now?"

"To my knowledge, I am the last queen of Queensland. Perhaps the last survivor. There's no way to know where the others are."

"How long have you been in the wild?" I ask.

"I escaped from the north when I was eighteen," she says. "I am now twenty-nine."

"Eleven years?" I ask. "You survived among the Golyats for *eleven* years?"

"Not alone," she says. "Not at first. The last of my people died two years ago. I have been patrolling the Divide ever since, hoping to make contact, or find a way across. I was convinced it would never happen until I saw the balloons in the sky."

Bake seems very well educated on our history—both as a people, and personally. Her knowledge lends credence to the idea that her people were privy to the Prime Law's contents, and this Second Law's contents. What she doesn't know is the history of Kingsland, or how its customs and laws have been changed over the years.

I'm about to ask her about the symbol on my knife when I feel a vibration beneath my feet.

While Dyer and I snap to attention, Bake rolls back, gets to her feet and looks ready to bolt. Her instincts are sharp and her reaction time quick.

"Where'd that come from?" Dyer asks.

Bake points to where the distant orange rope reaches the cliff's top. A lone figure is sliding down the rope with none of the speed or grace demonstrated by Bake. A second appears at the top as the ground shakes again. Far above the small figure, a Golyat head slides into view above the trees, black eyes downturned, oblivious to anything else.

A massive black hand severs trees as it reaches out. Rather than be caught by the massive hand, the desperate person leaps out over the cliff and plummets. The person dangling from the rope screams, the high-pitched sound echoing through the valley.

The Golyat reaches out for the person falling in silence, resigned to his or her fate. When it steps on the cliff's edge, stone crumbles. The rope breaks free, sending the second victim falling, pursued by a wave of boulders, and then...the Golyat.

As the giant topples, I see a second form rushing up behind it.

And another.

The battling Golyats, having seen new prey, have given up the fight for the chase, and it's leading them straight into the Divide.

When the first Golyat lands, crushing the two fallen people, the ground shakes with a violence I have never felt. A cloud of dust explodes up and out, concealing the monster and any clue as to whether or not it survived the fall.

But a moment later, I have no doubt that it did.

In the dark shadow of the miles-deep valley, the orange glow from countless Golyats is easy to see. It builds in brightness as the ancient beasts wake to find themselves partially contained in soil, and as hungry as ever.

44

"Go!" I shout, backtracking several steps before turning to run. While I've never seen a volcano, my father taught me about them. Stone so hot it melts, glowing orange. The shaking earth. The explosions of ash into the air. That's what the Divide looks like now, full of rising dust from the fallen Golyats, orange light from the monsters waking up, and a continuous, violent quake as more of the beasts plummet.

I wonder if that's what my father will see. With his clear view of the Divide atop his hill, will he think the Divide is erupting?

Not if he can see the Golyats falling into it.

I'm not sure how far we are from Essex and my father's hill. I know we were aiming further north, but we also reached the Divide far sooner than planned.

I hope he can't see it.

I hope no one can.

A volcanic eruption would be preferable to the Golyats.

"This isn't good!" Dyer says, running between me and Bake. "They're waking up! I think they're all waking up!"

While I disagree about the number of Golyats waking up—some are definitely dead for good—there are more than enough to take care of us, and the rest of humanity.

I follow the trail left by Shua and the others. It's a winding path through tufts of resilient grass and scrub brush, waking Golyats, and ancient human remains.

Hard packed soil explodes against me as a twenty-foot long arm bursts out of the ground. A two-fingered hand reaches for me, but falls short. The monster controlling the limb is locked in the ground, its mouth chewing on dirt, its partially buried torso glowing bright. But with half of it still underground, it fails to rise. It will eventually, of that I have no doubt, but for now, the solid earth trapping the Golyat is our salvation.

The stench of the Golyats fades with a cool breeze blowing north-ward through the valley. When I hear the sound of rushing water over stones, I understand why. We're about to reach the Karls River offshoot that spills into the Divide before reaching Boston.

Cresting a small rise, the river comes into view. It's fifty feet across, but only a foot deep. Easy to cross, but no help against the Golyats. Not that it could help, even if it were one hundred feet deep. There are Golyats on both sides, all of them waking up.

"Keep going!" I shout, rushing toward the river. At a sprint, we can catch up to the others and regroup at the wall. If we're lucky, they'll find an alcove, or a cave for us to hide in. While most of the waking Golyats can't see us, those we pass can. When they pull themselves from the ground, maybe they'll tear each other apart in anger.

Then again, thousands of raging Golyats could very well collapse the Divide completely. Without sheer cliffs, the distance would be crossable.

We should have never come, I think. *Micha and the Law were right all along. We've doomed humanity.*

But we could still save it.

And set it free.

If we can survive long enough.

Traversing the river is harder than I thought it would be. The bed of round stones is slick and loosely packed. Every step is a twisted ankle waiting to happen.

"Shit," Dyer says with each cautious, but hurried footstep. "Shit. Shit. Shit."

Halfway across, a loud slurp draws our attention down-stream. A Golyat rises from the river. At thirty feet, it's not nearly the tallest, but it's deadly enough. Water sluices around the body as rocks tumble away. The saturated riverbed gives way far faster than the crusted earth, allowing the beast to rise to its full height in moments.

The creature's stomach flares bright, the color snaking down through its bowels.

Teeth chatter and all throughout the valley, Golyats struggle to stand, returning the hungry call.

Dyer's string of curses increases in frequency as we speed. If we don't risk injury now, we'll die.

But then, none of us are moving, and it's not because of the stones, or the water, or injury. We just can't turn away from the Golyat as it takes a step toward us and loses most of the meat on its leg. Great sodden sheets of black, rubbery flesh peel apart and slap into the water, carried downstream.

The Golyat doesn't seem to notice and brings its other leg forward. Its foot, still contained in mud, remains in place, detaching from the limb with a pop. Muscle, sinews, and skin slurp away from bone like a tall boot. When it lands on its exposed, blackened ankle, the rest of its waterlogged body starts to come undone.

Great heaps of once-desiccated, now swollen, flesh fall into the river. Lumps of viscous liquid ooze from broken and exposed veins. The stomach and entrails fall from its core and burst upon a rock, the orange glowing contents surging down-stream.

"Wow..." Dyer says, fear morphing into fascination.

With a final step, the Golyat pulls its skeleton right out of its body. The bones waver for a moment as the eyes slide from their sockets and splash into the river. Then it collapses in a heap.

"That's why they avoid water," I say to myself.

"It was under there for a long time," Dyer says. "I wonder how long it would—"

"A minute," Bake says. "A minute in the water and they start to come undone. Three minutes and they fall to pieces. Walking through this water, some will lose their feet, but the big ones will make it through."

Most of the Golyats in the valley are smaller than the behemoths seen above. Thinking about them pulls my attention back. I turn around just as another plummets from above, the impact shaking the stones beneath my feet. It nearly drops me. The creature lands atop two Golyats that had already fallen, pushing them back down. But there are others, to either side, including the moss-covered giant, that are getting to their feet.

In a valley filled with thousands of Golyats, those falling from far above are the greatest threat.

When yet another great beast follows the line over the edge, I can't help but watch. It doesn't look frightened. Doesn't flail. It just reaches out—toward us—and falls.

"They know we're here," I say.

"Of course they do," Bake says. "They *all* do. With nowhere to hide, we will not be safe until the night, and with this many of them, even the night will not be dark enough to hide us."

The falling Golyat strikes the mound beneath it. One of its outstretched arms impacts the shoulder of a much larger, now rising giant. The limb is wrenched away from the body and catapulted in our direction.

"Shitty cupcakes," I grumble, and I start running across the river. I stumble a few times, but don't stop or slow.

A splash and a rumble draws my eyes back for a moment. The colossal arm has crashed into the river behind us.

Upon reaching the far side, we slow for just a moment to look back. The moss-Golyat is nearly free of the tangle created by the still falling creatures. Its black eyes burrow into me. I can feel its desperation.

Sucking in air, an exasperated Dyer manages a smile. "You did it..."

"Did what?" I ask, starting to move again.

"Cupcakes," she says. "Shitty cupcakes. I'm so proud."

To my surprise, Bake gives a laugh before sprinting ahead.

"You should go ahead," Dyer says when she notes I'm not also sprinting.

"I'm not leaving you here."

"I'm coming," she says. "Just not as fast." She rolls up her sleeve, revealing a blackened arm, from shoulder to wrist. The flesh is starting to shrink down and tighten.

How long until she loses her mind? Until we have to separate it from her body?

"Still not leaving you," I say.

"Woman," she says, and then shakes her head. "I'm going to eat you first."

She starts running again. It's several minutes before we catch up with Bake again, but we do. Not because we've out-paced her, but because she's stopped. Despite the situation growing more and more precarious with every passing second, she can't proceed any further.

When Dyer and I round the body of a permanently dead Golyat, I spot the others gathered by the cliff face at the center of a clearing, free of giant bodies. They have their weapons drawn and are facing Bake. Del has an arrow nocked and aimed.

They must have assumed the worst when Bake showed up without me or Dyer. I wave my hands as I step out and around Bake. Weapons lower and we hurry toward them.

"Who are you?" Plistim says to Bake as we get closer, both bewildered and suspicious.

"No time," Bake says. "We need to leave. Now."

"Leave?" Shua says. "Night is nearly upon us. There is a crevice in the wall. We can—"

"You are fools to travel with the sun," Bake says. "Darkness *is* the best defense against the Golyats, but it will not be our friend tonight." She motions to the valley around us. While the sky overhead has turned purple with the setting sun, and the valley is completely sunless, it is actually brighter than when we arrived.

A shake draws my attention back to the moss-Golyat, still fighting to escape the rain of bodies falling from above.

They just keep on coming...

If it, or any of the other giants, head in our direction, we will have minutes at best. "She's right. We need to leave."

"But where?" Salem asks.

In reply, Bake and I both look up.

"In the dark?" Shua asks.

"Better to fall from a cliff than be eaten by a Golyat. And..." Bake holds her hand up, wiggling her fingers to reveal her shadow on the cliff base. "...it will *not* be dark."

"Not dark enough," I say, understanding. "Not nearly enough."

A chatter rises up and a chorus joins in. The sound becomes an endless pressure on my ears, but I don't hold my hands against them this time. There isn't time to acknowledge the pain. The moss-Golyat is nearly free. And it's not alone. The flow of monsters from above has stemmed.

"Shua!" I point to the cliff. "Now! As fast as you can!"

No one argues as Shua grabs the gear he needs and rushes to the cliff, starting up with the agility of a squirrel. We take what we need to climb, leaving everything else behind. Once Shua's got the first anchor station in place, we snap our grips onto the rope. Bake takes her sword from Dyer, sheaths it on her back, and launches up the wall first, using the rope without a grip. The rest of us, either inexperienced at climbing, or injured, heave ourselves up with the rope grips, using them in reverse.

We're three hundred feet up and rising when the Golyats finally untangle and storm toward us.

45

"I can't do it," I tell my father.

The look of disappointment leveled at me is enough for me to try again. Small fingers dig into tree bark. I can feel my nails bending, close to breaking or being torn away. Wouldn't be the first time. Fear of that pain makes me hesitate again.

"You are held back only by the limitations you have already set for yourself. You believe yourself weaker because you're a woman, that you're slower because your legs are shorter, that you are less significant because you are my eighth child."

Just a few feet off the ground, I lock myself in place and turn to my father, tears brewing. "I *am* less significant because I'm your eighth child."

"Only because you believe it," he says. "Laws can't be broken without consequence, but they *can* be proven incorrect. They can be risen above. Just like you can climb this tree and any other obstacle in your path just as soon as you decide it's possible. Who will you be, Vee? Someone controlled by the laws of men and nature, or someone who climbs above them?"

He steps back and waits while I cling like a squirrel, deciding who I will become.

The memory comes and goes as I pull myself up the orange line left behind by Shua, who is somewhere above, climbing in the dark, locking ropes and cams into the cliff.

I fell from the tree that day, just a few feet higher. My father said it didn't matter that I fell, only that I tried to climb, that I fought against gravity's pull. At the time, I thought he was just a harsh teacher. As a young woman, I believed his early instructions had been fueled by a flair for the dramatic. But now, hanging from a rope, inside the Divide, dangling over a mob of hungry Golyats, the lesson feels wise, appropriate, and a little prophetic.

By the time the Golyats reached us, we had completed a three hundred foot vertical sprint and pulled the ropes up behind us, putting us five hundred feet above the valley floor, out of reach, and apparently out of sight. The monsters searched for us, but in the dull orange light cast by their innards, we had melded into layers of darker stratum. And when we rose through that period of geological history, we were truly out of sight—at least until the sun rises.

It also means we're climbing in the dark, which is easy for those of us climbing the rope. Assuming Shua does a good job planting our anchors, we just need to reach up and pull, over and over.

But even that's harder than it sounds, especially in my current condition. My body is raging against me. Days of abuse are taking their toll. Right now, the only thing keeping me going are those lessons from my father. But even his inspirational words have a limit. I'm still human, after all, and some laws can't be surpassed.

I'm sure Shua is taking breaks. Each time he locks in a new cam, he could clip on, hang in place, eat, drink, and then move on. Despite that, I never gain on him, and I no longer see the others above me. And since I haven't seen Bake fall past us, I'm assuming she's still climbing like a machine. I thought I had been hardened by the world, made strong and resilient, but after years of living among the Golyats, Bake surpasses me, except maybe when it comes to giving and receiving headbutts.

"You okay up there?" Dyer asks.

I use the question as an excuse to stop and rest. I release the grip and slide down a little before coming to a stop, held in place by the ancient device, a strip of fabric, a carabiner, and a harness that is making itself comfortable in regions of my body where I'd prefer a gentler touch. But I don't bother readjusting. The effort would be too great, and wasted. The straps will pinch and slide their way back. Better to just accept the discomfort and move on.

"Tired," I admit. "Going down was easier."

I look down and see Dyer silhouetted by the orange glow from below. The hungry Golyats are still active and agitated. Some scour the valley, looking for signs of life. Others are still fighting against their bonds, receiving no help from their risen brethren. But the monsters that frighten me most are the bunch that fell into the valley behind us. They're...fresher, stronger, maybe even more intelligent. They're standing below, heads turned up, like they're waiting.

I think it's because they suspect we've climbed the cliff, but without seeing us, they're not sure. So they wait for confirmation...and then what?

When I've seen enough of them, I turn my eyes upward. Clouds mar the sky, blocking most of the dust ring's reflected light. Had the sky been clear, the Golyats might have already spotted us.

"Give me some room," Dyer says, pushing her way up under my legs.

I move to the side, my legs complaining about even this subtle effort. When she's beside me, I go limp again. "What are you doing?"

"Good news," she says. "My dead arm is strong. And it doesn't get tired. I can barely feel it at all."

She holds her decaying arm out over the orange glow below. I can't see details, but her muscly hand is now thin and gnarled. She flexes her fingers a few times.

I fail to see how that's good news. While I do have my machete, I'd rather not have to decapitate my friend while hanging above the Divide. Not only would it break my heart, but it would also send her head tumbling to the Golyats below. If they're looking for confirmation about where we fled, I think a severed head falling from above would do it.

"Can you hold on to me?"

"I'm not sure this is the right time for you to make a move." My smile is as weak as the rest of me, but it feels good.

"Bitch, if I decide to get frisky you'll know it, and you won't mind it."

Despite our situation, I have to fight to not laugh aloud. The sound would carry in the valley, further agitating the Golyats. I wrap my arms over Dyer's neck and my legs around her waist. I'm surprised when she unclips me from the grip and secures me to her. The device can handle the weight. They were designed to support many more pounds than they'd ever have to carry.

"Now," she says, "check this out."

Holding the grip with her blackened hand, she hoists us both up with little effort. Using my grip with her still human hand, she holds us in place while she reaches up and pulls again. "I could do this all frikkin' night and never have to rest."

"That's good," I say, "because it's what you need to do."

As Dyer pulls us upward, tripling my previous pace, I wonder how my father would feel about me getting help. I climbed that tree on my own, two weeks later. After reaching the top, there wasn't a tree I couldn't conquer. But I've never climbed a miles-high tree after taking a beating—physical and emotional—for three solid weeks.

While trying to channel my father, seeing him standing by that tree, urging me to persevere, I fall asleep.

My dreams are dark, yet fleeting, lost in a confusion of images that even while sleeping, I wonder if they're real. Standing at the foot of a Golyat that's gnawing on Shua, I ask, "Is this a dream? Because sometimes I have dreams like this."

"No!" Dyer shouts at me, her arm healthy, dressed in flowing white. "It's not a dream."

I open my eyes and see purple. *Another dream?* I wonder, expecting Dyer to shout at me again. Instead she says, "There you are."

Her voice is close and calm, warm on my face.

"It's a nice morning," I say.

"Haven't really stopped to notice," she says, and I look away from the sky.

Gray stone slides past, triggering the memory of where we are and what we're doing.

"I got you," Dyer says when I tense. Her arms are wrapped around me, holding the rope grips behind me. Her legs are pressed against the wall.

Walking vertically, her Golyat arm does all the lifting.

Stretch, pull, stretch, pull. Her pace is constant. If it weren't horrific it would be impressive. That said, we're actually moving very slowly. "What's wrong?"

"Light," Dyer says. "We've been moving slowly since the sky lightened, but we're nearly done." She tilts her chin up. "Look."

I lift my head. The Divide's top is just twenty feet above us. Shua stands at the edge, pulling Salem to safety. Despite starting behind Salem, Bake is missing.

"Did Bake..."

"Climbed ahead as soon as she could see. Didn't really need the ropes. I'm not sure where she is now."

"You climbed through the whole night?"

"There were a few stops along the way," she says. "They all fell asleep twice."

"You didn't?"

"I...don't freak out...I'm not tired. Like not at all."

"It's spreading?" I ask.

"Haven't really had the opportunity to look." Dyer glances at the harness holding her body and clothing in place. "But that'd be my guess."

"Do I look delicious yet?"

She smiles. "You always look delicious, cupcake."

"Aww," I say. "You can use it in a nice way, too?"

"It's a versatile word, and a dessert."

We're both smiling when a Golyat chatters below us. The sound echoes through the valley, setting off a chain reaction.

Dyer freezes and waits. "Do me a favor and let me know if they're looking this way."

I turn my head down, moving slowly. The Golyats are looking up, but I don't think they're focused on us. Not yet, anyway. "Hold still."

"What are they doing?" Dyer asks.

"Trying to flush us out." It's a guess, but it's what I would do if I were hunting hard-to-spot prey. Stillness, and slow motion, is hard to spot. But an animal on the run stands out. But can the Golyats even reach us all the way up here?

A groaning scuffle breaks out when one Golyat bumps into another, spilling it into a third. Limbs flail as monsters with the self-control of toddlers thrash their neighbors, the violence spreading like an echo.

When the last of the watching creatures turn away, I say, "Go!"

Dyer launches us upward and in six rapid heaves we reach the top. Shua reaches over and pulls me up. Thanks to Dyer letting me sleep through the climb, I have the strength to help and turn around with Shua to help Dyer. But she doesn't need it. She digs her thin, black fingers into earth and drags herself over the top.

Relief washes over me as we step away from the ledge, heading for the forest-line thirty feet away, where Plistim, Salem, and Del wait. When I see their faces, my relief fades. Something's wrong.

Plistim drops to his knees and lowers his head to the ground, placing his ear against the stone.

"What is it?" Shua asks as we approach.

Plistim lifts his head. "Horses."

"What's wrong with horses?" I ask. Herds of horses are common in New...in Kingsland. They're harder to keep up with, kill, and transport, so shepherds don't bother with them, and they keep to themselves. I've always admired them, but have never feared them.

"With riders," Plistim says.

"*Riders?*" I'm aghast. "The Prime Law strictly forbids—"

"There was a lookout positioned to the south," Plistim says. "He left at our arrival. The sound of approaching horses so soon after is not a coincidence. A stable is kept in Rockingham. Only the elders know of it. There are a hundred horses kept for times of emergency. There has rarely been a need for their use, but last night...we created an emergency beyond any faced for five hundred years. All of New Inglan will be on alert."

Before we can discuss the subject further, or run away, the horses and their riders emerge from the forest just a hundred feet away. They turn in our direction and then shuffle to a stop, the horse hooves clomping on the exposed stone. 'Too loud,' I want to say, but then I make eye contact with the lead horseman and forget about dying at the Golyats' hands. If the giants make it up the Divide they will find our bodies already rotting.

When the horses stop, the lead horse struts in a circle, forcing the rider, who looks uncomfortable atop the steed, to twist his head. But he never loses eye contact for more than a moment, maintaining a steady, bloodthirsty glare that puts the Golyats to shame.

Then he draws his sword and says, "Hello, wife."

46

Micha looks both haggard and frenzied, like he hasn't washed or groomed himself in weeks. I suspect I look similar, but he has a wildness about him. Dried blood is spattered on his loose-fitting, deer leather pants. His hairy chest is matted with clumps of dark brown coagulation, as is his beard. He is drenched in blood.

"You don't approve?" he asks, looking down at himself.

"Who have you killed?" I ask.

"Anyone and everyone suspected of colluding with Modernists," he says, like I should have already known. "Not since the great Cull has my sword had so much practice."

Micha draws his long sword. It's still wet with blood, the tip dripping as it comes free. "I started with your father."

I draw my machete and make it one step before Shua catches hold of me and yanks me back into his arms so I can't move.

"Your father didn't die for nothing," Shua whispers. "Neither should you."

Micha snarls at the interaction. "You would have been proud. He admitted nothing and provided no information. But his whore...she sang for me."

Shua tightens his grip on me, but it's not necessary. I've seen Micha do this before—bait his enemies into attacking, tricking them into foolish actions. I won't play into his hands...at least not until I have the chance to cut them off.

Shua lets me go when I relax and give him a nod.

"No trial?" I ask. "What of the Prime Law?"

I'm buying time now, sizing up the enemy and trying to come up with the plan. The others are doing the same, I'm sure, but they're probably coming to the same conclusion I am—we've survived the Golyats to be slain by my husband.

There are fifteen men with him, all on horseback, most with swords or spears, and some with bows and arrows, though none nearly as powerful as Del's. They could run us down with the horses alone, but raised above us, atop the mighty animals, they have us at a severe disadvantage, not to mention outnumbering us nearly three to one.

"The Prime Law came to an end the moment *you* decided to cross the Divide!" Micha's voice booms with righteous indignation, and on this point, he's not entirely wrong. But he also doesn't know what we know.

"And what law governs the land now?" Plistim asks.

"My law." Micha raises his sword. "The law of the sword. Of blood. And now, of vengeance."

Sensing Micha is about to charge, I blurt out, "I didn't decide to go across the Divide. I was forced. Knocked unconscious."

He studies me. "You were seen with your father just days earlier, after I left for Boston, and yet you beat me there, killing two men on your way."

"I went there to kill my son," I say, "before you could torture him."

The truth of this statement resonates. He knows the depth of my loyalty to the law. I might have despised him, and betrayed him, but I would have never willingly joined the Modernists.

"That might be true," he says, but then he motions to Salem. "Yet, here he stands.

"Did you ever find your father, bastard?"

In response, Salem does the worst thing possible. Despite keeping his mouth shut, he looks right at Shua, who moments ago wrapped his arms around me, whispered in my ears, and calmed me.

Micha's laugh bellows out over the Divide. "Three generations of traitors."

"You must listen to us," Plistim says. "There is little time. The Gol—"

"If the Golyat poses a threat to us, it is only because you have summoned it here, and thanks to the volume of your actions, you have summoned us as well." Micha motions to the men around him. "It is fitting, don't you think? The end of humanity begins with the end of a feud."

"Give me your sword," Dyer says to Shua. "I can hold them."

"You wouldn't last more than a few seconds," Shua says.

Dyer holds out her blackened arm. I can now see streaks of black at the base of her neck. "I can probably throw a horse with this thing. And I'm feeling hungry."

Shua looked ready to argue until those last words. Is the change happening now? Or is she simply trying to convince Shua to let her die now, doing what she can to let us escape. But it won't be enough, and Shua knows it.

"Silence!" Micha shouts, but instead of obeying, Shua turns to his father. "Take Salem the rest of the way. Finish what we've started!"

After a moment's hesitation, Plistim nods, and Shua draws his sword. I draw the machete and toss it to Dyer, who catches it in her human hand. I then draw my knife. I don't see her move, but Del already has an arrow nocked and aimed at the men on horseback.

We will kill some of them, but can we slow them down enough for Plistim and Salem to escape? It seems doubtful, but there is nothing left to do but try. Freedom or death. It's time to put the ancient motto to the test. When I die, will my last thoughts be of regret, or pride that I died doing what was right?

Micha takes a moment to size us up, his horse agitated, ready to charge. Then he turns back to his men and says something too quiet for us to hear.

Archers adjust their aim, and fire.

The first arrow sails past my head, and I think they're aiming for me, but then I hear a wet thud and a grunt.

Plistim staggers back, an arrow in his chest and a look of surprise in his eyes. A second arrow strikes his shoulder, and he stumbles back again, just feet from the Divide's edge.

"Freedom for you..." Plistim says to Salem. "Freedom for all...is at Mount Fletcher. Go, boy. Go!"

A third arrow strikes his throat, snapping him into a state of shock and pushing him back even further. Teetering on the edge, Plistim reaches out to his son. Unable to speak, he offers a proud smile, and then falls.

"What have you done?" I scream.

"You mourn the man you detested for so long?" Micha is equal parts outraged and surprised.

"Have you even *looked* over the edge?"

The blank stare on his face says that he hasn't.

How long will it take for Plistim to reach the bottom?

How much longer until the Golyats understand where his body came from?

And what will happen when they do?

To his credit, Salem runs. Even I don't think he'll make it far, but he knows that his mind is not expendable. Without it, we're lost. It's not fear that drives him, it's duty, and even as he flees, I'm more proud of him than ever.

Micha opens his mouth to order the charge, but I shout, "Del!" before he can. The quick girl launches two shots before anyone can react. Two archers at the back fall from their horses.

Just as she's about to fire another arrow, a blur descends from the trees above Micha and his men. It drops down onto the back of Micha's horse, which startles and rears up.

"Atta—" Micha's command is cut short when an arm wraps around his throat as he holds on, keeping himself and his attacker atop the horse.

When the steed drops back down, I have no trouble recognizing Bake, even though she's pulled a black hood and mask over her head, concealing every bit of face save for her blue eyes. She places her blade against the skin next to Micha's eye.

"Order your men to dismount and you have my word they, and you, will not be harmed," Bake says.

"We going to honor that promise?" Dyer whispers.

I won't like it if we do, nor will Shua, but I will not betray the honor of our friend from beyond the Divide, certainly not after she has saved us all.

"Who are you?" Micha growls.

Rather than declare herself as she did with us, Bake says, "The woman who will impale your face if you do not obey her."

"Do you know who I am?" Micha asks.

"Are you a descendent of Sig?"

Micha's face screws up. "Who?"

The blade cuts into the skin beside his eye, drawing blood. "Ten seconds."

After three, Micha relents. "Dismount!" he shouts, fuming as his men climb from their horses.

When they're all down, Bake says, "And now your weapons! On the ground."

The men obey her faster than they would if it were Micha giving the command.

"Back away!" Bake says, and when they do, she motions for us to approach. "Come!"

The horses look even bigger up close.

"How the hell do we do this?" Dyer asks, but then she intuits the situation and yanks herself into the seat that's buckled to the horse's back. I follow her lead and pull myself up.

It's then that the Golyats react to Plistim's body. I don't know if he just landed, or if they've had time to put thought into his sudden arrival. But a great wailing chatter booms out of the Divide, spooking the horses. With a communal whine, the horses without riders bolt, which is for the best. Those with riders buck and twist about, panicked, but well trained.

Bake tosses Micha to the side and slips into his seat. She takes up the straps resting on the horse's back, gives them a snap, and taps her heels into its sides, saying, "Heyah!"

She's done this before, I think, when the horse starts forward at a good pace. I do the same with my horse, only gentler, and the steed starts moving, following the direction in which I tug the straps, which I now see are attached to a device in its mouth.

I guide my horse toward the Divide.

"Vee!" Shua shouts, fighting to control his horse. "Let's go!"

The ground shakes from an impact deep within the Divide. Are the Golyats fighting over Plistim's body?

Up ahead, I see Dyer ride up behind my still-fleeing son. She reaches down with her black arm, yanks him up, and deposits him on the horse behind her, keeping pace with Bake. Del, on a horse of her own, looks uncomfortable on the creature's back, but is holding on and keeping pace.

"I need to see!" I shout back, inching the horse closer to the edge.

When the dizzying drop is revealed, the horse complains, but doesn't run. If anything, it calms down. I lean out and look down, just as the earth shakes again. I'm glad the horse is looking the other way when I see what's below. If it could see what I do now, it would no doubt fling me from its back and run until reaching the sea.

"Heyah!" I shout, thumping my heels into the horse's sides. It whinnies and takes off running in the opposite direction from Micha and his men, who will no doubt regroup and pursue.

When I catch up to Shua, he shouts, "What did you see?"

Both of us appear to be naturals on horseback, and at any other time, I'd enjoy the experience. Right now, I barely notice it. "The Golyats," I tell him, the ground shaking from another impact. "They're climbing."

47

Traveling on foot seems quaint after an hour on horseback. I'm a little sore between the legs—less so after removing the climbing harness—but the ground we've covered more than makes up for it. A day's journey can be completed in an hour. A week's in a day. With Shua in the lead, navigating woods he seems to know well, we make rapid progress. The beasts even make short work of the rivers we cross, swimming while still mounted.

What's not great about horses, and the reason for their banishment under the law, is that they leave an easy to follow trail. I don't know how far Micha had traveled from his camp, but if the lookout summoned help so quickly it couldn't be too far. And I have no doubt there will be more horses and men. Micha doesn't travel toward danger without a veritable army at his side. My dislike for the man wavers for a moment when I realize that in the face of danger from the Divide, he rode toward peril, rather than away from it.

But bravery does not supersede brutality, murder, subjugation, and abuse, or the fact that if he catches us, our deaths will be long, painful, and pointless.

Thinking about what Micha will do to us reminds me of my father's demise. Of Grace's. Never were there two more loving, sweet, and wise people. When images of their deaths are fabricated by my imagination, I control the narrative, seeing Micha putting his sword through their chests, or taking off their heads. Quick deaths.

I know the truth is far worse, but for me, it's unimaginable. The images conjured by my mind, though fictitious, would undo me. The tears running steadily over my cheeks would be joined by sobs, making us even easier to spot. And my sorrow is shared. Shua for his father, whose death may have very well ignited the very threat he sought to defeat permanently. Salem for both his grandfathers. Dyer for her husband. Del for the family who accepted her and attempted to take her to a new and better world. The only one among us whose countenance is unaffected by recent events is Bake. Living alone in the wild, among the Golyats, with her people scattered or dead, she has been hardened and sharpened to the point that I doubt anything could shake her resolve.

I'm pulled from my thoughts by my horse's whinny. Instinct fuels my search for danger, and I find it right away.

The rumble. Despite the distance traveled, the Golyats' rise can be felt in the air itself. *They're coming,* I think, picturing them scaling the Divide's walls far to the north and south.

Of course, the rumble could have another source. Horse hooves. And a lot of them. While we move in single file, navigating toward a destination only Shua knows, Micha and his men can follow our trail as fast as their horses can run.

Feeling doom creep up my back, I ask for the first time, "Are we nearly there?"

Shua slows his horse to a stop, body rigid. He raises his hands slowly. "We're already here."

"Identify yourself," a man's voice says. I look for the speaker, but see no one.

Shua, who had wrapped his head and face to keep out insects, slowly unravels the fabric. "You know who I am."

When his face is revealed, a slender man, no more than ten feet away from Shua steps away from a tree trunk. His clothing is camouflaged in a way that let him blend into the tree, undetectable even up close. "When the air turned strange this morning, I suspected we would have visitors. I did not expect *you.* Have you not yet departed?"

"We have returned."

When the stunned man ingests the news, an impressed Bake asks, "How did you—"

"Hide?" the man asks, recovering from Shua's revelation. "It's what we do."

"We?" Dyer asks.

In answer to her question, twenty more men, women, and children emerge from the trees around us.

"You're the Keepers," Salem says with a sense of awe.

"Salem, grandson of Plistim, I am Berube, keeper of secrets. It is an honor to meet you." Berube turns to Shua. "And where is your father?"

"Dead," Shua says, dismounting. "Slain by the men who are now pursuing us. When we have what we came for, you need to flee this place for a time. And leave no trace."

"We are not incapable of defending ourselves," Berube says. "We've been set upon many—"

"The man coming is my husband," I say. "And his army."

Berube levels his gaze at me, looking over my face. "And you are..."

"Eight," I say.

He doesn't flinch at the news, but he knows the name, understanding that I am the daughter of Jesse and wife of Micha.

"Why...is *she* with you?" Berube asks.

"She is Salem's mother," Shua says, and this time Berube looks surprised.

"You...the elder's wife? Your son is..." He shakes his head but moves on to another pressing question. He points to Bake. "And who is this strange creature?"

"Further explanations will have to wait for another time," Shua says. "We need access to the library."

"For what purpose?"

"A map," Shua says.

"Leave the horses," Berube says, and then to Shua. "You trust them with this secret?"

"More than anyone else," Shua says, and he waves for us to join him.

Berube leads us through a path only he can see. I see no signs of previous passage, and we're careful to leave none behind us. After a few minutes hike, we stop by an oblong mound upon which nothing grows.

"If any one of you reveals the location, I will have no choice but to hunt and slay each and every one of you."

Dyer snickers, but her smile fades when Shua says, "He's not joking." Then to Berube. "They understand, and will die before revealing our secrets."

Our secrets.

Berube is a Modernist, perhaps even a key figure.

Berube's skeptical eyes focus on me.

"I'm one of you now," I say, and I'm a bit thrown by the earnest admission. "My husband will torture and kill me whether I tell him what I know, or not. He will learn nothing from me, and if I get the chance, I will avenge Plistim and my father."

"Your father?" Berube sounds nervous. "What of Jesse?"

"Slain," I say, "by the man no doubt closing in on us."

"A father slain by a husband," Berube says. "You now understand the sacrifice all Modernists make." He reaches beneath a very normal layer of leaf litter, grasps hold of something hidden, and pulls. A hatch opens upward, perfectly concealed. "Inside. Everyone."

The small room on the far side is dark and cramped. We're plunged into darkness when the hatch closes. There is a scaping sound, and then a light shining down from above. I look up at the clear rectangle through which I can see blue sky and trees. "Is that glass?"

"We saved more than books," Berube says.

"Books?" Salem asks, some of his burden lifted.

Berube smiles and opens a second door. Light streams down from rectangles in the ceiling, revealing thousands of books contained in glass cases. "Welcome to the library. Well, not *the* Library. One of many. But..." He waves his hand like he smells something foul. "...you understand."

When Shua sees us fanning out to admire the collection of books, documents, and images protected by the rows of glass, he snaps his fingers. "We are here for a reason, and time is short."

"What are you looking for?" Berube asks, "or rather, where are you trying to go?"

"Mount Fletcher," Salem says. "That was the Old World name for it. It won't be too far north from here."

"Mountains," Berube says, crouching by what appears to be a very wide and deep metal drawer. "Mountains... New Hampshire... Here." He pulls open a drawer, flips through a collection of maps coated in something clear and shiny, and pulls one out. He holds it up, inspecting a large drawing of mountains from above, all of them labeled. "Rattlesnake... Stinson...Fletcher. Found it!"

He lays the map on a clear table and points to the mountain. "Right there."

"Where are we?" Salem asks.

Berube traces his finger south, then taps the map. "Here. Perhaps an hour's journey on horseback, accounting for corrections you'll have to make on the way." He winds his finger back and forth, following a winding path to our destination.

"Why can't we just go straight?" Dyer asks.

"My dear," he says, oblivious to her blackened arm, which she's covered. Even her hand is wrapped. He points to the areas he'd wound his finger around. "These are mountains. Thousands of feet tall. It will be far faster, and easier on your horses if you go around, rather than over."

Shua retraces the route with his own finger and then looks to Salem. "Do you have it?"

Salem nods.

"We'll need this." Shua rolls up the map.

Berube is mortified. "But—"

"The mountain might provide the freedom we've sought," Shua says.

"Your father has sought to undo the Golyat for decades," Berube says. "What has changed that he gave his life, and you've come to me? What did you find over there?"

"The Golyat is not an individual," Shua says. "There are thousands of them. Hundreds of thousands. Perhaps more across the world."

"And..." Berube says.

"They're coming," I tell him, in no mood to mince words. "That is what you felt this morning. Not my husband and his deadly masses, but a horde of giants scaling the Divide's wall. If we do not stop them now, there will be no future for mankind and no place for you to hide."

Berube stares at me for a moment, and then turns to Shua, who gives a nod of agreement. "Should have damn well said so from the start." He gives Shua a shove toward the door. "Quickly! If Micha is following you, we will slow him—"

Shua opens his mouth to object.

"—without risking our lives. They cannot fight what they cannot see." He shoves Shua again. "Now go, before it's too late!"

As we hurry to the door, Dyer stops by Berube. "Do you have any books about cupcakes?"

Berube is flabbergasted into a fit of sputtering before saying, "Cupcakes? What's wrong with you, woman?"

"Do you or not?"

He blinks several times, and then says, "Three."

"I'll be back," Dyer says, heading for the door again. "Well, probably not. Shit."

We leave the library behind, its windows and hatch closed once more, invisible to all who pass by. In the short time we've been gone, our horses have been fed and watered. But the rumble in the air has changed. It's now underfoot as well.

Micha is gaining, or perhaps worse, the Golyats.

Back on our horses, we break into a gallop, striking out north as Berube and his people melt into the forest. At this pace, we'll reach our destination in far less time than predicted, but I suspect we might simply be hastening our own deaths. If we don't find a solution at Mount Fletcher, we will have hastened the demise of all of Kingsland.

48

We ride hard, slowing on occasion to consult the map, which Salem is using to navigate in tandem with mountain peaks that are growing more distinct the further north we travel. We stop in a clearing of tall grass, and the horses start munching, oblivious to the danger behind us. While we've seen no sign of Micha, rumbles still roll through the ground.

When Salem slides from the back of Shua's horse, I drop from mine and stand beside my son. He inspects the map and then looks up from one mountain to another.

"We're nearly there?" I ask.

"I think."

"You *think?*"

"Identifying mountains on a map from this perspective is difficult."

"We're not lost..."

He shakes his head, but lacks confidence.

"Let me look," I say, leaning in.

"You haven't spent a lot of time with maps," he points out.

"True," I say, looking over the bird's eye view of the region. I find the path pointed out by Berube and follow it, glancing at the peaks around us. "But I have spent a lot of time in the wild."

Imagining the flat image rising from the page, standing among the flat mountains, I picture the scenery. "We're here." I point to the map.

He nods.

I look at our surroundings again, this time imagining the mountains from above. I match my mental map to the one in Salem's hand. Unable to read the labels, I ask, "Which one is Fletcher? On the map?"

He points to our destination, and then I point to the real world mountain that matches. "That's Fletcher."

"You're sure?"

"I can see it," I tell him. "If that makes sense."

"Actually," he says with a smile, "It does." He looks at me with a kind of admiration that makes me uncomfortable. "It's how I describe most of what I can do that other people don't understand. It explains a lot." He leans in close and whispers, "We both know I didn't get it from father."

We share a laugh that isn't lost on Shua, who's been watching us. "If you are done telling jokes..."

"There," I say, pointing to our destination. "That's Fletcher."

As Salem and I return to the horses, he says, "I can teach you to read. When there is time."

Bake perks up atop her horse and turns to me. "You can't *read?*"

"Most people can't," I say, climbing onto my horse. "Only elders and those brave enough to break the Prime Law."

"*The* Prime Law had no such decree to break," Bake says. "*Your* Prime Law is shit."

"Later," Shua says, and he sets his horse galloping across the field.

As we cross the field, Mount Fletcher rises up before us. It's not the tallest mountain, nor is it steep, but it is covered with an endless sea of pine trees.

How are we going to find what we're looking for in that mess when we're not even sure what we're looking for?

On the clearing's far side, back in the forest's shade, Bake comes to a sudden stop. She turns back in what I've now learned is called a saddle. "Trouble at six o'clock," she says, and I'm relieved when no one else appears to understand her either. "Behind us."

Emerging from the forest a mile back is a line of men on horseback. At their center is Micha, his horse trotting back and forth as the group halts. I can feel their tension from here, equal parts anger and terror.

They're chasing us, but what is chasing them?

I get my answer in the form of a distant chatter. Unlike a Golyat in the Divide, the sound is crisp, clear, and without echo.

There is no doubt. The Golyats have invaded Kingsland.

And they're coming this way.

"Fan out," Shua says. "Every thirty feet. We'll go up this side, down the other, and then split into two groups, working our way around the top, and then again and again until we reach the bottom. The multiple paths might slow them down."

Our progress is slowed by the steep grade, the horses constantly trying to walk along the mountain's side, but we make steady progress. I study every tree, stone, rock, fern, and game trail, hoping to spot some sign of ancient habitation. As much as I'd like to find an entrance as obvious as the FEMA bunker, that structure stood on the far side of the Divide. For this site to have remained hidden in Kingsland means it is *well* hidden. How many hunters, shepherds, and explorers have traversed this mountain without stumbling upon it?

When the trees thin ahead, signifying our approach to the summit, my discouragement blossoms. Searching the entire mountain could take days. And the mountain is capped by exposed granite, where we would also be exposed.

Shua gives his horse a kick and climbs into the clearing first with the kind of urgency that suggests he's seen something. Our group converges, horse hooves clattering on the stone.

The view ahead opens up, revealing distant mountains and lakes. But the sight doesn't interest Salem at all. His eyes are drawn downward, to the stone.

A collection of symbols have been etched into the gray rock. Spirals, crosses, letters, and even more intricate designs. There are also several piles of rocks stacked into pyramids.

"What is all this?" I ask.

"Markers," Shua says. "Left by travelers. It's a tradition in the northern counties, to mark our passage. Each symbol is a different person, and you can see who visits most often."

He points out a star inside a circle that's been carved at least a dozen times.

"Do you know who they are?" I ask.

Shua dismounts. "If you know the symbol."

He crouches atop the stone slab and puts his hand on a symbol consisting of two vertical lines and two horizontal. "This was my father's." He shakes his head. "He stood right here. So close. Without ever knowing."

A scratching sound pulls my attention to Bake, who has silently dismounted, picked up a stone and begun carving her own symbol in the stone. She draws a circle, and a star within, and then inside that, a skull. It's crude, but easy enough to see. "The symbol of a Queenswoman. To mark our passage, and our existence on this planet."

"Not that the pictures aren't nice," Dyer says, "but shouldn't we be—oh, holy cupcacks! I mean—cupcakes! Holy humpcakes!"

I follow Dyer's wide, downturned eyes to the gray stone and spot what she's already seen. It's faded and partially covered by someone else's work, but the circle with two lines in it is still visible, as is the equally old arrow etched beside it.

Bake scurries over to the symbol, looks it over for just a moment, and then looks in the direction the arrow points...right back the way we came.

"Missed something," she says.

"What does it represent?" Salem asks, as Bake and Shua return to their horses.

"In the Old World, it was meant as a warning, left behind in places where people had no business treading. In that way, it was a symbol of protection. Later, in the end, it became a symbol of hope. Of direction."

"Which is it now?" Del asks, and it's not a bad question.

Bake's answer does little to quell our fears. "Does it matter?"

A heel thump to my horse's side and a pull on the reigns turns me around. My intent is to answer her question by heading toward the forest and my murderous husband. But the view ahead staggers me and sets my horse rearing up onto its hind legs in shock.

A Golyat rises up over the top of a distant mountain, eyes locked in our direction, but down, toward the base of the mountain. It's following Micha. He's led them straight to us.

The monster chatters as it rises up higher, and is then joined by a second and a third, one of which has two arms dangling from its ribs, the other covered in moss.

"Down the mountain," Shua says, urging his horse past mine as it gains control of itself. "Hurry!" We ride over the crest moving down, straight toward danger, and maybe hope.

Once again, we scan for signs of something—anything—that will reveal an entrance.

Ten minutes later, as a chorus of chatters cuts through the forest, I see it. I think I see it, because it could also be nothing at all. "Here," I say, drawing the others to me and possibly wasting time. "Look."

The thick pine is hundreds of years old. If I'm right, it's more than five hundred years old. Ten feet above the ground is a round eye where a branch once hung. The bark has grown up around the wound, but the two vertical cuts can still be seen at its core.

"Could be," Bake says, but doesn't sound convinced.

"Search the area on foot. Fast as you can. If we find nothing, we'll keep moving." I dismount at the base of the tree. When my feet strike the ground, a hollow thud booms beneath me. I look down at the ground, lift my foot and stomp. The sound repeats.

"It's hollow," I say, stepping back to solid ground.

The others leap down from their horses and we scour away centuries of dirt and decaying pine needles. When a sheet of metal is revealed, we double our efforts, clearing away a hatch that bears the symbol of my ancestors.

But is it a warning?

Or an invitation?

Not needing an answer, I find the still solid handle and pull.

49

Like Berube's library, the open hatch leads to a small, dark space, the way forward blocked by another metal door. Unlike the first, which has weathered the elements for five hundred years, if not more, this second door is pristine. Its gray surface is aglow in the light of day streaming through the still-open hatch.

I rap my knuckles against the surface.

"You think someone is going to answer the door?" Dyer asks. "Pretty sure no one is home."

I don't bother replying to the jab. In fact, I barely hear it. My focus remains fixed on how to cross the threshold. The door has no handle. No lock mechanism. "Doesn't look like it was made to be opened."

"Not from the outside," Shua agrees. "Perhaps there is a lever?"

A quick search of the empty walls turns up nothing. There is a door, and beside the door, a flat panel of what looks like black glass.

"We need to think like our ancestors," Salem says. "This site was secret, and based on the revelations in Lew's journal, it contained technologies that were more advanced than what was publicly known about at the time of the Golyats' emergence, including a possible solution..."

"Which was never put to use" Bake says. "Have you considered that it was never used, because it was never ready?"

No one has voiced the concern, but I'm sure we've all considered it. I know I have.

"At the very least, this structure might provide a place in which we can survive the coming slaughter." Bake frowns at the door. "If we can get inside."

Salem steps to the front of our group, inspecting the glass. "The Old World had what they called computers. They were machines...but smart. They could think, in a way, and displayed information visually, through sheets of glass."

"I read about them," Shua says. "The concept never made sense to me. Why couldn't people just think for themselves?"

"Computers just did it faster, in some cases," Salem says, leaning toward the sheet of glass. "They interacted with the computers using small tactile devices, but could also speak to them, and..." He reaches his hand out to the screen. "...touch the screens."

His fingers push against the glass.

Nothing happens.

A heavy, unseen weight falls over us, filling the small space, applying pressure.

"Shit," Salem says, and withdraws his hand.

The moment his skin parts with the glass, it glows to life.

Shua, Dyer, Bake, Del, and myself respond by drawing weapons and preparing for a fight.

Salem leans closer as a dot spins around in circles, leaving a trail behind it, looping around and around. "How? After all this time? It still works. Still has power..."

I'm not sure what kind of power he's talking about, and I don't get a chance to ask. The screen turns white and displays a single word. "What does it say?"

"Passcode," Salem says.

"What is that?" Del asks.

"It's like a password." Salem inspects the glass again. "I don't see a way to input text."

"Is there anything in the Prime Law about a passcode?" I ask. "Something that would have been passed down over generations."

"Not in the true Prime Law," Bake says, "And I doubt it was included in your sham of a Prime Law."

"It wasn't," Shua confirms.

"Perhaps it is not a word?" Del asks. "With no way to input text, it would have to be something else. You said you can touch the screens?"

"The symbol," I say. "Of Sig."

Salem reaches out for the screen, one finger extended.

"Wait," Bake says with enough force to lock Salem's finger in place, just an inch above the screen. "I would like to try something. To know we were not forgotten."

After a moment's hesitation, Salem steps aside. "Don't break it."

Bake glowers at him a moment, and then reaches her finger out. When she touches the screen, a black mark is left behind. She touches it again, drawing a circle. Inside the circle, she draws a star.

The 'we' she spoke of was not humanity as a whole, or even Kingsland. She's drawing the symbol of a Queensdaughter, finishing it off with a skull. When she withdraws her finger, points of light blink at all of the junctions and the crude finger-drawing is refined as though by magic.

Text scrolls onto the screen, and Salem reads it. "Welcome, Queen."

The door *thunks* as it unlocks.

The door opens to darkness.

"Great," Dyer says. "Anyone have a torch?"

A glaring bright light erases the darkness, and then snakes down a long, straight hall. My eyes squint as rectangles that appear to contain the sun itself illuminate everything. While the rest of us tense once again, Salem steps through the door like he's returning home after a long journey. He points at the glowing box above him. "These are lights! They're powered by electricity."

"Elec-what now?"

"Electricity. Like lightning." Salem lifts a hand, stopping our questions. "They had ways of generating it, without a storm. They could contain it. And somehow, though I doubt we'll ever understand how, stored it at this site in a way that defies time."

He steps further into the hallway, waving for us to follow. "C'mon. We don't have much time."

Despite our fears, and the strangeness of this place, Salem is right. I'm not sure Micha would follow us inside, but he will certainly be waiting for us when we exit...if he and his men haven't been consumed by a Golyat by then.

"What are we looking for?" Shua asks, as we move down the hallway.

"Someplace that looks important." Salem glances into rooms as we pass through. They're full of ancient, but modern looking desks, chairs, cabinets and darkened computers.

"Geez," Dyer says, looking through a door on the right. It's twice as thick as the rest and has a lock mechanism similar to the one that gave us access to the facility. But this lock was disengaged long ago, and the door left open, revealing racks of weapons that are both ancient and modern. Amidst the strange, black metal weapons are an array of blades, two bows, and more arrows than Del could fire in a week. "Can we stop?"

"Keep moving," Shua says. "We can resupply on the way out."

I look into the next room and find more oddly shaped equipment for which I cannot guess the purpose. "These all kind of look like they were important once."

"The space we're looking for will be bigger," Salem says. "Something...I don't know. Something like..." He stops in his tracks, peering at two doors mounted side by side. He's looking through glass windows. "Something like that!"

Salem pushes through the doors, and as he does, I register a faint vibration in the floor. The Golyats are closing in, which means Micha is, too. "We need to hurry."

I follow my son through the doors and stagger to a stop. The space beyond is massive, far larger than the FEMA bunker and so well-lit that the space—and everything inside it—can be seen.

"What is that?" Dyer asks, looking at the massive object to our left. I can't tell much about it other than it's black and crescent shaped.

"A plane," Salem says. "I think." And when he sees our baffled expressions, he adds, "It could fly. But that's not what's important." He points to the other side of the room. "It looks a little makeshift, but I think this is a laboratory, where they would conduct experiments and study the results."

Several computers are coming to life, their screens glowing blue. They stand atop long desks that are covered in an array of machines, devices, and equipment that I can no more describe, than use. "You're not planning to use these computers..."

As smart as Salem might be, understanding the technology to the point of finding what we need is unlikely.

"That could take weeks," Salem says. "Maybe months."

"Then what are we looking for?" Del asks.

"Lew," Salem says, standing on his toes to look over the dozens of desks, their equipment and the chairs strewn between them. At one point, this facility would have contained hundreds of people. Maybe more.

How many of them worked at these tables, trying to find a way to stop the Golyats' advance? How many of them left before the end, helping to found the first counties of New Inglan? How many of them died here?

I don't see any bodies. The space is fairly immaculate. Just a thin layer of dust.

"Well, not Lew," Salem says, "but evidence of him. If we can find where he worked, that's where we'll start."

We break into groups of two, scouring each aisle, trying to make sense of what we're seeing and searching for signs of a man none of us have met, who is long since dead, yet remains the source of all our hope.

Twenty minutes pass without a single discovery we can understand. Even Salem has trouble comprehending everything we're seeing, though he remains confident he could figure it out. Should we survive the coming battles, I have little doubt Salem will spend the rest of his days in this place.

Which means I will, too. I spent far too long apart from my son, and if I'm honest, I have grown fond of his company.

I pause my search to look at the ceiling. For the past ten minutes, vibrations have shaken the mountain's insides. The Golyats are above us now, and they don't appear to be going anywhere. They're either tearing Micha and his men apart, or raging at having lost track of them.

While we saw three of them, there could be more—a *lot* more—and there's no way to know if they're coming toward us, or spreading out through Kingsland.

"Hey, what about this?" Dyer stands at the laboratory's core, surrounded by an abnormal amount of computer screens, some of them large and curved. She holds up a familiar looking book. It looks just like the one Salem found at the FEMA bunker, the one belonging to Lew, which led us here.

Before anyone can reply, Dyer grips her chest with her blackened arm and collapses to the floor.

50

Salem and I reach Dyer at the same time, but only one of us tries to help her. She's sprawled on her back, twitching, eyes rolled back. Her breaths come in rapid-fire gasps. Sets of three. "What's wrong with her?"

When my question gets no reply, I turn to Salem and find him flipping through the book Dyer discovered. "Salem, help me!"

"I am!" he shouts back, and for the first time in my life, I hear anger in his voice directed toward me. "She's becoming a Golyat. I don't know how to stop it, other than cutting off her head."

When Shua arrives, sliding onto his knees beside me, Salem steps away, sitting in a chair that swivels. Shua's gentle touch surprises me. He takes Dyer by the back of her head, lifting gently. "Listen, asshole, it's not your time yet."

Dyer's body spasms. I fear she'll injure herself when she bites her bottom lip, but no blood comes from her mouth. Instead, there is a drawn out, "Ffffffff," followed by a pained, "-uck you."

Dyer's eyes roll forward and focus on Shua.

"Careful," she says. "Vee's the jealous type, and I'm not really in a position to defend myself."

"Just hang in there—"

"Oh, god. Vee, are those *tears?*" Dyer asks. "Is he crying?"

I glance at Shua. He doesn't bother trying to hide the tears.

"I've lost too much family already," Shua says. "I'm not going to lose you, too."

"Not sure you have much of a choice," Dyer says, lifting her dead hand to her chest. She grips the fabric, and with a strength that defies her condition, she tears the garment away. Bare chested, Dyer looks down at her changing body, but instead of despair, she shows relief. "The girls still look good."

While 'the girls' are not yet touched by the Golyat blight making its way through her body, the desiccated blackness has passed her shoulder, sending tendrils out toward her neck, down her ribs, and around her heart. She doesn't have much more time.

"Here!" Salem shouts, looking in the journal. "I found it. I mean, *he* found it. Lew. There's a lot here, but..." he turns the page, reading quickly. "He was infected during the course of his experimentation. He was an old man by then. Close to a solution. He created an...inoc... inoculation. I don't know what that means. But it prevented people from changing. At least the few he tried it on. But...it didn't work on him. He was too advanced for it to save him. He says, "The inoculation failed to stop my transformation, but it did slow it down, hopefully long enough to finish my work on the Golyat solution. I've sent everyone to live outside while I finish my work. If I die before finishing, I will at least be trapped in the base and unable to hurt anyone.'"

"Help me look," Bake says. She's standing at the lab's wall, looking at a row of shelves behind glass doors. Salem and Del head for her. "An inoculation is an injection that protects your body. I don't know how. But we need to find vials of liquid, and syringes."

"I don't know what those are," Del says.

"Uhh, clear cylinder with a needle on one end."

Del opens one of the glass doors and reels back. "It's cold!"

"Refrigerators," Salem says.

The word is lost on me, but Dyer lets out a gentle gasp. "I bet this place has an amazing kitchen."

"Go help them," I tell Shua. "I can't read."

He gives a nod and transfers Dyer's head into my hands.

"Not going to screw this up?" she asks me.

"Screw up saving you?"

She rolls her eyes. "We both know I'm done. I'm talking about Shua, father of your child. A good father. And probably a good husband. You've had a shit deal for a long time. Doesn't matter if you're 'married' already, or what your birth order is. Fuck tradition. You can't—"

Her body goes rigid for a moment, teeth grinding.

When she relaxes again, I say, "I know, and I won't."

"Won't what?"

"Save you."

She smiles. "You little shitcake."

"Move!" Salem says, and all but bowls me over as he drops to his knees. He holds a small, brown glass jar in one hand and a strange looking device in the other, a long needle sticking out of the end. He stabs the needle through the cover, and pulls the back end out, sucking the liquid into the cylinder. When there's none left, he withdraws the needle and positions it over Dyer's heart. He shifts to the side a little, says, "Sorry," and then jabs the needle in, squeezing the liquid into Dyer's chest.

She winces as the needle is withdrawn and says, "Well, that was horrible, thanks. But I don't think—"

Dyer's whole body convulses, her arms and legs thrashing about.

"Hold her down!" Shua shouts, leaping atop her Golyat arm before being tossed away. He sails fifteen feet, clears a desktop with his body, and tumbles to the floor amidst a torrent of metal, plastic, and shattering glass.

The rest of us just stare at Dyer. How can we hold her down when she's strong enough to toss us away? Before anyone can come up with a solution, she goes still. Del reaches for her neck, checking her pulse the way she might slain prey.

"Alive," Del says.

"Father," Salem says, "are you still alive?"

Shua groans and pushes himself up.

And then the world trembles. The Golyats are raging.

"We need to hurry," I say.

"We are safe," Bake points out. "We have time."

"While we're safe down here, people are dying up there. And not just the people trying to kill us. Salem, keep reading. The rest of us will keep—"

"Holy shit," Salem says, staring at the book. "He did it."

"You found it already?" Shua asks, working his way back to us.

Salem shrugs. "I started at the back and worked my way forward. The last entry describes Lew's final moments of conscious-ness. It's... disturbing. The entry before is what we're looking for, but he was too weak to leave. He never got to tell anyone."

"He can tell us now," I say, and I motion for Salem to read.

"I'll paraphrase," he says, and then, looking at me, adds, "That's when you—"

"I *know* what it means," I say, pride telling me to argue my intelligence, common sense telling me to suck it up.

He scans the pages. "Okay...the transformation into a Golyat first occurred with a genetically engineered bacteria created to rapidly dispose of waste, of which there was millions of tons. The bacteria was designed to burn through organic and inorganic waste without producing harmful smoke or gases, reducing it all to a liquid slurry that could be absorbed by the ecosystem without harmful effects. After a week, it should have died out."

"But it didn't," Bake says.

Salem shakes his head. "Most of it did, but there were rats living in all that trash. When they were exposed, most rats died, but some didn't. They became hosts for the bacteria, extending its life long enough for it to mutate. For it to evolve. It only took a few years for the rats to spread the bacteria to other creatures, which in turn spread it to humanity, and that was the beginning of the end.

"Lew says finding an antibiotic to combat the bacteria was so difficult because its various parts were something he calls 'rare materials.' It contains elements of bacteria gathered from the indigenous population of North Sentinel island, a creature he refers to only as 'Prime,' and a genetic modification called RC-714. 'These are the elements that made the bacteria so resilient, adaptable, and gave the Golyats their emaciated form, fueling their hunger and making them able to grow so large.'"

"Where is it?" I ask.

Salem looks up. "Where is what?"

"The antibi...anti..."

"...biotic," Salem finishes, and doesn't bother asking me if I know what it is. No one here does. "I don't know where it is, but he references a dart gun."

Now, that I understand. Poison darts are a useful hunting tool. "So we find the darts, shoot the Golyats, and what?"

"I don't know," Salem says. "He never got to try them, but the antibiotic worked in the lab. The inoculation is similar, giving the human immune system the ability to identify and destroy the bacterial cells. But I think you captured the essence of what our next steps are: find the antibiotic darts, shoot one into a Golyat, and see what happens next."

"What happens next," says a growling voice from behind us, "is that all of you die."

I spin around, machete in hand, to find my husband and twenty men standing between us and the exit. They look haggard and beaten. Many are bloody, but each and every one of them churns with fury. Since their number has been greatly reduced, I can only assume that these men have witnessed the horror that's been brought to Kingsland—brought by us.

"Micha, wait." As much as I would like to put my machete through the heart of the man who killed my father, I lower it instead. "We can stop them. The Golyats. The people who made this place figured it out."

"And yet the Golyats now rampage through New Inglan." He stalks toward me, weapon drawn, still drenched in the blood of Modernists.

"They died before they could use it," I say, and I motion to my son. "Salem knows how. He understands all this." I motion to the equipment around me. It's a gross exaggeration, but I need to convince him to try. I might loathe my husband, but if he and his men were taught how to slay a Golyat...

"Consider the bastard spared, then." Micha is nearly upon me. I raise my machete again, as Shua, Del, Bake, and even Salem prepare for a fight we cannot win. The twenty men spread out, closing the distance, sizing us up.

Somewhere behind the crescent-shaped plane, something falls, clanging on the hard floor.

While the sound makes me wary, Micha doesn't notice. He's lost in rage. Micha brings his sword up to hack at me, while I prepare to defend myself. As soon as our weapons clang, the attack will begin.

But Micha doesn't swing.

While he might have missed the sound of something falling, he's already attuned to the chattering teeth of a Golyat. Sword still raised, he's an easy target. I could gut him where he stands. Instead, I say, "One of them got inside. We'll need to fight together."

I can tell the suggestion disgusts him, but when I turn to face the sound, he doesn't strike me down.

"How can we kill it?" he asks, over the sound of shuffling feet.

"With our ancestor's solution: a special poisoned dart." It's a crude explanation, but accurate enough. "With what we have now, take off its head."

When the lone Golyat steps out from around the plane, I realize that might be easier said than done.

51

"I want its head!" Micha shouts without taking the time to assess the situation. His shortsightedness is displayed once more when he adds, "And then the Modernists' heads!"

Hearing the term 'modernist' spoken with such disgust now sounds off. Antiquated. The term isn't even accurate. Plistim and his followers aren't obsessed with modern technology, they're committed to undoing the sins of our ancestors no matter the cost, even if that includes breaking the Prime Law, and using any resources available.

Micha's men form a wide arc, but they don't rush into the fight. Who could?

The Golyat is no bigger than Shua, but it is far from a man. While it lacks the emaciated form of its larger brethren, the creature's skin is pitch black. Its black eyes and blacker pupils shift from one person to the next, rather than fixating on a single target. While its stomach burns bright, it stalks toward us, into the empty space between the makeshift laboratory and the giant, black, flying vehicle.

Teeth chatter.

The glow blossoms.

Stomach juices roil.

And then, it stops, almost as though it's fighting itself. It sneers, cracking open flesh on the sides of its nose, which is when I notice it still *has* a nose. Fists clench as its muscles twitch.

It's fighting against something.

"What are you waiting for?" Micha shouts, pushing his way to the front of his men. "Cowards!"

I think his men are simply being realistic about their odds of walking away from this fight. The Golyat might be small, but its movements are fluid, and something about it feels almost intelligent. At the least, it is not driven by pure instinct, and from what I can see, it appears to be resisting those instincts.

What are you? I wonder. *Why are you different?*

The answer comes to me at the same time Micha charges, and his men follow, somehow more frightened of my husband's wrath than a Golyat's hunger.

The Golyat's fearless eyes snap up, watching the incoming men.

Its mouth twitches, separating lips—it has those, too—to reveal black teeth.

He's trying to talk.

"Stop!" I shout, but I'm too late.

Micha leaps into the air, plunging his sword ahead of him. The blade slips through the creature's ribs and out its back.

Before Micha can withdraw the blade and strike again, the Golyat grasps his wrist and squeezes. With a snap and a scream of pain, Micha is separated from his weapon and then tossed aside. His men, emboldened by my husband's apparent wounding of the beast, charge headlong into their collective doom.

As the Golyat turns to face the men, the two halves of Micha's sword protruding from the creature's body bend toward the floor and then fall away. They clatter to the smooth concrete just as the first man does. I barely see it happen. One moment, the first of Micha's men to reach the Golyat is swinging a sword, the next he's in two halves, sliding in different directions, streaks of blood and gore forming a V.

The rest of the men, either numbed by horror, or simply not seeing what happened, press the attack.

Swords and spears whoosh through the air, some of them connecting, most of them not. Men scream out throaty battle cries and then high pitched shrieks. The Golyat battles with a savage disregard for the pain it's inflicting, and something more—skill.

For every blade that touches the creature's body, many more miss, and not because Micha's men aren't experienced fighters. If they're here with Micha and survived the Golyats above, then they are well trained. Some of them are probably veterans of the Cull. But the Golyat ducks and dodges faster than the men can attack, counter attacking with deadly force. Each strike is measured, brutal, and efficient. Every man that drops to the floor, does not get back up.

While I cannot identify the fighting style, I know that's what it is. In some ways, it reminds me of how Shua fights, but with less flair, and more power.

"Vee..." Shua sees it, too.

"I know."

"How?"

I shouldn't have an answer to this question, but I've known since first noticing this creature was different from other Golyats. I look at Salem, who is glancing between me and the battle. "It's Lew."

Salem's eyes lock on me. "Lew?"

"The inoculation didn't just slow the transformation," I say. "It left some of him intact. I think he remembers. Maybe not much, especially after five hundred years, but he isn't a mindless predator."

There's no way to know that for sure, but I can't think of a better explanation for a Golyat that is equal parts man and monster in a sealed facility, where Lew's own journal revealed he was here alone, transforming into the thing he spent a good portion of his life trying to defeat.

"You're right," Salem says, and his voice echoes through the suddenly silent space. We'd been shouting to be heard over the sounds of battle, but the clang of weapons, the screams and the snarls have all stopped.

Lew stands in a field of dismembered bodies, his black skin now red with blood and unidentifiable bits of Micha's men. Not one of them remains standing, and aside from Micha himself, not one is left alive.

That's not true. There is one man still living. He's suspended in the air, his quivering feet dangling six inches above the floor, dripping blood and piss. Lew's hand is inside the man's gut. When the man is lifted higher, I understand what's happening. Lew has punched through the man's insides and grasped hold of the man's spine. The wound is fatal, but not instantly.

Lew stares up into the dying man's eyes. Then he grimaces, clenches his eyes shut.

His stomach flares with a violent gurgle, his hunger fully awakened.

When Lew opens his eyes again, all hints of the man that was are gone.

His teeth chatter—desperate and excited—and then open.

If Lew has been down here all this time, by himself, then he's never eaten anyone as a Golyat. Perhaps that's why there is still a vestige of the man left?

"Lew!" I shout.

Dripping teeth pause just inches from the dying man's neck.

Lew's black eyes shift toward me.

A dry hack catches in his throat.

"We're here for the cure," I tell him. "To stop the Golyats. We want the same thing."

His stomach responds for him, burning bright, the color working its way downward. *How long can he resist it?* I wonder, and then I realize that he *is* resisting.

With a rigid, jittering movement, Lew turns his head and stares at something behind us. Despite the danger Lew presents, I look back along with Salem. Is he looking at the lab? And then I spot an aberration—a door.

Salem looks back at me. "Do you think?"

"Go," I tell him, and then to Bake I say, "Go with him. Keep him safe.

She resists the request for a moment, looking between Lew and the door he pointed out. I sense the battle in her, between curiosity and the desire to fight. Her dual nature is both intellect and warrior. In the end, she decides to follow the path without which even the warrior cannot prevail.

Salem and Bake sprint off toward the door, just as Del's bow releases an arrow.

"Del!" I shout. "Why did you—" I have my answer when I look at Lew and find the arrow poking out of the now dead man hanging from his arm. The arrow was an act of mercy, and despite the situation, I adore her all the more for it.

Lew cranes his head to the side, looking at the now lifeless eyes.

His stomach growls, the brightness spreading.

He fights it, but only for a moment. His skin shrivels as his insides begin to melt inside himself. Hunger awakened by the presence of so much food, he's finally begun to eat himself and complete the trans-formation.

His jaws open again, and this time there's no stopping him. The dead man's skin stretches beneath Lew's teeth and then gives way. A fist-sized lump of meat and sinew is wrenched away from the neck. Lew throws his head back, snapping at the chunk and then swallows it whole. His excited roar is cut off when he dives back in for a second bite.

"What should we do?" Shua asked, and I'm a little surprised he's asking. But his father did put me in charge of situations like these...not that there has ever *been* a situation like this.

"Follow Micha's orders," I say. "Take his head."

Despite knowing exactly how to kill Lew, Micha's men aimed to disable before cleaving off the man's head. I'm not sure I could pull it off either, being shorter than most men, but Shua has the height, strength, and skills.

As does Micha, who is climbing to his feet behind Lew and is reaching down for a dropped sword.

Lew groans in monstrous ecstasy as he devours his prey, the meal stopping his own body from further eating itself. For no reason I can discern, he becomes discontent with his meal, tossing the corpse away and focusing on me once more. But this time, the near-intelligent eyes are gone. All that remains is the single-minded focus of a Golyat.

52

The facility rumbles as Lew takes his first step toward me, but the shaking has nothing to do with the lone subterranean Golyat and everything to do with those above. I thought the violence above us had peaked, but I was wrong. Despite being under a mountain of solid granite, vibrations move through the floor and everything upon it, including the laboratory. Everything not locked down or too heavy to move jitters over the hard table tops. Somewhere behind us, glass shatters. And despite all the noise and the potential for a cave-in, Lew continues toward me, picking up speed with each step.

I back away, weapon raised. "Lew! Don't do this!"

He keeps on coming, closing the distance. I have just seconds.

"We can stop this, but you have to let us!"

"Vee," Shua says, voice quiet, but urgent. He stands to the side, sword drawn, not foolish enough to get in Lew's path, but ready to strike. "It's not thinking anymore."

It's more of an observation than a strategy, but it's something. Lew had fought Micha and his men with a high degree of skill. He's still strong, immune to pain, and ravenous, but the mind that guided his previous attacks appears to be clouded.

A shriek and flare of orange sends me diving to the floor. Lew's outstretched arms and open jaws sail over me. His airborne legs collide with my side. The weight and speed of his body, bends and snaps two of my ribs, but it's a small price to pay. The alternative was to have a piece of my body sliding down his throat.

Lew catapults head over heels.

His face impacts with the hard floor. Something cracks. Still in motion, his limbs bend up and over his face-planted body, and for a moment, the sickening angle of it makes me hope his neck will snap. But then he tumbles over onto his back. With a whack of his arms against the floor, Lew flips over and then shoves himself back to his feet. His sneer reveals black, shattered teeth.

Shua's sword sings through the air, the blade biting into Lew's neck. For a moment, hope exists, but then is blotted out, first when I see the blade has only cut an inch deep, and second, when a spritz of Lew's blood slaps against my arm.

The pain is instant. The three dots of blood are small, but the agony they trigger is system wide, and for a moment, it undoes me. I drop to the floor, vaguely aware of Shua shouting and Del responding.

I force my clenched eyes open in time to see Lew charging me again, unfazed by Shua's attack. I try to move as the pain becomes more localized, but my muscles are twitching. Feet scrabble, useless on the floor.

Lew reaches down, his hunger unwavering.

A blur barrels into the Golyat, tackling it to the side. I didn't see much, but the clothing was definitely not Shua's.

I roll over, trying to push myself up, and watch my rescuer roll away from the sprawled Golyat.

It's Micha.

"Don't make me regret saving you," he says, climbing to his feet in time with Lew.

I push myself up, enraged at the idea of being indebted to Micha. My arm throbs with the effort, but it's once again under my control. I glance at my skin. Three small points on my forearm are smoldering, hairs of black already snaking out.

Is Lew's Golyat blood somehow more potent, perhaps refined by the inoculation that failed to save him?

If so, we can't risk any more of his blood touching another person.

"No blades!" I shout, stopping Shua mid-swing. The interruption keeps him from making a killing blow with his now shrunken blade. But with Lew's decapitation would come a spray of poisonous blood that would either kill us on contact or transform us into Golyat far faster than the few flecks on my arm.

Micha lets out a battle cry, slamming his fist into the side of Lew's head. The impact sends the Golyat reeling. I don't think it hurt, but the force of Micha's meaty fist was enough to knock Lew off balance.

Micha presses the attack, driving his fist against the monster's body, never in the same place twice. The attacks are unpredict-able, and for a moment, unstoppable. Then, as though growing impatient, Lew snatches the front of Micha's shirt and tosses him to the side, all the while looking at me. Despite having several options for who to eat first, it's still locked onto its first target, perhaps drawn to me because of my arm's singed flesh.

Shua rushes in, but the Golyat sees him coming. A vicious backhand sprawls him to the floor.

Lew comes at me again, and though I've regained my feet, I have no idea how to defend myself. I could dodge his charge—maybe—but that will only buy me a few seconds. I could use his momentum against him, flipping him up and over me, but again, it wouldn't do much more than delay what now seems to be inevitable.

In the end, I decide to handle Lew the same way I would any predator I came across in the wild—matching its lethal violence. Ignoring my own advice, I raise my machete and swing it toward Lew's neck. The cut probably won't sever the head completely, but I just need to get it through his spine. If I'm successful, Lew's blood will spray all over me, but Golyat bacteria has already worked its way into my skin.

With Shua and Micha a safe distance away, I put all my strength into the strike. But I've misjudged Lew's speed. Instead of the blade striking flesh, my fist collides with Lew's shoulder. The machete is wrenched from my hand at the same time Lew collides with me.

When I was a girl, chasing Bear through the woods, he dodged hard to the left and when I watched him go, I collided with a tree. Being struck by Lew is worse. I'm flung back to the floor, sliding for several feet before rolling to a stop.

More ribs are broken. My head feels like it has been caved in, though I know it hasn't been because I'm still conscious. But the hurt caused by Lew is small compared to the agony wrought by his blood. It feels like a hungry rat has been let loose inside my body, tearing at me, trying to escape. Instead of checking over my body, I glance at the arm. Black lines streak up under my clothing and down to my hand.

Damn it, I think, but then I realize it doesn't matter what I'm turning into, because long before the transformation is complete, I'm going to become a meal.

What I'm not going to do is die lying on my back. I get to my feet and brace myself. It's all I *can* do. When his open, drool-dangling mouth approaches my face, I close my eyes and wait for the suffering to end forever.

Only it doesn't.

The pain ravaging my body from the inside and out remains just as poignant.

When I open my eyes again, a black arm is stretched out in front of my face. It's long and slender, the skin rough and textured like bark. It's a Golyat's arm, but it's not Lew's.

"Hey, Vee," Dyer says. She's clutched Lew by the throat and lifted him off the floor. He's holding onto her wrist, but shows no sign of concern. "I got this."

Lew's black eyes with even blacker pupils shift toward Dyer. Something in his expression shifts. The mania is gone.

"Dyer," is all I get out before Lew drives his foot into Dyer's still human body. Good news: the inoculation appears to have worked, stemming the Golyat bacteria's advance before it reached her heart. Bad news? She's knocked to the floor.

But not for long. Gasping, she rises to her feet and stomps toward Lew. With some part of his human mind returned to deal with Dyer, who he must see as a challenger—something no Golyat ever lets stand—his single-minded focus on me fades. That's a good thing, because I can barely stand, and not because of my physical injuries.

My legs wobble and I fight not to fall again. The pain increases, but then something else does as well—my strength. It's like the rush I feel before facing off with a predator. *How can I be growing weaker and stronger simultaneously?* I think, and then I realize the truth. While the human part of me is growing weak, the Golyat part of me is getting stronger. *How long until my skin shrinks in and darkens? Until I crave my friend's flesh? Until Lew sees me as competition? Until I digest and shit out my own insides?*

My legs give out. I don't feel my knees slam into the hard floor.

For a moment, I forget my pain, as Lew tumbles past me. His rolling body is pursued by Dyer, who's bleeding from three slices on her cheek, but she looks undaunted as she throws her partially Golyat body into battle.

Beyond the fight is Micha, back on his feet, bewildered by what he's seeing. I don't know if he's ever met Dyer, but he no doubt recognizes her humanity—and is probably already plotting to kill her if she defeats Lew. Hell, several weeks ago, I would have, too.

As bad as Micha is, I'm loathe to admit that I was once not much better.

Of course, I'm soon going to be much worse.

Shua catches my eye. He's moving toward me, but cutting a wide circle around the action. As skilled a fighter as he is, he doesn't stand a chance against Lew. The best thing any of us can do is stay out of the way and hope that Dyer's newfound strength combined with her brutal fighting style is enough to defeat Lew...who is equally strong, if not stronger, and whose combat skills are uncanny, for a Golyat, or a human.

Shua is shouting something at me, but I can't hear him. My heart is pounding, blood rushing past my ears.

I focus on his lips, trying to forget my pain.

The words slowly resolve. *I...love...you.*

My face screws up with disbelief and pain. *What? Really? Now?*

I try to call him an idiot, but then collapse in on myself. When I do, his voice reaches my ears, delivering a three-syllable message that is very different from the first, which I now realize I misread.

"Be...hind...you."

I turn to look and catch sight of Del for just a moment before she plunges something sharp into my back.

53

The pain in my back is nothing compared to the anguish of Del's betrayal. It flares far brighter and hotter, but lasts only a moment. With my newfound strength, I fling Del away. Before she hits the floor, I see the now empty syringe clutched in her hand.

Del was not my betrayer. She was my salvation.

But perhaps, like with Lew, the cure has come too late?

My insides twist, curling me in on myself. I can feel my muscles tearing and knitting themselves together, the transformation continuing undaunted.

A shout that is equal parts anger and pain draws my eyes open in time to see Dyer sail past and crash to the floor. She's breathing, and then moving, but she's not going anywhere fast. As strong as her arm might be, the rest of her is still human.

Lew on the other hand...

He roars toward Dyer, but he doesn't pursue her. He searches the space for new threats. With Micha and Shua no longer pressing the attack, he turns his attention back to me.

Shua takes a step toward Lew, and I manage to thrust a hand out at him. "No!"

I push myself up, fighting the pain. If I'm becoming a Golyat, my life is already over. If Lew kills me, it will be a mercy. And if he eats me alive...

He won't, I decide. I'm too far gone. I can feel it, the hungry itch, the ravenous drive.

Shua must see it, too, because he obeys my command.

On my feet, Lew faces me, and for a moment, he looks confused. He doesn't know whether to eat me or kill me as competition.

Then he attacks, mouth closed, claws extended.

Competition, then. Even he knows I'm too far gone. Golyats are many things, but they're not cannibals.

I face him head on. Knowing my skills as a fighter—against people—are lacking, I try for an unconventional approach. While he swings a hand, I launch my whole body, locking my arms over my head and curling up. We collide hard, and I'm surprised when I'm not the one flung backward.

When I open my eyes again, I'm on the floor and Lew is sliding away, his black skin squeaking over the smooth surface.

I get to my feet again, moving fast.

"Vee..." Shua says. He's looking at me like I'm a mountaintop sunset. Or am I misreading him again? When he smiles, I know that I'm not. "Look at yourself."

I don't get the chance. Lew leaps from his position on the floor, tackling me around the knees. Before I can recover, his strong hands grasp my ankles and pull. I'm yanked off the floor, spun in a half circle and flung.

This is it, I think, tumbling who knows how far. There's no time to think anything else, or ponder my regrets. I slam into something solid, but it gives under my weight with a metallic crunch that hurts my ears more than the impact does my body.

I sit up inside a crater created by my body on the aircraft's wing.

And I barely felt it.

I look at my arms now. My dark skin is still intercut by veins of black, but it hasn't spread, nor has my body become desiccated. If anything, I simply look...stronger.

I *feel* stronger.

The inoculation worked.

I'm not going to become a Golyat!

But there is still a very good chance I'm going to die here and now.

Lew roars as he leaps into the air, following my course. When he crashes into the plane, leaving a dent of his own, I've already fled.

I land on the floor, twenty feet below, without needing to roll. It's no harder than if I jumped up and down. And I'm fairly certain I could leap back up. But there's no time to try.

Lew is upon me, and he's still more savage, and less human than me. Claws slice through my clothing, catching the side of one breast and enraging me in the process. I drive a knee into Lew's crotch and discover the blow has far less effect on Golyat men than it does the standard variety.

As trails of blood race down my torso inside my shredded clothing, Lew drives a fist into my gut and then the side of my head. The blows drive me forward, and then sprawling to the side, but they hurt far less than they should.

"Vee!" Shua says, rushing to my aid, and if he gets much closer, to his own demise.

"I can handle this!" I shout with a bit more anger than intended. But he stops short, once again respecting my wishes. It's one of the things I like most about him. In a world ruled by violent men, Shua is a welcome and gentle aberration. He should see another day, even if I don't.

Lew rushes in, as I get to one knee. I throw a punch at his gut and connect, but his forward momentum carries him into me, his knee driving into my chin with enough force to really hurt. My head cracks against the hard floor when I'm sprawled back. Lights spiral above me, and then Lew stands over me.

I reach up for him through a haze, hoping to grasp some part of him and squeeze. Instead, my hand is pinned beneath his foot. Then I see the bottom of his other foot, rising up to stomp on my face. *How many stomps will it take? To crush my face? To kill me?*

When his heel drives into my nose, I know the answer is: *more than one.* The taste of blood fills my mouth. He's broken my nose. The foot rises again. My instinct is to close my eyes, but I don't. Instead, I look up at Lew, into his charcoal eyes, and say, "It's not your fault. You did your best."

There's a moment of hesitation, and then the foot descends.

But it never lands.

Lew arches in pain, his foot crashing to the floor beside my face as he attempts to stay on his feet. He reaches back over his shoulders, grasping for something out of reach. A roar of frustration bellows from his mouth, but becomes a sharp shrieking sound. He spins around, still reaching, to reveal an arrow embedded in his back.

Damn it Del, I think, looking for the girl. She's lowering the bow, a hundred feet away. When he forgets about the arrow, and me, she'll be his next target. Possibly his next meal.

But she's not alone. Salem stands with her, both of them in danger. But then I see Bake, their protector, weapon drawn and as ready for a fight as ever. But it's still a fight none of them can win.

Why is no one backing away?

They just stand there, watching.

Waiting.

What the hell for?

That's when I spot the glass cylinder in Salem's hands. It's full of a viscous black liquid.

"I think it's working," Salem says, eyes hopeful, like when he would ask me about the world, and unlike my father, I stayed silent. How often did I see this look, only to crush it? It's no wonder he left. Even before Plistim's influence, he longed for freedom. And now, here he is, fighting for that long elusive idea that had been so important to our ancestors, and so dangerous to survival under the Golyats' rule.

Lew stops reaching for the arrow in his back when something far more painful and unseen wracks his body. He convulses in waves, stumbling back, gripping his head. He screams, and for a moment, I hear an echo of his former human self.

His skin dries out and begins curling back in sheets. Clear liquid oozes out through fresh fissures crisscrossing his body, torn wide with every agonized movement.

The pain of his Golyat unbirth appears even worse than the transformation I had been going through, and when he speaks, I know it's because the still-human part of him remembers and regrets his actions.

"I am...sorry." Lew's voice is raspy. Barely there. But I can hear him because the apology is directed at me.

"Not your fault," I tell him, and he looks even more wounded by the grace I've extended to him. "You've done more than anyone else could."

He falls to his knees, quivering. His end is near.

"How long?" he asks.

How long what? I wonder and then I guess. "Five hundred years. Roughly."

He closes his black eyes. "But we survived..."

"We did," I tell him. "And thanks to you, we can finally fight back."

"Kill him," Micha says. He's snuck up behind me, fists clenched.

Shua answers for me, holding his partially digested sword toward my husband's chest. The fact that Shua would like nothing more than to strike my husband down is easy to see. Micha has a hard heart and lives by an archaic law that I now know to be corrupt at heart, but he's no fool. He opens his hands and takes a step back.

"You did this?" Lew asks, looking at my son.

Salem nods.

"You understand what needs to be done?"

"I found your journal at the FEMA bunker," Salem says. "And here. We know about the inoculation." He points to Dyer, who's picking herself up, and then to me. "It worked on both of them. And the anti-bacterial...it worked on you."

Lew shudders, grinding his black teeth. "I can...see that..." Lew motions for Salem to come closer, and my son obeys. Despite the obvious danger, I let him. Lew is back, and I can't help but trust the man whose five hundred year old action provided the hope for our future.

"You'll need to make more," Lew says, his voice growing faint. "You'll need the keys to my kingdom.

"Login: DeepBlueCT, all one word. D, B, C, and T are all capital letters. You understand?"

I have no idea what he's talking about, but Salem says, "Yes. You're talking about the computers."

Lew nods. "This will give you access. The password is..." Lew coughs as his stomach peels open, spilling dull orange liquid over his lap, the fury taken out of it. "...JackSiglerWasHere, all one word, capital letters on the J, S, W, and H."

More liquid burbles from his gut as he laughs.

Jack Sigler. The Sig.

"He was my ancestor," I say, and then I point to Salem. "And his."

Lew smiles at this. "You have his eyes." His eyes drift to Bake and his smile grows. "Know your eyes, too."

With that, he collapses forward, landing in a puddle of himself. The room is silent for several seconds, as we watch for signs of life.

We see none.

The silence is broken by Shua shouting, "No!"

Once again, I'm struck from behind and stabbed with something sharp, but this time it's not Del, or a syringe.

It's my husband, and a knife.

54

The pain is intense, but localized, and compared to the agony of Golyat transformation, more of an irritant than incapacitating. It's logic that keeps me frozen in place. The blade is an inch inside me, severing skin and muscle, but nothing vital yet—I think.

"Any of you make a move and I'll gut her," Micha says.

Shua tenses, but remains rooted in place. Despite his stillness, I can see him working through his options. There are plenty of strategies and attacks he could employ to disable or kill Micha, but every single one of them ends with me dead.

Bake inches her way closer, slow enough to not be noticed, but she'll never get close enough to make a difference. Salem and Del obey the command, but I can see Del's eyes wandering, looking for arrows on the floor. She won't find any.

"Haven't really thought this through," Dyer says. She's the closest to Micha and in the best position to act, but I doubt I'd survive. She flexes her charred arm, already comfortable with the horrific, but powerful partial transformation. "She dies, you die."

Dyer holds her open hand up toward Micha's head, curls her slender black fingers like she's squeezing it, and then crushes her hand together. It's not an idle threat, either. She has the strength to do it.

And so do I. While I've been spared a full physical transformation, my brown skin is still marbleized with black streaks. But on the inside... I suspect the change is more significant. My mind and hunger are unaffected, but the density and strength of my muscles has increased to the point that when Micha moves me between himself and Dyer, the muscles in my back contract, gripping the knife. I'm not sure Micha could push the blade any further without an intense effort.

I'm also feeling less pain. That doesn't mean the damage is any less severe, as far as I know, but despite the knife in my back, I'm not overcome by the pain like I should be.

The mountain shakes from the violence above. Something in the floors above us cracks. It's followed by the rumble of a cave-in. The facility can't take much more abuse.

I'm about to lecture Micha about the futility of what he's doing, to explain that we have a real chance to defeat the Golyats, to offer a truce. But he knows most of that already and still proceeded with his treachery. His allegiance to the Prime Law is blind and unwavering. There was a time, perhaps when the Law was untainted by the desires of men, that his commitment would have been commendable.

Still, if I can just make him see...

"You're being foolish," Salem says, beating me to the punch. "You're an elder. Your job—your *only* job—is to ensure that the people of New Inglan are protected."

"Says the Modernist bastard responsible for bringing hell to my land." Micha spits at my son, but the wad falls short. He nods at Lew's motionless form, "Who colludes with our enemy. If there are people alive to remember our history, I will ensure it is your name they associate with the destruction of New Inglan. My only mistake was not slitting your puny throat when you emerged from your adulterous mother. I was merciful then. I will not make the same mistake now."

He gives the knife a twist, but I grip it in place by clenching up my back.

Theory tested, my confidence grows.

The room shakes again. This time, dust falls from above. Little chunks clatter off the lab and computers, which I still don't know how to operate, but I understand their importance. If they're destroyed, everything we have sacrificed and accomplished will have been for nothing.

"Go," I tell the others, "Leave me."

"What?" Shua and Micha say together, both men equally baffled.

"The laboratory is more important than my life." I turn to Salem. "You have what you need to stop them?"

He looks mortified, but he nods and holds up the black liquid. "We just need a delivery system."

"The arrows," Del says, looking back at the doorway that leads to the armory and the exit. "It worked on Lew."

Shua catches my eye, his gaze asking a silent, 'Are you sure?'

I give the slightest of nods and say, "I'm okay. You all need to go..."

The ceiling booms, and this time I swear I hear a Golyat chatter through the earth and stone surrounding us.

"Now!" I shout.

When Bake all but drags Salem and Del toward the exit, and a slightly more reluctant Shua and Dyer follow them, Micha grips my arm tighter and shouts. "Stop! Now!"

He's not used to being disobeyed, but defying the Prime Law's authority, and those who represent it, is our specialty. And Bake, well, she's guided by a different set of laws that says ours is a bad joke. She's also been fighting this fight far longer than the rest of us, and she understands that my life is worth sacrificing if it means ridding the world of Golyats. Lew understood that, too, as did our ancestors, who created the safe zones and passed my family's knife down through the ages.

The knife of Sig—of Jack Sigler—which is still tucked into my waist.

"Stop!" Micha roars, as Bake waves the others through the door, gives me an approving nod, and then hurries after them.

"I'm going to kill you now," Micha whispers through clenched teeth. "And then I'm going to slit—"

"Do it," I say, clenching my muscles. "If you can."

"You believe I won't?" he asks, confused by my resignation. "That I have *feelings* for you? That I ever did?"

He's trying to get a rise out of me, but our marriage has always been loveless.

"Love is a concept beyond your comprehension," I say.

"Does he understand it?" Micha lets go of my shoulder to point at the exit.

Almost, I think, inching my freed arm toward my waist.

"*All* of them do," I say. "It's what guides them. Makes them strong. It's why they'll defeat the Golyats. And it's why I'll stay here, with you."

"You're not dying for them," he says, and I can feel his grip on the knife tightening. "You're dying *before* them."

"One of us is," I say.

Micha's moment of confusion coincides with a quake that rattles the floor beneath us. Drawing my blade from my waist, I spin.

Micha is fast but slowed by his confusion for only a moment. Even as I spin, he thrusts the blade, but it's caught by cords of solid muscle and pulled from his grip.

My blade sings through the air, glinting in the room's overhead lights for just a moment, before being coated in red.

Micha staggers back, eyes wide, questioning: 'What did you do?' He gets his answer when he tries to ask the question aloud. A bubble of air pops from his open neck, spraying blood to the floor at my feet. His hands clutch the slippery flesh as a curtain of blood flows down his body. He gives up when his frantic hands slip inside the gap, filling his throat.

Micha drops to his knees, his breaths hissing through his neck.

"When the day is done, Kingsland will be saved and I will make sure that history will not remember you, or the Prime Law, *at all.*" He slumps to the floor, lifeless. I take little satisfaction from his demise. He could have helped unify Kingsland against the Golyats. I would not have enjoyed his presence, but I would have accepted his help.

A Golyat roar rolling through the exit hallway twists me away from the sight of my dead husband-no-more. I run for the open door, unsure of what to expect. I race down the hall, passing the armory without stopping, and a moment later I re-enter the light of day.

Through squinted eyes I behold a sight far more horrific than I'm prepared for.

The moss-coated, colossal Golyat stands just one hundred feet away, downhill, putting its head seventy-five feet above me. If there were any trees left standing, the beast would be hidden from view, but the mountainside has been cleared by Golyat tantrums.

Two more goliaths, including the monster that has pursued us from the start, arms still dangling from its ribs, race up the mountainside toward their staggered brethren's back. Their teeth chatter as their stomachs roil with fluids and orange light. Their eyes aren't on the wounded moss-Golyat. They're focused on the collection of people just ten feet in front of me.

"It's working," Salem shouts, as the mossy Golyat sheds its greenery, and then its flesh. Great sheets of greasy, black meat peel away from the bones, thudding to the tree-littered ground. The air is an odd mixture of Golyat tang and fresh-split wood, both pleasant and repulsive at the same time.

The Golyat roars, raising its arms as if to say, 'Why me?' and then the arms slurp from their sockets and fall to the ground, shaking the earth with the force of fallen trees.

"Everyone move!" I shout.

The group spins to face me, relieved and surprised.

"You're—" is all Shua gets out, before I shout, "It's coming down!" and I shove Shua to the side. A shadow falls over us as the mossy monster topples toward us. Its black eyes slide from its head, falling first. Then its remaining skin and muscle sheds, falling straight down and leaving its black skeletal form to plummet toward us.

The ground convulses beneath our feet when the moss-Golyat's bones strike. I stumble and recover, but everyone else falls. Bake is a little more graceful than the rest, rolling back to her feet.

She points downhill. "Incoming!"

Del scrambles up, nocking an arrow from her replenished quiver. "Salem. I need more—"

"We have a problem!" Salem shouts, arms spread wide, eyes turned down. The glass vessel in which he held the antibiotic sludge is shattered, its contents filtering into the toppled tree's branches and pine needles.

"Can we get more?" Shua asks.

"It will take too long." Salem motions to the facility's entrance. The fallen mossy Golyat's leaking skull lies atop the opening.

Before the viscous liquid can drain away, I stab my knife into it, coating it in a thick layer of the stuff. While Del does her best to coat her arrow tips, I turn to Dyer and say, "Throw me."

55

"Say again?"

"My whole body is as strong as your arm," I say, turning to face the incoming Golyat, blade dripping black. "Now, throw me!"

"Mmm, okay." Dyer grabs the back of my belt, hoists me off the ground, spins once, and lets me fly. Thanks to her inhuman strength and our elevated position on the mountain, I sail toward the Golyat that I don't recognize from our past encounters. It's a hundred feet tall and now missing an arm, no doubt lost when competing against his larger brethren for Micha's men.

I careen in an arc that takes me higher than the one-armed monster's head and then drops me straight toward it. Black eyes track my progress through the air. Its head turns up to greet me, teeth chattering, the sound nearly powerful enough to slow my progress. But gravity has me now, and pulls me toward the monster's chomping jaws.

As strong as I might now be, a single bite from those massive teeth will pulverize me. Before I have the time to fully regret my rash strategy, an arrow whistles past beneath me. The one-armed Golyat stretches for me, mouth gaping open to swallow me whole. Then the arrow pierces its left eye. Fluid bursts out, deflating the orb and blinding the beast on one side.

The creature's teeth slam together, narrowly missing my reaching arm. I catch hold of a curl of skin and hold fast. The ancient, stretched flesh peels from the face as a long sheet, lowering me to the monster's shoulder, where I drive my blade into its meat. When

I withdraw the knife, much of the black fluid is gone, but a thick smear remains—as does the blade. I'm not sure if the antibiotic fluid works fast enough to stop a Golyat's insides from melting the blade, if the thick goo acted as a shield, or if my ancestor's weapon was forged from a Golyat-resistant metal, but the blade shows no sign of degradation.

That's good, because I'll need it again.

The one-armed, and now one-eyed Golyat beneath me wails in agony. For the first time in who knows how many hundreds of years, it's feeling pain. It lets loose a shriek tinged with despair. Perhaps, like Lew, some small part of the man it once was still remains. Freed from a mental prison that had been guarded by a burning desire to consume, he is now free to express sorrow for the things he has done, and the many people he has reduced to steaming piles of waste.

Just as the monster starts to come undone, it's tackled from the side by the beast pursuing me since setting down on the Divide's far side. The jarring impact topples the mortally wounded one-armed Golyat, and knocks me from its shoulder. I drop past the attacker's lowered head and see its eyes track my descent.

If I survive the impact with the ground, and the maze of tree trunks and jagged limbs, the first Golyat we faced, still adorned with the hooked arms of a former opponent dangling from its ribs, will set upon me. With its one-armed counter-part's skeleton falling out of its shedding flesh, the rib-Golyat's attention will return to its prey.

I strike out hard with the knife, digging into thick black flesh. After slicing through several feet of skin, the blade catches and my fall comes to a stop high above the ground. I wait for the agonized scream of another Golyat being undone, but I'm disappointed.

The rib-monster roars, but not in pain.

I see the incoming hand just in time, leaping away as long, slender fingers take hold of the limb dangling from the massive ribcage. I land against the over-sized ribcage and dig my fingers into its bark-like skin.

"Shitty cupcakes," I grumble, when I realize I delivered the antibiotic to the arm of a long dead Golyat.

The ribs I'm clinging to flex outward as the Golyat grasps the hanging arm and yanks. The hooked elbow remains fixed in place, and the beast is far too stupid and lost in hunger-lust to maneuver it free. As a result, the rib is detached from the sternum, yanked out through the skin, and cracked in half.

The Golyat shows no reaction to the self-inflicted wound other than tossing the arm and its own rib away, and then turning its attention back to me.

Holding on with one hand, and my toes, I lift the knife, ready to plunge it into the monster's flesh. I stop short of striking when I see the blade, cleaned of antibiotics when it slipped through the dead arm's flesh.

The Golyat reaches for me again. Unwilling to part with the ancient blade, I slip it into my belt and scurry across the jagged ribcage. With my newfound strength, and the Golyat's rough but pliable skin, I'm able to move across the torso with the ease of a squirrel on a tree.

I take refuge behind the second dangling arm, ducking away when the Golyat grabs for me.

With experience and frustration guiding the Golyat, it yanks the arm away with staggering force. Another rib breaks in half, jutting out of the chest from different angles, forming a bony triangle. Black blood spatters from the wound, flung from the bone's marrow. Most of it rains to the forest floor, eating up whatever it lands on, but a fist-sized glob strikes my shoulder.

I freeze up, waiting for the pain to come, and then the anguish of transformation. But all I feel is wet and warmth.

I'm immune, not just to the change, but to the liquid's digestive abilities. I'm not sure if that would extend to the glowing orange fluid of its gut, and I don't plan on finding out.

I climb a little higher and turn my attention downward. Shua and Salem are trying to find a way past the Golyat skull blocking the entrance. If they can get inside, they'll be able to return with more antibiotic. They can't see it from ground level, but the only way back inside is through the skull's hollowed eye socket.

Del and Bake yank back tree limbs, trying to get at the spilled antibiotic. As much as I hope they succeed, I don't think they'll be coming to my rescue any time soon.

And then there is Dyer. She's standing still, head turned up, hand over her eyes to shade the sun. When she sees me looking down at her, she smiles, extends her hand and gives me a thumbs up.

I nearly laugh, but then I have to move again, climbing higher to avoid being plucked away and eaten. The giant fingers scratch and squeeze, trying to grasp me. The Golyat pummels itself, but continues the chase everywhere I flee.

How can we stop it?

Without the antibiotic, the Golyat is unstoppable. Short of a giant sword to cut off its head, the giant cannot be killed.

Not by a human, at least.

I glance up toward its head and find those big black eyes and somehow blacker star-burst pupils staring back at me. The teeth chatter in excitement. A black tongue inside waggles back and forth inside the mouth. Froth flings out with each chomp.

Every instinct I have screams to get as far from that hungry maw as possible. Instead, I head straight for it.

The dark eyes widen like those of a man about to climax. The moment it has been tearing itself apart for has nearly arrived.

Hands reach up for me from both sides, both of them squeezing air. If they grasp hold of me, I will pop like a frog in the hands of a malicious child, my guts bursting from my mouth.

I scramble up and over the enlarged ribcage, moving to its shoulder once more. Jaws snap, the teeth coming together with such force that one of them shatters. I'm belted by tooth fragments, but the larger pieces miss me.

As I leap toward the back, where long bones grow from the creature's spine, one hand pursues me and the other reaches around the head to intercept.

I slip once as my foot digs into the old flesh and scoops away a chunk, but then I jump, sailing from its back to one of the long spine bones. I hit hard, which was my intent, but I'm dazed by the impact and I fail to grasp hold. I land atop the next spine bone down, my back nearly breaking. The fall is painful, but lucky.

The Golyat hands clasp around the area where I had been a moment before, locking on to the bony protrusion. Had I not fallen upon impact, I would have been little more than a smear. But the Golyat doesn't know I'm missing, and as with the ribs, it takes hold of what it finds, and pulls with savage force.

A roar of frustration transforms into an odd kind of shriek, and then back again. The warbling sound continues as it vacillates between its mindless drive to consume me, and the fact that it is pulling itself apart.

Orange light flares from below, coupled with a roiling gurgle. Somewhere inside it, a waterfall of digestive fluid calls out for food. The light is so bright that it flares through the creature's back.

If this doesn't work, I think, *it might actually digest itself to death.*

A loud crack and a wet slurp silence the growling gut. The vertebrae connected to the long spire of bone is torn from the Golyat's back, just below its neck.

The orange light goes dark.

The gurgling stops.

Limp arms fall downward, carrying the dislodged bone with them.

I cling in place as the Golyat topples forward. When it hits the mountain, I'm slapped against its back, dazed once more. Thanks to my altered body, I recover quickly and get to my feet, as a curtain of pine needles flutters back toward the ground.

As the debris clears, I see Shua and Salem, staring back at me from their position by the Golyat skull's eye socket. Then there are Bake and Del, crouched in the trees, eyes on me. Dyer stands her ground, just a few feet away from the fallen Golyat's shoulder.

"Fucking cupcakes!" Dyer shouts with a grin. "Someone get this woman some chocolate pudding!"

I walk over the monster's back, heading toward Dyer. "What is pudding?"

"I read about it once," Dyer says, as I jump down beside her. She gives me a pat on the back with her blackened arm. "So, next order of business, find out if this place has a kitchen, right?"

I look at each member of our family gathering around, each one stunned by what they've witnessed.

"Now..." I say, looking south toward the distant sound of raging Golyats. "Now we take the fight to them."

Epilogue

One Year Later

"Two Goliaths at eleven o'clock," Salem says. "One more, and a Behemoth at three. They're working on the wall. That's what I can see, anyway." He lowers the binoculars and turns to Del. "Can you hit them from here?"

"Can I—" She shoots her young husband a look. Over the past year, she has proven herself to be an uncanny shot, utilizing powerful bows found in the underground base in combination with arrows crafted by our ancestors. We've all become good shots, using bows and arrows more than bladed weapons since crossing the Divide a second time, but no one can match Del's accuracy, or range.

Del nocks an arrow, draws the string back, and lets the antibiotic-coated projectile fly.

After gaining access to the base's computer systems, thanks to Lew, Salem was able to uncover the method for creating the antibiotic and the inoculation. Three of Micha's men survived the events at Mt. Fletcher, and spread the word about what they'd witnessed throughout all the counties. The next army to arrive in search of those responsible for bringing the Golyats across the Divide were volunteering to fight with us—not against us. We had taken down a few Golyats on our own, but with an army at our disposal, Kingsland was cleared of the beasts, and peace restored in less than a month.

We then set our sights on the world beyond the Divide.

'Freedom or death' took on a new meaning, and the world felt lighter, despite the Golyats' presence in it. For the first time in five hundred years, the people of Kingsland were truly united behind a cause more noble, worthy, and empowering than hiding.

When it came time to find volunteers to cross the Divide, we had to turn people away. Bake selected a hundred men and women based on fighting and survival skills. And then she taught them about the Golyats, about surviving beyond the Divide, and about our true history and our scattered brethren.

Armed with countless antibiotic arrows, our army marched the Divide's length. From high above, they rained down permanent death upon the Golyats. Some attempted to scale the walls, but none made it to the top.

To re-cross the Divide, we repeated Plistim's hot air balloon stunt, peppering Golyats as they descended. Reunited on the far side, fifty men and women left in heavily armed groups of ten. Their mission was to systematically clear the land beyond the Divide, and I have little doubt they are getting the job done.

The rest of us have a much different job—one that we're close to accomplishing.

Del's arrow drops from the sky a half mile away. I don't see it hit the Golyat's back, but there's no mistaking its violent reaction. Loud wailing echoes off the wall as the giant thrashes about, reaching for something it can't reach. Even if it could, there's no stopping the antibiotic. It spreads through the creature's system, killing the bacteria driving its hunger and holding the whole thing together. Golyats don't simply fall over dead. They fall apart in a heap of ancient flesh, slime, and exposed bones.

It's a sight I have yet to tire of, not because I enjoy the gore, but because it means we're making progress.

"One Goliath down," Del says, nocking another arrow, "One more to go."

Goliaths are Golyats ranging in size from fifty to one hundred feet. Anything over that is called a Behemoth. Salem came up with both names, but it was Dyer who insisted anything under fifty feet be called a 'little bitch.'

Del's second arrow finds its target and sets the second Goliath wailing. The creature falls back, slipping out of itself until it crashes into the lush forest, which reminds me of home, but is far more lush and wet. Two deep pockmarks are revealed on the wall when the Golyat falls. They've been pounding against it for who knows how long, chipping their way through the massive barrier, which ascends at an angle.

No way we're scaling that, I think.

It's Shua who voices the concern. "I don't think we're going over the wall." He slips an arm around the small of my back. Before crossing the Divide we were married in Essex... by my father.

Micha had been lying about his death. While he *had* captured my father, and tortured him, he had stopped short of killing him. The Golyats' awakening in the Divide interrupted my father's interrogation, and Grace had not yet been touched. Of all the positive turns of event over the past year, my father's life being spared was the most joyous.

After the wedding, my father resumed his role as Essex's elder, organizing the counties and educating the people about the past, ensuring that everyone could read. He was very impressed with Bake, and together they updated the Prime Law to more closely match what our ancestors had intended—especially when it came to the Golyats and reunification of the five safe havens.

Which is what inspired our journey across what had once been called the United States of America, but is now known simply as the wilds. After months of travel, and fighting, and hunting, we finally spotted the wall, as massive and unnatural a barrier as the Divide, only in reverse. Upon first seeing it, we thought it nearby, but it took days to reach it and now, just after noon, we stand in its shadow.

"Why do you think they're beating on the wall?" Dyer asks.

"They know what's beyond it," Bake says.

These two women have become like sisters to me. I trust them in all matters, which is good, because I'm the leader of this small army, and thanks to their input, Shua's support, and Salem's knowledge, we've only lost two men. They are also deadly to Golyats at close range. When the forest is too thick for arrows, they wield antibiotic-laced weapons in a way that none of the beasts can defend against.

Shua would argue that he is equally skilled against the Golyats, and he's close, but his true value is as a leader of men. While I *am* in charge, because of what I've done, what I'm capable of, and what I look like, Shua is far better at inspiring people. My marbleized skin doesn't let anyone forget that part of me is Golyat, and that if the hunger ever awakens in me, the antibiotic might not work. The response to Dyer's arm had been similar, but enough of her still looks fully human, and her sense of humor puts people at ease. She also figured out how to make cupcakes, which made her a lot of friends and brought more than a few suitors to her hut's door. She turned them all away, claiming to be focused on our continuing mission, but she is still faithful to Holland, who had been her life. I hadn't understood the concept when she first explained it to me— I lean into Shua's arm—but I do now.

"How could they know what's beyond it?" Salem asks, head craning high. The top of the wall is cloaked in clouds.

"We should search the area for signs of habitation," Bake says, and before Salem can complain about that she adds, "People coming and going. Just because the Golyats don't have a way through doesn't mean people don't."

"And there's no way in hell we're getting over that thing," Dyer says, and then she looks at me. "Well, maybe *you* could."

I look up at the unclimbable height and realize that I probably could ascend the wall, even at an angle. I don't really get tired. I'm strong enough to crush stone. And I've had some experience climbing—having ascended and descended both sides of the Divide, making several trips before taking our army across. But it's not without its risks. Loose rock could send me plummeting, and while I can fall from great heights— I turn my head up... "Let's call that a last resort."

"Del," Shua says, "Finish the job. Then we'll scout the area for signs of passage. If nothing turns up, we'll split into two groups and trace the wall's exterior to search for gates and tunnels."

All eyes turn to me, those of the people who have become my close family and dearest friends, and those of the forty eight people standing behind us. As the heir to Plistim's legacy, I feel strange having the final word, but in the new world, being the eighth of anything no longer matters.

I nod and say, "Do it," to Del. Then I turn to the warriors and hunters behind me and add, "We've journeyed long and fought hard, sacrificing blood and loved ones. And now, our destination is finally in sight. Our brothers and sisters, severed from us five hundred years ago, lie on the far side of that wall. And when we've reunited with them, we will not stop until we've located the safe zones in the south..." I look at Bake. "And those left in the north. We will not rest until every man and woman can live in freedom. And if we die in the effort, so be it. There are worse things than death, and we will never return to that sorry state. Freedom or death!"

"Freedom or death!" the warriors repeat, thrusting bows and blades in the air.

Dyer leans in beside me. "Did you rehearse that?"

"Salem helped me write it," I whisper back, and then give Del a nod.

Del lines up her third shot. We'll have to track down and recover the arrows—our supply is limited—but Behemoths and Goliaths are never hard to find.

With a snap of the bow, the arrow sails over open forest, headed for the third Goliath's back.

A scream rips through the forest.

Too soon, I think. *And too high pitched.*

I look back, scanning the face of every man and woman. No one is missing.

"That was a woman," Shua says, poised to run toward the sound.

"Little bitch!" Dyer shouts, pointing her sword downhill toward the forest's edge. A black form, thirty feet tall, but on all fours, crashes through the trees. I see it for just a moment, but the shape was canine. As the beast runs into the forest, the orange glow of its stomach marks its path.

I draw my machete, its sheath always full of black antibiotic.

"Follow," I tell Shua. "But carefully."

He nods and I break into a run that only the largest of Golyats, striding through the open, could match. When it comes to moving through the forest, I have no match. I slip into the trees and follow the fresh path left by the ravenous Golyat.

Leaping fallen trees and rounding those that still stand, I close the distance, turning hunter into prey.

The Golyat hound comes into view. It's a shriveled canine with so much peeling skin, it almost looks like hair. Its claws are long and black, matching its teeth. The rib cage is expanded, and tall bones grow from its back, matching its previously human counterparts. The glow of its gut moves in a nearly straight trajectory toward its ass, and I can't help but wonder how fast the little bitch could work its way through a line of people, gobbling them up and shitting them out—a mobile, steaming fountain.

When the Golyat stops, I nearly collide with its shriveled tail. Rather than dodging, I leap up, clearing its backside, sailing past its spines and landing on its neck. Skin crunches beneath my feet, splitting beneath the force of my landing.

I plunge the machete into its flesh and give it an unnecessary twist. The beast goes rigid, spasms, and then turns its head to the sky and howls. The dry, ragged sound becomes a wet gurgle, and then it falls silent. The creature collapses beneath me, and I'm forced to jump away before falling into its liquifying form. I land, sense motion, and look up into a pair of narrow eyes.

The woman is a few inches shorter than me, slender, and dressed in green-dyed clothing that would let her blend in with the canopy above. Straight black hair hangs to her shoulders, giving her a sleek look. Her dark brown eyes are slender, and nervous. She looks from my eyes to my skin, her hand inching toward the knife sheathed on her side.

"I'm not going to hurt you." I stab my machete in the ground, raise my hands and step away from the weapon. When she doesn't respond, I ask, "Why are you out here? Beyond the wall?"

"Saw you coming," she says, pointing at the wall above. "From there."

I look up and spot a small hole, through which a second face looks down at us. Revealing the hole is a poignant show of trust. I wave to the person watching, and he—or she, I can't really tell from here—offers a furtive wave back. A smile, too.

"I came to warn you," she says, and she motions to the Golyat. "About them, but..."

A Golyat screaming in agony as it's torn asunder by one of Del's arrows finishes her point.

"Who are you?" she asks.

"Vee, of Kingsland," I tell her. "Ancestor of Sigler. Friend of Queensland."

A mix of relief and sadness overcomes her. "We have waited a long time to hear from you. From anyone. We thought we were all that was left."

I step closer and she doesn't flinch or go for the blade. "We are here now, and there are many more in Kingsland."

"And you can *kill* Golyats?" she asks, looking beyond me now as the flesh peels away from the Golyat's fallen skeleton.

"I can kill them all." I smile. "*We* can kill them all."

She climbs to her feet. "I am Bek, of Knightsland, descendant of Shin."

Despite a lifetime of hardening, suffering, and perseverance, my heart breaks upon hearing those words. Tears in my eyes, I open my arms to embrace her and say, "Sister."

Bek steps into my embrace, repeating my declaration of our bond. "Sister."

Held in the arms of a stranger, I experience the tangible legacy of Plistim's life: freedom is worth fighting and dying for, but it's the bonds of family—and the love at our core—that endures.

Even when freedom is lost.

A NOTE FROM THE AUTHOR

Dear Reader,

As the father of the 'kaiju thriller' literary subgenre, I feel a lot of pressure to come up with new and original kaiju stories involving monsters the likes of which no one in their right mind would ever want to come across...yet still can't get enough of. My solution this time around was the Golyats. They're big and nasty in the most visceral ways I could imagine. I mean, sure, Nemesis eats people, but at least she takes her time digesting them. Being eaten by a Golyat...it's just a violation of what it means to be human...and that's exactly what they're supposed to be. They're the worst of us gone awry and allowed to steep for hundreds of years, but they're also a reminder that freedom, when it's not defended, can be taken from us, by hubris, by our own government, or by hordes of giant monsters.

I hadn't meant for *The Divide* to be any form of political commentary, but I suppose the massive, insurmountable gulf that separates pockets of humanity from each other is a metaphor for the state of America and the world at large. Wouldn't it be nice if we could cross that divide before our world falls apart and ends up looking more like Davina's? If you're part of a book group: discuss!

If you enjoyed the novel and would like to see more kaiju thrillers (I've got more in the works), be sure to post a review on your online retailer and on Goodreads. Each and every one helps a lot. The more reviews the books get, the more retailers recommend them to readers, the more they sell, and the more I get to write...which, if you enjoy my novels, is a good thing for all of us.

Thanks for reading!

—Jeremy Robinson

ART GALLERY

To help inspire and evolve the Golyats into the most horrific monsters I could conjure, invoking hints of past creatures from some of my other novels, I turned to Liu Junwei, who goes by Shayudan (Shark the Painter). He's the amazing artist behind the covers for *Project Hyperion*, *Project Legion*, and *Unity*. He's also the cover artist for *Project Nemesis* and *Project Maigo* in China. Shark helped refine the visual look of the Golyat and my vision for them. The following art gallery includes designs for the Golyats, the Golyat bear, and Vee, as well as a few scenes from the story. Hope you enjoy them as much as I do!

Side note: if you're seeing the full color images in the e-book (the Golyat head, and Vee), I colored those myself, so if you think the coloring is horrid, I'm to blame.

—Jeremy

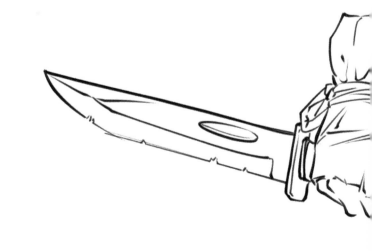

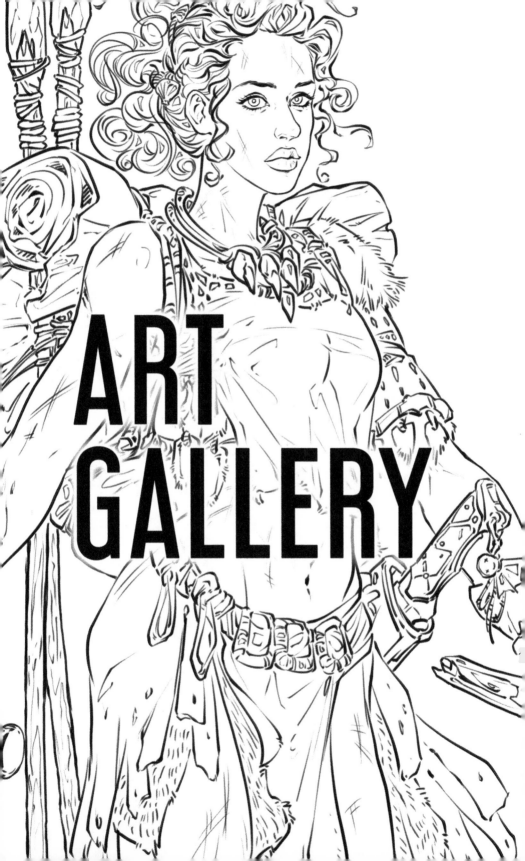

ART
GALLERY

ACKNOWLEDGMENTS

Thanks to Kane Gilmour, for putting in the extra effort to clean this one up. Now we know what happens when I write while on vacation! Big thanks to my amazing team of proof readers: Roger Brodeur, Jeff Sexton, Kelly Tyler, Julie Cummings Carter, Dustin Dreyling, Elizabeth Cooper, Lyn Askew, Sherry Bagley, Dee Haddrill, Becki Tapia Laurent, and Sharon Ruffy. You guys help me look like I can actually type! Extra big thanks to my fam (Hilaree, Aquila, Solomon, and Norah). Your creativity inspires and motivates me to keep my novels original. Love you guys.

ABOUT THE AUTHOR

Jeremy Robinson is the international bestselling author of sixty novels and novellas, including *Apocalypse Machine, Island 731*, and *SecondWorld*, as well as the Jack Sigler thriller series and *Project Nemesis*, the highest selling, original (non-licensed) kaiju novel of all time. He's known for mixing elements of science, history and mythology, which has earned him the #1 spot in Science Fiction and Action-Adventure, and secured him as the top creature feature author. Many of his novels have been adapted into comic books, optioned for film and TV, and translated into thirteen languages. He lives in New Hampshire with his wife and three children. Visit him at www.bewareofmonsters.com.

CPSIA information can be obtained
at www.ICGtesting.com
Printed in the USA
LVHW110008160119
604106LV00002B/296/P

9 781941 539354